FOOL ON
THE HILL

Matt Ruff

FOOL ON THE HILL

A Novel

A MORGAN ENTREKIN BOOK
THE ATLANTIC MONTHLY PRESS
NEW YORK
·

Published simultaneously in Canada
Printed in the United States of America

Library of Congress Cataloging-in-Publication Data

Ruff, Matt.
  Fool on the hill.

"A Morgan Entrekin book."
  I. Title.
PS3568.U3615F66   1988   813'.54   88-16620
ISBN 0-87113-243-5

Design by Laura Hough

The Atlantic Monthly Press
19 Union Square West
New York, NY 10003

FIRST PRINTING

A DEDICATION:

*to the Bohemians, with gratitude,
to the Grey Ladies, with affection,
and to Lady Chance,
    with deepest love*

AUTHOR'S NOTE

Cornell University is a real place, of course, and any number of interesting true stories could be, and have been, told about it. But *Fool on The Hill*, while making mention of a number of actual events and local legends, is first and foremost a work of fiction. The Cornell depicted within these pages is a shadow Cornell, like the real one yet unlike it; the characters who live and love here never existed, though perhaps they could have.

History buffs are warned in advance that even where the author has strayed into the realm of real events, these have often been altered to better suit the story. One example that requires mention has to do with the '69 black students' takeover of Willard Straight Hall. In this book, the mythical fraternity Rho Alpha Tau is credited with the Saturday morning "commando raid" in which a group of whites attempted to retake the building; in real life, the majority of the raiders were from Delta Upsilon. Despite the substitution, the author in no way means to imply that D.U. is in any other way similar to his Rho Alphas. Hopefully no fraternity is, though it might be nice to find a real Tolkien House out there somewhere.

Thanks are due to the following individuals and organizations, with apologies to anyone I've forgotten: Professors Bob Farrell, Alison Lurie, Lamar Herrin, and Ken McClane of the Cornell English Department, as well as my agent, Melanie Jackson, and my editors, Anton Mueller and Morgan Entrekin, for seeing this book through to the light of day; the City of Ithaca, Cornell University, and Prudence Risley Residential College, for giving me something to do for four years; Jeff Schwaner and Lisa V. for best friendship, poetry, and cheap beer when I needed it; Susan Hericks for being the only real saint in town; Thalia for motherly advice; Suzie Q. for loss of innocence, Julie K. for loss of confidence, and Muffy for the real McCoy; Chuck for more cheap beer; and Jenny New Wave for just being himself.

Thanks also to Erica Ando, who I really did write a book for; to the people at the Dewitt Historical Society who helped me do some last-minute research; to Brad Krakow of Risley Dining, who kept me wired on free coffee; to the Risley Hall maintenance staff, who number with the angels; and finally to the members of Cornell Public Safety and the Ithaca Police Department, who helped out on some technical stuff and who are actually far more relaxed and less Clint Eastwood–like than depicted here. Should they ever get around to sending my girlfriend's fingerprints back, I will like them even better.

List of
Major Characters

Stephen Titus George, *a storyteller*
Aurora Borealis Smith, *a nonconformist's daughter*
Mr. Sunshine, *a Greek Original*
Calliope, *the most beautiful woman in the world*

The Bohemians
Lion-Heart, *The Bohemian King*
Myoko, *Queen of the Grey Ladies*
Ragnarok, *Bohemian Minister of Defense*
Preacher, *Bohemian Ministry of Ministry*
Z.Z. Top, *Bohemian Minister of Bad Taste*
Fujiko, *a Grey Lady*
Woodstock, *Bohemian Minister of Impetuousness*
Panhandle, *Bohemian Minister of Lust*
Aphrodite, *Bohemian Minister of Love*

Other Human Beings
Jinsei, *Ragnarok's love and Preacher's lover*
Walter Smith, *Aurora's father*
Brian Garroway, *Aurora's boyfriend*
Officer Nattie Hollister, *an Ithacop*
Officer Samuel Doubleday, *an Ithacop*
Shen Han, Amos Noldorin, and Lucius DeRond, *the Three Presidents of
  Tolkien House*
Larretta, Curlowski, and Modine, *the three Architects*
Catherine Reinigen, *Aurora's friend*

The Sprites
Hobart, *Eldest and keeper of the Chimes*
Zephyr, *his granddaughter*
Puck, *Zephyr's lover*
Hamlet, *Puck's best friend and romantic counselor*
Saffron Dey, *Puck's mistress*

Canines and Felines
Luther, *a mongrel dog*
Blackjack, *a Manx cat*
Excalibur III, *bewildered Sheepdog and Dean of Canine Studies, Cornell University*
Gallant, *a St. Bernard*
Skippy, *a Beagle*
Rover Too-Bad, *a Rastafarian Puli*
Bucklette, *a right-wing Collie bitch*
Rex Malcolm, *King of Luther and Blackjack's home neighborhood*

Black Hats
Rasferret the Grub
Thresh, a Rat, *General of Rasferret's army*
The Green Dragon
The Rubbermaid
The Messenger
Dragon, *an Irish Wolfhound*
Jack Baron and the brothers of Rho Alpha Tau
Laertes, *the vengeful brother of Saffron Dey*

Cameo Appearances
Denman Halfast IV, *Ithaca's premier slumlord*
Fantasy Dreadlock and the Blue Zebra Hooter Patrol
Joe Scandal, *a black activist*
and
Ezra Cornell as himself

FOOL ON
THE HILL

1866—TWILIGHT
IN THE VALLEY

Mr. Sunshine first enters the city near dusk of a spring day in 1866, after heavy showers have turned its dirt roads and streets to mud soup. This is not the sort of weather that Mr. Sunshine prefers, but he is drawn on by a smell, a sweet smell that cannot be covered or washed away by the scent of fresh rain: the smell of Story.

The city lies in a valley along the shore of a long lake, and takes its name from a Greek island so distant as to be little more than a dream. Ithaca, home of the fabled Ulysses. Mr. Sunshine appreciates this name, for he, like it, is Greek, a Greek Original in fact. When he was younger he got around quite a lot in the World, but these days he spends most of his time in his Library, except when he feels the urge to go out and hunt up new material.

And so it happens that he walks east into the heart of the city along Owego—soon to be renamed State—Street, while the sun sets behind him and all around gas lamps are lit against the coming darkness. Crossing Fulton Street a horse and buggy have become hopelessly mired, but Mr. Sunshine passes through the mud unhindered. Likewise he is unhindered by the Ithaca citizenry, who would surely form a mob if they were to notice his odd dress—the ancient sandals on his feet are alone enough to mark him as some sort of freak. Yet while he sees and is seen by many people on his walk into town, he receives no un-wanted attention, encounters no trouble.

Along Corn Street two policemen are chasing a renegade hog; formerly the family garbage disposal at a nearby house, the swine has decided to try life as a freelander. Mr. Sunshine watches it charge up the block, cops floundering in tow, and then, turning away, takes his first long look at The Hill. There are many hills surrounding the city, but only one is of concern to Mr. Sunshine. This hill, The Hill, rises along the east edge of downtown Ithaca. It is cut by two Gorges, Cascadilla and

Fall Creek, but other than these natural wonders there is little to recommend it . . . yet.

But there will come a man there, Mr. Sunshine thinks, looking down the paths of the Future not quite so easily as he looks down this quagmired street, a man of daydreams, in love with love, a man with a kite and the name of a saint. And a woman with the name of a princess, who could use what he might give her . . .

He sees other Characters besides these two: a peculiar pack of modern-day knights who will ride up this very street, a dog in search of Heaven, a faerie with a flying wing of pinewood and gossamer. But they will be a long time coming yet; the Story which has drawn him will not have its true start for over a hundred years. It is all right; it will give him time to prepare, to Meddle a bit.

Twilight. The last glow of day leaches from the sky, revealing star-studded velvet. There is no moon, which Mr. Sunshine finds depressing, but one can't have everything. By gaslight he nears the intersection of Owego with Aurora Street, where the Ithaca Hotel stands (it, along with dozens of other neighboring buildings, will burn to the ground during an all-night conflagration five years hence). Two men stand out front of the Hotel arguing, or rather, finishing an argument.

"You're a goddamned fool," the shorter, wider man shouts, "if you think the people of Ithaca will sit still at the creation of an—an Oberlin within their borders!"

"Co-education is a sound plan," replies the other man more calmly. He is tall, dressed in a black coat and top hat, a man of wealth with a grey beard as long as his adversary's face. "I doubt our fellow Ithacans will complain once they see the University in operation. In time we hope to offer instruction in every study . . . to any person, male or female."

"Well you may rest assured, Sir," the short, stout fellow says with a note of finality, "that none of my children, male or female, will ever patronize such an institution."

"No doubt," the tall man agrees. "By 'every study,' I do not, of course, mean to include the study of how to act like a pompous ass, which is the only study to which your offspring are likely to be inclined."

So much for civilized discussion. The short man puffs out his cheeks as if trying to explode and take the tall man with him; when no blast is forthcoming, he makes a gesture with his hands that is seldom seen in these parts, turns to go, tangles his feet, and falls flat out in the mud. Once again wishing he were a bomb and failing, he picks himself back up, dripping mire and horse manure from his own not inexpensive black coat, and stomps away (squelch, squelch, squelch) into the gathering gloom.

Mr. Sunshine moves closer, letting himself be noticed, though the tall man, seeing him, still registers no surprise or shock at his outfit. "Denman Halfast," the tall man explains by way of greeting, indicating his retreating adversary. "Local landowner; if only his mind had expanded along with his property holdings he might be a pillar of the community."

"And your name, Sir?"

"Cornell." The tall man tips his hat, then coughs; he is not a young man, and hasn't been for a long time. "Ezra Cornell."

"The millionaire," Mr. Sunshine nods, not offering his own name in return. "One of the founders of the Western and Union Telegraph. I know of you. And did I hear you say something about the opening of a University?"

"Up there." Cornell points to The Hill, little more than a shadow-shape now; the sun is vanished entirely below the horizon and full dark is minutes away.

"Up there," Mr. Sunshine echoes, nodding again. It makes sense. "Many people will come here in the future. Many Characters . . ."

"I don't believe I've seen you before," says Cornell. "You're a traveler?"

"Sometimes," Mr Sunshine agrees.

"What brings you to Ithaca?"

"Story," comes the answer. "I'm a Storyteller, looking for a new Tale to pick up on."

Ezra Cornell frowns ever so slightly. "Storyteller. You write fictions?"

"I Write, yes. You don't approve?"

"Well," Cornell clears his throat, "I do appreciate fine literature—"

"So do I," says Mr. Sunshine. "I especially like dabbling with the classics: Chaucer, the Norse Sagas, the lives of the Saints, Shakespeare, Greek mythology of course—"

"—of course," Cornell butts back in, "but I've always thought popular fictions to be a waste of time and learning."

"No need to fear, then," Mr. Sunshine assures him. "You must understand, I'm no ordinary storyteller, no hack toying with cheap fabrications. I'm a Storyteller; I Write without paper, and all my fictions, Ezra, are true."

Cornell looks at him quizzically, not understanding, and Mr. Sunshine responds with a smile.

"It's all right," the Greek Original says. "Come, walk with me. I wish to see this Hill of yours . . . and see what I can do with it."

Book One

THE ROAD
TO THE HILL

THE PATRON SAINT
OF DAYDREAMS

I.

On a windless summer day in an uncertain year, more than a century after the founding of Cornell, a man who told lies for a living climbed to the top of The Hill to fly a kite. He was a young man, a surprisingly wealthy one even for a professional liar, and he lived alone in a gaudy yellow house on Stewart Avenue.

The liar (who was also known as a fiction writer) walked up Libe Slope at a brisk pace, so used to the incline that he barely huffed and did not puff at all. Halfway to the top he paused to check the sky; it promised rain, but not for a while. He continued his climb.

It was a Sunday, and he was on his way to the Arts Quad, which he unabashedly believed to be the heart of the University. During the year the Quad saw more activity than any other part of campus, from the Greek Festival in September to the burning of the Green Dragon in March, and besides, the Arts Quad was where it had all started. The first three University buildings to be erected—Morrill, White, and McGraw Halls—sat at the crest of The Hill like old grey men, keeping a weary eye on the town below. Just south of them the McGraw Chimes Tower poked at the sky from the side of Uris Library, another sentinel. The Chimes were a heartbeat to go with the heart, though that beat was sometimes off-key.

The Arts Quad was also one hell of a place to fly kites, even on a day with no wind.

Reaching the top of the Slope, the man who told lies for a living passed between Morrill and McGraw. Squat boxes, the two Halls were a tribute to Ezra Cornell's total lack of aesthetics—and they also went a long way toward explaining why more artistically minded architects had been hired to design most of the other University buildings.

7

Once on the Quad, the professional liar saluted the memorial statues of Ezra Cornell and Andrew White, and sat down in the grass to assemble his kite. At this hour—the hands on the McGraw Tower clock stood at five past noon—he was the only person up here. Cornell was going through its annual hibernation, the hiatus between the time when the last summer students left and the first regular students arrived for the fall term. The largely residential North and West Campuses were ghost towns now; Central Campus was occupied only by a smattering of professors here and there, most of whom were still in bed, visions of research grants dancing in their heads.

The dogs were out, though. As always. Back in the late Thirties a man named Ottomar Lehenbaur, one of the original stockholders in the Ford Motor Company, had donated two million dollars to Cornell's Engineering School. Because "Lehenbaur Hall" would have been a bumpy-sounding mouthful—and perhaps a bit too German-sounding for that day—the Board of Trustees convinced Ottomar to set a different condition on the donation. After thinking it over he created a codicil that granted free run of the campus to any and all dogs, "be they stray or otherwise, for as long as this University shall endure." Due largely to the codicil, the canine population on The Hill had grown until it was now about three times the average for that part of New York State.

The man who told lies for a living looked up from his kite and saw a St. Bernard eyeing him from beneath a tree. He gestured to it, at the same time reaching into the Swiss Army bag that hung over his shoulder. He brought out a handful of dog biscuits and scattered them on the ground.

"You hungry?" he asked the dog. The Bernard got up, trotted over unhurriedly, and after a quick sniff ate the biscuits. Then it flopped down and allowed itself to be petted.

"Good boy," the man who told lies for a living said, scratching the Bernard's stomach. "It's always nice to have some company. You want to hear a story about how I got to be rich and famous?"

The dog barked noncommittally.

"Oh, come on. It's a good story, really. And it's got a beautiful woman in it. Seven years worth of beautiful women, in fact. What do you say?"

The dog barked again, sounding more positive.

"Good! That's the spirit!" the professional liar said. The liar's name was Stephen Titus George, though on the cover of his first book this had been shortened to S. T. George. A critic—a very kind critic—had taken things one step further, referring to him as "St. George."

This was more appropriate than anyone would ever know.

II.

"I never knew my parents," George began, assembling the kite as he spoke. "I grew up with my Uncle Erasmus. Erasmus was sort of the family black sheep because of his profession, but he was also the only one who'd take responsibility for a kid that wasn't his. He was a sculptor, talented, high on ambition, though actually he made most of his money selling concrete animals, which you'd think wouldn't be too profitable but hey, we were living in New York City. Three days a week he'd drive his van out from Queens to Manhattan, set up a table on some busy sidewalk, five dollars apiece for solid cement squirrels, chipmunks, pigeons—Urban Jungle Art, he called it. Most impractical souvenir I've ever heard of—who wants to lug a concrete pigeon around the sights all day?—but the tourists were crazy about them, especially the Southerners. Never took Erasmus more than three hours to sell out his entire stock, and then he'd come home and fill up the molds again, make another batch. Left him plenty of time to do the sculpture he really wanted to do, and we never went hungry.

"He turned me on to the arts when I was still very young. 'The thing to remember, George,' he used to say, 'is that artists are magical beings. They're the only people other than the gods who can grant immortality.'

"That got me psyched, you know? Everyone wants to be like God, at least until they reach puberty. For a while I tried sculpting, but it wasn't really to my taste. Then one day I had to write a short story for a sixth-grade English competition, and something just clicked. I went and asked my Uncle if he'd mind my becoming an author, and he gave me his blessing, bought me a ballpoint pen for my very own. So I started writing, slowly and without much talent at first, but—"

The Bernard raised his head and barked twice.

"I'll be getting to the lady in just a minute," George promised. "Be patient. Now as I was about to say, my biggest problem in the beginning was that I was too content with my life. Writers need anxiety to draw on for inspiration; if everything's going peachy, you're sunk. Fortunately in my case, puberty came early.

"In my sophomore year of high school, I fell absolutely and hopelessly in lust with a girl named Caterina Sesso. I'd like to say I fell in love with her, but I won't lie to you: 'lust' is the honest term. She was an Italian, and in those days Italian girls were all the rage. Later on redheads came into vogue, and just now the fad is Asians, but in high school the state-of-the-art girlfriend was an Italian. All of which is racist and sexist as hell, but I've never actually met anyone who didn't have a preference, have you?

"Caterina was Italian, but she was also Catholic (the two sort of go together), which was a bad break for me. Catholic girls are all taught to avoid lust, and things were made even worse in my case because I came from a semi-Protestant background. I tried all the normal approaches and she refused to have anything to do with me. Then, after torturing myself over her for weeks on end, I sat down with my pen and wrote her a story. Twenty-three pages. And it was good, too—best thing I'd written up to that time. I typed it up, Xeroxed it, and gave a copy to Caterina.

"Four months later, on my sixteenth birthday, she gave in and had sex with me." (Here the Bernard barked again, and George nodded.) "I know. Surprised me too. It wasn't just the story that did it, you understand, but that definitely opened the door, convinced her to give me the time of day. We went together for a while, and then the night I turned sixteen there was this party at my Uncle's with all my friends. When that broke up around midnight, Caterina and I wandered over to Flushing Meadow Park. We sat and drank beer until two, and then we lay down underneath that big steel globe they built for the World's Fair, and started making out, and just kept going.

"Next thing we knew it was sunrise, and someone had come along and stolen the leftover beer."

The Bernard barked twice, questioningly.

"What happened then? Well, for a week I couldn't write a single word. Life was perfect, not a care in the world, so I had nothing to drive me. That problem solved itself quickly enough, though—after her next confession Caterina decided that we'd committed a mortal sin, and broke up with me.

"I spent the next seven years, right up to today, trying to get back to that birthday night under the World's Fair globe."

Bark.

"Simple. My luck did a complete reverse. Maybe I broke a mirror without realizing it. All I know for certain is that every time I got near a woman after that I thought about how it'd been with Caterina and wound up trying too hard, scaring them off. But my writing style kept getting better and better, mostly from all the practice.

"When I was seventeen a woman I'd never seen before ran up and kissed me on Fifth Avenue, then took off before I even knew what had happened; I went home and wrote my first published short story. Just before the end of high school I saw a redhead tooling around the neighborhood in a Corvette and *The New Yorker* paid me three hundred dollars for the result. And then I came here.

"Sophomore year at Cornell I fell madly in lust again, this time with a Taiwanese punker. Incredible-looking woman. I wrote her a novel over Christmas vacation. Burned off four hundred pages in a month. I didn't get to sleep with her, never even knew her name, but the book got published and it bestsold. So did the next two books . . ."

The Bernard stood up and shook itself furiously.

"Swear to God!" George told it. "Why would I lie to a dog? When I go home to Queens for visits my Uncle just smiles at me. 'You sure took after me, didn't you, George?' he says. 'It's a good thing your father isn't still around, or he'd probably accuse me of some funny business.' I'm twenty-three years old, I have enough money to live off for the rest of my life, the critics like me, I'm graduated with extra honors, and now Cornell's taken me on as a writer-in-residence. And all for the want of a steady girlfriend."

Wagging its tail, the dog licked George's hand. Whined.

"No," said George. "Not unhappy. How can you be depressed in a world where a man makes a living selling concrete wildlife? Lonely, maybe. Sometimes. Restless all the time. But I have this theory, see, that Whoever's in charge is setting me up for something big—*Moby Dick, Part Two*, with wheels, say, a novel to change the course of history—and once I get it done, the Editor will ease up and let me have sex again, maybe even fall in love for real. Only, after about a month of perfect bliss, He'll turn around again and give me something else to be anxious about. . . ."

The kite was now fully assembled. George held it up so the Bernard could see. It was a traditional diamond shape, with the head of a dragon painted on a white background, and red rays projecting out from the head. A red and black tail trailed from the bottom.

"I just picked it up last night," George said. "Let's see how she flies, eh?"

He stood up and the dog began to bark again. There was still not so much as a ghost of a breeze in the air.

"I know, I know. Don't you worry. I may not have much luck with women, but the wind and I are old lovers."

And while the Bernard looked on doubtfully, George stared up into the sky, as if searching for a familiar face there. He began to turn in place, holding the kite in one hand and a spool of heavy twine in the other, facing first west, then north, then east, then south. Three times around he turned, smiling all the while, as if casting a spell that was as amusing as it was powerful. In a sense he *was* casting a spell, though whether it was fueled by magic or coincidence he could never have said. All he knew was that it worked.

He stopped turning and gazed deep into the face of the sky once more. "Come on," George coaxed softly, and the wind began to blow. It came out of the west where it had been waiting all along, and lifted up the kite with unseen hands. The Bernard began barking furiously.

"Something else, isn't it? Scared the shit out of me the first time I did it. Now that I'm used to it, though, it's kind of fun."

He stood and listened to the wind, the wind which probably would have blown anyway but which never failed to come when he called, not since his Uncle Erasmus had taken him to fly his first kite when he was twelve.

"Maybe it's not so strange, eh?" he said. "Hell, in a book or a story I can make the wind blow just by typing a single sentence. And you figure the world, real life, that's just another story, one that doesn't need to be written down on paper."

George laughed and winked at the Bernard, while above them the kite soared higher and higher, a dragon in a diamond cage trying its wings for the first time.

III.

"George is feeling lonely again," Zephyr observed from where she stood in the McGraw Tower belfry.

"Is he?" her Grandfather Hobart said absently. Hobart was busy making his daily inspection of the chimes. "That's nice."

"It's a very optimistic lonely," Zephyr added, "but still lonely." She sighed and rested one hand comfortingly on the hilt of her sword, which was actually a two-inch stickpin that had been set into a miniature ivory handle. Zephyr too was a miniature, only a half-foot tall and invisible to human beings, save for the very drunk and the very wise. There were many names for her race—elf, gnome, faerie, Little People—but *sprite* was the common term. There were well over a thousand sprites living on The Hill, anonymously helping the humans run things.

"I wish there was something I could do for him," said Zephyr. It was part question, and when Hobart didn't immediately offer any suggestions she whirled around, intending to be furious—but of course Hobart wasn't the sort of person you could bring yourself to be furious with.

"Grandfather!" she whined, settling for mock anger. "Are you listening to me?"

"With one ear," Hobart told her. "No offense, dear, but you've been repeating more or less the same thing for the past six months."

"Do you think it's wrong of me?" Zephyr asked seriously.

"To love a human being? No. If that were a crime, I'd be more guilty than you. I loved one too, in my time. Why do you think I've spent the past century taking care of these bells?" He looked affectionately at the chimes. "Dear sweet Jenny McGraw. How I do miss her."

Zephyr leaned forward, interested. "Was she beautiful?"

"To my eyes, at least. Not, mind you, as beautiful as your Grandmother Zee, but very close."

"Did she . . . did she ever see you?"

"On her deathbed I think she might have. Consumption took her while she was away traveling the world; she came back to Ithaca to die. I was her most constant companion during her final days, more constant than her own husband. And toward the very end, I think, when she'd really begun to slip away, she seemed to take notice of me."

Hobart's eyes grew distant, and a little sad.

"That's the problem with loving a human being," he said. "Most of them can't see you except in extreme circumstances, and even then they don't always believe what they're seeing. Dear Jenny . . . I'm almost sure she thought I was nothing more than a hallucination."

"I think George could see me," said Zephyr. "I don't think he'd have to be drunk or dying, either. He's not crazy, but he . . . he has strong daydreams."

"Strong daydreams." Hobart chuckled. "And what if this daydreamer *could* see you, what would you do then? You can't consummate love with a giant, dear. Several times I tried to imagine what it might have been like between Jenny McGraw and myself, and the picture I got was rather embarrassing, to say the least. Some things really aren't meant to be."

"But . . . if only there were something . . ."

"As for that," Hobart went on, "why do you feel you have to *do* anything for him? You say he's lonely, but look. He's laughing down there."

"But he was just talking to a dog. People never talk to animals unless they're lonely."

"Your own father used to hold conversations with ferrets."

"Yes, but Father *understood* ferrets."

"Did he really? It always seemed to me that if he'd really understood them, he wouldn't have wound up being eaten by one. But perhaps I'm just too old and muddleheaded to see the truth of it."

Zephyr lowered her eyes. "Now you're making fun of me. You really do think I'm silly, don't you?"

"No more so than the rest of us," Hobart assured her. "It's just that the best you can hope to accomplish is to find George a human woman to fall in love with. But that's a job best left to Fate. I can tell you from experience that a sprite meddling in the personal affairs of a human almost always brings bad luck."

"But we always—"

"*Personal* affairs. There's a difference between helping the University Administration keep its files straight and playing matchmaker. Meddling in that area causes more trouble than it's worth, Zephyr. Ask Shakespeare if you don't believe me."

"Then what am I supposed to do?"

"Let him handle his own business. He's got the wind on his side; he'll do all right. And once you fall in love again—with a sprite, this time—it won't hurt nearly as much as it does now."

Hobart paused for emphasis, then added: "Puck's been asking about you."

"Puck's an idiot," Zephyr said automatically.

"Puck has his faults. He has his good points, too. You used to know that."

"Maybe I'm not the same as I used to be."

Hobart shrugged.

"As you wish," he said, knowing that there was no point in arguing. "But I can tell you honestly, finding Zee was the best thing that ever happened to me."

"The best thing," Zephyr repeated. "But you still tend Jenny McGraw's chimes, don't you?"

"Well . . ."

"When George leaves, I want to follow him in the glider. Is that all right?"

"I suppose," Hobart said with a sigh. "But he'll probably go down to The Boneyard. I don't want you in there, not even flying overhead."

"Fine. If he does go there I'll just turn around and come back. I promise. OK?"

"All right," Hobart agreed, uneasily.

He went back to his inspection of the chimes, while Zephyr stood at the edge of the open-air belfry, unmindful of the seventy-foot drop.

"Grandfather Hobart?"

"Yes?"

"What's so bad about The Boneyard? What's in there?"

For a long time he didn't answer.

"Nightmares," Hobart said finally. "Old nightmares."

IV.

George stayed on the Quad for the better part of an hour. When he finally reeled in the kite and disassembled it, the wind did not stop. It blew steadily, summoning cloud after cloud until the sky was steely grey. The rain was much closer now.

"Give me an hour," George petitioned the clouds. "I want time for a walk." He cocked his head as if listening for a reply, then put the pieces of the kite back into the Swiss Army bag and started heading back the way he had come. "So long, buddy," George said to the St. Bernard, which had wandered back under the tree. "Thanks for your company."

As he passed Ezra Cornell he snapped another salute, smiling at the thought of the legend: it was said that if a true virgin passed between the Quad statues at precisely midnight, Ezra and Andrew would come to life and shake hands with each other. Oversized footprints painted on the path between the two statues paid tribute to the notion. *But you'd have a hard time deciding what to do if I came by, wouldn't you?* George thought. *Once as a teenager and then seven years of abstinence, a man's virginity might spontaneously regenerate after all that time. Hell, some people develop a third set of teeth.*

Pondering this, George left the Arts Quad behind him and hurried down Libe Slope toward The Boneyard, while in the sky the clouds took a vote and decided to hold their water a little longer.

V.

The glider, an ancient contraption of pinewood and gossamer, was stored in a secret hangar in the Tower peak above the belfry. Zephyr reached it by means of a hidden ladder and staircase. At the top of the stairs she pulled a lever in the wall, setting in motion a group of counter-weights that opened the outer hangar doors.

Sitting in the farthest recesses of the hangar, the glider looked about as aerodynamically sound as a winged sneaker. Designed to be as invisible as the sprites, the glider's pinewood frame was anorexically thin, and the gossamer wings—woven from Midsummer's Eve lake fog—shimmered only slightly even in the brightest daylight. The single passenger rode in a narrow sling suspended beneath the main body of the craft, controlling direction by pulling on two threads . . . but it was the wind that did most of the steering.

Zephyr climbed into the sling without hesitation or fear. She loved to fly; it was certainly a more convenient method of transportation than walking or squirrelback. Why the great majority of sprites remained earthbound was a mystery to her.

Puck did a lot of flying, she knew—though his was a more mechanical and less magical bent—but she purposely tried not to think about that now. She had refused to see or speak to Puck for months since she'd caught him fooling around with Saffron Dey inside one of the display cases in Uris Library. Coincidentally or not, her feelings for George had first surfaced at about that time.

Zephyr launched the glider with a thought. Like George, she too was on intimate terms with the wind, and didn't even have to bother spinning around to summon it. She merely called to it in her mind and a river of air flowed into the hangar, floating the glider gently out, like a cork leaving a bottle in slow motion. The hangar faced north, giving her a splendid view of the Quad as she entered the open air; then she banked to the right, descending in a series of wide spirals around the Tower.

"Be careful of the weather!" Hobart shouted to her as she passed the level of the belfry. "And remember—stay away from The Boneyard!"

Zephyr raised one hand to wave, not bothering to yell back that she'd understood, and then she was lower, circling the clock faces of the Tower. *I love you, Grandfather,* she thought, at the same time wishing that he wouldn't worry about her so much. But old sprites seemed prone to worry, and at 172 years of age, Hobart was the oldest surviving sprite on The Hill (Zephyr, only 40, was just finishing adolescence), old enough to have seen action in the

Great War of 1850 against Rasferret the Grub, the most terrible conflict in remembered history. Zephyr wished he would learn to relax.

She leveled out at an altitude of about thirty feet and flew after George, who had reached the bottom of Libe Slope and was crossing West Avenue into the temporary ghost town that was West Campus. She had closed more than half the distance to him when a low droning reached her ears. Recognizing the sound, Zephyr looked for cover to hide behind, but there was none close enough. A moment later a propeller-driven biplane pulled even with the glider.

"Hello, Zeph," Puck called to her. His plane was a single-engine scale model, the type hobbyists build and fly by remote control. In this case, however, the miniaturized controls were located in the cockpit. "Long time no see. I've been hoping we'd bump into each other up here."

"Goodbye," Zephyr replied curtly, yanking the glider's nose up. This slowed the craft's speed considerably, and Puck, unable to copy the maneuver without stalling his engine, shot past her. The biplane began a wide U-turn while Zephyr lowered the nose again and headed for the bottom of the Slope, calling on the wind for extra speed.

"Come on, Zeph!" Puck pleaded. "I just want to talk to you!"

"*I* don't want to talk to *you!*"

She sailed over West Avenue and under the arch between Lyon and McFaddin Halls, then hung a sharp right, hoping to lose Puck among the West Campus dormitories. George, who had also gone through the arch but continued on straight, paused in mid-step as the glider passed near, though of course he could neither see it nor hear it. He did hear the drone of Puck's biplane a few seconds later, but dismissed it as a mosquito and kept walking.

"Come on, Zeph!" Puck shouted again. But instead of answering, Zephyr began weaving between buildings, pulling tight turns and other acrobatics in an attempt to shake him off. Puck brought the biplane up to full throttle and hung on. He was a good pilot, as good as she, and knew that eventually she'd have to give up.

But he'd forgotten about her tenacity, and her friendship with the wind. The wind kept Zephyr's glider moving at an incredible speed, while giving no similar aid to the biplane; it was all Puck could do to keep pace with her. Then, after making a particularly tight turn, he saw Zephyr pass between two close-growing trees. Barely a hairsbreadth of space existed between them, but a convenient breeze spread the branches to make room for the glider. Zephyr passed through the opening, and Puck attempted to follow.

The branches closed up in front of him.

"Terrific," said Puck. He tried to pull up and succeeded only in stalling his engine; the biplane plunged belly first into the branches. For a few seconds all was tumbling and chaos, and then, by some miracle, the plane reemerged on the far side of the trees with its wings and propeller intact. It was still stalled, however, and immediately went into a dive.

"Terrific," Puck said again, as the biplane stubbornly refused to level out. It was too heavy to glide effectively, and with the ground rushing up to meet him like a relative at a family reunion, there was no time to restart the engine. He was going to crash into the sidewalk.

"Terrific," Puck said, for what should have been the third and final time.

The wind saved him. It billowed up underneath the biplane like a cushion, forcing it to straighten out, holding it steady. Puck wasted no time asking questions; he pounded the starter button until the propeller kicked over and began to turn. As soon as it did, the wind cushion faded, leaving him to fly on his own power again.

"Are you all right?" Zephyr asked. The glider was alongside him now, close enough so that they didn't have to shout over the drone of the biplane's engine.

"I'm still breathing," Puck told her, not ready to concede anything more than that. "You are a *nasty* one when you get upset, you know that, Zeph?"

"It's your own fault." Now that it was clear that he was all right, some of Zephyr's anger came creeping back in a muted form. "That thing's a death trap, anyway. You should know better than to trust physics. If I hadn't talked the wind into saving you—"

"*Saving* me!? You're the one who got me into trouble in the first place."

"Yes, well," Zephyr protested in a lame voice, "you could have gotten into trouble yourself just as easily. And then where would you have been?"

"I have a parachute," Puck informed her, although this, too, sounded a bit lame. They fell silent for a moment, banking left to avoid another cluster of trees. A sparrow looked up at the sound of the biplane and chirped.

"That's another thing," Zephyr said. "You're too noisy and too easy to see."

"Maybe. But human beings have a way of not noticing obvious things. Even that George character—"

"Don't you say a word about George!" Zephyr warned.

"Fine. But people don't scare me, Zephyr. They really don't."

"What about animals? They notice you. Most of them would probably be too scared to do anything, but a pack of crows, or an owl . . ."

"God, Zephyr, are you really that worried about me?" Puck grinned at her, and she gave him a black look. "Well listen, I was thinking about crows and owls myself, so I got Cobweb to help me rig something up."

He brought the biplane up a few feet so that she could see two black cylinders that were mounted under the lower wings.

"What are they?" Zephyr asked. Like all sprites, she was fascinated with weapons.

"They're mini-cannons. Cobweb hooked them up to an electronic firing circuit and loaded them with buckshot. Should be enough to stop an owl."

"Or blow your own wings off."

"Maybe. But there's always my parachute. . . ."

Zephyr looked at the cannons again. They certainly were an interesting idea—even if they were also dangerous—and she had to admit that no similar weapon could be mounted on the glider.

"Neat, aren't they?" Puck asked, reading her thoughts.

"Pretty neat," Zephyr admitted. "I—"

As if suddenly awakened from a dream, she realized that George was no longer in sight. Both glider and biplane had begun to drift out of West Campus in the direction of Fall Creek Gorge. Without bothering to say good-bye, Zephyr broke formation and began angling back in the direction of The Boneyard, where she knew George would be by now.

"What—?" Puck said, abruptly finding himself flying alone.

"Go home, Puck," Zephyr called back to him. "I don't want to talk to you."

"Terrific," said Puck, watching her speed away. He opened up the throttle once more and turned to follow her. "Jesus, Troilus, and Cressida—here we go again!"

VI.

The thing to remember, George, is that artists are magical beings. They're the only people other than the gods who can grant immortality. . . .

The Boneyard was located below Stewart Avenue, about halfway down the side of The Hill. George had discovered the place several years ago, and had visited it regularly ever since, using it for inspiration. He would walk among the tombstones, pausing frequently, reading names, dates, epitaphs, and asking himself questions: What was this person like? How did she die? It says here she was married; were they happy together? This one over here died young; did he enjoy what time he had? What did he do on his sixteenth birthday?

Hundreds of tombstones here; hundreds of stories, each individual one far too long to ever tell in its entirety. But every so often George would see something that would stick in his mind, maybe just an unusual name, and the next time he sat down to write, that person would become part of a new tale, one step closer to eternity.

Strangely, for all the time he had spent in The Boneyard, he was constantly discovering new things. On this particular day he came across two unusual stones that he had somehow never noticed before. One was a standard rectangular piece of marble that bore the words:

DEDICATED TO THE LOVING MEMORY

OF HAROLD LAZARUS

1912–1957

BY HIS ADORING WIFE

GOD GRANT HIM REST

The inscription was kind enough, even a little touching, but the embellishments were grotesque. Beneath GOD GRANT HIM REST was an etching that depicted some sort of demon with a bow and arrow chasing after a doe. More demon figures floated in the upper corners of the stone, and the whole was topped by an intricately carved gargoyle figurine that leered at the onlooker.

George shook his head, trying not to laugh. Poor Harold Lazarus. What had he done to deserve such a monument? Or had his wife just had exceedingly bad taste?

"What do you say, Harold?" George asked, crouching down beside the stone and taking out a notepad. "How'd you like to live forever?"

He made a rough sketch of the gargoyle, softening the features so that it looked unlucky rather than fierce. Underneath the sketch he wrote: "LAZARUS—HAS ADORING BUT TACKY WIFE." George had no idea what story might come out of it, but he would endeavor to give back some of Harold's dignity.

The other stone had no humor in it. It was set on the top of a small rise, and in comparison to the stones around it—expensive, tall things that looked like scale reproductions of the Washington Monument—it was hopelessly crude. It didn't even have a definite shape, but appeared rather as if someone had started with a boulder and knocked bits and pieces off until it was small enough to be used as a marker. Likewise, the inscription had been chiseled in the roughest manner, but was still legible. George stared at it for a long time.

> HERE LIES ALMA RENAT JESSOP
> BORN APRIL 23, 1887
> DIED APRIL 23, 1887
> HER FATHER LOVED HER

The sky continued to darken. The rain would not wait much longer, and George still wanted to visit a particular spot at the far north end of The 'Yard. But for a few moments more he stood before the stone, studying its rough, hammer-hewn surface, until at last he understood.

"You son of a bitch," he whispered, awed. "You made it for her yourself."

VII.

"This place is supposed to be dangerous, you know," said Puck, trying to keep up with Zephyr as she weaved among the gravestones. They had landed the glider and plane back by the entrance to The Boneyard and begun following George on foot. Puck could no longer remember the reason for this, but reflected that it couldn't have been an intelligent one. "It has rats in it."

"You're not afraid of rats, are you?" Zephyr asked him.

"No, of course not. Not if there are only a few of them, anyway. *I* know how to take care of myself."

Zephyr laughed for the first time since he'd been with her that day. "If you're hinting that I don't know how to take care of myself," she said, "just remember who taught you fencing."

"Your Grandfather taught me. You were just a sparring partner."

"Yes, but you never beat me in practice, did you? Not once . . . oh, come on, Puck! If you insist on tagging after me at least try to run a little faster."

Puck grunted and tried to put on extra speed, but Zephyr moved extraordinarily quickly even without her glider. And Puck had a bigger load to carry—in addition to his sword, he also bore a needle-firing crossbow that seemed to gain weight with every step.

"Listen, Zeph," Puck wheezed, nearly tripping over a blade of grass. "I've been meaning to ask you . . ."

"The answer is no, but what do you want?"

"Well, Cobweb and I and a bunch of others were thinking of holding another Lab Animal Freedom Raid in a couple weeks, and I was wondering if you wanted to—"

"No thank you," Zephyr cut him off. "That's just a big prank anyway, and you know it. Why don't you ask Saffron Dey? I'm sure she'd love to go with you."

"Look, Zeph, Saffron . . . Saffron's a hell of a nice sprite, and all, and I have to admit that I was a little taken with her for a while, but when you get right down to it, she's not even in your class!"

"You think so?" Totally disinterested.

"I know so! Look, I'm really sorry if your feelings were hurt, but I can't believe you're still upset. . . ."

"*Upset!?*" She threw a look back over her shoulder that would have curdled root beer. "*Upset!* You were doing it with her in a *display case*, for God's sake! How do you expect me to feel?"

"So it was in a display case, so what? Nobody could see us! Nobody except Cobweb, of course, and he traded me two thimblefuls of tequila so he could w—"

Puck trailed off abruptly, wondering not for the first time what wrong he had committed that his tongue should run so very much faster than his brain. Zephyr said nothing further, simply picked up the pace even more until Puck was nearly hyperventilating.

Ahead, a concrete walkway spanned a narrow, stream-filled gully. George was just crossing it, drawn by something on the other side. Zephyr hurtled after him, energetic as ever, while Puck plodded doggedly in her wake.

They both felt it at the same time.

It was a presence, a cold radiation that came at them from across the gully, as if a small black sun had been placed somewhere on the other side. Both sprites stopped dead in their tracks, sudden terror rolling over them like thunder.

"What is it?" Zephyr whispered, as if afraid of being overheard.

"I don't know." Puck had set down his crossbow and was shivering. "It's bad . . . there's something very bad over there."

Across the gully, George continued to walk along unconcernedly.

"How can he stay over there?" Zephyr wondered aloud. She too had begun to shiver. "Can't he feel how bad it is?"

"Maybe he can't. And maybe if he can't feel it, it can't hurt him."

"Do you think it knows we're here?" Zephyr said.

As she spoke, two graveyard rats, big ones, sprinted out of hiding from behind a nearby tombstone. Puck saw them coming and scooped up his crossbow, managing to kill one with a shot that was more luck than skill. The other rat continued charging forward, leaping into the air at Zephyr as soon as it was close enough.

"Zeph!" Puck shouted. "Look ou—"

But she was already turning, sword in hand.

VIII.

George had found what he was looking for.

It was a plain white marble square laid flat against the ground, more a plaque than a proper gravestone, and weathered by many years. He had no idea why such an unremarkable thing should seem so special to him, yet it was true that he had never visited The Boneyard without coming by here to look. One strange thing he'd noticed—all the other standing gravestones in the area had sagged, seeming to lean away from this one like petals from the heart of a strange flower. Surely that was just coincidence, but it added to the illusion that this was, well, the *center* of something.

The stone bore no date, and only a single name, seven letters carved by some long-ago hand:

PANDORA

George hunched over the burial site, feeling nothing but a strange and inexplicable fascination. Zephyr or Puck, placed in the same location, would have died instantly of fright, but George merely thought to himself: *What story does this one hold?* It almost made him wish he could really resurrect the past, rather than just make up fictions. *What story? I'll bet you it's a good one, whatever it is.*

He ran his fingers over the marble surface, tracing each letter. Lightning flashed in the distance.

IX.

Zephyr cleaned her sword with a piece of a dead leaf. She had killed the rat in one stroke, sidestepping and piercing it through the heart as it finished its leap.

"You see?" she said to Puck when her sword had been resheathed. "I can take care of myself."

"Sure," Puck said, still shaken. The bad feeling from across the gully had subsided a little but remained in the background, like a lingering nightmare.

"There's one thing I'm curious about," Zephyr went on. "It doesn't look like many people get buried here anymore, does it? Most of the space is already taken. But then why would there be rats? Don't they need lots of fresh . . . you know."

"I couldn't tell you, Zeph. But there've always been lots of rats in The Boneyard. Always. It really isn't safe to stay here. More of them will probably be coming this way soon."

"Let's go home, then," Zephyr said, after a pause. "I want to go home now."

She had lost all interest in tailing George, at least for today, something for which Puck was silently grateful. He didn't delude himself, though, knowing that he still had a long way to go before he would be back in her good graces.

They scurried back the way they had come, keeping a sharp eye out for rats, and it was only when they were airborne again—Zephyr with the help of an uphill gust of wind—that Puck began to feel safe.

X.

George made it home just ahead of the storm. No sooner had he set foot on his front porch than rain began thundering off the sidewalks and car rooftops hard enough to raise mist. This was accompanied by an amazing electrical show.

It being Sunday there was no mail—thankfully; the flow of fan and hate mail was slow but steady, and it took a lot of time to read—but his landlord had left a note on his door:

TENANT,

PLUMBER COMING SOMETIME DURING THE WEEK TO INVESTIGATE LEAKS. WINDOW REPAIRMAN NEVER THERE WHEN I CALL; PERHAPS YOU COULD TRY. AS FOR THE OTHER, I DON'T UNDERSTAND WHAT YOU MEAN BY "ROACHES IN KITCHEN." WE FUMIGATED ONLY LAST JANUARY.

YOUR LANDLORD,
DENMAN HALFAST IV

George smiled ruefully and shook his head. Denman Halfast . . . he remembered one time when he had given the man a copy of one of his books. It had been returned a week later, with the same sort of impersonal note: "TENANT, TOO FANTASTIC AND TOO MUCH PROFANITY. YOUR LANDLORD . . ."

Perhaps it was time he gave up renting and simply bought a house in Ithaca; he had money enough. But he wasn't sure he liked the idea of putting down roots here, even tentative ones. He was still young enough to consider himself a wanderer, and as Uncle Erasmus had once said, wanderers rent or flop, they never buy. Besides, this particular house was where he had been living—with three friends—back when his first book, *The Knight of the White Roses*, had been published. He had read the *Times Book Review* every Sunday on this very porch, watching his novel climb the bestseller list a notch at a time until it reached a peak at number three, outdone only by Jackie Collins and the latest Stephen King.

He got himself a Coke out of the refrigerator and came back out on the porch to watch the storm. The rain smelled fresh and clean, like the promise of an exciting new year. And though neither George nor anyone but a certain Mr. Sunshine could know it in advance, this year would be the most exciting Ithaca had ever seen.

Oblivious to this, George sat on his porch, and drank his Coke, and made daydreams out of the rain. He wondered about the book he would write this year, and he wondered—not too desperately—whether love would find him at last and let him rest for a time. But he smiled all the while he was thinking about it, because at the core he was happy enough just to be alive and watching the storm, and this one thing made him special.

In other places, both far and near, others had begun to turn toward Ithaca. New students, old students, vacationing professors, soon it would be time for them to come and bring Cornell out of hibernation, give it life for another year.

But not all who traveled the road to The Hill that late August came in search of learning, and not all of them were human.

LUTHER ON THE ROAD TO HEAVEN

I.

Blackjack crouched perfectly still in a dark corner of an abandoned basement. His breathing was soft and controlled; his whiskers did not move, his claws did not tap the floor, his tail did not twitch. He had, in fact, no tail at all.

The rat was about ten yards off to his left, still moving carefully, but beginning to believe that the coast was clear. Blackjack fought hard to control his eagerness. He had been waiting motionless for almost an hour now, and didn't want to blow it with a stray sound or thought. Keep cool, that was the ticket. And when the rat had moved away from the wall, toward the middle of the floor where it was more likely to become disoriented, he would pounce.

A minute or so later the rat began to do just that. It picked up the smell of food, a rancid scrap of cheese lying amidst other debris left behind by some passing wino. There was cat scent in the air as well, which a more cautious rodent might have noticed, but the lure of the cheese was strong and by the time this rat recognized its peril it would be too late.

One uneven portion of the floor was awash with sunlight. The building above had been almost completely destroyed in a fire, and the sun's rays leaked in through a gash in the basement ceiling. The rat paused at the shore of this bright lake, sniffing the air and making a final decision. The cheese was on the far side.

Wait, Blackjack cautioned himself, careful not to let the thought slip outwards. *Wait until he's in the light and blinded. Then creep up as close as you can and . . .*

"Blackjack?"

The word came from the direction of the partially collapsed basement stairs. The rat froze, thought it over for perhaps a second, and bolted for home.

"Fuck." Blackjack launched himself forward, knowing he was already too late. The rat caught a glimpse of the coal-black Manx bounding after it and put on an extra burst of speed, reaching safety with room to spare. Blackjack skidded to a halt in front of the rat hole and pawed at it in vain.

"Blackjack?"

The cat turned around, seething. A mongrel dog—a bitch—stood at the foot of the stairs, watching him.

"This had better be good, Riva," Blackjack warned her. Had he been using speech, he would have been almost shouting. "You just cost me lunch."

"Malcolm wants to see you," she told him. His eyes widened just the tiniest bit, but his anger over the lost rat did not diminish.

"Malcolm wants to see me, eh? Good for him. You go tell him I'll drop by when I get a chance. Like maybe next week."

"Malcolm wants to see you *now*," Riva insisted.

Blackjack considered another retort, but thought better of it. Cats—street cats, at any rate—had no fear of dogs, but Malcolm was the baddest of the bad in this neighborhood. It would not be wise to cross him, or his messenger. Likewise, he would not have sent for Blackjack unless something truly important had come up.

"Soon," Blackjack relented. "I'll be there soon. You go tell Malcolm—"

"I ain't yours to order about!" snapped Riva, who had little patience with felines. "Malcolm says come back with me, so you come. Now."

"What is it? What does he need to talk to me about?"

"Come and ask him yourself, damn it! You think I know?"

But Blackjack stared at her, and in a moment she dropped her eyes. "It's Luther," she told him. "Something gone wrong with Luther." The Manx nodded, or performed the feline equivalent of a nod. The news did not surprise him; a lot of things had gone wrong with Luther lately.

"All right," he agreed. "I'll come with you . . . but Malcolm owes me a rat."

II.

A word about animals, and telepathy.

Many storytellers, from Aesop to Richard Adams, have spun tales in which animals hold conversations with one another. There is little evidence of this in real life, however; while some animals can produce an amazing variety of distinct sounds, and some sort of basic communication is possible through this, the idea of two dogs barking back and forth about the meaning of life is a fairly laughable one. It is no wonder then—never having overheard two horses discussing their sexual difficulties—that most people view animals as less intelligent than humankind, if still lovable.

In fact, all living creatures—human beings included—are born with a latent power of telepathy. The power never develops in most humans, however, because speech takes the place of its main function. It is in those animals most closely associated with humanity—cats and dogs in particular—that telepathy becomes a refined and useful tool.

However, while cats and dogs are able to "think" to one another without difficulty, there are a number of important differences in their perception. One of these differences is that cats are, for some unknown reason, able to understand human speech, whereas dogs are not. Some cats also learn to read—another impossibility for dogs—although obtaining and manipulating books is obviously difficult for them.

A great dichotomy has sprung up because of this. Dogs, able to empathize with human emotions but not comprehending the complexity of human thought, have come to hold human beings in awe and think of them as at least partially divine. Cats, on the other hand, after witnessing the magnitude of human foolishness for centuries, have grown aloof and individualistic, dealing with human beings only—or so they think—on their own terms. Cats are also far less religious and superstitious than dogs; Blackjack was a hardcore atheist.

It might seem at first that such diametrically opposed groups would be forever at war. But, despite a general lack of respect, close friendships between individual cats and dogs do occur from time to time. Just such a relationship existed between Blackjack and Luther, and it was for the sake of that relationship that Blackjack went to see Malcolm right away that day, instead of delaying long enough to get even for the loss of the rat.

It was out of the same feeling of friendship, furthermore, that Blackjack ultimately wound up joining Luther on a quest, a quest to find something that the Manx did not even believe existed.

Heaven.

III.

Malcolm held court in the decaying shell of an abandoned church. ("Abandoned" was a word that could be applied to the majority of the buildings in this neighborhood, one of the poorest ghettoes of the South Bronx.) Riva led the way, though Blackjack knew it well enough. As they approached the church's front steps, several lazing dogs—all of them mongrels—turned to look. At the sight of the Manx they all shied back a little.

One of the first things Blackjack had done after taking up residence in this area had been to get into a scrap with a notorious dog by the name of Fearless Bledsoe. Bledsoe was an avowed cat-hater, and upon first seeing Blackjack with Luther he had flown into a rage. As a result of the ensuing fight, Blackjack had a long scar etched permanently into his left flank. Fearless Bledsoe, however, now went by the name of *No-Balls* Bledsoe, and rumor had it that he had not so much as glanced at a cat since.

"You can all stop shaking," Blackjack said (thought-said) to the dogs as he climbed the church steps, secretly proud of his reputation. After what he had done to Bledsoe, there wasn't a stud within five miles who didn't get nervous when he sauntered by.

Except Malcolm.

They entered the church. Most of the pews had been overturned by vandals; none were undamaged. Several fierce-looking mongrels crouched among the ruins, and at the head of the nave Malcolm himself lounged before the shattered altar, flanked by the four best-looking bitches in the neighborhood.

"Hello, cat," Malcolm said. He was part German Shepherd, part Doberman, and part Mastiff . . . with a trace of timber wolf, if you believed the stories, which Blackjack didn't.

"I have a name," replied Blackjack. "Use it."

"Little testy today, cat? Let's see . . ." He concentrated for a moment. "Has somethin' to do with a rat you didn't catch, mayhap?"

"Yes," said Blackjack uneasily. For the most part telepathy was only useful for discerning projected thoughts, but Malcolm was one of those rare animals who could actually probe into another mind—how deeply, only he knew.

"And mayhap," Malcolm continued, "you think it's my fault."

"Oh, it's her fault," said Blackjack, indicating Riva. The bitch snarled at him. "She's the one who scared the rat away. But since she was on your business, and since she seems to be your property—"

"My *property?* Oh, cat, you hurt my feelings. Bitches as property . . . that's a 'Bred notion if I ever heard one. An old mix like me has got better things to do than own other dogs."

Blackjack looked at the four bitches gathered around the altar. When their time of heat came, no stud was permitted to touch them without Malcolm's invitation and approval.

"You're so liberated," Blackjack said.

"*We-e-ell* . . . nobody ever promised I was *perfect*, cat. But just so as you'll know what a generous fellow I am . . ." He turned to one of the dogs among the fallen pews. "Get this tom something to eat."

The dog vanished into what had originally been the church sacristy, returning a moment later with not one, but three dead rats dangling from his mouth. He deposited them on the floor at Blackjack's feet.

"They're a little stiff," apologized Malcolm, "but they're plump, too. Lot of plump rats around here lately."

"What's wrong with Luther?" Blackjack asked. A gift of three whole rats made him suspect the worst.

"He wants to go lookin' for Moses."

"Oh . . ." Moses was Luther's sire. He was also deceased. A car had run him down three days ago, and just yesterday morning his body had been removed by two men in a sanitation truck. "He wants to go visit the garbage dump?"

"That's what I thought at first," Malcolm said. "But I looked him through real careful, and now I'm thinkin' that mayhap he's got a longer trip in mind. A much longer trip."

"And how do I figure into this?".

"You're his friend, cat. Closest thing to family he's got now that Moses passed on. It's your job to watch out for him."

"My job . . ." Blackjack's anger returned; he did not appreciate having responsibility forced on him. "Just roll that thought back, Malcolm. I like Luther, but I'm not *going* anywhere with him."

"Talk him out of it, if you can. But if he walks, so do you, cat. The world's a hungry thing; mayhap it wants to eat Luther for breakfast, and I don't plan on lettin' that happen. I owe Moses that much."

"But *I*," Blackjack insisted, as if explaining something to a retarded kitten, "*I* don't owe Moses anything."

Malcolm stopped lounging and stood up on all fours, facing him. For the first time the dog showed signs of losing his own temper.

"You listen, cat, and listen careful. I won't repeat myself. You're *goin'*, even if you got to walk Luther halfway 'round the world. Hell, that dog's got no fight of his own. And he ain't never been told about 'Breds—Moses didn't want him to know. How long you figure he'd last without someone to watch his back? Now *you*, cat, you got fight enough for two or three."

"Don't try to flatter me," said Blackjack. But he was softening.

"I ain't flatterin' you, cat," Malcolm replied. "I'm just tellin' you what I see. You're like a glass to me, you know. The glass gets too cloudy to look through in parts, but those parts that I can look through . . . well, you ain't quite worth *flatterin'*, but I wouldn't be in an all-fire hurry to throw you on the junk heap, either. And Luther, he's goin' to need your help if he leaves this place."

No response.

"You got your own tongue, cat?" Malcolm asked. "Or are you just noddin' your head without movin' it?"

"I'll talk him out of leaving," Blackjack said, more to himself than to Malcolm. "No need for either of us to go anywhere. I'll talk him out of it."

"You better eat those rats, then. His mind's set tight, and you'll need a full stomach to even budge it."

But Blackjack had lost his appetite.

"Where is Luther, anyway?" he asked.

"Luther's down the block, at that building where they used to have all the meat," said Malcolm. "He's on the roof."

IV.

"Luther?"

Blackjack entered the former House of Morris Butcher Shop, one of the last stores in the neighborhood to close. There was a dog sitting just inside the doorway, but it was not Luther.

"Get out of my way, Isaac," Blackjack warned, as the mongrel blocked the entrance.

"You get out," Isaac commanded, shaky but possessing enough hatred to make up for it. Isaac and Fearless Bledsoe had come from the same litter. "Ain't no need for you here, cat."

"Malcolm sent me to talk to Luther," the Manx told him. After a pause he added: "I would have come on my own anyway, sooner or later."

"Malcolm sent *you* to talk to him? What is he, crazy?"

"Why don't you go ask Malcolm that yourself? Look, my friend's on the roof, so just get—"

Isaac bared his teeth . . . and reeled back, bleeding from a slash across his muzzle.

"Stupid," Blackjack said, retracting his claws. Isaac scurried out of the way like a spooked puppy. "Don't ever threaten a cat unless you mean business. That was your brother's mistake."

He walked on toward the back of the shop without another word, and Isaac gave him no further trouble. Blackjack sniffed the air, detecting the ghosts of Kosher Bacon and Liverwurst Past. The smell was even stronger in the back room, and Blackjack remembered pleasantly how the head butcher had used to feed him scraps. That butcher had been a capital fellow, for a human being—he'd never made Blackjack beg or do tricks for the food, nor had he ever tried to pet him. You could almost come to respect a human like that, one who let you keep your dignity and still eat.

He found the stairs leading up and began to climb, his stomach growling . . . now he wished he had eaten the three rats, or at least one of them. The stairs led to the roof, which had actually been the second floor once. The original roof had collapsed, and only one wall remained standing, the one overlooking an alley on the left-hand side of the butcher shop. Luther was there, gazing down at the alley through a jagged hole that had originally been a window. He was a medium-sized dog, his short-haired coat a confused mottle of black and white.

"Luther?"

"Blackjack," Luther greeted him without looking up. He projected his thoughts softly and distinctly, as Moses had taught him to do. "You came. I knew you would."

"It—it wasn't actually my idea. I didn't even know you were up here until Malcolm told me. Er . . . why exactly *are* you up here, Luther?"

"I was just looking at the spot where Moses died. He crawled into the alley after he'd been hit, you know."

"Did he?"

"He spent his *whole life*," Luther continued, the thought tinged with reverence and sorrow, "his whole life trying not to be a bother to anyone. In the end I think he didn't want to leave his body lying in the street."

"I doubt anyone would have cared," said Blackjack, moving up to sit next to him. "Not in this neighborhood. I am sorry about it, you know. I know I told you that before, but I meant it."

"There's nothing for you to be sorry for. It's not your fault he's dead. Raaq's the one to blame."

"Who?"

"Raaq. The Deceiver."

"Oh." Blackjack was really not in a mood to discuss the canine version of Satan.

"He's not the same as Death, you know," said Luther, who was in a religious mood. "But the two of them do travel together. Death's job is to collect all the souls. It's Raaq who does the actual killing, though. Whenever a car hits a dog, Raaq is the driver. Oh, it's a human—a Master—but for that one instant, he becomes Raaq. And the car becomes Raaq, too. . . ."

"Luther," Blackjack interrupted gently.

". . . He makes dogs fight one another, makes them sick. He's in the rabies. He makes litters come out stillborn. He—"

"Luther!"

"Huh!?" Luther jerked his head around, as if shaking off a particularly bad dream. "Wh-what did you say?"

Blackjack studied Luther's eyes for a long moment. Luther did not look well. If dogs had been capable of crying out of emotion, his face would have been streaked with hysterical tears.

"It's not fair, you know," Luther said, and the thought was quiet, meek. "I was the only one in my litter to survive past the first month. And my mother, she just disappeared. Moses always thought the 'catchers had gotten her. Lately I've been wondering if it wasn't something worse. What if she was out at night sometime, all alone, and she met up with Raaq in person?"

"Raaq isn't real, Luther," Blackjack told him patiently. "Raaq's only a bad dream that some caveman put a name to. Then a cat overheard the caveman talking about it, and just for laughs he told a dog. And you've been scaring yourselves over it ever since."

Luther listened to this with equal patience. Cats often said strange things, especially in reference to the Masters. A good dog nodded and took it all with a polite grain of salt.

"You'll still be my friend, won't you, Blackjack?" he asked, when the Manx had finished. "You're all I've got left now that Moses is gone."

"I'll be your friend," Blackjack promised. And because cats can't hug, he bit Luther playfully on the ear. Then he said: "Now what's this I hear about you going to look for Moses?"

"Well . . ." Luther lowered his eyes, embarrassed. "Even with you as a friend, you understand, I still miss him a lot. I want to see him again."

"His body, you mean?"

"Oh no!" Luther looked frankly surprised. "Why would I want to see that? What good's a body if nobody's in it?"

"Then what—"

"I want to see his soul again, Blackjack."

"His soul." Blackjack shifted uncomfortably on his haunches. "And where might that be?"

"In Heaven, of course."

Now Blackjack looked surprised. As he happened to glance down into the alley, a terrible thought struck him.

"I hope you're not stupid enough to be thinking of jumping," he said solemnly. "Even if suicide were a rational option, I can tell you right now that two floors isn't high enough. It'll hurt, but unless you land on your head it'll probably just cripple you, not kill you."

"I'm not going to jump, Blackjack. What made you think that? You don't jump to Heaven. You walk there."

"Pardon?"

"I had an idea," Luther explained. "It came to me yesterday, right after they took Moses' body away. I was down in the alley itself, sniffing around where he'd been lying, and I could still smell him."

"Of course you could. The weather's been clear, so there's no reason why the scent should fade quickly. What does that have to do with Heaven?"

"Well," said Luther, "I was standing there thinking, 'If I can smell Moses' body, I wonder if I could sniff out his soul.' And then I thought, 'What if I could sniff out Heaven itself?'"

"Oh . . ." Understanding was beginning to dawn.

"So I came up here, you see, to scent for Heaven. I suppose a taller building would have been better, but I like this spot, and Moses did too.

"Anyway," he continued, "for a long time I didn't get anything. All last night and this morning there was nothing but exhaust smell from the Lower City. And then, just a few hours ago, a breeze sprang up, and it brought a new smell. Very faint, but it was there.

"I smelled Heaven, Blackjack! It's up north. Up north so far that I'm not even sure the world quite reaches it, but I think I can make it . . . or we can, if you want to come with me."

Blackjack watched Luther nervously during this entire thought-speech, and soon realized that there was no way he was going to talk him out of making the journey. Every possible argument—that Heaven didn't exist, that if it did exist there would be no way to reach it alive, that it probably wasn't worth rushing to anyway—was blown away by the slightly romantic, slightly crazed look in Luther's eyes. He realized also, grudgingly, that his own somewhat tarnished but still honorable conscience would not allow him to stay behind while Luther went out into a world he was too innocent to survive in alone.

"Tell me one thing," Blackjack said, trying to resign himself to the idea of the journey and knowing he would get no sleep tonight.

"Sure," replied Luther, wagging his tail. "What do you want to know?"

"This Heaven place. What did it smell like?"

"Like rain," Luther told him wonderingly. "Rain and hills."

"Gee," said Blackjack. "That sounds just swell."

V.

They left three days later. Most of the other neighborhood dogs, and some of the cats, gathered to see them off. Good-byes were exchanged, good luck wished, and then they were on the move. Malcolm accompanied them for the first mile, reeling off some last-minute advice that was mostly intended for Luther.

". . . Now remember that you don't have collars, neither of you. That ain't a bad thing at all, ain't no man ever put a collar on me, but the 'catchers will know you for strays right off. Keep a sharp eye out for them, and remember that some of them can gun at you from a distance.

"Also," he said cautiously, as if crossing thin ice, "you got to watch out for 'Breds."

"'Breds?" asked Luther. "What are those?"

"Purebreds," said Blackjack, keeping his eyes on the road ahead. "Pure-bred dogs."

"What are—"

"Has to do with blood, mostly," Malcolm told him. "Me, I got blood from three or four strains of dog in me. You, Luther, you got even more—so much that it'd likely take God and a helper to get it all straignt. But a Purebred—that's a dog with only one strain, or so much of one that he can pretend that's all he's got. It's called havin' pedigree, and they think it makes them better than those that don't have it."

"But how can you tell who has pedigree, if it's just the blood? By smell?"

"Oh, you'll know, Luther. Purebreds come in a lot of types, a lot of flavors, you might say, but all the ones of the same type look the same. Not exactly the same, mind you, but there's a normal, a perfect, that they're trying to be. And they hate dogs like us. Mixes."

"Are all Purebreds like that?"

"No," Blackjack interjected. "He's exaggerating."

"Not by much, cat," insisted Malcolm. "Not by much at all. But you'll know the really bad ones—the ones that want to kill you—by a thought in their minds. You'll hear that thought clear as a bell, even if they're tryin' to cover it up with other thoughts."

"What thought?"

"*Mange*," Malcolm said. "That's what they call us. *Mange*. You hear that thought in another dog's mind, you feel it, smell it, taste it, then you'll know that dog is your enemy. Get away from him as fast as you can, kill him if you have to."

"Kill him?" Luther's eyes were wide with shock. "A dog that kills another dog lets Raaq into his heart, Malcolm. You know that. You can't—"

"Mayhap Raaq does get in. But as long as a dog's still alive, he can still hope to get Raaq back out. A dog killin' another dog happens all the time, Luther. And *you* know *that*."

Luther said nothing. He knew it, all right, but he also knew, as Moses had taught him, that things didn't have to be that way.

"Mange," Malcolm repeated, with a distaste that he did not try to hide. "You remember that word, Luther. Write it on your heart. And listen for it."

They had reached the outer limits of their home territory. Familiar smells faded into obscurity and were replaced by strange new ones. Other animals, other things.

"This is as far as I go," Malcolm told them. "You all remember what I told you, though, and take care. I'll miss you, Luther. Mayhap I'll even miss you, cat. You're no son of a bitch, but you do grow on a fellow."

"I'm flattered beyond belief," Blackjack said."

"Don't say good-bye, Malcolm," Luther said. "You never know, we might be back someday."

"I don't think so, Luther. Not that I don't want it that way, but that ain't how it feels."

"Making predictions about the future now?" Blackjack chided him. "I suppose that's appropriate, since we're heading off to find a mythical place."

"That's one thing about you, cat," replied Malcolm. "For a smart animal, you surely are stupid sometimes. How do you know I can't read the future? Ain't I read *you* pretty well? The future's a darker glass, less clear, but it ain't all secret."

"And you don't think we'll be back?" Luther said, saddened.

"No," said Malcolm. "You got big things ahead of you, Luther. Who knows, mayhap Heaven is waitin' for you out there. But I doubt as we'll meet again in this world."

"If there's another world besides this one," put in Blackjack, "I'll probably be in so much shock that I'll even be glad to see *your* ugly muzzle again, Malcolm. You *are* a son of a bitch, but I suppose you grow on a fellow, too."

"Take care then, cat. You too, Luther. Good-bye now."

"Good-bye, Malcolm," Luther said, and turned away. Blackjack followed at his heel.

Night was falling as they left. The sky was overcast but rainless, and the clouds glowed dully with the light reflected from Manhattan to the south. Malcolm stood at the edge of the home territory, his territory, and watched until both dog and cat had vanished into the gathering darkness.

As he walked back alone to the church, a light wind began to blow.

PRINCESS AURORA . . .

I.

On the morning that his daughter was due to leave for her last year of college, Walter Smith rose ahead of the sun, dressing quietly and slipping out into the chill Wisconsin morning before dawn could get a grip on the sky. Walt was a factory worker rather than a dairy farmer—and a retired factory worker at that—but his property bordered on one of the biggest cow pastures in the state. He headed there now, vaulting two fences and wading a shallow stream in defiance of his age. Arthritis had mercifully passed him over, for now, but he suspected that not even painful joints could have kept him indoors. Early morning was his time of rebellion. Especially this morning.

Hopelessly ordinary in most respects, Walter Smith's life could have served as a definition for the word *average*. Born in the early Twenties to Lutheran parents who were neither rich nor poor, he had lived through the Great Depression, the Second World War, the McCarthy witch hunts, the Civil Rights Movement, the Vietnam War, and the Watergate Era, national upheavals from which he felt barely a tremor. He married at twenty-five, settling on the outskirts of the sleepy Wisconsin town where he and his wife and daughter still lived. The next forty years of his life were spent working at a production plant for the Great Midwest Paint Company (and the most exciting event at the plant in those forty years had been the introduction of a brand new line of wood stains—Great Midwest Wood Stains, they were called). Walt had become a recognized and respected face in town, not the sort of person you'd vote for for mayor, but one you'd be sure to invite to your church social. A good, run-of-the-mill type fellow.

That was what everyone thought, anyway. Not even Walter's wife Prudence knew of his occasional habit of doing things that were, well, not quite so run-of-the-mill. These *digressions*, as Walter had come to call them in his mind, were never very frequent or large-scale. He knew in his heart that he was not cut out to be anything but regular, but over the years he had come to feel a deep appreciation for those lucky individuals who broke the mold. The

35

digressions were a salute of sorts, a tip of the hat to rebelliousness, craziness
. . . differentness.

Perhaps the impulse had always been in him, like a latent kidney
disorder, but it had come into its own rather late in his life. Walter would
never forget the day in 1955 when he had first fallen down the rabbit hole of
unorthodoxy, driven to the breaking point by the ruthlessness of Dick Stark,
an ex-marine and newly hired manager at the Great Midwest Paint Plant,
who must surely have numbered Attila the Hun among his ancestors. Walter's Primal Digression was simple; it involved nothing more than jumbling
the numbers on Stark's weekly delivery manifest, the huge, pale green ledger
in which the paint orders were logged. Pure chance brought Walt to Stark's
open and unguarded office, and he seemed to barely think as he performed
his act of sabotage, but the results were wondrous to behold: over the course
of the next two weeks, a Detroit funeral parlor undergoing renovation received a triple order of cheerful Lemon Yellow Latex; the congregation of a
newly built church in Ohio found itself awash in Electric Purple; a Great
Midwest Paint store in downtown Milwaukee got truckload after truckload of
Susan B. Anthony Pink . . . a shade not unlike that of the pink slip that Dick
Stark was given, unceremoniously, at the end of the month.

Walter had spent a good deal of time worrying over his sanity after this
stunt—it was the first time he had ever done something even remotely out of
line with the Straight and Narrow (and what a first!)—but the incident also
filled him with a strange sense of elation. For those few moments in the
Delivery Office, frantically altering the manifest, Walter Smith had had a
taste of the World of Unorthodoxy, and though it was not his world, it surely
did feel grand all the same.

Large-scale "digressions" such as this had remained few and far between
in the many years since then, but Walt had managed to pick up one or two
daily quirks as well. One was the habit of getting up very early and going out
to walk while the rest of Wisconsin—even the dairy farmers—still slept. And
now, in the age of his retirement, he had discovered something else, something deliciously rebellious and perfectly suited for the dark, private hours of
pre-dawn.

Sitting on a lonely tree stump at the border of the cow pasture, Walter
Smith reached into his jacket pocket for a plastic ziplock bag. Inside the bag
were four pre-rolled marijuana cigarettes. He bought them from an old
factory buddy named Don Mezz for a dollar apiece, coming out to the stump
and getting a buzz on on those mornings when the spirit moved him. Don
had been completely taken off guard the first time Walter approached him to
make a purchase, and Walt was particularly pleased with the memory of that
reaction.

He took out one of the joints, placing the bag on the stump beside him.
Lighting it with a tarnished Zippo, Walt inhaled deeply to get the coal going.

He held the smoke in his lungs for as long as he could, exhaling a clean white column. He was getting good at this; he no longer coughed after each drag.

For the next twenty minutes Walter did nothing but smoke. Usually he limited himself to one joint, but this morning he went considerably further than that; this morning he was worried about his daughter. His one and only daughter, whom he had often prayed would turn out to be a true rebel, not just a part-timer.

She had come into the world on a seemingly endless night some twenty-one years ago. The labor had lasted thirteen hours, and at one point Walt had wandered out of the waiting room in a nervous fit, looking for something unusual to do. He wound up buying a pack of Marlboros from a nearby candy store—in those days the thought of marijuana had not even crossed his mind, but as he was a non-smoker, tobacco was digressive enough—and nearly choked to death on his first inhale. Then, walking back to the hospital, he had looked up at the night sky and seen a glow: the Northern Lights, come down from Canada for a guest appearance.

The baby girl was christened Aurora Borealis Smith.

II.

"—so Brian said he thought that was a pretty sick thing, having magazines like that for sale in a family store where kids can walk right up and look at them, and Mr. Garfield said maybe that was true, but it wasn't Brian's store, and Brian could take his business elsewhere if he didn't like it. Then Brian asked him what he'd do if a lot of people started taking their business elsewhere. That's when it really started heating up. Mr. Garfield started talking about the First Amendment, and Brian whipped out his Bible, and they were arguing for the next hour or so—"

She was tall, pale, with blond hair that hung almost to her shoulders. Her lips were thin and pleasant, her cheeks well formed, her eyes bright blue like the noon reflection on a lake, or a cornflower in the lapel of a Duchess. Everything was nearly just right, as if she needed only one more ingredient to take her from pretty to beautiful.

Walter Smith watched Aurora as she made breakfast, not really hearing her words. Mrs. Smith was still in bed, suffering though her annual Cornell sick-in. At the beginning of Aurora's freshman year they had all driven out to Ithaca together, and their first sight driving into North Campus had been that of two women, standing on the East Avenue bridge above Fall Creek and exchanging an open-mouth kiss in broad daylight. Furthermore—as if God were trying to emphasize some point—they were an interracial couple, in addition to being homosexual. Walter had conceived great hopes for Cornell's radicalizing potential as a result of this, but his wife Prudence had nearly fainted. Now she grew violently ill every year as the beginning of the fall term approached, and had refused to set foot on the campus again until Aurora's graduation day.

"—afterwards we walked around and talked for a while. I wasn't really feeling too good about what had happened. Brian was right, of course, but scaring an old man like Mr. Garfield . . . well, you've got to think about him, too, not just about some kids who might pick up a *Penthouse*. I mean, *somebody* must buy them for him to have them in the first place, and maybe he thinks he needs the business—"

Walt was still playing touch-and-go with reality. He'd overdone it on the stump, smoking two joints and getting a good start on a third, not realizing until too late how hard it was going to hit him. He felt numb all over, his thoughts heavy-limbed; the most annoying property of a marijuana high was that it became impossible to concentrate on more than one thing at a time, and even that one thing had a way of slipping out from under you.

Aurora scrambled eggs and went on about her date last night, while Walter's mind pinwheeled back to the past. To his sons. Aurora had come along very late in the game, a surprise package of a birth, but earlier on Walter and Prudence had made two boys together.

Ed, the eldest, was a straight arrow, more run-of-the-mill than his own father (Walter had watched him carefully for any signs of the occasional digression, but there had been none). He lived in Minnesota with a sedate Methodist wife and two children of his own, worked as a consultant for an insurance firm, and sent a card every Christmas, Mother's, and Father's Day.

The other boy, Jesse, had come out of the womb only after a long and drawn-out delivery, screaming bloody murder. A world-beater from the very first. During the Vietnam War Jesse had been at Berkeley, marching in protest, getting arrested on an average of once a month. He had written home frequently about his exploits, sending newspaper clippings, and once his face had appeared briefly in a crowd on an evening newscast. Toward the end Walter had begun to suspect that Jesse had a boyfriend out there, as well. This had never been confirmed, but Walt had felt a touch of pride over it all the same—it would have been wonderfully unorthodox, though what Prudence might have thought . . .

Four days before his graduation, Jesse had been struck and killed by a car just outside of campus. The driver had not been drunk, merely looking the wrong way at the wrong time, and to Walter that seemed the cruelest thing of all—that there should be nowhere to lay blame, no one to shake a fist at, except perhaps Fate. He had cried a long time over Jesse, in a way, he had to admit to himself, that he could never have cried over Ed. And he might have proved inconsolable if not for something that Aurora, barely five at the time, had done for him.

She had stolen him a bouquet. Not just gathered it, but stolen it, crawling under fences and sneaking into private gardens all over town—and in one instance, according to her story, playing hide-and-seek with a very big Doberman Pinscher—to bring back a diverse collection of flowers: roses, marigolds, tulips, daffodils, peonies, others he couldn't even name. She gave him the bouquet and told him all about how she had come by it, and told him he could stop being so sad now, everything would be all right. He still had every one of the flowers, pressed between the pages of a hardbound copy of *The Adventures of Tom Sawyer* that lay in his bottom dresser drawer. He also still had the kernel of hope for her that had been born in him that day, for she'd had Jesse's look in her eyes, dormant but there all the same, waiting to be brought to life.

If only it hadn't been for Brian Garroway.

"—so Brian said—"

Brian was Aurora's steady boyfriend, had been since high school. To be brutally honest, he was her fiancé, in everything but name. All that remained was the buying of a ring and setting a date, a formality that would probably be taken care of by Thanksgiving break, Christmas at the latest. And then . . . then it would be too late.

"—and Brian—"

Walter was quite aware that to most parents, Brian would have seemed like perfect son-in-law material. He was a good fellow, clean-cut, about to graduate with a degree in Hotel Administration from one of the better universities in the country. Brian was also a born-again Christian, a steadfast believer who had no patience with drugs, alcohol, cigarettes, or pornography. Or world-beating. To see Brian marching in support of a liberal protest, Walt was convinced, would be a sure sign of a coming apocalypse. A nice kid, all things considered, one who would never break the rules, one who would marry, take his place as a productive member of society, raise a nice, average family, and never do anything noteworthy in his entire life.

"—and we—"

We. That was another thing about Brian: he seemed to be in love with the first person plural. We this and we that. If you let him, he'd do your talking (and even your thinking) for you. Walter feared this especially, that Brian would wear away to nothing, out of the best of intentions, whatever remained of that little girl who had once stolen him a bouquet.

The marijuana high (actually more of a low) tinged all these thoughts with a deeper sense of paranoia and desperation than usual, and as Aurora set a steaming plate of scrambled eggs and bacon before him, smiling unsuspectingly, he resolved to talk openly with her before she was off to Cornell and beyond his reach. As she got her own plate of eggs and sat down at the table he caught her glance, held it, making it perfectly clear just from the look on his face that he had something of the utmost importance to say to her. Walter opened his mouth to speak, but his state betrayed him, and the words that came out were perhaps not the best:

"If you ever were to decide you were a lesbian," he told her in all seriousness, "I'd understand."

Because she did not, in fact, have any plans of becoming a lesbian, and because it wasn't the sort of subject she thought about regularly, Aurora's response to this was perhaps predictable: the one-word question "What?" either blurted out, stuttered, or spoken calmly. It took her a moment, though—as it might have taken many people a moment—for her ears to run a test and make sure they'd heard correctly.

"What?" she said, splitting the difference between blurting and calm speech.

Walter looked at her across the table, his eyes red and watery—and not all of that was from the pot.

"Daddy," she said, her voice still uncertain how to compose itself, "Daddy, what's wrong?"

His tongue froze on him. He balled his hand into a fist and struck his thigh as one might strike a defective tape recorder, forcing himself to concentrate, and the words came out in a flood:

"Jesse. I was just thinking about your brother Jesse, how he . . . how he had this smile, this special smile about him. One of the clippings he sent us during the War protests, I still have it, it shows these two policemen dragging him away after he screamed out that Lyndon Johnson was a pig. They were dragging him away to a special police bus, and one of the cops had just clubbed him, but he was smiling, smiling and shouting all the same, as if it were the greatest thing in the world. That smile, it was an *I'm alive* smile, I guess you'd call it, because he *was* alive . . . he . . . he . . ."

The words faltered again, and Aurora shook her head, still struggling.

"Daddy, I don't—" she bit her lip. "Are you trying to say that Jesse was gay, or . . ."

"No, no!" Walter burst out. "No! I mean, he might have been, you can always hope, but that's not the point, the point is . . . the point . . . it was the smile, the smile! Jesse never tried to conform, he was *different*, different in a dozen ways, and that being different made him *alive*, made him smile. Ed, he smiles and laughs too, but never that way. Not everyone is meant to smile that way, maybe. Oh, but if you've got it in you, the potential, and you don't . . . don't . . ."

He reached across the table and took one of Aurora's hands, clasping it tightly.

"I can remember," he continued, "I can remember two years after Jesse died, and we took a trip to Minnesota for Ed's wedding. At the reception all the bridesmaids were lined up like birds at one side of the hall, with these big yellow bonnets on their heads, and you got one of Jesse's *I'm alive* smiles on your face and asked me what would happen if someone went and started knocking those girls' hats off. And I . . . I would have let you do it, you know, let you try jumping up and knocking hats off. But your mother overheard, she was already upset over some of the relatives she'd had to talk to, she told you to behave and stop thinking things like that. When . . . when did you start listening to your mother, Aurora?"

"Daddy, *what* . . ."

"I just don't want you to wake up thirty years from now," he told her, squeezing her hand almost tightly enough to hurt, "and realize that your chance to have more of a life, your chance to smile the way Jesse smiled, all the time, has gone by. I don't want you to feel that loss. Do you see? Do you understand?"

III.

"Don't worry about the damage, Mr. Smith," Brian Garroway was saying. "The left headlight's out, but the engine's fine and we won't be driving after dark. You can thank my younger brother for this, by the way. His sense of responsibility belongs in a Crackerjack box."

Brian carried Aurora's bags to the back of his station wagon, which was parked in the Smith's driveway. The wagon had a bumper sticker that said "JESUS IS MY BACKSEAT DRIVER." It also had a pronounced dent in the left side of the front fender; the headlight was mortally wounded.

"Are you sure you're going to be all right?" Aurora asked her father in low voice, as Brian unlocked the back of the wagon. "I swear I thought you were having some kind of a nervous breakdown at breakfast."

"I'll be fine," Walter said. She studied him uncertainly, and noticed for the first time how very red his eyes were. A thought struck her, one which she dismissed immediately as ridiculous.

"What would you say," Walter went on, "if I offered to drive you?"

"Drive me where, Daddy? You don't mean to *Ithaca*, do you?"

"The car's in the garage," said Walter. "Tank's almost full. We could go a fair piece down the road before we even had to stop. And we could talk, just you and me, about anything you want. My 'nervous breakdown,' for instance."

"Daddy . . ."

"I mean it. Back at breakfast I wasn't too clear-headed, but I'm feeling better. I might like to rest a little bit more before we take off, but I *will* drive you. Really."

"But . . . well, what about Brian?"

"Let him drive his own damn car," Walter replied, and Aurora would have laughed at this if it were not for the fact that he was dead serious.

"Daddy," she said again, "Daddy, you've got to realize how silly this is."

Walter lowered his eyes, nodding.

"It is pretty silly, isn't it? Pretty damn silly, yes . . ." He looked up again. "But what do you say?"

For the briefest instant—only an instant, mind you—Aurora considered accepting his offer, leting him drive her all the way to Ithaca if it was that important to him. And maybe, just maybe, it wasn't only for his sake that she considered it.

"Let's go, Aurora!" Brian called, breaking the spell.

"I love you, Daddy," Aurora said, kissing Walter on the cheek. Then she was hurrying to the station wagon, pausing to yell back over her shoulder: "I'll call as soon as we get there, all right? . . . I promise."

Walter nodded again, and had to fight hard to keep his fists from clenching. He felt worn out, beaten.

"You take care now," Walter said.

Aurora opened her mouth to speak, but Brian Garroway said: "We'll be fine, Mr. Smith. Don't worry yourself."

The two climbed into the station wagon, slammed the doors. "Seat belts," Brian said automatically, even as Aurora was reaching for hers. He turned on the engine, put the station wagon in reverse, and began to back gingerly down the driveway. Walter waved from the house and Aurora waved back . . . and as they approached the end of the driveway, she reached over to the steering wheel and honked the horn twice.

"Cripes!" Brian said, startled. His nervous system did a few quick jumping jacks. "What'd you do that for?"

"Just saying good-bye," she told him.

"Well please do it some other way. I'm in a very edgy mood about this car right now."

Aurora made no response to this and waved to her father one last time. Then the station wagon was moving down the road, leaving home and parents behind. There was silence in the car for the next few minutes.

"This is going to be a good year," Brian finally said. He smiled and squeezed her hand. "Maybe the best year so far."

"I hope so," Aurora said. She smiled back, and Brian never even noticed how forced it looked. "I really hope so."

She suddenly wished very badly that she'd taken her father's offer.

IV.

As for Walter Smith, his morning ended in prayer. Not the orthodox, "Lord we beseech thee" style of prayer, but something much closer to true conversation. Walter, had not been to church in some years—though Prudence still went regularly, and Brian Garroway frequently urged him to do the same—but he still retained a fair amount of faith; surely the world could not have become so wonderfully mixed-up without a guiding, jester's hand.

When the station wagon was out of sight, Walter sat down on his front porch and stared at the stretch of driveway where Brian had been parked.

"Listen," he began. "I need a really big favor, I think. . . ."

. . . AND LADY CALLIOPE

Day ran on into night again, and that evening, in Delaware, the most beautiful woman in the world left the capital city of Dover and walked north on U.S. 13. Her name was Calliope, and on the long road behind her she left a string of carefully broken hearts, like diamonds cut to a finer shape by a master lapidary.

Cut to a finer shape . . . she too was finely shaped, custom-made in a sense. In the city she had just left there lived an out-of-work mechanic, a man of little ambition and even less courage. Shy but possessed of a depth of passion that was his one strength, this mechanic favored women with fiery red hair, milk-white skin, and silver eyes, women of medium height whom he could kiss without stretching or stooping; Calliope fit this description exactly, more exactly than might have been believed possible. Even for those whose fantasy lover was different, Calliope had a heart-catching edge to her, a perfect, irresistible something. That she walked tonight was a fact of her own choosing; no motorist, regardless of their hurry, would have denied Calliope a ride had she desired one. But she did choose to walk, wanting to be alone for a time, as she always did after an Exit.

Back in Dover, the mechanic would soon return from a day's wandering to find his lover Gone. Not gone, but Gone. Photographs of the two of them together now showed only one person, him; a jacket saturated with her scent now smelled only of must; their bed was made, as if never slept in. He would search for her frantically, and when he realized that she was truly lost forever, the Hurt would begin. Calliope had seduced him well; he would Hurt so badly that at first he would think he was going to die. But when death did not come, he would find himself being transformed by his Pain, and in the end for the sake of lost love he would be drawn into an act of great heroism, of consequence. Exactly how this was to come about and for what purpose Calliope could not have said . . . she knew only that it had something to do with a Story. As always. But she was not the Storyteller; she was part of the Tale.

Calliope turned her thoughts ahead, to the next Meeting. This upcoming Love promised to be an important one, and more complicated than the last. She cleared her mind and walked, duffel bag slung over her shoulder, a tiny silver whistle hanging from a chain around her neck.

There was no moon that night. Calliope traveled far, in darkness. By eleven forty-five she had reached the small town of Talbot's Legacy, some twenty miles outside of Dover. The road was deserted, and she passed through the town's center with no company except for the scant streetlamps that cast faint circles of light on the asphalt every thirty yards or so. And the wind, of course. The wind was always with her.

The Turning began at exactly twelve o'clock.

Far to the north, so many miles distant that no natural creature could have heard it from here, a set of tower chimes marked the passage of one day into another as the clock touched midnight. Calliope's ears perked up at the sound.

A moment later she walked beneath one of the streetlamps, and her hair was longer. Longer, and darker—it covered her ears, nearly touching her shoulders. And that was not the only thing different about her, though for a moment it was the most noticeable.

Thirty-some paces in the shadows, and another streetlamp captured her. Her hair, black as the new moon, now hung halfway down her back. Her skin had taken on color, and her eyes were phasing from silver to dark brown.

More paces, more changes. Calliope's entire stature began to change, becoming shorter, thinner; her skin continued to color, taking on a rich olive cast; her breasts grew smaller, more compact, but still perfectly proportioned; her nose widened.

The entire metamorphosis took perhaps five minutes. When it was done, Calliope stopped under another streetlamp and looked at her reflection in a nearby storefront. It had been a long time since she had been Asian; she liked what she saw.

"I'm on my way, George," said Calliope, executing a graceful pirouette in the lamplight. "I'm on my way."

A SIDETRIP
THROUGH HELL

I.

For Luther and Blackjack, New York City had become a memory left far behind. Led by the mongrel's nose and the Heaven scent, they had been traveling for some days now, in a zigzagging but roughly northwesterly direction. This particular morning they had come upon a town, the name of which they never learned. They had passed through a residential area—rows of neat houses, each with its own well-kept yard and garage—and were now nearing its center. Blackjack was unusually calm after their stroll through the peaceful neighborhood—which had been mercifully free of petting children and hose-spraying old men—but Luther found himself growing suddenly tense. His anxiety took a quantum leap when he saw a white van cross through an intersection about two blocks ahead.

"I can feel Raaq in this place," Luther began to say. "Maybe we should—"

"Oh, hell!"

"What is it?" said Luther, thinking that Blackjack must have smelled danger too, or seen something.

"Heat," Blackjack told him. "Just caught a whiff of it. There's a puss in heat around here. A street puss, if I'm lucky." He looked at Luther hopefully. "It's kind of tempting, you know. Would you mind if I just nipped off for a moment and . . ."

"There's danger here, Blackjack," Luther replied. "Can't you feel it? Raaq . . . Raaq's somewhere close."

"Raaq," the Manx repeated, unimpressed. "Well listen, Luther, isn't Raaq only supposed to bother dogs? I mean, he's your devil, not mine. So I don't have anything to worry about. And if he *does* show up, I'll hit him broadside while he's concentrating on you and knock him senseless." A poorly constructed chain of logic, but Blackjack was in a hurry to get laid now and didn't want to waste time arguing over nonsense.

46

Luther looked away, disappointed. "OK, Blackjack," he said. "You go ahead, if you want to think I'm being superstitious. I'll wait here for you as long as I can. But if something does happen—"

"Please, please don't try and make me feel guilty, Luther. I came with you on this trip, didn't I? And I promise I'm going to stick by you until we find your Heaven, but right now I want a little heaven of my own. That's not too much to ask, is it?" He began backing away in the direction of the heat-scent, all the while looking at Luther with wide, imploring eyes. "I'll be back before you know it. Cats don't take that long anyway and I can be fast when I'm pressed for time. I'll be right back."

"Go on, then," Luther said flatly. "But it's a mistake, Blackjack. This is a bad place."

"We'll be gone soon enough," Blackjack called back, vanishing into an alley.

Luther crouched nervously beside a telephone pole, not at all reassured by Blackjack's words. He watched the street, wondering from which direction Raaq would come at him, and in what form.

Directly above him, a handbill had been stapled to the pole. Luther glanced at it once and then ignored it. Perhaps Blackjack could have made sense of it, but to him it was just a meaningless collection of symbols.

The handbill read:

ATTENTION
Town Ordinance #101-bb
passed 4/13 this year:
Due to a large number of incidents involving stray
animals, a revised leash law has been passed by City
Hall. Any dog or cat discovered roaming free within the
town limits will be taken to the Animal Shelter. If the
animal has a collar with proper identification, the owner
will be contacted and a fee imposed for return
of the animal.
Unclaimed animals, and those without any
identification, will, after a period of
thirty (30) days, be either sold or destroyed.
LEASH YOUR PET—IT'S THE LAW

II.

Half an hour later, Blackjack had still not returned. Luther found himself caught in a great dilemma, for trouble had arrived, and though he wanted to run, he was not at all certain that he could find Blackjack, or that the Manx would be able to find him. But to stay here much longer might bring even worse consequences.

Luther remained crouched beside the telephone pole. Across the street, two German Shepherds lounged—not too casually—in front of a vacant lot. They were watching him. A Boxer had been with them earlier, but he had hurried away down a side street as soon as Luther had been spotted.

Now, at last, Luther understood what a Purebred really was. The Shepherds *did* look alike, and their coats were sharp and clear, as opposed to the random, muddied coloration of the mongrels Luther had grown up with. He could see how such dogs might develop a certain pride in themselves— they were beautiful, no denying that.

But Raaq was in them, or he had been in them before and left a mark on their hearts, and that dimmed their beauty to nothing. *Have you killed others of your kind?* Luther would have asked them, had he not been so afraid. *Other dogs? I think you have.* And that thought that Malcolm had warned him about—*Mange*—filled the Shepherds' minds like poison as they watched him.

Luther looked at the alley, wondering how far Blackjack had had to go to find the puss.

"Blackjack?" Luther said with sudden hope, as he heard a noise in the alley. But it was only a newspaper blown by a light breeze. Then the breeze died, leaving the paper scattered on the sidewalk like a dirty white shroud.

Blackjack, Luther thought to himself. *Blackjack, where are you?*

And where were the people? Surely some kind Master would save him if the Shepherds chose to attack. But there were no people on this street, no one coming in or out of the stores.

It was as if someone—Raaq?—didn't want him to escape.

More noise from the alley. It was definitely an animal this time, and Luther knew he had waited too long, because it was a big animal, too big to be Blackjack.

A Great Dane padded out of the alley. The Dane stood almost three feet high at the shoulders, more than a foot taller than Luther.

"Hello, mange," it said.

Luther began to move then. He walked along the sidewalk, away from the Dane, and the big dog did not attack him. It simply followed him, at a distance of about ten feet. Across the street the Shepherds had stopped lounging, and they too were trailing him.

Luther walked, slowly gaining speed as panic took him.

"Hello, mange."

The greeting came from a vacant lot on his right. He had thought to turn in there, but saw that a Golden Retriever and two Schnauzers were waiting for him. He kept on straight past the lot. The Retriever and the Schnauzers fell in beside the Great Dane.

Now it was worse. Now they were talking about him.

"Kind of runty-looking, isn't he?" This from one of the Schnauzers, who was actually a good bit smaller than Luther.

"Sort of," the Great Dane agreed. "But I'll bet he's got some fight in him."

"All manges do," said the Retriever. "Where do you suppose he came from?"

"It doesn't matter. Manges are everywhere. There's too damn many of them."

"What do you think Dragon'll do with him?"

"That isn't hard to figure out."

"*I'd* feed him to Cerberus, if I were Dragon."

Forced to listen to them, Luther suddenly heard other words, deeper down in his mind where his best memories lay. Moses' words.

"You don't ever kill another dog, don't ever even fight with one. A day may come when you feel pressed, when you feel there ain't no other way out, but remember that a dog that lets Raaq into his heart is dead anyhow."

"But Malcolm says—"

"Don't you listen to Malcolm. Malcolm ain't anything special, nothing special at all. Just think how easy it is to give yourself over to hate, and then remember that the easy thing is never the right thing. Never. And that's what Malcolm's all about.

"You mark me well, Luther. God gave a dog four legs so he could run, and he gave him a mind so he could pick the right way to run. You know which way that is?"

"Any way but Raaq's way."

"That's right. You keep that well."

"—stupid mange, I wonder if he'll beg as much as the last one." Luther quickened his pace still more. Up ahead was an intersection, and if he bolted at just the right moment he might yet escape. They had him flanked, but so far the Shepherds hadn't tried to cut in front of him. A quick zigzag into a convenient alley and he could—

The Boxer, the one that had been with the Shepherds before, appeared on the sidewalk at the intersection, panting heavily. He was followed by a Dalmation, an Irish Setter, and a Bull Terrier.

There was no way out, now. The Shepherds crossed the street, closing the ring tightly around him. Luther backed up against a storefront—a butcher shop, it happened to be—and waited as the other dogs moved in toward him.

"Hello, mange," the Boxer said.

III.

"State your pedigree, Booth."

The Cocker Spaniel cowered in the center of a narrow courtyard which had been formed incidentally from the placement of several connecting buildings, most of them warehouses. No windows overlooked the courtyard, and the only exits were one padlocked back door and two alleyways, one of which was blocked off by a chain-link fence. The air in the place was still and hot, and the walls and ground were stark in the noon sunlight. A pack of various kinds of Terriers had arrayed themselves along one wall like a jury, and two Bull Mastiffs stood guard at the open alleyway; various other Purebreds stood or crouched in random places. At the far end of the court, three Doberman Pinschers ringed a high mound of gravel. Sitting atop the mound was the dog that had just thought-spoken—an Irish Wolfhound, the largest of the breeds. It measured nearly seven feet from nose to tail, and stood a yard high at the shoulders. Its coat was pure white, and unlike some of the other dogs in attendance, it wore no collar.

"Booth!" the Wolfhound exclaimed when the Spaniel did not answer immediately. "State your pedigree!"

Still the Spaniel hesitated, and a Bulldog with only one ear ran up and nipped at his flank.

"Dragon's given you an order!" the Bulldog said, barking furiously at the same time, "Answer him!"

This only terrified the Spaniel further, and the Bulldog began snapping at his flank again, driving him around in a circle. The other dogs watched this with great amusement.

"Judas!" the Wolfhound finally said, and the Bulldog came to immediate attention. "Leave him be."

"Of course, Dragon. As you wish." The Bulldog gave one more bark and backed off. The Spaniel was now bleeding from a tear in its hind leg.

"Now, Booth . . ." the Wolfhound began.

There was a disturbance at the entrance to the courtyard. A new pack of dogs had arrived, led by a Boxer and a Great Dane. Luther was in the pack, forcibly hidden in the center. He was to be a surprise. The guards allowed the pack to enter, and after a quick glance the Wolfhound paid no attention to them.

". . . let's make this simple," he continued. "I asked you for your pedigree, but we both know it, don't we? Your sire and dam were both Purebred Spaniels, correct?"

"Y-y-yes," the Spaniel said. He was not terribly bright, and close inbreeding had given him a peculiar mental defect—the telepathic equivalent of a stutter.

"What was that?"

"Y-yes, Dr-dr-dragon."

"And your grandsires? All Spaniels?"

"Y-yes."

"How many generations back? How many that you know for certain?"

"Seh-seh-seven. M-maybe eh-eight."

"That's pretty good," the Wolfhound told him. "Eight generations. That's even better than old Judas, there." The Bulldog glowered at this, but did not protest. "You're a real Purebred, Booth. And tell me, what is the law for Purebreds?"

"N-n-n-not . . . n-not t-t-to . . ."

"Not to what?"

"N-not to m-m-mate outside the br-br-br-br-"

"Breed! Breed!" snapped Judas.

"-br-br-breed."

"Very good, Booth." The Wolfhound showed teeth that were nearly as white as his coat. "And what is your crime?"

The Spaniel did not reply.

"Come on, Booth," the Wolfhound cajoled him, warning back Judas with a glance. "What is your crime?"

"I-I b-broke the br-br-breeding l-law. I . . . huh-huh-had re-luh-lations . . . w-with a b-b-bitch outside m-my br-br-breed."

" 'Had relations.' " The Wolfhound pulled the corners of his mouth back so far that he seemed to be smiling. Then, with sudden fury: "You *impregnated* her, you idiot! And *by* impregnating her, you forced me to destroy what was otherwise a perfect animal."

"Destroy?" Luther said, trying to see better over the dogs that surrounded him. "What does—"

"Shut up, mange," the Great Dane said sharply.

In the center of the courtyard, the Spaniel had begun to cringe again. "Dr-dr-dragon," he tried to say. "Dr-dragon, i-i-it—"

"You broke the breeding law, Booth," the Wolfhound overrode him. "You broke the highest law there is. Now tell us, tell everyone here, what is the penalty for breaking the highest law?"

"I know!" Judas piped up. "A dog who breaks the breeding law, who risks the creation of manges, has betrayed the entire Purebred Order as well as his own breed. For this treason he shall be torn apart, even as he sought to tear apart the foundations of decency."

The Wolfhound nodded.

"Cerberus," he said.

At the word, the three Dobermans stood up as one. Luther caught a clear view of them and immediately noticed something strange, both in the way they moved and in the way their eyes looked. He watched them stride forward and circle the Spaniel. Even when the three were not making identical motions, they seemed to be moving eerily in tandem with one another . . . almost as though they were possessed of a single mind.

"Dr-dragon!" the Spaniel pleaded, pawing vainly at the ground as if to dig a hole to hide in. "Dr-dr-dragon, p-please! Wh-when Assa d-d-died, you pr-promised t-t-to g-g-get m-me someone n-n-new: Y-you pr-pr-promised: I-I-I-I c-couldn't w-wait any-muh-more: I-is th-th-that s-s-so bad? I-i-is th-th-tha—"

"Gut him," ordered the Wolfhound. The Dobermans fell on the Spaniel from all sides.

Luther closed his eyes and turned his head away. This did not prevent him from hearing the sounds, but fortunately the execution took only a moment. During that moment, a strange thing happened; Luther felt his fear slipping away, to be replaced by an oddly spiritual calm. Moses' words began echoing in his mind again.

"Enough!" the Wolfhound commanded, and the Dobermans backed off, their teeth and muzzles bloody. What was left of the Spaniel did not much resemble a dog, or any other animal for that matter. The Dobermans returned to their places surrounding the mound, and one of the Bull Mastiffs came forward to drag away the carcass.

"So," said the Wolfhound, "what's the next order of business?"

The Great Dane in front of Luther barked tentatively.

"Hello, Aleister," the Wolfhound greeted him. "You have something for us?"

The Dane and the other dogs who surrounded Luther moved aside, revealing him to the crowd. The Wolfhound's eyes widened, and the Dobermans began barking in earnest.

"*Mange*," said the Wolfhound gleefully. "Aleister, you've found us a *mange*."

"Oh, well, it wasn't just me," the Dane disclaimed, trying to seem modest. The Boxer and the two Shepherds looked at him in irritation. "I had help capturing him."

"We shall have to reward all of you, then. Where did you find him?"

"Right out in the street," the Boxer interjected before the Dane could reply. "He was just sitting there, like he was waiting for something."

The Wolfhound digested this. "Could he have been waiting for another mange? Or a group of them?"

"I don't know, Dragon." The Boxer looked nervous, as if he were afraid of being punished for the oversight. "I suppose it's possible. I'm sorry, we didn't wait around to see."

"We'll have to make a search later on, then. After we've taken care of this one. Can't have manges wandering loose in the town." He focused his attention on Luther. "Step forward, mange."

Still inexplicably calm, Luther did as he was told, moving to the place the Spaniel had occupied. Blood stained the ground before him.

"What is your name, mange?" the Wolfhound asked.

"They call me Luther."

"You say 'they'—were there others with you before you were captured?"

"I'm the only . . . the only 'mange' . . . that I know of in this place."

The Wolfhound squeezed his eyes down to slits, concentrating.

"You're lying," he said. "No, not exactly . . . but you are hiding something. You were traveling, traveling with a companion. Who was it? What type of animal?"

He can see into me, Luther realized. *Just like Malcolm. But his sight isn't as strong as Malcolm's was.*

"Why don't you figure it out for yourself?" Luther challenged him. "If you can."

"Do I detect a touch of impertinence? Or is that a show of courage?"

"You mean to kill me," Luther replied. "I don't have to look into your mind to see that. You'll fancy it up and make a big deal of it, maybe, just so you can have some fun, but in the end it'll still be dog killing dog. Raaq is in your hearts, all of you, and I guess it doesn't make any difference if I'm 'impertinent' or not."

Several of the Terriers howled in amusement at this, while the Dobermans growled continuously. The Wolfhound merely nodded.

"Impressive speech. My name is Dragon, if you haven't already gathered that. I am Pack Leader of this domain. I don't suppose I have to tell you your crime, do I?"

"There's nothing to tell."

"You are a mange. An unnatural and disgusting intermingling of breeds meant to be kept forever separate. Under our law, your very existence is a crime."

Now Luther barked mirthfully. "If you mean to say that I committed a crime by being whelped, you must think I'm God. Creation is His responsibility."

"The crime," continued the Wolfhound, "is punishable by destruction."

"Destruction is God's responsibility too. Dogs can only murder. That's what you really meant, isn't it?"

Dragon studied him. "You have spirit, mange. Much more than Booth did. Can you fight?"

"Absolutely not."

"You can't, or won't? I somehow find it hard to believe that you're a coward."

"I won't join you in killing. Raaq may take my life, but he won't have my soul in the bargain."

"Not a coward, then. Merely stupid. That's another mange quality. You see now why we have to be so stringent in our breeding regulations."

"Booth didn't look all that smart," Luther observed.

"Booth was a sad exception to the rule," replied the Wolfhound. "But in a way that's your fault, too. The more manges in the world, the fewer Purebreds, and the smaller each Purebred line. Booth's ancestors were forced to breed too closely, due to a shortage of Spaniels in the area."

"And it backfired," Luther pressed him. "So maybe it's not such a good system."

"Oh, mange. Even a crippled Purebred is infinitely superior to your kind, don't you understand that?"

But Luther refused to be baited. "If that's true," he said, "then you must have to check out every new member of your Order carefully, to make sure his ancestors were all all right. . . ."

"Pedigree," said the Wolfhound. "All Purebreds must have a clean pedigree going back at least five generations. We have ways of making sure they're telling the truth about it."

"But only *five* generations?" said Luther, feigning surprise. "That's hardly anything. Where I come from, the Purebreds have to check out to *twelve* generations."

This stunned all of them, in a way Luther would not have imagined possible. More than a few of the Purebreds started to get very nervous, as well.

"*Twelve?*" exclaimed Judas, twitching uncomfortably. "Twelve, that wouldn't be right, not at all. How could you expect any dog—"

"He's lying!" the Wolfhound said, probing Luther's mind. "The pesthole he comes from doesn't even have Purebreds."

"But why are you so jumpy?" Luther inquired. "You're Pack Leader, Dragon. *You* could trace back twelve generations, couldn't you? Or is there a stain somewhere in your pedigree?"

"My pedigree is flawless!" Dragon insisted. "And you, mange, you're dead. Slowly and painfully." He glanced at the Dobermans. "Cerb—"

The command was interrupted by a new thought-voice, loud and frightened, which came from the unblocked alleyway.

". . . missa dog, ya don't wants to botha me. I's jes an ol' cat, an ol' puddycat what don't botha nobody, nobody 't'all. Ya ain'ts gonna wanna *hurt* ol' 'Jack, is ya? I sho do hope—"

"Move it!" ordered another.

A black cat with no tail tumbled past the guards into the courtyard, followed by an angry-looking Malamute. It took Luther a moment to realize that the cat was Blackjack, because the Manx was moving and holding himself in a way that he had never seen before. Luther finally put his paw on what it was: Blackjack was acting humble, and a scared humble at that.

"What do we have here?" asked Dragon.

Judas barked joyously. "It has no *tail!* Look at that! A cat with no tail!"

Blackjack crouched low to the ground, not hissing or defensive, but appearing to be more terrified, if that were possible, than the Spaniel had been. "I found this . . . this *tom*," the Malamute explained distastefully, "wandering in the street. It asked me if I'd seen a mange named Luther. I thought you'd want to know about it, Dragon."

"So," the Wolfhound said, making the connection, "*this* is your traveling companion."

The Malamute seemed perplexed for a moment, then growled as it caught sight of Luther.

"Move the mange off to the side!" Dragon ordered. "We'll do the cat first, and let him watch!"

It was no sooner thought than done. Luther was hustled to the sidelines by the Great Dane and the Boxer, and Blackjack was shoved violently forward until he occupied the spot where the Spaniel had been killed.

"What's goin' on?" the Manx asked, shuddering. "What's y'all plannin' to do? I's jes an old puddycat, ya don—"

"Stop your whining!" the Malamute snapped.

"Cerberus." said Dragon. The Dobermans rose. "You are at your own discretion, Cerberus—but make it entertaining."

Blackjack's fur stood on end as the Dobermans approached him. He tried to back away, but the Malamute set up a fierce barking that scared him out of his retreat.

"Please, missa dog," Blackjack groveled, prostrating himself. "Please, ya don't wants to hurt me, does ya? I's never done nothin' to a dog, never *would* do nothin', no, not this puddycat. . . ."

"Now I know where you get your courage, mange," Dragon said. "You must have stolen *his*."

Luther made no reply. He was studying Blackjack, wondering what in hell had happened to him. Could something have driven him mad?

"Please, missa dog, please . . ."

The Dobermans encircled him now. They spent a few moments snapping at him, teasing him and driving him back and forth. Then one of them, one that was slightly larger than the other two but otherwise identical, moved in until he and Blackjack were almost nose to nose. Like Dragon before, the Doberman's lips were drawn back so far that he seemed to grin. Saliva dripped from his exposed fangs.

"I bet he's going to take his balls," Judas offered. "Hey cat, he's going to take your balls!"

"Really?" said Blackjack, sliding his claws out and locking them. "I'm afraid he'll have to do it by smell."

"Cerberus!" Dragon warned, too late. "Cerberus, look out!"

The last thing the Doberman had been expecting—the last thing *any* of them had been expecting—from the panicked cat was an attack. As a result, the dog did not even have a chance to defend itself as the Manx reached past its muzzle and calmly and professionally tore out its eyes.

"Much too easy," said Blackjack. The Doberman whipped its bleeding head back and howled in agony . . . as did the other two Dobermans.

Blackjack began to run. The two unwounded Dobermans regained their composure a moment later, and leapt blindly for the spot where the Manx had been. Not finding him, they began to bite and tear at each other instead.

"That," said Blackjack, looking back over his shoulder, "is the stupidest fucking thing I have ever seen. Luther! Come on!"

Luther heard the call and ran for it, momentarily unimpeded. The sight of the ruined Cerberus held the Purebreds entranced. Luther caught up with Blackjack, and the two of them had actually gotten almost two-thirds of the way to the alley before Dragon awakened to their escape.

"Stop them!" the Wolfhound ordered. "Tear them apart!"

Now the other dogs all rushed forward, and it might have seemed that Blackjack and Luther had no chance. But if there was one thing that the Manx had learned long ago, it was that a task that can be performed easily by a few often proves impossible for an army. The air was already heavy with a blood smell, and this drove a number of the Purebreds into a killing frenzy—or perhaps the spirit of Raaq entered them. Those that did not immediately find their intended victims in many cases turned and attacked one another.

Luther somehow slipped through the initial wave of attackers. Later he would suggest to Blackjack that God or Moses' ghost had aided him, and out of politeness Blackjack would say nothing. Once through this front wave he was caught in a press of dogs, all straining to get into the fray. He was bitten any number of times—the frenzy had spread to all the Purebreds by now—but none seemed to realize that he was the dog they were trying to get to. Little by little he began to work himself through the crowd toward the alleyway, which was now unguarded.

Blackjack saw two German Shepherds coming at him from the front, a Great Dane and a Malamute from the right, four assorted Terriers from the left, and an unruly and uncountable mob from behind. He picked the tallest approaching dog, stayed low, and shot right under it. Taking advantage of the ensuing chaos, he too skirted around toward the alleyway, disabling any dog that attempted to stop him.

Dragon shoved his way through the throng, searching. Two big dogs reared up on their hind legs in front of him, grappling with one another. He separated them, then dove on an animal he thought was Luther. It was not; it was the Boxer who had helped bring Luther in. Dragon had picked it up by the neck and worried it to death before realizing his mistake.

Then, by chance, he glanced at the alleyway, just in time to see Luther and Blackjack scurrying away. No one else had noticed their departure.

"No!" he cried. "They're escaping! They're escaping! Stop fighting each other and go after them! Stop fighting each other. . . ."

But it was a while before he could get the Purebreds to listen to him.

IV.

"What happened to you, Blackjack?" Luther asked as they scrambled out of the alleyway. "You were gone so long I thought something had gotten you."

"Something almost did," the Manx told him. " 'Catchers. A pair of goddamned 'catchers in a big van. They got the puss. I had her spotted and was just about to make my move when they came along and nabbed her. A minute later and I guess they would have gotten me too—caught me in the act, so to speak."

"Did they see you?"

"That was why I was gone so long. One of them came after me on foot. Ran pretty fast for a two-legged. He was shooting at me with some funny kind of gun and once he almost hit me. By the time I shook him and found my way back, the 'Breds had already grabbed you. So I found that Malamute and let him grab me."

"You did a good job acting scared, Blackjack. You almost had me convinced you'd lost your mind."

"It wasn't that hard to act," the Manx admitted. "I've never run into a group of dogs like that before, but if there are more of them scattered around the countryside, I can see what Malcolm's so paranoid about."

They zigzagged through the streets, following no definite path but being careful not to double back. Luther scented for Heaven, but could find no whiff of it in this place.

"I can't find Heaven, Blackjack," Luther said. Blood ran from a dozen wounds on his body, all of them minor. "What are we going to do?"

"Get out of this town as fast as we can, is what," Blackjack replied. "We can worry about Heaven later."

A grey-haired man with a cane spotted them as they turned the next corner. He noticed that they were without leashes or collars, and, remembering how a stray cat-and-dog team had torn up his garden two months earlier, he went to the nearest pay phone and called the Animal Shelter.

V.

"Well, Lucrezia?"

The Bloodhound bitch sniffed the ground carefully, then the air. "North," she said finally. "They're heading roughly north from here."

"Good," said Dragon. "That's what I think, too, but I wanted to be certain. They've got a good lead on us, but the way they're going they might just blunder into the Maze, and that should delay them long enough . . . all right, then. Lucrezia, Aleister, Perdurabo, and Manson come with me. Judas, you go back to the court and tell the others to disperse and head home.

No more patrols today. We'll have another meeting tomorrow to discuss all that's happened."

"But . . ."

"But what?" the Wolfhound snapped impatiently.

"Well . . . it's just that I kind of wanted to come along too, and I'm sure most of the others would—"

"No. No packs roaming the streets. It's afternoon, there'll be more people out, and we're in enough trouble with the 'catchers as it is. If you have no word from me by tomorrow, tell Therion that he's in charge. And start looking for a replacement for Cerberus."

"Yes, Dragon," said Judas, still visibly disappointed. "As you wish."

"Now," Dragon said, as the Bulldog padded away, "let's go take the mange. And that damned cat."

VI.

"Damn it! This is the third time we've been through here."

"The streets are all tangled, Blackjack."

"I don't care how tangled they are, we should be able to find our way out. Getting lost is for people."

"I have a feeling Raaq doesn't want us to get away. At least not me. And who knows, maybe he *can* hurt cats."

"Forget Raaq and help me figure out—Wait! Look over there!"

Luther looked. A man in overalls had just come out of a nearby house. He paused at the front door, saying an affectionate and extended good-bye to a half-dressed woman within. Parked at the curb was a green flatbed truck, on the side of which were painted the words: BEATRIX, INC.

"What do you think?" Blackjack asked. "We could hop in the back and hitch a ride. If he drives back the way we came then we get out in a hurry, but if he heads out of town—"

"Yes!" Luther said, as if he'd just had a revelation. "That's it, Blackjack! That's how we get out!"

The overall-clad man still tarried at the front door. He and the woman were hopelessly absorbed with one another, and neither noticed the mongrel dog and the tailless cat scrambling up the back bumper of the truck. A tarpaulin had been tossed carelessly into one corner of the flatbed, and Luther and Blackjack hid themselves under it.

Blackjack felt something poking his side and turned slightly. He saw a large metal box with the word "Phillips" stamped on the top, and by the dim light seeping in under the edge of the tarpaulin was able to make out the further inscription:

> With love and affection during
> those lonely nights on the road.
> My thoughts are always with you.
> —Your Pookie Bear

"A tool box," Blackjack said, and would have snickered had he been capable of it. "What a touching gift."

"What?" Luther asked.

"Never mind. I have a feeling this truck is leaving town, though. Who knows, maybe it'll even take us closer to your Heaven."

"I think it will," Luther replied.

VII.

"We have them!" Dragon said triumphantly as he led the others into the web of curving streets known as the Maze. "How far do you think, Lucrezia?"

"Not far," the bitch assured him. "Smells like they got just deep enough in to get lost."

"We have them!" Dragon repeated, quickening his pace. "We have them!"

The sound of an approaching engine grew behind them. Dragon charged onward, oblivious to it, but Perdurabo turned to see what was coming.

"Hey Dragon . . ." he said.

"The cat's going to be the only problem," the Wolfhound briefed them on the run. "We'll fall on it from all sides and kill it straight out. . . ."

"Dragon, I think . . ."

". . . the mange shouldn't put up much of a fight. We can take our time with him. I'm going to—"

"Oh, hell!" Perdurabo exclaimed, as a white van came roaring into view. "'Catchers! 'Catchers!"

"What?"

Dragon finally turned to look, but it was almost too late to do anything.

VIII.

"Say hey, Dante, look at that!"

The glassy-eyed, battle-scarred, World-War-II-veteran-turned-dog-catcher hunched over the steering wheel and grinned at what had just been pointed out to him.

"Hah-um," he said.

"Five dogs, Dante!" his companion went on gleefully. "Five, and not a single collar! That beats shit out of a stray cat-and-dog pair any day of the week in my book!"

"Hah-um."

"Check out that big one in the front, there. Ain't he a beauty? Virgil's gonna have himself a happy fit when he sees what we brought in."

Dante's companion, still in his teens, reached behind his seat like a kid rummaging under the Christmas tree and brought out a pistol with the word "Lethe" stamped on the grip. Placing the pistol on the dash, he reached behind again and brought out a rifle, similarly stamped. Neither the pistol nor the rifle were supposed to be used except in emergencies—and certainly not while the van was in motion—but to the young and the shell-shocked life is a continual emergency.

"Hold her steady, Dante!" the rifleman cried, leaning out the passenger window.

"Hah-um."

"Whooooo-haaah!" He pulled the trigger, and a small dart struck the closest dog in the flank. Perdurabo, whose name meant "I will endure to the end," stumbled more from shock than from the immediate effects of the tranquilizer, and was crushed under the front wheels of the van.

"Hah-*um!*" Dante cried triumphantly.

"Oops," said the rifleman, sounding a bit more concerned. "I don't know if Virgil's going to like that." Then, with renewed spirit: "But what the hell! This is fun, ain't it, Dante?"

"Hah-um!!!"

"All right, good buddy. Floor it!"

Dante floored it. As the van accelerated he began to hum *La Forza del Destino.*

IX.

"Raaq's near!"

"Jesus, Luther, don't worry about it. We're moving. Nothing can get at us now—not unless Purebreds can fly."

The flatbed moved steadily along, bouncing with the occasional pothole but otherwise riding smoothly. Then without warning it slowed, as a weak barking reached their ears.

"That sounds like Dragon," Luther said.

"Jesus," the Manx repeated. "Wait a minute! Luther, don't!"

But Luther had already crawled out from under the tarpaulin. He lifted his head up high enough to see over the side of the flatbed.

He hardly knew how to react to what he saw. It was as if some great avenging angel had come tearing through here, leaving ruin in its wake.

Farthest up the street, Perdurabo lay dead like a torn rag doll. Perhaps fifteen yards in front of him was another lump of roadkill that had once been Aleister the Great Dane. Lucrezia had been a bit more fortunate—though struck by a dart, she had managed to move out of the van's path before collapsing. Nearest of all, Dragon stood shakily in front of the now idling van, two darts sticking out of his side. The 'catchers had stepped out of their vehicle and were trying to throw a net over him.

You watch, Luther. Raaq ain't to be trusted. Sometimes he turns on his own.

So Moses had said, and so it seemed. Only Manson had escaped.

"You brought this on yourselves," Luther thought, trying not to feel too much pity for the dead. "You would have been happy to see us run down."

"Wh—" Groggy, Dragon intercepted the thought. He looked up and saw Luther riding past in the flatbed. *"MANGE!"*

The Wolfhound launched himself forward, a leap that would, under normal circumstances, have carried him up into the truck. Drugged, he only went about three feet, falling heavily on the concrete. As the flatbed sped away and the 'catchers moved in, he fired a parting threat at Luther, fragments of a thought like shrapnel:

". . . kill you, mange . . . find . . . I . . ."

Then he faded into greyness.

"Well," said Blackjack, joining Luther, "looks like there is some justice in the world after all. How about that?"

Luther made no reply. He was staring at the remains of Perdurabo as they cruised past.

"Don't lose any sleep over them, Luther," Blackjack advised. "They deserved what they got. And this way you don't have to worry about fighting them."

Still Luther made no reply. He crawled under the tarpaulin and did not speak again for several hours. The truck rolled on, passing through a short tunnel at the edge of town and beginning a long ascent out of the valley.

They were back on the road to Heaven.

THE RIDE
OF THE BOHEMIANS

I.

If some peace-loving millionaire were someday to sponsor a search for the quietest quiet little town in all Pennsylvania, one of the runners-up in the competition would almost certainly be the town of Auk. (The *winner* of such a competition would, without question, be Thanatos. Officially incorporated in 1892, Thanatos, which is located thirteen miles outside of Scranton, is literally a graveyard. The town's one living resident is Desmond Emery Sargtrager, a groundskeeper, and he does not even snore.)

Though Auk can never hope to surpass the perfect serenity of Thanatos, on a good day it comes very close. No major highways pass within ten miles of it; the surrounding countryside is plain Pennsylvania forest, without a single cave, ski slope, waterfall, or other potential tourist attraction. The sole industry is the manufacture of jigsaw puzzles, surely one of the world's less action-packed businesses. Perhaps the finest demonstration of Auk's peaceful nature, however, came during the town's hundredth anniversary, which was celebrated in a calm and orderly fashion just a few years before the time of this story. There were no fireworks, no marching bands or parades, and only one speech, which lasted for exactly two minutes and thirty-seven seconds, making it shorter than the average FM pop tune.

While outsiders might consider this a boring state of affairs, the people of Auk—many of them senior citizens or at least middle-aged—are quite content with their lives. They need no change of pace, thank you very much, and if they feel a need for high adventure they can always subscribe to cable television, which has been available for some months now.

But nobody ever gets what they want, not all the time. Two days after Luther and Blackjack had their run-in with Dragon, the town of Auk received a century's worth of excitement in the space of two hours. It was an event that Auk's citizens still talk about—and fear the repetition of—to this very day.

The incident was born out of a mad tea partier's recipe of travelers who arrived in Auk one after the other, like succeeding waves of an assault group: three hunters, two bear cubs, four nuns in a renovated limousine, one full-grown bear, seven and a half refugees from a Rhode Island motorcycle gang war, and two vacationing Methodists, one of whom was suffering from hemorrhoids.

And, caught right in the middle of things, Cornell University's self-appointed guardians of non-conformity.

The Bohemians.

II.

For Jed Cyrus, the town Constable, it started out a very ordinary day. He woke up promptly at 6:00 A.M., showered, shaved, dressed, kissed his wife on the right cheek as she continued to sleep, and left the house at precisely 6:20. He walked up Cherville Drive, one of Auk's four side roads, until he reached Main Street and turned left toward the center of town. That was at 6:25. If things had continued on in the usual way, he would have stopped at the Canterbury Café at 6:30, spent fifteen minutes sipping lazily at a cup of black coffee—he always drank half of it and threw the rest away—and then gone on to the station house to begin the morning's paperwork at 6:55.

The first sign that things were not going to go so routinely came when, during his walk down Main Street, Constable Cyrus got a pebble in one of his boots. They were tight-fitting boots, snug and comfy, and how a pebble ever managed to get into one of them was something of a mystery, but it lodged itself behind his heel and became impossible to ignore. By the time he removed it and got his boot back on, he was two minutes late to the Canterbury.

A small thing, you might think, and of course you'd be right. But later, when they were cleaning up the debris, Constable Cyrus' mind kept going back to the pebble and wondering if it hadn't been some sort of omen, a warning to turn around and go back home to bed.

Jankin Badewanne and his wife Alison, Auk's most elderly—and earliest-rising—couple, were playing checkers on the porch in front of the Canterbury Café when the Constable arrived.

Morning, Jed," they said in unison, without looking up. The Constable tipped his hat to them, as he did every morning, and then paused on the porch steps. He took a quick look up and down Main Street to make sure that none of the buildings had disappeared overnight. None of them had, not even Farrell's Bar and Grill, which always looked ready to blow away at a moment's notice. Satisfied, he tipped his hat to Jankin and Alison one more time and went into the Café.

The big clock that hung behind the counter read 6:32 as he came in. Perry Bailey, the proprietor, took one look at the Constable and hurriedly set the clock back two minutes.

"Morning, Jed," said Bailey, handing him a ready-made black coffee. Constable Cyrus gave him thirty cents and a tip of his hat. Then he went over to a table by the front window and sat down. He sipped his coffee contentedly, thinking that this was surely one of the nicest parts of his day.

The hunters showed up five minutes later, and the Decadents were not far behind.

III.

The Risley Hall Bohemians had left their summer lodgings in SoHo just over a week ago, crossing New Jersey along the back roads and cutting through Northeastern Pennsylvania on their way to Binghamton, New York. At present there were only six of them on the move, but their number would triple once they reached Binghamton, and quintuple by the time they finally rode into Ithaca.

The temperature had been cool for a summer week, which was fine with them. A Bohemian's clothing is important, and the hint of fall in the air had allowed them to wear their longcoats comfortably during the journey, at least during the early and evening hours of the day. They made a colorful procession coming into Auk.

Lion-Heart, the reigning King of Bohemia, rode in front on a magnificent black stallion whose mane had been clipped in Mohawk fashion and dyed bright purple. The horse was a certified Thoroughbred, foaled in England, but Lion-Heart himself was much more difficult to classify. Due to an extremely liberal-minded set of ancestors, he had genes and features from just about every race on earth: dark brown skin, tight-curled red hair that he kept very short except for a single long braid-tail in back, green, almond-shaped eyes, sharp nose, thin lips, narrow jaw, and long, well-muscled arms and legs that were almost hairless. He was not handsome by any usual standard, but he was so refreshingly different that this went unnoticed. As befitted his status as King, his longcoat was as purple as his horse's mane.

Myoko and Fujiko, the Grey Ladies, rode beside Lion-Heart on horses that were no less magnificent than his. Both women were mixed Asian, but while Fujiko was small and wore her red-tinged hair trimmed above the ears, Myoko stood near six feet and had hair cascading like black midnight halfway down her back. Their longcoats, naturally enough, were grey.

Ragnarok, the Bohemian Minister of Defense, and Preacher, the Bohemian Minister of Ministry, rode side by side behind the Ladies. Ragnarok, blond and light-skinned, was the only Bohemian not mounted on a horse. He drove a jet black motorcycle instead, patiently keeping pace with the others; he wore a black vinyl trenchcoat and dark sunglasses, even at this early hour when the sun was barely above the trees. Preacher, a tall, heavy-set black, wore a white longcoat and rode a white stallion.

Z.Z. Top, the Minister of Bad Taste, was a study in soiled leather. Bringing up the rear on a grumpy burro (a San Diego Padres baseball cap had somehow been affixed to the animal's head, which did not improve its temper; neither did the personalized plastic Disneyland license plate—CHICO 69— dangling from its tail), he looked like the cloned offspring of James Dean and Fidel Castro after a quick trip through a garbage disposal. He gave the impression of seldom having bathed in his lifetime, and this impression was not incorrect. One of the Great Unwashed, the Top had filled his saddlebags with can upon can of the most loathsome beer money could buy: Black Label Light, Iron City, Utica Club. God bless this swill. He was kind to children, though.

The Bohemians entered the Auk town limits at about half past six. They had been on the move since four that morning, hoping to cross the border into New York by mid-afternoon. A quick breakfast was first in order, however, and as they moved through the still-sleepy town they kept an eye out for a restaurant or Café.

By the time they found the Canterbury, the mad tea party had already begun.

IV.

At 6:35, Constable Jed Cyrus was still sipping his coffee, but he had stopped thinking how this was one of the nicest parts of his day. Instead, he stared out the window of the Canterbury Café at the three men who had pulled up in front of Wayne's Texaco, wondering if he ought to go and arrest them. Crises of responsibility like this one always gave him an upset stomach; he could feel the coffee turning to acid already.

The three men—hunters, by the outfits they wore—looked both ugly and stupid enough to have been children of incest. They stood in front of the gas station, scratching their heads in puzzlement. Every so often one of them would reach inside the pickup truck they'd come in and honk the horn for service. Apparently they hadn't bothered to read the five-foot-high sign that said WAYNE'S TEXACO / OPEN 8 A.M. to 10 P.M.

The Constable couldn't have cared less about their dubious parentage or their lack of intelligence. These things were not crimes, at least not the sort that you made arrests for. What did bother him was the makeshift steel cage trailer that the hunters had attached to the back of their pickup. There were two live bear cubs in it. Now Constable Cyrus was no hunter, and not terribly familiar with the latest gaming regulations, but he felt reasonably certain that late August was not bear season. Even if it was, he had a sneaking suspicion that capturing live cubs might not be legal.

He was weighing the moral consequences of simply letting them go, letting the police in the next town take care of the arrest and the associated paperwork, when his morning suffered a further bad turn. All at once the air was filled with the buzz of approaching motorcycles, and the three ugly hunters looked around as a pack of even more unsavory men on Harley machines rode into view.

Constable Cyrus had never seen a bike gang outside of the movies before, and was not overjoyed to have this status quo revoked. They were not Hell's Angels, but looked relatively fearsome all the same—shoulder patches on their leather jackets identified them as THE RHODE ISLAND DECADENTS. Constable Cyrus did not ask himself what such people were doing out of New England; he was too busy trying to keep his knees from knocking.

The bikers numbered seven. In the grand scheme of things their true names are unimportant—call them Sleepy, Sneezy, Sleazy, Grumpy, Dopey, Bashful, and Doc (a further patch on Doc's jacket proclaimed him DUKE OF THE DECADENTS). Ravenous after an all-night ride, they drew up in front of the Canterbury, their grit-spattered Harleys the most menacing vehicles Constable Cyrus had ever laid eyes on. A sidecar was attached to Sleazy's bike, and in it rode a bound trunk topped with a funeral wreath. Scrawled on the trunk's side was the epitaph: FRED—NO BRAKES, TOUGH SHAKES.

As the Decadents hopped up onto the Café porch, the Constable took a moment to mourn the fact that he was not carrying his revolver. In truth, the weapon had been left locked in his desk drawer at the station house since he had first taken office ten years ago. He wasn't sure he would have had the courage to use it anyway, but at this point in time it would have made him feel a lot better.

"Hey, hey," said Sleazy, stepping up beside Jankin and Alison Badewanne as they continued to play checkers. He snatched a black piece off the board and bit it neatly in two, spitting the checker halves into the street. Both Badewannes looked up angrily, saw the tire chain Sleazy held coiled in his right hand, and said nothing.

"Hey, hey," said Grumpy as he slammed open the Café doors and strode inside. The sight of Constable Cyrus brought him up short.

"Hey, hey," said Duke Doc, joining Grumpy. At this point Constable Cyrus made the great mistake of standing up; Doc noticed immediately that he wore no sidearm and began to smile.

"Hey, hey," Doc repeated, bringing out a switchblade and pressing the stud. Eight inches of steel sprang forth, gleaming dully. "Good morning, officer." In contrast to the weapon his voice was polite, almost cultured.

Perry Bailey stood frozen behind the counter, praying silently that he

would be ignored. The Constable swayed a little on his feet, and sputtered: "I
. . . I . . ."

"What's that?" Doc asked, running his fingers lovingly over the knife
blade.

"I . . . c-c-could . . ."

"Please, sir," said Sleazy, stepping into the Café with the tire chain
wrapped around his fist. "Please speak up."

"I-I-I-I . . ."

The other four Decadents crowded inside, weapons out.

"Officer?" asked one of them. "What are you trying to say?"

The Constable pursed his lips, and with great effort shouted at them: "*I
could have stayed home this morning!*"

That said, he fainted dead away.

"What a shame," Grumpy sighed. "No spine."

"Fucking tragedy," Sleazy agreed.

"Tell us," asked Doc, glancing over at Perry Bailey. "Does he always
collapse under strain?"

Perry Bailey began to do some stuttering of his own, but he was spared a
fainting spell by the passing of the four previously mentioned nuns in the
limousine. Like the pebble in the Constable's boot, the nuns were nothing
spectacular—they drove straight through Auk without stopping, looking
somewhat out of place in the big car, which had been donated to their convent
by a rich miller in the hopes that God would forgive him his wealth—but
they did have some small effect on the course of events.

The Decadents moved back out on the porch to watch the nuns go by.
They waved, and one of the nuns waved back, giving them a quick blessing
out the car window. Then, as the bikers watched the progress of the limo up
the street, their collective gaze was drawn for the first time to the Texaco
station, the hunters, the pickup truck, and, most interesting of all, the bear
cubs in the steel cage trailer.

Doc took one look at the cubs and forgot all about Perry Bailey and the
unconscious Constable.

"Hey, hey," he said softly.

V.

The street outside the Canterbury was soon littered with broken glass. When
the Decadents first advanced on the Texaco station, one of the hunters
foolishly reached into the cab of the pickup for a shotgun. Four bikers
disarmed him and knocked him senseless. Grumpy went running up the
street shooting out windows; when the last shell had been fired, he tossed the
empty shotgun through the glass front of Farrell's Bar and Grill, demolishing
a neon sign that foretold THE BUD SHALL INHERIT THE EARTH.

"Where'd you get the cubs?" Doc asked one of the two hunters who were still standing.

"It was Fred's idea!" the hunter said fearfully, pointing at his fallen companion.

"Fred?" Doc smiled, and looked affectionately over his shoulder at the trunk in the cycle sidecar. "Fred, meet Fred."

"He said we could sell 'em!" the hunter babbled on, his eyes wide. "We found out where they lived, tracked them to this cave, and Fred, he had a what-do-you-call, a trankilizer gun—"

"A trankilizer gun," Doc repeated.

"A trankilizer gun," echoed the other Decadents in unison.

"We knocked 'em out," the hunter continued. "Knocked those cubs right out. But it was dark as hell, and they were awful heavy carryin' back to the trailer. And then the mother bear showed up . . ."

"The mother bear," said Doc.

"The mother bear," echoed the Decadents.

"Yeah . . . yeah, the mother bear. She showed up, but we got away with the cubs anyhow and shit mister are you gonna kill us or what?"

"We'll see," Doc replied. "Pick up Fred here and get into the middle of the street, please."

"W-what?"

"Get into the middle of the street. Both of you. And Fred."

After a moment's hesitation, the two hunters lifted up Fred and dragged him into the middle of the street with them. Four Decadents mounted their cycles and began circling the hunters like sharks. Sleazy and Bashful jumped up on the back of the trailer and began yanking on the triple-padlocked door of the steel cage. One of the cubs stuck a paw out at them and Sleazy whipped it back with his tire chain.

"Hey!" the wide-eyed hunter called to them, eager to do anything that might improve his chances of survival. "Hey, I got the keys to that if you want 'em!"

"That won't be necessary," Sleazy said, continuing to yank at the door. All three padlocks were beginning to give.

Doc got back up on the Café porch to watch the festivities. This was the most fun he'd had since being chased out of Providence by the Firedrakes, a rival gang. Looking into the Café, he saw that the Constable was still out cold, though Perry Bailey was doing his best to revive him.

"Good," Doc said to himself. If the Constable was typical of the Auk citizenry, they should have at least another half hour before someone heard the commotion and got up enough courage to call the State Police. The bikers could be safely across the line into New York before the first trooper showed up.

The four Decadents tightened their circle around the hunters. One cyclist broke formation entirely and cut down the middle, slapping the wide-eyed hunter lightly on the shoulder and getting a shriek out of him. Doc laughed at this, and as he did one of his thighs struck the Badewannes' checker board. He suddenly realized that the two old folk were gone.

"Oh hell," he said. They were nowhere in sight; it didn't take a genius to guess what they'd gone to do. Breaking into a light sweat, Doc looked up the street, half expecting to see the State Police sneaking up on them. He saw the Bohemians instead, and they were somehow more disturbing.

"What . . ."

"Good morning!" Lion-Heart greeted the Rhode Island Decadents in a strong, clear voice. The cyclists stopped circling, and all eyes turned to Bohemians. They were strung out across the street in a line, all on foot now with the exception of Ragnarok, who revved the throttle of his motorcycle patiently.

Lion-Heart continued: "Any of you who don't belong in this town should feel free to leave. Right now."

The Decadents looked at him in disbelief. Grumpy searched for an ethnic slur to use on him but couldn't choose among the many possibilities. He finally came out with: "What the fuck did you say, asshole?"

"GOOD MORNING!" Lion-Heart repeated, louder and slower this time, pronouncing each word carefully. Preacher and Z.Z. Top echoed his words in sign language for the benefit of the hearing impaired. "YOU CAN ALL GO NOW."

"Who the *fuck* are *you?*" In a burst of rage, Grumpy revved his cycle and accelerated down the street toward the Bohemians, swinging a chain.

"Fuji," Lion-Heart said calmly. Fujiko, who had taken a collapsible Lucite quarterstaff from her saddlebags and assembled it, stepped forward into the path of the biker. The Decadent came right at her, realizing too late that her reach was longer than his.

The riderless motorcycle continued down Main Street almost fifty feet before crashing into a mailbox and stalling.

"Who's next?" Fujiko asked. She stood over the fallen Grumpy, who was trying to rub the bump on his head and the bump on his ass at the same time.

"Holy goanna jism," Sleazy whispered. "She took him down."

Both bear cubs threw themselves at the cage door just then. The padlocks gave completely, and Sleazy and Bashful were hurled to the ground.

"Holy *fuck!*" Sleazy yelled. He rolled out of the way just in time to avoid being squashed by an escaping cub.

Chaos resumed; the Bohemians broke formation and moved in, as did the three remaining cyclists. Sleazy and Bashful scrambled to get to their own bikes, while both Doc and the bear cubs seemed momentarily at a loss for what to do. The two unarmed hunters ran for the safety of the pickup truck, dragging Fred behind them.

The mad tea party hit full stride:

Two more cyclists charged Fujiko. One of them changed his mind at the last moment and swerved away; the other kept coming, hefting a long crowbar, planning to run Fujiko down. Lion-Heart came at him from the side, hauling him off his bike and body-slamming him before he knew what had hit him;

Z.Z. Top, ignoring the melee around him, headed off to make the acquaintance of the bear cubs. He was halfway there when a biker turned and bore down on him. Almost casually, the Top picked up a chain that one of the other Decadents had dropped and threw it into the spokes of the biker's front wheel, catapulting him head over heels onto the asphalt;

Bashful ran for his cycle and came face to face with Myoko. Like all Grey Ladies she had an inner glow that made her beautiful, and in the roselight of early morning she looked angelic enough for Bashful to momentarily forget that they were on opposite sides. "Hello," he breathed, fighting a blush. "Hello," Myoko replied sweetly, and, like the angel in the Bible who wrestled with Jacob, she touched the hollow of his thigh and dislocated his left leg;

With a Confederate yell another biker tried his luck against Fujiko, and lost;

Constable Cyrus, revived at last from his faint, staggered onto the porch of the Canterbury Café and looked in disbelief at what was happening in his peaceful little town. The one sight that remained clearest in his mind years later was that of Z.Z. Top shambling up to the cubs with a big smile on his face. "Hello, bears," he heard the Top say, and then the Top began to pet them;

Sleazy, mounted and moving at a fair clip, was jumped simultaneously by Lion-Heart, Fujiko, and Preacher. The cycle and sidecar spun out of control and flipped over, spilling Fred's trunk into the street. Mercifully, the trunk remained closed;

The three hunters began to cheer from the cab of the pickup. At the same time, a number of Auk residents, some still dressed in their nightclothes, began drifting into the area to see what was going on. In the distance, the sound of approaching sirens could be heard;

Finally, in desperation, Duke Doc of the Rhode Island Decadents—the only member of the gang still up and about—leapt to his cycle, planning to get the hell out. He raised his switchblade and waved it about as a warning to anyone who might try to stop him, but the Bohemians had cleared off the street.

All except Ragnarok, who still sat patiently astride his own bike at the end of the block.

"You get out of my way, now," Doc said, a tremor in his voice. Ragnarok cooly removed his sunglasses, wiped them with a black handkerchief, and put them back on. Then he reached down to a small tubular rack on the side of his bike and took out a carved black rod. It looked like a scepter or a short cane, but served equally well as a mace.

"Come and get me, partner," Ragnarok said evenly.

Doc thought it over for a minute. The growing noise of sirens decided him.

"All right!" he snapped, laying one hand on the bike throttle and brandishing the switch with the other. "All right, here it comes for you, then!"

They gunned their engines at the same time, flying down the street toward one another. As the gap closed, Doc began to smile, because he'd done this sort of thing before—in fact, he'd taken out the Second Lieutenant of the Firedrakes in just such a contest, in the days when the Decadents were still holding their own. Long before he reached him, he visualized in his mind how the knife would cut into Ragnarok's coat and beneath it, sending him twisting and screaming off his cycle. Doc smiled with the satisfaction of it before it ever happened.

He was still smiling when Ragnarok swung the mace up gracefully, catching him on the wrist and knocking the knife out and away. As the bikes passed parallel to each other, the Bohemian Minister of Defense kicked out with one black boot and struck Doc in the thigh, knocking him off balance.

The Duke of the Rhode Island Decadents toppled off his motorcycle and bounced once, twice, three times. His bike slid, struck sparks against the ground, and came to rest beneath a NO PARKING sign.

"Jesus H. Christ on a Yugoslavian water buffalo," Constable Cyrus said, summing things up.

Ragnarok slid his mace back into its holder as the first State Police car came into view. The trooper car was tooling along at a fair pace, and the screech of its brakes was very loud as it swerved to avoid a white Buick sedan that cut onto Main Street off a side road. A bumper sticker on the Buick's front fender read: "WE ARE METHODISTS AND DAMN PROUD OF IT."

"What now?" Perry Bailey moaned, huddling by the Badewannes' checker set.

The sedan stopped short in front of the Café; three fishing rods fell off a rack on the back and clattered in the street.

"It's the damnedest thing!" the driver shouted at the Constable, squirming uncomfortably in his seat. "The damnedest goddamn thing!"

"What is?" Constable Cyrus asked fearfully. But the answer was already in sight—a full-grown bear had appeared, coming from the same direction as the Buick, and was presently attacking the trooper car.

"The den mother!" one of the hunters cried. Z.Z. Top moved hastily away from the cubs. The hunter tried to start the pickup to drive away, but the engine only wheezed and hitched.

Constable Jed Cyrus looked over his shoulder at the clock in the Café. It was now 7:05. Half an hour ago he had been contentedly sipping his coffee.

"Jesus Herbert," he said, recapping his summary.

"You OK, man?" someone asked. It was Preacher, walking up the steps of the porch.

The Constable took one look at him, worked his jaw up and down a few times, and asked: "Who the hell are you people? Some kind of Lone Ranger outfit?"

Preacher smiled innocently.

"No sir," he said. "We're Bohemians."

A PEEK AT
MR. SUNSHINE'S
LIBRARY

The Library was, like Mr. Sunshine himself, a Greek Original. It stood on the top of a hill far taller than The Hill, a hill without rain, where the season was always summer and the time always just past noon on a Saturday, a good time for a bottle of retsina or perhaps some hemlock tea if you were in a more philosophical mood. A gentle breeze wafted the scent of laurel through the open windows of the Library, and from outside could be heard the lowing of cattle and the occasional chord from a distant lyre.

Mr. Sunshine sat in the Library's Composing Room, at his Writing Desk, laboring over his latest Manuscript, a Story tentatively entitled "Absolute Chaos in Chicago." Despite the name, Mr. Sunshine's Writing Desk was not at all similar to an ordinary writing desk; likewise, the Manuscript was unlike any manuscript that Stephen George had ever produced. Stephen George told lies for a living, but all of Mr. Sunshine's fictions were true, and though he sometimes checked his spelling, his Stories were not Written on paper. The finished Volumes of his work were not bound like ordinary volumes; and the Books in the Library were not catalogued or shelved like ordinary books. It was all very abstract, but not really.

If you could take a peek at Mr. Sunshine at his Desk, and if your mind was such that you could comprehend his work, you would understand that "Composing" really meant "Meddling." For a fictitious fiction story, the kind of lie that Stephen George told, requires the hard labor of its author to be completed; but a *true* fiction, such as those that Mr. Sunshine dealt in, will, like a watch already wound, tick along quite nicely by itself without any further help. Mr. Sunshine's Storytelling, to extend the metaphor, consisted of occasionally—or more than occasionally—moving the hands of the watch, and seeing what interesting forms of mayhem this resulted in.

Because his Stories went on without him, he could switch from one work in progress to another without falling behind in either of them. Those works he tired of for the time being he gave to the Monkeys.

73

The Monkeys, all blind, deaf, and mute, yet dissimilar to any ordinary handicapped monkeys, were arrayed around Mr. Sunshine's Writing Desk in vast (but not infinite) ranks. Each Monkey sat at a Typewriter, which was of course unlike any ordinary typewriter, and Meddled. Because they had not the slightest clue what was going on, however, the Meddling of the Monkeys was entirely random and generally meaningless. That was all right; the Stories went on regardless, and once in a while they did hit on something. A Monkey puttering over "The Life of Catherine the Great" had chanced to insert a bit about a horse that had put Mr. Sunshine in stitches for days, though Catherine herself probably did not find it nearly so funny.

The Monkeys labored; the afternoon breeze wafted. Mr. Sunshine paused to check a word in his Dictionary, and then, suddenly remembering something, he set "Absolute Chaos in Chicago" aside for a moment. He got up from his Desk and strode out among the Monkeys, checking working Titles, searching for one in particular. In between "World War Three: The Prologue" and "The Life of Anita Bryant" he found it: "Fool on The Hill," an odd piece he had started more than a century ago and whose Plot was finally starting to cook. There had been major Meddling already and more yet to be done—after which he might just go down and take a ringside seat to watch the climax—but for now, only a few touches were needed.

First things first. Taking the Monkey's place at the Typewriter, Mr. Sunshine Wrote:

A fine cottage awaits Her arrival; champagne & feta in fridge.

And then:

George bumps into Aurora early one morning. Wouldn't they make a much nicer couple than Aurora and Brian?

Satisfied, he let the Monkey take over again and returned to his Desk. Concentrating once more on Chicago, Mr. Sunshine took his Dictionary and flipped toward the back.

"Let's see now . . . T-R-I-S-K- . . ."

AT HEAVEN'S GATE

I.

The first to return to Cornell, some as early as mid-August, are the Orientation Counselors and Residence Advisors, those whose job it is to make the army of newcomers feel at home and see them safely through their first year. Then on August twenty-third the dorms open, and the Freshmen begin to arrive, wide-eyed and unsuspecting. They have one free week in which to sample the pleasures of Ithaca—swimming in the gorges, hiking the countryside, drinking in the Collegetown bars if their phony I.D. is good enough, drinking in the dorms if it isn't—and once again the brick and cinderblock of West Campus echo with the pitter-patter of little Nike-clad feet. On North Campus there is a smaller-scale parody of this, most of the noise coming from Mary Donlon and Clara Dickson Halls (and, of course, Risley, the Bohemian dorm).

That August twenty-third, and the twenty-fourth and -fifth also, it rained hard most of the day, as if Ithaca were making a special effort to acquaint the Freshmen with its climate. During those three days, when the showers were interspersed with periods of heavy mist, Stephen George went for long walks in the town proper as well as on the campus. He sorted through the faces he passed, searching for old friends, making a few new ones. He flew his kite often, regardless of the weather, and only once did the wind fail him. That time, the early afternoon of the twenty-third, he gave up no more than ten minutes before a monster thunderstorm swept through the area. Two Ithaca men who had chosen the wrong day to go sailing were struck by lightning and killed on Cayuga Lake, but George was safely indoors, sipping tea in the Temple of Zeus in Goldwin-Smith Hall.

On the morning of the twenty-fourth he wandered down to The Ithaca Commons at the foot of The Hill and stopped for breakfast at McDonald's. While he sat in meditation over three pancakes in a beige styrofoam tray, a

75

grizzled old man with an Eddie Bauer T-shirt came into the restaurant. The old man was obviously a McDonald's regular whose name, it quickly became apparent, was Wax. The women behind the counter nearly fell over themselves greeting him and presenting, with much fanfare, "Wax's morning coffee." George craned his neck to see if the coffee were black or with cream (for as a writer, such minor details held great significance for him). Wax accepted the styrofoam cup, bowed deeply, and found a seat alongside a chubby woman who looked to be in her seventies.

"Howdy," he said to the woman, who was a librarian in decline. "My name's Wax. Know why they call me that? 'Cause I'm *so* slick . . ."

Two minutes and he had her giggling like a schoolgirl. Three minutes and they were sharing hotcakes and sausage.

True love, George thought, and caught sight of a familiar face two booths down from where Wax was putting on his moves. "Stay here," he told his pancakes, and went over to say hello.

"Hey, lady." Aurora Smith looked up and smiled as George slid into the booth.

"Hi, George," Aurora returned the greeting. They had met two years earlier on the Arts Quad, George literally knocking Aurora off her feet as he moved to avoid a Bohemian on a runaway mare, and become good friends. They got along well, although George had never been completely comfortable with Aurora's boyfriend. "How was summer? Write any more stories for strangers?"

"One," George admitted. "I whomped something up for my landlord's daughter, of all people. Short novella. The editor of a fiction magazine over in Vermont wants me to make a serial out of it. Oh, and then there's this."

"What is it?" Aurora asked, as George took a folded envelope out of his pocket.

"Claims to be from a professor of Eugenics at the University of Iowa. She liked my first novel and wants to breed me with some of the women from the Writers' Workshop there."

Aurora laughed, louder than she might have in the presence of her boyfriend. "Are you going to take her up on it?"

"Nah." George shook his head. "I'm too much of a wimp. No stamina. U. of Iowa has a *big* Writers' Workshop. Maybe if I had Mormon blood . . . Anyway, how about you? How was your summer?"

"Oh, you know . . ." she trailed off, shrugging. It was a common gesture with her; George got it almost every time he asked her something even remotely personal. "Life is good. I'm happy."

"Yeah?" George said.

"Yes, really . . . hey, I finally read one of your books!" She brightened. *"The Knight of the White Roses.* I found a copy of it in a Milwaukee bookstore when we drove up there in July."

"What'd you think of it?"

"I loved it," she told him honestly. "How did you ever come up with the idea for th—"

"What are we all talking about?" said Brian Garroway, appearing suddenly. The McDonald's men's room was located in the darkest reaches of the building, and Brian, so to speak, had been on safari.

"My action-packed literary career," George replied, as Brian sat down beside Aurora and put an arm around her. "Aurora was just telling me about how she read one of my books."

"*The Knight of the White Roses?*"

"That's the one. You read it, Brian?"

"I skimmed it."

"And what'd you think?"

"You have a fair writing style," Brian granted him. "It's good in an unpolished sort of way. Other than that I thought your entire premise was far-fetched—a New Wave Camelot?—and there was way too much profanity. The whole thing struck me as being too romantic, too, by the way."

George was impressed. "All that from just a skimming? You missed your calling, Brian. You should have been an English major." He looked at Aurora. "Did you think it was overly romantic?"

"Well . . ." Aurora said. She shrugged automatically, inadvertently throwing off Brian's arm. "Not really. It was all *supposed* to be a little exaggerated like that, right?"

She shrugged again, then went back to picking at her hash browns. Brian laid a hand lightly on the back of her neck. A moment later he said:

"You about ready to go? I'm supposed to be up at Dickson pretty soon to talk to Michael Krist."

"Sure," Aurora said, putting her fork down. "I'm done."

"Good, Let's go." He stood up. "Sorry to rush off like this, George."

"That's all right. You'll probably be seeing me around on campus this semester."

"I hope we will. You're teaching this year, right?"

"That's right," George agreed. "I get to pass along some of my unpolished writing style. Should be fun."

Brian laughed politely. "Good luck. See you around, George." Aurora stood up, gave George a small wave. "You take care," she said. He nodded to her, and then Aurora and Brian were on their way out of the restaurant. As the front door swung shut after them, a voice spoke up behind George. "Now there's an unhappy marriage shaping up."

George looked back at the sound. The ever-popular Wax was sitting alone while his newfound librarian went to powder her nose.

"What do you mean?" George asked.

"The expressions on their faces," Wax explained. "The look in their eyes.

It's subtle, you understand, but it reminds me just exactly of my brother and my sister-and-law before they tied the knot. Bad shakes, my young friend."

"What happened to your brother and your sister-in-law?"

"Too much tension. Made for a bad match. Third night of the honeymoon she got fed up and shot him in the leg. Hell of a thing; he hasn't walked straight since."

Wax shook his head and sighed, then turned away. "You want to be a Good Samaritan, young man?" he added, giving his coffee a stir. "Steal that woman's heart away for yourself—save that boy from a lifetime of limping."

"Right," said George. He too shook his head—grinning—and a moment later went back to his pancakes.

II.

"How do I look?"

"Absolutely ridiculous, if you want the truth."

"I'm serious, Blackjack. Do I look like a Purebred?"

"You look like a neurotic dog who went and dipped himself in a mud puddle. Which proves that looks don't always deceive."

The flatbed had taken them upstate, to the vicinity of a town the humans called Watkins Glen. Now they were walking due east, with only a short march left until they would be at the site of what Luther still insisted was Heaven.

"Funny, I was expecting a much longer trip than it's been," Blackjack said. "But if Heaven is so close, Luther, then why even bother trying to disguise yourself? If it's what you say it is, you won't have any trouble with Purebreds there."

"This is just in case," Luther told him. "You never know, Raaq might have some sort of guard around it, to keep dogs from getting in."

"But if Raaq's guards kill you," Blackjack pointed out, "won't you wind up in Heaven anyway?"

"Well . . ." The thought was unsettlingly logical, but Luther didn't want to give up his disguise. "Well, I might, but there's no sense taking chances."

"As you like it, then. But I think it'd take a pretty stupid Purebred not to notice there was something unusual about you, Luther."

Luther did, as Blackjack had said, look like he'd just been dipped in a mud puddle. He'd rolled in one, actually a thick brown pool left by recent rains. Two squirrels had watched him curiously as he'd done it. Now his coat stuck out and curled in odd ways that bore no resemblance to natural hair growth, but at least the color was uniform. On a good day he might have passed for a Terrier of some sort, a Terrier who had just bulled his way through a dirt wall.

"I just feel more comfortable this way, Blackjack," Luther said. "If Dragon were to walk by now, I bet he wouldn't even recognize me."

"You're probably right. Not that I plan on seeing him again, the way those 'catchers were treating him. But you smell like shit. I wouldn't be surprised if there was some in that puddle."

"I don't care about my smell. I can still smell Heaven, stronger than ever, and that's what counts. We'll be there soon, tomorrow maybe, and then everything will be fine. It'll be so good to see Moses again. . . ."

Blackjack said nothing for a moment. Part of him, the carefully guarded part where he kept his conscience and sympathy hidden, was beginning to wonder what would happen if they didn't find Heaven. Obviously, the cat thought, they *couldn't* find it, not the traditional Heaven anyway, and it was equally impossible that Moses would be there. The events of the journey had done nothing to dispel Blackjack's atheism. If anything, the run-in with Dragon had strengthened his disbelief; surely no just God, or gods, would allow such mindless prejudice to exist.

"Listen, Luther," he began, "if . . . if Heaven really was only a short distance away from here, wouldn't there be some sort of sign by now?"

"Sign?"

"Like the lights from the City reflecting off the clouds. Heaven ought to be bigger than Manhattan, at least, but still we haven't seen any sign of it, any change. Oh, the air's cleaner here, but it's been that way for days. There's no change in the countryside, no sign that we're leading up to something big. And don't you think there should be, if we're so close?"

"What you're trying to say is, you still don't believe Heaven exists?"

Blackjack stared down at his paws.

"And," Luther went on when he made no reply, "you don't want my feelings to be hurt when we don't find it?"

"Luther . . ." Still he did not look up. "Luther, you're a good friend, and you know I don't want to see you hurt, but . . . I can't believe such a place is real. Not some big doghouse in the sky, full of angel-dogs or whatever and the souls of the dead. It's too much like something you'd see in a dream, and it'll take more than a short march for this landscape to melt into something dreamlike."

"Why did you come with me, if you didn't believe we'd find Heaven?" Luther asked. The question was emotionless; Blackjack couldn't tell if Luther was angry.

"Because you're my friend," Blackjack replied, as if ashamed to admit his own emotions. "And maybe . . . maybe because I thought the journey might be worth it. Not that I minded living in the slums, you understand, that's good ratting territory, but I could get enthusiastic about settling somewhere with real trees, and grass that doesn't just grow up in the sidewalk cracks. I'm sure this place we're going to is nice, Luther. Maybe even nice enough to justify this damn trip. I know your nose wouldn't lead you completely wrong. But Heaven . . ."

"You don't believe we'll find Moses, either, do you?"

"No," Blackjack said, as gently as he could. "I don't think Moses exists anymore, except as a memory. That doesn't lessen him any, though, because we're all going to cease to exist sooner or later . . . sorry to be so blunt, but I don't want you to be too disappointed when we don't find him. I hope you aren't angry with me."

"Angry?" Luther sounded surprised. "You're just saying what you feel, Blackjack, and after all, you're a cat. Even if you turn out to be right, that won't be your fault. I know you don't *want* Moses to not exist anymore."

"No, I don't," Blackjack agreed. "I want us to find him. But when we don't—"

"*If* we don't," Luther insisted. "Let's say if, until we're actually there. Who knows, it might still turn dreamlike. Maybe we'll have to do something special, yet, before we're really there. Like . . . I don't know, like a cross a magic river, or climb a mountain. It smells like it's got big hills, at least. You should really try to be more optimistic, Blackjack," he said as they started off again. "*I* think things are definitely improving."

"This from a dog who looks like something out of a swamp."

"Blackjack, you—"

And so it went, the two of them arguing back and forth good-naturedly as they made their final approach to Heaven.

III.

"Am I dreamin'?"

Just past seven on the morning of the twenty-fifth. An Ithaca Police patrol car was idling by a downtown intersection, watching an army on horseback ride up West State Street in the direction of The Commons. The rain had taken a short rest break, and the Bohemians appeared out of the mist like a phantom parade.

"No, you're not dreaming," said the officer behind the wheel of the car. She was a slim black named Nattie Hollister; her partner, Samuel Double-day, was pale, middle-aged, and had a remarkable rash of freckles on his cheeks.

"They sure are colorful, aren't they?" added Hollister.

"Who are they? *What* are they, I should say."

"They call themselves Bohemians."

"Is that some new kind of Communist thing?"

"Not exactly. They're a good bunch, really. Never had to run one in."

Doubleday hawked and spat out the window. "Maybe they just never got caught. I don't like 'em."

At that point Ragnarok cruised in front of the patrol car on his bike. He saw Hollister through the windshield and raised a hand in salute.

"God bless all Ithacops!" he cried.

"Hail, Caesar!" shouted some of the other Bohemians.

"You see? You see?" Doubleday growled. "Just like those fags down at The 'Wave. No respect for authority."

"Oh, they respect us," said Hollister. "They just show it in a unique way, that's all."

"That one there," Doubleday went on, as Z.Z. Top trotted by on his burro, "Marxist or child molester. No question."

"Don't trouble yourself over it, Doubleday. They're harmless. You want to cruise over to the State Diner and pick up some coffee?"

"Yeah. Yeah, sure. As soon as this damn intersection is clear, that is." His mouth was drawn down in an angry bow; Hollister was beginning to wonder if the man ever smiled. "Ah, hell!"

"What now, Doubleday?"

"It's raining again!"

Hollister threw back her head and laughed.

IV.

"Let's hear it for the rain!" Lion-Heart cried as they rode through The Commons, and the downpour received a solid round of applause. They had been applauding everything from woodchucks to Greyhound buses for the past five miles, so happy were they to be back. For many of them, including Lion-Heart, this would be their last year at Cornell, and they wanted to start off on as positive a note as possible.

Lion-Heart still led the way, Fujiko and Myoko flanking him, the other Bohemians and Grey Ladies following in a disorderly fashion. Sweeping through The Commons they cheered the row of stores, cheered the McDonald's, cheered the sidewalks beneath them. In front of Iszard's department store—which stood on the site of the old Ithaca Hotel—they encountered George, who had risen very early that day.

"Morning, storyteller," Lion-Heart said, nodding to him. He held up a hand, and the procession halted. "What brings you out? I thought we were the only ones crazy enough to beat the sunrise."

"What sunrise?" George said pleasantly, glancing up at the clouds. "Besides, I figured it was about time for you to be coming back. Got a welcome-home for you." He hoisted a bottle of Midori up to Lion-Heart.

"Well now," the Bohemian King said. "Can't help but respect a man with good taste in liquor."

"Hey George," cried Z.Z. Top, trotting up to the front of the line. He held a newspaper in one hand. "Got a good one for you. You heard the latest from Chicago?"

"No. What gives?"

"All right," the Top said enthusiastically. A fan of *The Knight of the White Roses*, he loved sharing odd news items with George. "Dig it, there's this guy out to the Windy City owns a huge house in the suburbs, he comes home two days ago and the place is burning up. There's not a fire truck in sight, and his kid, who's been left home alone, is screaming out a top-floor window for Daddy to come save him.

"So he's a concerned father, he ought to just run in and see if he can save the kid, right? Only thing is he's got this mental problem, he's a what-do-you-call, a tri— . . . a trisko— . . . ah, fuck!"

"Triskaidekaphobe," Myoko offered.

"Right! Right, that. Triskawhatever. Which basically means his asshole goes into toxic shock over the number thirteen. And there's smoke pouring out of exactly thirteen windows of the house."

"He counted them?" George said skeptically.

"Hey man, it's right here in the paper, inquiring minds want to know. This guy's house, it's a special effects representation of the number thirteen, and his spinchter starts to get all tight . . ."

"Nice, Top," said Fujiko.

" . . . and there's no way in hell he can make himself go in, not even with his own child in line to be a barbecue. So he goes back to his car, see, gets a spare gas can out of the boot, grabs a pop bottle from the gutter, rips a strip off his Brooks Brothers suit, and makes himself a suburban Molotov cocktail. Lobs it into a part of the house that hasn't been touched yet, *whoosh*, fire, smoke, the number thirteen becomes the number fourteen, his asshole simmers back down and now he can be a hero. Gets the kid out fine but the fire guts the house, and the final kicker is the insurance company doesn't want to pay off because the guy committed arson, technically. They're going to have one hell of a time in court with that one."

"Quite the tale."

"No shit. But if you put that sort of thing in one of your novels, zap!, into the penalty box for lack of realism."

George shrugged. "Can't beat real life for suspension of disbelief."

"No shit. Lots of weird stuff going down in Chicago lately. We'll have to get together for some beers, pop a few Black Label Lights while I tell you about it."

"Need a lift up The Hill, storyteller?" asked Lion-Heart, when Z.Z. Top was through.

"No thanks," said George. "Think I'll hang out here a while longer."

"As you like. Hey, you got a woman yet?"

George reddened the tiniest bit.

" 'Fraid not," he admitted. "I'm still trying, though."

"Yeah, well I got something for you, make us even for the Midori." He brought out a velvet pouch, and from it produced a fortune cookie which he tossed to George.

"What's this?"

"Open it, storyteller. Don't ask questions."

George cracked the cookie open. He took out the slip of paper inside and read it aloud.

"Beware the Ides of March," he read, looking puzzled. "I don't get it."

"Huh?" said Lion-Heart. "Shit, I must have given you the wrong one." He rummaged again in the pouch and got another cookie. "Here."

This time the slip of paper inside made more sense.

" 'Redeem for one (1) Woman of Your Dreams. This coupon void where prohibited by law.' Wow. Just what I needed."

"Those are magic fortune cookies, storyteller," Lion-Heart informed him. "I had this Wicca chick in SoHo make 'em up special for me. If that doesn't help you, you might as well give yourself up as a lost case."

"Thanks for the vote of confidence, Li," George said.

"You just take it light, storyteller." The Bohemian King gave his horse's reins a shake and got moving again. "Come up Risley way and visit us sometime soon."

"I will," said George. He moved out of the way and watched them go by, waving at those Bohemians that he knew, blushing when a Grey Lady named Kiri smiled at him. Soon they were all past, making a slow-motion charge up The Hill, first to the Cornell stables and then to Risley.

George folded both fortune cookie messages carefully and placed them into a dry part of his wallet.

Then he hunkered down under a storefront awning to watch the rain.

V.

Calliope arrived in Ithaca sometime during the rain, though only she could have named the exact hour. A small cottage awaited her in a grove along Triphammer Road, north of North Campus. It was cozy and suited her perfectly, though she knew she wouldn't be needing it for long.

After putting away her few possessions she showered, washing away the smells of the road, almost polishing herself until her skin glowed. Clean, she investigated the cottage's refrigerator and found the champagne and cheese, smiling at the discovery. Thoughtful of him. She ate and drank while the sun went down, its descent hidden by the cloud cover.

Long after sunset she dressed in a pair of moccasins and a curious silver-threaded robe that looked like a cross between a kimono and a long cloak. She went out into the night.

The rain had once again given way to mist, this time for good, and in her robe Calliope was nearly invisible. Three times she passed strangers on the road. None of them saw her, but each paused in her wake, feeling a deep sadness as if some great love had just been lost to them.

Prudence Risley Residence Hall stood on the north edge of Fall Creek Gorge, to the left coming off the East Avenue bridge that led to Central Campus. The residents were holding a Mist Party in the rear courtyard, and the whole building blazed with light.

Lion-Heart mingled and drank at the party for about an hour, then staggered out onto the front lawn to get a break from the music, a non-stop stream of "alternative" rock bands. Not that such groups weren't good—most of them—but they were feeling, paradoxically, a little too trendy lately. Now that disco was officially dead, it might be a good idea for the Bohemians to resurrect it, just for the shock value.

Sipping Midori from a shot glass, Lion-Heart stared drunkenly at the dorm. Erected in 1913 as a women's dormitory, Risley had gone slowly radical over the course of the late Sixties and the early Seventies, eventually becoming a co-ed haven for misfits. Three years ago a conservative element had begun to creep in, and Lion-Heart, then a Freshman, had formed the Bohemians to combat it. True, much of what the Bohemians did was not original—Lion-Heart had freely borrowed clothing styles from the Greenwich Village neighborhood where he had grown up, as well as borrowing from his parents' considerable Old World fortune to finance the cavalry aspect of the group—but the sight of a purple-garbed rider on a purple-maned horse was still different enough, even at relatively liberal Cornell, to raise eyebrows and restore Risley to its former reputation.

But while history might be made to repeat itself, it never stopped moving. With most of the hard-core Bohemes graduating this year (including Lion-Heart and his bankroll), he had begun to wonder how long it would take before the remainder drifted apart, or collapsed into a clique. He wondered about the dorm, too, how it would fare without such wonders as Z.Z. Top's electronic Jew's Harp.

Even as Lion-Heart pondered Bohemia's role in Risley and larger society, Calliope appeared out of the mist, revealed for a moment in the glow from the dorm.

"Ho . . ." Lion-Heart gasped, frozen by the sight of her. The shot glass dropped from his hand and the ground lapped up the rest of the Midori.

"Ho?" Calliope caught his gaze and smiled, tearing his heart. For she was the loveliest woman he had ever seen, ever would see, and yet he suddenly knew with an iron-clad certainty that she was not to be his. When she teasingly blew a kiss at him, Lion-Heart lost all control of himself.

"Who are you?" the King of the Bohemians demanded, springing forward to catch her. "At least tell me who you are. . . ."

"I'm just a dream on a lonely night," said Calliope, laughing. As he reached out to grab her she spun, the cloak/kimono slipping easily through his fingers, and then she simply wasn't there anymore. He stumbled and fell hard to the ground.

"Wait!" he called into the mist, not sounding very much like a King now. "Wait . . ."

Her laugh echoed once in the distance—she sounded as if she were crossing the bridge—and faded. Lion-Heart thought about chasing after her and soon rejected the idea, knowing he could never catch her unless she wanted him to. And besides, he was just drunk enough to believe that something bad might happen to him if he became too persistent and annoyed her.

"Go easy on him, though," the Bohemian King said thickly, struggling to his feet. "Whoever it is you did come here for." No sooner was he standing than Myoko came around to the front lawn looking for him, and Lion-Heart thought he had never been so glad to see anyone.

"Are you real?" he asked her, still dizzy from the fall.

"What?" Myoko glided up to him. "You been into something heavy tonight, Li?"

He didn't answer, but reached out gently to touch her, as if fearing that she too might whirl and vanish. He clasped her hand in his, marveling at the feel of solid flesh and bone; he brushed his fingertips against her cheek.

"What is it?" Myoko asked, surprised and flattered by the expression of awe on Lion-Heart's face. He'd gone through a cold phase recently, being short on affection in the past week or so; now it seemed to have passed.

"You *are* real," Lion-Heart said, taking her in his arms and kissing her. And so they remained, clasped together with the faint sounds of the party drifting over to them from the courtyard, for the better part of an hour. When at last they ended their embrace and turned to go inside, all memory of Calliope had been erased from Lion-Heart's mind. He had seen no one that night but Myoko, and he loved her.

VI.

The Arts Quad was deserted when Calliope got there. It shouldn't have been; even with the majority of the night's activities—wild parties in particular—taking place at the dormitories, fraternities, and sororities, there should have been a few scattered individuals passing through Central Campus at any given time until well after midnight. But the Lady was in a mood to dance, to dance but not to be seen, and so all those who would otherwise have walked through the Quad suddenly got it in their heads to take a different route to wherever they were going.

She skipped along playfully, pausing beneath a cluster of trees in the northeast corner of the Quad, where mist and shadows mingled freely. She drew out her whistle, gently clutching the tiny charm in one perfect fist, and blew. It made no discernable sound, but the area before her glowed hazily, the mist forming itself into a phantom image of George.

"So that's what you look like," said Calliope, smiling. Physical appearance meant nothing to her emotionally; her eyes were such that she could see any person as perfectly attractive, just as she, with her special magic, could appear perfectly beautiful to them. But she did want to get a glimpse of him before actually seeking him out, for curiosity's sake if nothing else.

Done looking, she waved the apparition away and strode across the grass until she stood on the walkway between the two Quad statues. Andrew D. White gave her a stern look as she threw off her robe and stood naked except for the mocassins. These too were kicked away as she began to dance, a wild, Dionysian ballet the like of which had never been seen on any stage. Before long the wind began to blow, sighing a melody among the branches of the trees and beneath the eaves of the buildings. The wind did not part the mist and so none could see what was going on, but a number of the sprites heard the wind-song and wondered what it could mean. Zephyr's Grandfather Hobart remained frozen at the top of McGraw Tower throughout the performance, frightened for some reason he could not fathom. The wind blew around George's house as well, and he too paused to listen—but not in fear.

How long the dance went on is as uncertain as the hour of Calliope's arrival, but it ended at midnight. She landed back between the statues with a great somersault just as the Clock began to strike. While the chimes tolled out the change of days, Calliope looked from Andrew to Ezra, as if daring them to make a move. They did not. Then the chimes ceased and she quickly gathered up her robe and shoes, laughing as she ran back the way she had come.

"I'm here, George," she called to the night. "I'm here."

VII.

"Is this dreamlike enough for you, Blackjack?"

"It's interesting, I'll grant you that."

It was mid-dawn on the morning of the twenty-sixth, and Luther and Blackjack moved through a world of white, a thick fog that was the last gasp of the preceding three days' weather. Even at that moment the rising sun was beginning to burn the fog away, but for the time being it *was* like part of a dream, like moving through a tunnel to a hazy world that was slowly being brought into focus.

The two animals had walked most of the night, entering Ithaca under a dark gloom that almost prevented them from realizing they'd come to a town. Passing through the deserted Commons, the air had been rich with Luther's "Heaven smell," and as they reached the foot of The Hill the mongrel had proclaimed joyously that they were almost there, almost there. Once again Blackjack had been patient and polite in his response, but somehow he'd expected the Divine environment to be better lit.

Now, in a moment of perfect stillness, a gateway loomed up ahead of them. "Heaven's Gate!" exclaimed Luther. "It's the Gateway to Heaven, Blackjack! We found it!"

"St. Peter must still be sleeping," Blackjack observed quietly. Luther paid him no mind, running up to the Gate and barking in glee.

"We're there! We made it!"

"Are you sure?" asked Blackjack, examining the Gate closely. It was a rather plain construction of stone, with a wrought-iron span across the top. Not a trace of pearl.

While Luther barked and capered beneath the arch, Blackjack went over to the wall on the left side of the Gate. The fog was thinning rapidly, and the Manx was able to make out the words on a plaque:

SO ENTER

THAT DAILY THOU MAYEST BECOME

MORE LEARNED AND THOUGHTFUL

SO DEPART

THAT DAILY THOU MAYEST BECOME

MORE USEFUL TO THY COUNTRY AND TO MANKIND

Intrigued, Blackjack crossed to the other side of the Gate and examined the companion plaque:

THIS STRUCTURE DEDICATED

TO THE CONTINUED SUCCESS

OF THE CORNELL UNIVERSITY

BY ITS PRESIDENT

ANDREW D. WHITE

1896

"University?" said Blackjack. "Luther, this is—"

"We made it! We made it!"

The Manx could not go on. It took no great power of empathy to see how ecstatic Luther was over their arrival at "Heaven"; Blackjack would not rob him of this brief happiness. He would be forced to face the truth soon enough on his own.

Or so Blackjack thought.

"Listen!" Luther said suddenly, ceasing his barking. Now that he took the time to notice, Blackjack realized that there was water running nearby. And that wasn't all—somewhere up ahead, chimes had begun to play.

"The angels need music lessons, I think," Blackjack couldn't resist saying, as a bad note disrupted the melody. Once again Luther paid no attention to him.

Together they passed through the Gate and padded around the great bulk that was Cascadilla Dorm. Following the music, they crossed over Cascadilla Creek Bridge into Central Campus.

"I smell dogs," said the Manx. "Lots of them."

"Of course you do, Blackjack. But don't worry, there can't be any trouble here, not in this place. Do you smell Moses at all?"

"How could I . . . . I mean, no, I don't smell him."

"Neither do I. But there are so many . . ."

A strong scent of approaching dogs up ahead. Blackjack tensed automatically. Luther glanced into a puddle and noticed for the first time that the rain and damp had washed away his mud-disguise.

"Oh no! I'm—"

"There's nothing to be afraid of in this place, remember?" Blackjack said soothingly, casually sliding his claws out.

"But it just occurred to me, Blackjack. What if God's a Purebred?"

"I thought God was supposed to be more like a human being. Like one of the Masters, you'd say."

"Well . . ."

They topped a rise, and saw two dogs coming toward them. Luther relaxed immediately; one of the dogs was a mongrel, the other a Purebred, and they were not hostile to one another. The Purebred, a young Beagle, seemed very high-strung for some reason, jumping about as though the damp sidewalk were too hot for him, but it had nothing to do with antagonism. The thought-word *mange* was nowhere in his mind, not that Luther could see.

"Hello there," said the mongrel, nodding to them.

"Hiya!" piped the Beagle pup, whose name, they soon learned, was Skippy. "Hey, I've never seen you guys before. You new around here? Huh? And hey, Mr. Pussycat, what happened to your tail? Huh? Huh?"

"Hello," Blackjack replied to the mongrel, retracting his claws halfway. He eyed the Beagle reservedly.

In front of them, the last of the fog melted away all at once, and the light of the rising sun struck McGraw Tower, for an instant wreathing it in a halo. Luther caught his breath at the sight.

"We made it," he said once more.

With a discordant clang, the Chimesmaster shifted into her second song for the morning.

Book Two

TALES OF AUTUMN

1866—OUTSIDE
THE BONE ORCHARD

They begin climbing The Hill along a dirt track that will one day be known as University Avenue, but which for now is just more nameless mud soup. The going is hard yet Mr. Sunshine forges ahead—carrying a bright lantern he did not have with him when they set out from the Ithaca Hotel—still oddly unimpeded by the condition of the road. And Ezra, several decades from being a spritely youth, keeps close at Mr. Sunshine's heels, driven by an indescribable compulsion that first bloomed in him when he was invited on this night trek.

Their conversation is appropriately strange. Sometimes Mr. Sunshine asks question about Ithaca or the planned University, sometimes he speaks knowledgeably about them, and sometimes—this is surely the strangest thing of all—he will, after Ezra answers a query, nod and then add an extra fact or two as if he had known more than Cornell all along. And some of his comments are hopelessly beyond comprehension.

One such comment pops out as they come upon the gates to the City Cemetery. Gazing farther up the road, beyond the glow of his lantern, Mr. Sunshine says: "The Black Knight will live near here, in a Black House. Hmm, wonder what I can do with him?"

Turning his attention to the Cemetery, he continues by asking: "What's this place called?"

"I don't know that there is an official name," replies Ezra. "Though it's often referred to as The Bone Orchard. A nickname of sorts."

"Bone Orchard," Mr. Sunshine rolls the words on his tongue, testing their feel. "Bone Orchard, nice idea, but a bit of a bumpy mouthful, don't you think? It could be shorter."

Cornell shrugs. "People will call it what they will."

"People can change their habits," Mr. Sunshine says, "over time. I like cemeteries, though; I've had some good Stories involving them. You don't mind if we walk through The . . . Boneyard, do you?"

Again, the feeling of compulsion at the request.

"Not at all, sir," Ezra answers. "Not at all."

THE FIRST WEEK

I.

Monday, 5:50 A.M.

George cracked an eyelid at the first light of dawn. Still half asleep, wrapped snugly in a wool blanket against the morning chill, he was filled with a sudden elation, as if he had just embarked on some grand adventure. In a sense he had—he was due to teach his first class at 10:10 this morning— but there was something more, something that his waking half could not quite grasp.

A sparrow sat on his bedroom windowsill, peeping in at him, perhaps hoping for a bit of bread. George smiled at the bird, then glanced at the kite which was propped against a chair just to the right of the window . . . and again he felt that strange elation.

Something's coming, the part of him that was still sleeping thought. *Something's going to happen.*

School's going to happen, his waking half replied, and promptly rolled over to get another hour's rest.

Outside the wind stirred briefly, startling the sparrow into song.

II.

Monday, 6:30 A.M.

The delivery crew for the Cornell *Daily Sun* had already been on the job for nearly an hour. The masthead almanac for that first day of classes looked like this:

Weather
Miraculously
Warm and Dry;
Enjoy It
While It Lasts

The lead-off for the Sun's SUPER-EXPANDED EDITORIAL PAGE read:

Wanted—One (1) No-Spill Dragon
IT MIGHT SEEM APPROPRIATE on this first day of instruction for the *Sun* to offer some words of encouragement to newcomers just beginning their studies at Cornell. We at the *Sun* pride ourselves on freshness and originality, however, and since every variety of encouragement has already been offered umpteen times in the past, this year we've decided not to bother. Besides, a *Sun* poll taken only last week reveals that the Big Issue on everyone's mind—first year students included—has nothing to do with academics. Rather it concerns the raising of the legal drinking age from nineteen to twenty-one, effective this December first. The Questions: Is there life without the weekend bar scene? Will Collegetown survive? Will we, the under-twenty-one crowd, survive without a good round of doubles to buck us up after a failed prelim?

There can be no doubt but that lack-of-alcohol crises will occur. All we can do is try our best to avoid emotions-shattering situations and occurrences wherever possible. Case in point: the annual Green Dragon Parade. As returning Cornellians will know, this is a mid-March event in which a gigantic Dragon, constructed by the incoming class of the Architecture school, is taken on a circuitous tour of Central Campus and then burned to ashes on the Arts Quad. This traditional event, first dreamed up by Willard Straight '01, has been carried out faithfully and flawlessly every year—until last spring, when the oversized beast collapsed in on itself before getting ten feet from its starting point. Filled with shame, the Architects descended on the Collegetown bars to drown their sorrows. One favored hangout, the Fevre Dream Tavern, reported its entire stock of liquor depleted more than an hour before last call. The booze did its job, it seems; there were a number of disturbances of the peace reported, but no suicides. The Archies were too numbed to think of gorge-hopping.

But this year, a retreat to the bars *won't be possible*. With pub owners increasingly vigilant for fake I.D., defeated Architects and the like will find themselves out of luck. As a public service, therefore, the *Sun* is asking those concerned to already start thinking ahead to March. We need a few good women and men who can build a *real* dragon, one that will stand tall and not collapse or fall over until it's supposed to. And while we're on the subject, let's everybody study hard, pass those prelims, and put some style into those term papers. In the end we at the *Sun* are sure we'll all find that Diet Coke goes down just as smoothly as a Manhattan—when it's a victory celebration.

III.

Monday, 8:05 A.M.

Fujiko screamed as her alarm clock went off, and the exquisite anguish of a Southern Comfort hangover settled around her head like a vise. She groped around in the semi-darkness for a weapon, came up with a hockey stick—her ex-boyfriend had left it to her as a remembrance—and reduced the clock to its component parts with one good swipe.

After sluggishly pulling on a bathrobe and pawing through three drawers to find a towel, she stepped into the hall—and screamed again, as the sudden light nearly blinded her. Across the hall Z.Z. Top wandered out of his own room, clad in yellow swim trunks and extra-dark Wayfarer glasses. His foot struck a copy of the *Sun* that had been thrust halfway under his door, scattering it in a flurry of newsprint. He paid it no mind.

"Good morning," Fujiko fumbled out, just to be polite.

"Bullshit," replied the Top.

They entered the bathroom together, Fujiko ignoring, as was Risley custom, the sign on the door that said MEN. The only shower was in use (a steady chorus of Sex Pistols tunes competed with the sound of flowing water), and Preacher sat cross-legged on the floor, waiting his turn. Woodstock, the newly-installed Bohemian Minister of Impetuousness, lay flat out in a semi-daze alongside the row of sinks.

"Jesus," Woodstock moaned. Another victim.

"Which?" the Top inquired, joining him on the floor.

"Bacardi one fifty one," said Woodstock. "Backgammon for flaming shots."

"I'm going to throw up," Fujiko announced. She staggered into a toilet stall and began to do just that.

"Who's in the shower? asked the Top.

"Jim Taber and Ben Hull," Preacher told him. "Both of them a lot more lively than this Bohemian this morning, sounds like."

"It's your choice of breakfast cereal," suggested Woodstock.

"What about the tub? Anybody using that?"

"There's a lemon tree in the tub," Woodstock informed him. As if to prove the truth of his words, he produced a sickly-looking lemon from his bathrobe pocket and began sucking on it.

"A lemon tree," the Top repeated. "How did—"

Preacher raised an eyebrow. "You really want to know?"

"No. Fuck it. Hey, anybody got a beer?"

IV.

Monday, 11:15 A.M.

"Heaven, did you say?"

"—Gannett Medical Clinic, donated by the Gannett Foundation in honor of Frank E. Gannett, class of eighteen ninety-eight. Its main function is the prevention of unwanted human pregnancies. . . ."

Luther, Blackjack, and a ragtag group of mongrels and Purebreds new to the University followed after a silver-furred tabby named Sable, who served as their tour guide. Already they had made their way up to the Agriculture Quad, across Fall Creek to North Campus, down and around Fraternity Row to the West Campus dorms, and up again through Collegetown. Now they padded along Central Avenue, headed back toward the Arts Quad.

Sable dutifully reeled off the facts and dates concerning each building they passed, not really caring how much of it penetrated. In truth the dogs in the tour group did not pay much attention to what the puss was saying, preferring to either gape at their surroundings or talk among themselves. Only Blackjack remained attentive. He busily studied Sable, who earlier had informed him quite candidly that she would soon be going into heat.

" . . . on our right is the Olin Hall of Engineering, financed by a gift from Frankin W. Olin, class of eighteen ninety-six. It opened in October of nineteen forty-two. . . ."

"Yes, Heaven," Luther responded to the mongrel beside him. "That *is* what this is. It has to be; it *smells* like Heaven, and besides, Blackjack and I traveled too far for it not to be."

"I don't mean to argue with you, friend," said the mongrel, whose name was Denmark, "but I traveled a long way to get here too. Only I didn't come for angels, I came for knowledge. This is a learning-place, you see; special, but surely not Heaven. You must have taken a wrong turn somewhere."

"*You* must have taken the wrong turn," Luther insisted.

"Och, but I heard it was a learnin'-place too," said Nessa, a Scottish Terrier bitch. "They've got a series of Questions, they do, that one has to answer. I suppose that means it's like Heaven, in a manner of speakin'—the answerin' of big Questions has a certain divine ring to it."

"Questions?" asked Luther.

" . . . this huge building coming up on our left," said Sable in the backround, "is Willard Straight Hall, opened in November of nineteen twenty-five, and dedicated to Willard Dickerman Straight of the class of nineteen oh one. The building is home to a number of human student organizations, and one of the University dining halls is located here. Dogs are not permitted in the dining area, and it isn't a good place to beg for scraps anyway. . . ."

"They got Five Questions," said Joshua, another mongrel. "The dogs who run this place, that is. And before you go talking about 'divine rings,' you'd best check out exactly what those Questions are. The fourth one's a long way from being Godly, for some of us."

"The Fourth Question?" Luther repeated. "I don't understand any of this. This is *Heaven*. It's got to be."

"Wait until the Convocation on Friday. Wait and see if you still feel the same way after that."

" . . . we now angle to the right, and as we do you can clearly see Sage Chapel just ahead of us. Humans gather in this edifice on Sunday mornings to waste time. . . ."

Sable led them between Sage Chapel and the Campus Store, toward a strange encampment behind the Day Hall administration building. Ducking out of the way of a pimply-faced Freshman who was in a big hurry to get somewhere, Sable purposefully brushed against Blackjack, stirring him. She was not in heat—not yet, not yet—but Blackjack might have tried something anyway if Luther had not broken off from his debate with Joshua and turned to them.

"Hey," said Luther to Sable, studying the haphazard collection of trenches and barbed wire just ahead of them. "What's that?"

"They call it Hooterville."

"Hooterville?" Luther could not help but be pleased by the sight of it. The trenches and scattered sandbag lean-tos had a desolate quality to them that reminded him of the burned-out buildings back home. "What's a Hooterville?"

"It's part of an ongoing protest," Sable explained. "Protesters are human beings who complain about the way things are so that other human beings can get annoyed and kill them without feeling too badly about it. Eventually the cause of justice is supposed to be served by this."

"Oh," said Luther, without the slightest understanding. He paused to look at a sign at the edge of the encampment, made of warped plywood and painted with human words he could not read:

WELCOME TO HOOTERVILLE!
One of the last bastions of sanity in a world of
crazed conservatism.
We, the members of the Blue Zebra Hooter
Patrol, Cornell's only benign terrorist
organization, believe in the principle of
thought provocation through non-violent
confrontation.
To this end, we as a group provide a continual
thorn-in-the-side to the Cornell
administration, thus encouraging both the

University staff and the student body to daily
question the status quo.
This Week's Major Issues:
1) Divestment from all companies doing
business in racist South Africa.
2) Affirmative action and increased minority
admissions.
3) Self-defense training for baby seals. (It *can*
be done).
GET IN GEAR AND <u>THINK!!!</u>

V.

Monday, 11:20 A.M.

"Kind of lets you know you're at Cornell, doesn't it?" observed Z.Z. Top.

"Can't imagine it being anywhere else," George agreed, taking another bite of his sandwich. The two sat with their backs against a cement bunker, surrounded by the gentle devastation of Hooterville. Fantasy Dreadlock, the leader of the Blue Zebras and a former Bohemian, had designed the encampment to represent all the world's ugliness, while at the same time symbolizing the struggle to hold on and eventually set things right again. Three separate trenches gouged their way across what had once been green lawn and gravel walkway; blunted barbed wire was strewn around more or less at random. Set on a slight rise at the center of the camp was a spring-loaded cannon that aimed straight up, and which was capable at a moment's notice of filling the air with propaganda leaflets or whatever else came to mind. Scattered throughout the area were the Blue Zebras, in their distinctive blue-and-white-striped jumpsuits, and with them other prominent members of the Cornell community: Joe Scandle, Resident Housing Director of the Africana dorm, Ujamaa, took lunch with Fantasy herself; the treasurer of Gay People At Cornell (GayPAC) argued heatedly with Brian Garroway and one of the heads of Cornellians for Christ, while Aurora watched from the far side of a trench; the editorial staff of the *Sun* played stud poker in the shade of a sandbag wall. At the fringe of the encampment stood two officers of the Cornell Safety Division—watchdogs guarding against an unlikely peasant revolt—drinking coffee and exchanging jokes with the Zebras.

The creation of Hooterville, a year and a half ago, had initially been approved by the administration during a period of student unrest. At the time it had seemed a small enough concession to appease a number of people; those in charge of the decision had also seen nothing wrong with concentrating the campus radicals in an area where they could be watched. The one thing no one in power had counted on, of course, was that it would last so long. Since its inception, however, Hooterville—not to mention the Zebras—had in some way figured into over three-quarters of the demonstrations, debates, and rallies on campus. And the Blue Zebras not only supported protests, they looked for them. Earnestly. Where the Bohemians preached the gospel of unorthodoxy, Fantasy and her Zebras spread the good word about conflict and dissent—much to the administration's chagrin.

To date, none of the many attempts to remove Hooterville had been even partially successful. The original permit for the encampment had included no expiration date, a critical oversight. The site could not be condemned as a fire hazard because it contained no flammable materials other than the plywood sign; likewise, since the installation of a sanitary outhouse (the cement bunker), there were no qualms from the Health Department. A final clincher against administrative interference had come from a Sixties-alumnus-turned-corporation-owner, who had offered the University a five-million-dollar grant on condition that the 'Ville be left unmolested; this same alumnus had also posted a five-thousand-dollar bond against eventual relandscaping needed to fill in the trenches, should that ever become necessary.

"Pretty," Z.Z. Top observed, startling George out of his reverie. He had begun to drift, daydreaming about the political significance of Hooterville. When the Top saw the confused look on his face, he pointed across the trenches at Aurora.

"Oh," said George. "She's pretty enough."

"What's she like to talk to? You know her, right?"

"I know her. She's nice. Good person."

"Thought she might be," the Top admitted, and caught George totally off guard by adding: "You ought to steal her away from that guy she's with."

"Pardon?"

"Well if you don't mind my saying, I've seen the two of them around before, last year, and they just don't strike me as the peaches and cream couple of the century."

"What are you getting at?" George asked. He thought of Wax, at the McDonald's down on The Commons. "You're saying Aurora and Brian don't look like a good match?"

"Only a hunch. He has that *look*, you know, that Mr. Overbearing-type face. Not quite Hitler Youth but you catch my drift. And I know, I know, the lady looks pretty happy from here, but maybe if she got tight with an alternative sort of guy, a kind of left-wing fiction writer, say . . ."

"All right, Top." George scrutinized him carefully. "Who signed you up as matchmaker?"

Z.Z. Top studied the sky. "Oh . . . Lion-Heart might have told some of us to keep an eye and an ear open for you."

This brought another laugh. "That's perfect!" George said good-naturedly. "Just what I need: the bunch of you running around trying to fix me up."

"Don't knock it, George. You could do lots worse. Romeo didn't even have one Bohemian on his side, and look what happened to him."

"I know that. Don't think I don't appreciate it, either. It's just that I don't think it's going to happen for me that way."

"Could be," the Top said honestly. "Lot of people, you can't put the fix in, they just have to wait till the penny drops on its own. But there's no sin in looking around while you wait."

"I'm looking," George said. "Finding—that's the problem."

Without warning the cannon at the center of the encampment fired, spraying an amazing shower of white roses into the air. They fell in a twenty-five-foot circle, startling a number of the Blue Zebras and getting a jump out of Fantasy Dreadlock, who had ordered no such barrage.

The Top was laughing. "Oh *man*, George, oh *man*. Speak of the fucking devil, baby."

One of the roses had landed squarely in George's lap, as if precisely aimed. Tied to the stern of the rose with a thread—a scarlet thread—was a small note. Against all decent laws of probability, the outside of the note was addressed TO THE DAYDREAMER. Within were three more words: I LOVE YOU. The note was not signed.

"This is impossible." George said matter-of-factly. "This can't be especially for me." Not even the wind could have carried the rose from the cannon to him with certainty.

Somewhere near, a dog began to bark.

VI.

Monday, 11:25 A.M.

"Luther!" called Blackjack. "Luther, what the hell's gotten into you? Luther!"

Luther, transfixed and barking like a hound close on a trail, made no reply. He bounded past the plywood sign into Hooterville proper, drawn on by a tantalizing smell the breeze had brought him.

"Luther!"

The head of Cornellians for Christ was very nearly bowled over as the mongrel brushed past him. Luther paused briefly to sniff at Aurora's legs, then dove into a trench, tripping up no less than three Blue Zebras as he charged along its length. He came up again near the cement bunker, downwind of George and the Top.

George, who had begun to stand up, was knocked back on his ass and pinned against the bunker as the dog leapt into his arms. If it had been an

attack, George's career as a writer—and a human being—might have ended
right there. But Luther intended only the greatest affection, and in demonstrating this he licked George's face like a Tootsie Pop holding great secrets at
its center.

"Hi, dog," Z.Z. Top said casually, as George went down under a
barrage of slurps. The smell that had been ingrained in George and his
clothing during a long Ithaca residence—the smell of hills and rain—sent
Luther into a near frenzy.

"Whoah!" George protested, gasping for air. "Whoah, calm down! I
can't breathe, all right?"

He managed to pet the dog and shove it back a few paces in the same
motion. As Luther began nipping affectionately at his hand, George scanned
the encampment for a particular pair of eyes. Just before Luther's arrival, he
had been looking around to see who might have tossed the rose to him under
cover of the cannon shot, and for a moment he thought he had seen a face
peering at him from behind a pile of sandbags. But she was gone now, if she
had ever been.

"Thanks a lot," George said to the dog, trying to sound stern. But he
could not help smiling: Luther's front paws, jammed into his abdomen, were
tickling him. At any rate the mongrel could not understand his words, and at
the moment was too overjoyed to sense George's disappointment. For George
was permeated with the Heaven scent, and for a while, at least, Luther was
convinced that he had made his first contact with a genuinely divine being,
the canine equivalent of a cherub or seraph . . . or a saint.

VII.

Tuesday, 4:00 P.M.

Puck lay stretched out on the deck of a battleship as it moved off from the
shore of Beebe Lake. It was a small battleship, only eight-and-a-half feet long,
and its hull was high-impact plastic rather than steel, but it was still an
impressive thing.

The battleship belonged to Hamlet, one of Puck's best friends. Hamlet
had spent weeks assembling the craft from an Aurora model kit, then
modifying it and installing a generator so that it could actually be used rather
than just looked at. The ship had a whopping top speed of three knots, and
was sufficiently well armed to repel almost any animal threat, either swimming or flying. The ship's name was *Prospero*, and Hamlet was quite right-
fully proud of it.

"But what are you going to do when winter comes?" Puck asked as they
steered toward Hamlet's home, a small island in the middle of the lake. The

island was overgrown with reeds and had no suitable area that could be used as a runway; Puck's biplane was hidden among the brush on the lake shore.

"You mean when the lake freezes over?" Hamlet replied from the bridge, a partially covered area in mid-deck. "I hadn't given it much thought. Guess I'll have to dry dock her somehow. Or maybe I can put ski foils on her, turn her into an ice boat."

"Probably skate her right over the dam and down the falls," Puck said ominously.

"Where you'll no doubt join me when your wings ice up. But at least I won't have as long a drop."

Hamlet began to pull the ship up alongside the island, but Puck sat up and said: "Hey, would you mind if we just floated around for a while?"

"Not at all," said Hamlet, veering out toward the center of the lake. "If you trust me not to go over the falls by accident. Something on your mind?"

"Sort of."

"Is it sort of about Zephyr?"

"Who else?"

"I take it you haven't been too successful at trying to make up with her?"

"Well," said Puck, "for a while it looked like I was making progress. Even though she's still hooked on that George character . . ."

"George the human being?"

"George the blowhard," Puck replied sullenly.

"There, there, my friend," Hamlet cautioned. "A human being who happens to be on intimate terms with the wind is no one to trifle with."

"So what if he's a human being? Calling the wind is nothing so special. Hell, Zephyr can do it just as well as he can."

"Yes," Hamlet agreed. "And you trifled with her too, didn't you?"

"We-e-ell . . . well look, regardless of how this whole problem got started, the point is she was finally coming around again, beginning to see the light about what a perfect couple we are."

"What a perfect couple," Hamlet repeated.

"That's right: We were made for each other. That's the conclusion I've come to. And Zephyr was just getting ready to forgive me for what happened when she found out that Saffron Dey is going with us on the Raid. Now she's back to not speaking to me again."

"Who let the news drop about Saffron?"

"I guess I did. How was I supposed to know that Zephyr would react that way? I never thought—"

"That's been your problem all along, you know," Hamlet interrupted him. "You've been suffering from a serious thinking shortage. I never understood what you saw in Saffron Dey in the first place."

"I'll give you two large and firm guesses."

Hamlet nodded. "Granted," he said, "that good cleavage doesn't grow on trees, I still don't see the sense in it. Zephyr's shape isn't as exaggerated as Saffron's, but it's a nice shape all the same. And lest you forget, my friend, Zephyr has a personality. Saffron's is as shallow as the dimples on a golf ball."

"That's all true," Puck admitted.

"Then why'd you do it?"

"Look, it's not like Zephyr and I had a firm commitment. . . ."

"That," said Hamlet, "is one of the two dumbest statements made by males on this planet, be they sprite or human."

"I had *urges*, all right?"

"And that takes care of the other."

Puck twiddled his thumbs self-consciously, not sure what to say next. "By the way," Hamlet went on, "what in God's name possessed you to invite Saffron on the Raid, especially when you were trying to patch things up with Zephyr?"

"I didn't invite her. She's Cobweb's date, officially. I guess he liked what he saw when he was watching us go at it in the display case."

"Did you try telling Zephyr that?"

"She didn't believe me."

"Hmm. I guess that's not surprising, is it?"

"No, it isn't," Puck said gloomily. "But what am I supposed to *do*, Hamlet? I don't want her to go on hating me forever."

"I doubt she hates you. Oh, she's not too pleased with you right now, obviously. And as to whether she'll ever trust you again, well, that's a toss-up . . . I'm afraid I don't have any simple solution for you, Puck. The consequences of chauvinism, as they say, aren't easy to undo."

"And there's nothing I can do?"

"Nothing honest I can think of offhand. You could always try using another series of lies to repair the damage from the first series, but that usually has mixed results. I'd say your best bet is just to keep on being nice to her and pray that things work out. Or chuck her and go after a different sprite entirely."

"I can't do that, Hamlet."

"Well then, I guess you'll have to depend on Fate to see you through. Who knows, maybe—"

He broke off as there was a sudden splash in the water off to their right. It was followed by three others, as unseen objects plunked into the lake.

"What is it?" said Hamlet, preparing for evasive action.

"There." Puck pointed. "On the shore."

Four young boys, humans, stood on the shore, approximately twenty yards away from the battleship. They were throwing rocks, and as Puck watched them, one produced a slingshot from his back pocket.

"How'd they spot us?" Puck wondered aloud.

"Children are good at noticing things that others would ignore," Hamlet reminded him. "And this boat isn't tiny, either. I've had trouble a few times before. Hang on."

The battleship's starboard side faced the boys. Now Hamlet accelerated and began to turn toward them.

"Wait a minute," said Puck. "Shouldn't we be retreating?"

"Not to worry," Hamlet replied, throwing a switch. A panel opened near the bow and a catapult-like contraption rose up to the level of the deck.

"Holy shitmoley!" cried the smallest of the boys. "Its comin' for us! It's comin' for us!"

"Shut up, Mikey," suggested the slingshot wielder. He took careful aim and fired a shot that passed right above the catapult and thudded clumsily off the outer shell of the bridge.

Puck stared at the rock, which weighed nearly as much as he did.

"This is one of those times," he said, "when I almost wish I weren't invisible."

"What makes you think they'd stop if they could see us?" asked Hamlet. "Have you ever seen what they do to chipmunks? Now, pray for good aim!"

He threw another switch, and the catapult lobbed an egg-shaped object into the air. In fact it was an egg, one that had been drained of its yolk and refilled. It flew in a high arc and burst on the forehead of the smallest boy—Mikey—who proceeded to scream as if mortally wounded.

"Hamlet!" Puck cried. "What was in that—"

"Child repellent," Hamlet told him. "Don't worry, the effects are temporary."

Mikey began to swipe at his head now, staggering blindly back and forth and wailing pitifully. The other children ceased their rock barrage and gathered around to see if he would drop dead, or what.

"Care for some tea?" Hamlet asked, bringing the ship around and heading once more toward his island home. "Macduff got me a really special blend. Says he liberated it from one of the dorms. It's part Earl Grey and part Colombian Red."

"Sounds good," said Puck. "Who knows, maybe it'll give me some inspiration about what I should do."

"Just give it time," Hamlet advised him. "Women have a way of coming around."

"Uh-huh. Now who's being chauvinistic?"

Hamlet laughed.

"*Realistic*, Puck," he said. "Just realistic. And besides, my fellow chauvinist, I didn't say that *men* were any more sensible in handling their emotions, did I?"

VIII.

Wednesday, 12:10 P.M.

"Check *her* out, partner."

Preacher looked across the Arts Quad at the woman Ragnarok pointed out. Blond, medium height, with a Tri-Pi blazer.

"Decent," Preacher granted him. "Plastic, but decent. But you can keep right on dreaming, cuz."

"Why?"

"That flash on her wrist. Even if it's costume jewelry, it cost. And you see how the bottom of her ear winks every time the wind blows her hair back? That look like a diamond earring to you?"

"So she comes from money. So what?"

"So what is what's she need *you* for? Must be a whole line of nice white fraternity boys just waiting for a chance at her. You're nothing new, except you drive a bike instead of a Porsche, and you don't have a tie on. She'll probably figure that's 'cause you don't have money, and poor, my friend, is a *very* old story. Now if a man came along who could offer her a real change of pace . . ."

"They have black people in the Greek system too," Ragnarok informed him. "And Hispanics, and Asians, and Saudi Arabians." Ragnarok smiled. "You're nothing special either, Preach."

Preacher smiled back. "Well that's true," he said, "but I guess I wouldn't be going after that particular chick anyway."

"Oh, of course not."

"I mean it. Why don't you check her letters one more time before she gets away?"

Ragnarok shook his head, puzzled. "What's wrong with Tri-Pi?"

"Oh, nothing. Sweet little sorority, the Pis. But why don't you rummage around in that steel trap mind of yours and see if you can't remember who their brother fraternity is?"

"Brother frat . . . Oh! Oh, shit."

"That's right," said Preacher. "Good old Rho Alpha Tau."

"The Rat Frat. Shit."

"Not just that," Preacher continued. "Now that I think about it, I remember her from around the dance clubs. Guess who she goes high-stepping with on Saturday nights?"

"The Chief Rat?" Ragnarok made a wild guess. "Jack Baron?"

"The man himself. Still think she's cute?"

"Miles Walker!" a shrill voice called out to them. "Miles Walker and Charlie Hyatt! Hey there!"

Both men turned, knowing already from the sound of the voice whom it belonged to. Ginny Porterhouse, an Orientation Counselor of truly enormous proportions, jounced up to them like a tugboat coming into port over stormy water. She pulled a much smaller woman in tow.

"Miles, how nice to see you!" She swept Preacher into a clumsy embrace before he could duck away. Ragnarok was quicker, escaping with a mere handshake. Both Bohemians were, as usual, impressed by her display of affection—for though they knew from experience and observation that she had no real patience with weird cases like the Bohemes, Ginny always managed to act civilly toward them. For a brief period.

Ginny's charge for the day was a diminutive Asian lugging a huge shoulder bag, which looked as though it might tip her over at any time. Still, Preacher could see in her eyes that she was strong, and perhaps Ragnarok saw it too, for they both began to care for her—or at least lust after her in a friendly manner—at the same moment.

"Ginny P.!" Preacher burst out. "How's it goin'?"

"Oh, we're having a wonderful time today," Ginny replied in her most matronly tone. "Boys, I want you to meet Jinsei. Jinsei's a transfer student from Penn State, but before that she was born in mainland China, of all places!"

"No shit?" Preacher said, winking discreetly at Jinsei. "And here I had you pegged for an Australian."

"Jinsei," Ginny continued doggedly, "this is Miles Walker and his friend Charlie Hyatt."

"Hi," said Ragnarok. "We're from mainland America."

"The low-rent district," Preacher added. "Say, are you sure you've never been in Sydney?"

Jinsei smiled bemusedly at both of them. "Actually," she said, "I grew up in Pittsburgh."

"Yeah?" Preacher turned to Ginny. "Here's your chance to take some serious English lessons, Gin. Bet she could cure that California accent of yours in no time."

"I'm sure," Ginny said. She took a not-too-obvious glance at her watch. "Well my, look at the time. And we have a really busy schedule today. . . ."

"Don't let us hold you up," said Preacher.

"I don't think we could if we tried," Ragnarok pointed out.

"Nice meeting you both," Jinsei said pleasantly, following as Ginny began to walk away. Preacher and Ragnarok bowed deeply to her.

A moment or two passed. Then Ragnarok called out. "Hey! Hey!" Both women, already some distance away, looked back.

"Don't believe a word she tells you!" Ragnarok shouted cheerfully to Jinsei. "She doesn't know the first thing about life at Cornell!"

"She doesn't even go to this school!" Preacher added. "She's an Ithaca College spy!"

Ginny dropped all pretense and glared at them. Jinsei favored them with another smile, catching both their hearts.

"She likes you," Preacher observed.
"She likes you," Ragnarok replied.
"So what do we do, cuz?"
"Guess we take turns falling for her," said Ragnarok. He spoke jokingly, but as it turned out, he was more right than he knew.

IX.

Wednesday, 6:15 P.M.

The bus bearing the Cornellians for Christ to their first fall picnic arrived at Taughannock Park shortly before sunset. It pulled up by the shore of Cayuga Lake, where an assortment of tables, a wooden shelter, and a ready-made bonfire were waiting. The Christers—as they were popularly known, like it or not (though the *Sun* was careful to use a different nickname)—piled out onto the grass and, after getting dinner started, chose up sides for frisbee football.

Aurora passed on the game, and while Brian and Michael Krist flipped steaks over a charcoal fire, she crossed Route 89 in search of Taughannock Falls. A footpath led her alongside a wide stream, and she paused frequently along the bank. The water seemed alive; from time to time the Falls would dry up to a mere trickle and the stream would suffer with it, but not this season. It roared, turbulent and jubilant, but for all its ferocity, the melody it made as it crashed over the stones in its bed struck Aurora as distinctly feminine. So did the song the wind pushed through the trees.

All this was part of a delightfully unorthodox world view that would have pleased her father to no end, had he known about it. For despite the cross that hung above her breast, and all the dogma that went with it, she had always thought of God as being female (or rather, Female). The image that came to her mind when she bothered to conjure one was of a not-quite-old, not-quite-matronly woman with the universe set out before her like a floor plan on a drafting table. It was a romantic conception, one Aurora could never have explained, much less justified, to Brian and the other Christers. So she simply believed in it, quietly and to herself.

Across the stream at one point she spotted a peculiar fall of logs that, combined with the oncoming darkness, gave the illusion of a cottage. It reminded her of a scene from George's book, in which the White Rose Knight and his Squire stopped for the evening at a cabin in an enchanted forest. The beautiful occupant of the cabin turned into a grizzly bear with the rising of the moon, and the Knight was very nearly torn in half before effecting his escape. Aurora didn't know about that part, but the earlier descriptions of the forest and homestead very much caught her fancy. It would be nice to live in a magic wood, she thought, with an occasional wandering Knight for company.

I just don't want you to wake up thirty years from now and realize that your chance to have more of a life has gone by.

More than once in the past two weeks Aurora had given thought to her father's words on the morning of her leaving. Far from unraveling the meaning of everything he had said, she had nonetheless begun to understand the basic gist of it, in particular his fear of Brian Garroway and how Brian might influence her. Walter had made no mention of her boyfriend, but no mention was necessary.

Her feelings about this were varied. Above all she was touched that her father should care so much for her, for she knew that at the very root it was love rather than selfishness that motivated him. Oh, no doubt Walter dreamed of having a norm-breaker for a daughter, but the concern in his voice on that last morning had been more than that of a man losing a dream.

She was also amused at this further confirmation of her world view. God was supposed to be omniscient, but Aurora had never met a man with any talent for mind-reading. Her father had apparently decided that, since she showed no outward signs of radicalism, her capacity and desire to be "different" had somehow vanished. Here Walter was dead wrong. True, she had grown up peacefully enough, with little show of rebellion or deviation. Aurora did not bother with such displays; while she had a certain admiration for those who made argument their daily bread, she herself avoided confrontation except when absolutely necessary, and kept more to herself than most people ever realized. But her dreams were vast.

If Aurora could have stepped inside the world of George's book she would have done so in a moment. Why not? Cross the magic stream and enter a world of enchantment. And if a dragon or two had to be faced, then that was a worthwhile price of admission. But in real life there were other things, stronger even than dragons, to keep you from crossing that stream. Love, for instance.

Aurora loved Brian Garroway. Someone knowing the full scope of her dreams might not have understood this, but love kept its own secrets. To Walter Smith, Brian's bad points seemed all too obvious: impatience, his inflexible sense of law, general intolerance. Closer in, Aurora saw good as well. She had been witness to scenes Walt would never know: impatient Brian spending an entire Sunday afternoon on an elaborate funeral and burial service when his younger sister's pet rabbit had died; law-abiding Brian running countless red lights on the way to the hospital when the same younger sister fractured her ankle skating; intolerant Brian walking a mile to a friend's house to apologize when he realized he'd been too hasty in an argument. Such moments were touchstones to her, keys to really *seeing* Brian as opposed to just judging him.

And of course he loved her too, however poorly he sometimes demonstrated that love. This was perhaps the strongest compulsion of all; true love is hard to turn away, especially first love, even if the cost is high.

I don't want you to feel that loss. . . .
She would think the whole thing over yet. Carefully. She still had time to think. Not much time, for Brian would be proposing officially to her before long, but hopefully time enough. Time to weigh the good against the bad, time to balance what she would gain against what she would have to give up.

Aurora walked the rest of the way to the waterfall, stunned, as always, by her first glimpse of it, a hundred-foot silver cascade that turned the last rays of the sunset into a light show. She stood on a stone bridge and lost herself in the music of the flow. In its day Taughannock Falls had seen explorers, tourists, lovers, and, in 1903, a pistol duel. It whispered her a song of magic past, and magic yet to be.

X.

Friday, 5:30 A.M.
At an hour when no sane student or professor would wish to be awake—even the *Sun* deliverers had, after a week of classes, decided to sleep a bit later—better than a hundred dogs were gathered on the Arts Quad. Sergeant Slaughter, a Bulldog who served as mascot to the members of Cornell's ROTC, had been padding about the campus since four in the morning, waking Purebreds and mongrels alike for the Dog's Convocation.

They stood, sat, lay, rolled over, tussled in a rough semi-circle before Ezra Cornell's statue: Pointers, Retrievers, Hounds, Shepherds, Terriers, Spaniels, the odd Toy Dog, other more exotic breeds, and a tight knot of mongrels who clustered at the far edge of the crowd, watching defiantly for any sign of condescension from the Purebreds. Luther, Blackjack at his side, looked anxiously for his sire as well, but Moses was nowhere to be found.

As they waited for the ceremony to begin, Joshua and Denmark argued fervently with a Collie bitch named Bucklette.

"Explain to me again," Denmark said, "how the Fourth Question is supposed to be 'perfectly acceptable.'"

"It *is*," Bucklette insisted. "You dogs"—here Joshua bristled—"just don't understand the educational process."

"I guess I don't," Joshua agreed. "How about teaching it to me?"

"Look," said Bucklette, "it's not as if you were the only ones who had a right to be upset—*if* there was anything to be upset about. The Fourth Question implies prejudice against everybody."

"It implies prejudice against *you*. Maybe. Me, it doesn't even consider."

"Well then that's all the more to the point. The Fourth Question is an absolutely marvelous example of reverse cogitation."

"Reverse cogitation," Denmark repeated.

"Reverse cogitation?" Joshua queried.

"Yes, yes! Here, let me give you another example. Suppose a dog came up to you and asked, 'What's the best way of losing your left foreleg?' "

"My leg?" replied Denmark. "I guess any way would be pretty horrible."

"It's a stupid question," Joshua added.

"Exactly. And you answer it by attacking the foolishness of the idea behind the question—like the idea of prejudice. *That's* reverse cogitation."

"It's still stupid," observed Joshua. "How can you . . ."

And so on. Luther paid little attention to what was said, although the argument, and the general tension between the mongrels and Purebreds, disturbed him. It had been a long week of discovery, and despite the joy he had felt on encountering George, he had seen a great many other things that shook his faith in what they had found. Blackjack, sensing this, had begun gently to prod him in the direction of reality.

"Luther . . ." he said now.

"This *is* Heaven," Luther responded automatically. "Moses is here, and sooner or later we're going to find him and everything will be all right."

"I like it here," the Manx confessed. "The air's cleaner and I don't go hungry half as often as I did back in the City. Good scavenging, good hunting. But would it be so awful if it wasn't exactly what we'd come for?"

Luther did not answer, and shortly Blackjack gave up . . . for now.

At quarter of six there was a sudden hush, a stilling of thoughts. An Old English Sheepdog had entered the Quad, led by a pair of Doberman Pinschers. For a moment Luther tensed, unavoidably reminded of Cerberus and Dragon. But these Dobermans did not move in tandem; one of them was attempting to walk and lick his balls at the same time, while the other panted at each bitch he passed. The Sheepdog was even less threatening. With his eyes totally hidden under a veil of fur, he allowed his mouth to hang open and followed the Dobermans blindly, seemingly oblivious to his surroundings.

"Well," said the Sheepdog, as they came to a halt in front of the statue of Ezra Cornell, "have we left yet?"

"Yes sir," replied one of the Dobermans. "We're there."

"Really? Jolly good!" He faced a stand of bushes and proudly began: "Welcome, one and all! My name—"

While the Dobermans were busy reorienting the Sheepdog toward the crowd, Luther asked, "Who is that?"

A mongrel bitch—a quite elegant dog, really—named Lace told him, "That's the Head. The boss-stud of education."

"Our leader in the pursuit of higher knowledge," Denmark added with a touch of derision.

The Collie bitch snorted, and Lace gave her a sharp glance.

"You got a problem, sister? Something we can do for you?"

But the Collie made no reply. A moment later the Sheepdog began to address them again: "Welcome, one and all! My name is Excalibur, Excalibur the Third, and I am your Dean of Studies."

The crowd howled and barked its approval. The Purebreds did, that is, except for the St. Bernard, Gallant, who tried to maintain an air of decorum and merely gazed respectfully at the Dean. The mongrels too were silent, but their expressions held only reproach. Meanwhile, at the very front of the ranks, there was an intermittent flounce of tail and ears—Skippy the Beagle, leaping for joy.

"Now," Dean Excalibur continued as the noise died down, "before we get on to the matter of the Questions, I think it only fitting that we introduce some of the members of our staff. Yes? Yes." He turned to face the base of Ezra's statue. "Are the, uh, cats here?"

"Yes sir," said one of the Dobermans, turning the Dean around again. "Just a moment." He gave three short barks, and a group of seven cats padded into view. They all appeared quite bored.

"For those of you who are new to this place," said Dean Excalibur, when the Doberman nudged him to go on, "these noble felines serve as our official interpreters and orientation counselors. I'm sure you'll find that they're a jolly good bunch of fellows, once you get to know them."

One of the cats, a Siamese, stretched and yawned.

"As for the dogs on our staff—our canine philosophers, as we call them—we have at least one to assist you with each of the Questions you will seek to answer. Why, I was just talking to one of them the other day, Smooth I think his name is—"

"Ruff, sir," prompted the Doberman who had been licking himself.

"Yes, yes, Ruff, of course. Jolly good fellow, as I'm sure you'll agree when you get to know him. Well, well, we'd better get on to the business at hand, eh? The Questions. Is Yoda here?"

"Wog, sir. His name is Wog."

"Yes, yes, Wog. Wog, come forward!"

Wog was an Affenpinscher, a small dark-coated dog with a flattened face that would have looked at home on a monkey—that was, indeed, where the breed name had come from. Wog stood a mere nine inches at the shoulder, and did not appear to be the sort of animal who would be entrusted with any authority. Nonetheless he bore himself with dignity as he advanced to stand beside Excalibur, fixed his beady eyes upon the crowd, and yapped once for attention.

"Listen now," Wog began. "Listen to the tale of what was, and what came to be. . . ."

A moth chose that moment to flutter past the Affenpinscher's face. Wog snapped it up, crunched it briefly between his teeth, and spat it back out again.

"Listen," he repeated, directing at least part of the thought at the moth's remains. "Just listen, and be made knowledgeable . . . a long time ago, in a distant land on a far shore in a really, really hard-to-find country, there lived a dog named Sapientia Stultitia, or 'Double S' as he is often referred to. We know not to what breed Double S belonged, but it is said that he was strong and pure-blooded. . . ."

One of mongrels began to growl. Luther saw that it was Joshua.

" . . . Now Double S was a good dog, but he was constantly plagued by cats, most of whom had no respect for him or any others of his race. In that age a great enmity existed between canines and felines, far worse than any imagined difficulties of today, and cats used the knowledge they gained from the Masters to practice torment and deceit. . . ."

The cats, including Blackjack, listened passively to this. The sins of their ancestors held no interest or pain of guilt for them.

" . . . so it came to pass that Double S recognized the need for some sort of education, some grasping of fundamental and philosophical truths among dogs, if only to put them on an equal footing with their persecutors. In his own words: 'I would found a system by which any dog can learn to match wits with any feline.' To this end, Double S created The Five Questions."

The Affenpinscher paused for emphasis, then went on:

"This, then, is the purpose for our gathering here today. To inaugurate the annual search for the fabled Answers, a search in which all are invited to participate. And let all be reminded that, as Double S so wisely pointed out, the search shall purely prove as valuable, or more so, than that which is sought, that in the seeking there is as much to be gained as in the finding. . . ."

"Oh yea, oh yea," cried Dean Excalibur, inspired by the telling. "Verily, verily. And now, Wog, The Questions. The Questions."

"The Five Questions of Ultimate Wisdom," quoth Wog, and as he listed them he accented the first word of each:

"Question One: *What* is the true nature of the Divine?

"Question Two: *What* is the meaning of life?

"Question Three: *What* is the meaning of love?

"Question Four: *Which* is the superior breed of canine?

"Question Five: *What* is the best dog food?"

As tradition dictated, Wog gave the entire list without pause, regardless of the crowd's reaction. Upon the uttering of the Fourth the mongrels set up a great howling that belied their small number.

"Rebellion?" Dean Excalibur cried fearfully. "Rebellion?"

Gallant the St. Bernard looked upon the mongrels with sympathy, though he wished they would find a less vocal way of making their displeasure known; Sergeant Slaughter and his troop of attack Bulldogs and Boxers tensed, ready for trouble; Bucklette the Collie watched the Bulldogs and Boxers anxiously, wishing they'd go ahead and *do* something instead of

just standing there; the other Purebreds ranged in reaction from embarrassment to annoyance. Blackjack, like all the cats, kept a carefully neutral
expression, while Luther was quite openly flabbergasted.

"Now, now," said Excalibur timidly, trying to restore some semblance of
order. "Let's try to be calm and collected about this. . . ."

But if anything, the howling grew louder and more angry. Over in
Sibley Hall, a very sleepy-eyed janitor paused in the midst of his first
morning chores and glanced nervously toward a nearby window, convinced
that a monster had gotten loose and begun rampaging on the Arts Quad.

XI.

Sunday, 11:40 P.M.

The Kay-Fung Specialized Animal Research Lab was located at the far
eastern fringe of the campus. Bordered on three sides by the Cornell Plantations, it stood secluded and peaceful, knowing little official business at this
time of night. Oh, it had its share of unofficial visitors—when the weather
was warm, students with free time would come to make love among the
darkened groves of the Plantations, or to drink and watch the stars. But the
building itself closed down more or less around nightfall, at least until mid-
semester when some of the more involved research projects began demanding
round-the-clock attention. With the setting of the sun, the lab was left empty,
except for the animals.

And tonight, the sprites.

Not ten feet from where two post-graduates ground eagerly against each
other in the dark, their academic worries momentarily forgotten, a model
biplane lay hidden in the underbrush. Farther along, at the foundation of the
lab building, a metal grating had been broken and pried away, uncovering a
six-inch-square ventilation shaft. Too small for any human being to even
consider entering, the vent led, with many turnings and off-branchings, to an
underground storage room where a delivery of animals was being held before
dispersal to various research departments. Even now at that far terminus, a
second metal grating was weakening under the assault of two tiny sledgehammers.

"Aye, that's it!" a voice encouraged above the chittering of various
animals. "Aye, laddies, get your backs into it. Get your backs into it, I say!"

Twists of metal flew outward; the entire grating loosened in its frame.
Impatient, two pairs of hands dropped two hammers, and two shoulders
slammed hard against the grill. The grating gave way altogether and fell out,
followed by two sprites. Fortunately the drop was only about half a foot.

"Shit," Puck said, pushing himself up on bruised arms.

"Very astute comment," said Hamlet, rubbing his own sores. They looked up to see Macduff shaking his head at them from the lip of the vent opening.

"Aye," he told them. "That's too much back, lads."

"Oh, I don't know," said a fourth voice. "I think they look kind of cute, all rough and tumbled like that."

Saffron Dey moved into view beside Macduff. She wore a woven maple leaf safari outfit that put a minimal strain on the imagination; even with Cobweb holding her closely from behind, Saffron looked inviting enough up there to make Puck's heart (and not just his heart, oh no) waver one last time. It was a moment he remembered often after her death.

Then Cobweb squeezed some or other portion of Saffron's anatomy to get her attention and Macduff said, "Now, now, let's have none of that. We have business. Here, let's have a light."

Someone farther back in the vent shaft handed forward a softly glowing piece of quartz hung on a short chain. Macduff rubbed the stone and its glow increased until the full interior of the storage room was visible to them. It was a square, cinderblock-walled space, recently converted. The walls were lined with shelves that held row upon row of tagged cages (the vent opened above one of the highest shelves, which was partially empty). The single door, opposite the wall with the vent, was metal, with three different locks. As if in explanation of the precautions, a sign warned:

RECENT ACTS OF VANDALISM HAVE FORCED CORNELL'S ANIMAL RE-
SEARCH DEPARTMENT TO RESORT TO EXTREME SECURITY MEASURES.
ANYONE FOUND TAMPERING WITH THESE ANIMALS WITHOUT PROPER
AUTHORIZATION WILL BE SEVERELY PUNISHED.

"Recent acts of vandalism," Macduff chuckled, leaping down onto the shelf beside Puck and Hamlet. "Sure an' that's us, lads." To those still up in the vent he called: "Come on, sluggards! It's not as if we've got all of forever!"

Quickly the other sprites lowered themselves down, all of them armed with swords, some bearing tools as well: first Saffron; then Cobweb; then Cobweb's three brothers, Moth, Mustardseed, and Moonshine; adventure-seekers and Macduff-associates Lennox, Ross, Angus, Caith, and Menteith; animal-handler Jaquenetta; and her apprentices, Rosaline, Maria, and Catherine.

"Well now," said Macduff, when the last sprite was out. "Any questions before we begin?"

"I've got one," Hamlet volunteered. "Seems I remember the last couple times we did this we were on the first floor. Now that they've moved all this into the basement, how are we going to get the animals out? Herd them through the vent?"

"Some," Macduff agreed. "Some. And then there's the door, lad. Sure an' you don't mind barebackin' on a rabbit up a flight of stairs?"

"That door over there? What, you're going to blow the locks off with cherry bombs?"

"Anythin' more?" Macduff asked, tired of the discussion.

"Just a word of caution," Jaquenetta spoke up. "I know most of you have done this before, but I want to remind you: unless you're trained in animal control, don't free anything that's bigger than you. Stick to frogs and small rodents."

"Aye," nodded Macduff. "Well said, well spoken. And now . . . let's to it!"

With a shout the sprites set to work, scattering to various corners of the room, lowering themselves to various levels on the shelves. The first cage that Puck stopped at contained guinea pigs, earmarked for use in a Freshman Biology class. It put him in mind of one of the main arguments against Lab Animal Freedom Raids, the argument that, released in the wild, the typical lab animal would die of starvation or exposure very quickly. The counter-argument, of course, was that the animal would die even more quickly—and perhaps more painfully—if given a live dissection in front of an auditorium full of undergraduates.

"Hey-*ya!*" Puck cried, knocking free the cage latch. He opened the gate, and the guinea pigs, sleepy and sluggish at first, began filing out onto the shelf. Puck reached out and stroked one of them as it passed him, using the low-level telepathy that all sprites possessed. All he got was a mindless repetition of *Mother-mother-mother-mother*— Guinea pigs were not known for great intelligence; perhaps they did have deeper thoughts, but these were beyond Puck's ability to read.

Caith and Ross were hip-deep in white mice. The mice's surface thoughts had nothing to do with Mother; rather they contemplated cheese, treadmills, and sex, pretty much in that order. So preoccupied were they with these notions that a number of them walked right off the edge of the shelf, plummeting.

"So," said Caith, trying to prevent the rodents from high-diving en masse, "how are we going to get all these guys out of here?"

"Through the vent, I guess," Ross replied. "Maybe Jaquenetta can play pied piper, or something. Or we can get them all pissing mad at Macduff and let him run on ahead. . . ."

Jaquenetta was busy with things other than piping at the moment. At floor level she had found a cage of kittens, and was trying to decide what to do with them. Cats, even newborn, were extremely dangerous and unpredictable. They could see sprites, but due to their practical nature they invariably perceived them as something else—as rodents, leaves in the wind, mere shadows—anything but as tiny magical beings, the existence of which would

defy feline logic. Given this, no sprite could hope to control them, no matter
how skilled at animal-training. The cat would either see the sprite as a threat
and attack, or completely ignore it.

But these kittens, according to the tag on their cage, had been reserved
for neurological experiments, and Jaquenetta was not sure she could leave
them to such a fate. While she ran over the pros and cons in her mind, the
other sprites continued the task of releasing the less dangerous animals.
Menteith used a firecracker to blow the latch on a glass case, then laughed as a
cascade of frogs tumbled out, catching Angus in the avalanche.

"Ya fookin' ass!" Angus sputtered, fighting his way out of a pile of
amphibians.

On one of the highest shelves, Cobweb was showing off for Saffron Dey.
To be quite frank about it, since she had already taken a fancy to him it was
pretty much inevitable that he would wind up having his way with her by the
end of the night—whatever way that might be—but Cobweb believed in
hedging his bets to the fullest. With an eye toward impressing her, he
engaged in a series of daring somersaults, bouncing perilously close to the
shelf's edge, then springing back and raising cage latches with his feet.

"That's really amazing how you do that," Saffron said vapidly at some
point or other, "but why don't you save some energy for later on? Who
knows, you might need it for something. . . ."

She winked at him; Lennox, close enough to overhear her words,
grimaced at the absolute lack of subtlety.

"Whoo-*pee!*" Cobweb cried victoriously. Gerbils milled all about them,
but still he managed another series of somersaults. He bounded back, back,
back, coming to rest beside a particularly large cage. Macduff still had his
glowing chip of quartz, which shined brighter than ever, but he was far below
them and the contents of the cage were hidden in shadow. Not even bothering
to check the tag, Cobweb high-kicked the latch, keeping his eyes glued to
Saffron.

"You," he said. "You are the most beautifu—"

A huge rat, a brown Norwegian rat of the sort known to strip the bones
of human children, shot out of the cage like a furry bullet, sinking its teeth
into Cobweb and ripping off his arm before he realized what was happening.
At first he did not even cry out, merely stared at the bloody stump that was
his shoulder, frozen in shock.

Then he saw the rat's eyes, its teeth, and the biggest scream of his life,
his death scream, welled up in his throat, and in his extremity he could make
out the rat's thoughts clearly.

I Thresh, thought-said the rat. *Thresh ends you.*

"*THRESH!*" Cobweb shrieked mindlessly, as the rat tore his chest open.
Saffron also shrieked, but she did not think to draw her sword or to run to
Cobweb's rescue—not that he was very rescuable anymore.

"THRESH!" Cobweb shrieked again, his last. Angus looked up, Puck looked up, they all looked up in time to see Cobweb topple off the shelf. Halfway down he was dead, and in the nature of sprites, he faded—his body evaporated into nothingness, his clothes turned to grey rags that continued to seesaw downward. His pinsword struck the ground with an insignificant pinging sound.

"Aye, Lord!" Macduff croaked. "What's this, now—"

"*No!*" Saffron cried out from above. More rats swarmed from the cage, and two of them rushed at her. One of these fell dead instantly, struck by needles from three crossbows—Puck, Hamlet, and Mustardseed each carried one—but the other rat stayed far enough back from the edge that they could not get a bead on him. Somehow, above the din of all the animals, they heard the unmistakable hiss of Saffron's sword being drawn, but what happened after that they could not tell, for they had problems of their own.

Heedless of the distance to the floor, the other rats—nine of them, including Thresh—leaped from the shelf. One died of a crossbow wound in mid-air, and two more landed badly and were unable to move, but the other six scattered, looking for blood and a way out. Two of them bore down Mustardseed before he could reload his bow; he was dead in seconds.

After Mustardseed faded, only five sprites remained at floor level—Jaquenetta, her three apprentices, and Angus. Of those still up on the shelves, only Puck and Hamlet had long-range weapons. The rest hurried down as quickly as they could. Lennox went too fast, landed hard, and fractured his leg. A rat spotted him and moved in for the kill.

"Not bleedin' likely, you bastard!" Lennox cried, whipping out his sword and skewering the creature as it leaped for him. It twitched once and fell dead. "How do you like that?"

With those words he collapsed in a faint. Two frogs hopped over his prone form, croaking contentedly, oblivious to the battle around them.

"Aye, ye bastard!" Macduff jumped down onto a rat's back, driving his sword into the base of its skull like a spear. "That's for Cobweb!"

"And this is for Mustardseed!" cried Angus, not five feet away, as he swung one of the sledgehammers at another rat. It staggered back, stunned, then shot forward and tore a chunk of flesh from Angus' leg. As it opened its mouth for another bite Ross and Caith hit it from both sides, taking it down.

Two more rats advanced on Jaquenetta. Without hesitating she opened the kittens' cage door. *Help me*, she thought-pleaded with the first kit to emerge, a black shorthair. The kitten's purely logical brain caught this thought, interpreting it as a sudden hunger pang; the cat shoved past the shadow at the cage door and ran toward the rats.

The rats continued on fearlessly, knocking the kitten over and beginning to tear into it.

"Oh, Lord," Jaquenette murmured, drawing her sword. But before she could go to the kitten's aid, each rat was struck down by a crossbow shot from above.

Puck scanned the floor carefully, saw no more live rats among the milling sprites and lab animals, and turned his attention to the shelf where Cobweb had lost his life.

"Saffron." Speaking her name, Puck shouldered his bow, drew his sword, and clambered up to the high shelf as quickly as he could.

Saffron Dey lay in a pool of her own blood. She had not faded and was therefore not dead, but death did not look far away. The rat lay beside her, Saffron's pinsword buried firmly in its heart. She had killed it, but suffered badly in return.

"Jesus and Troilus." Puck knelt beside her. With one hand he stroked her forehead, expecting to see her fade without ever regaining consciousness. But as he touched her, she opened her eyes, and all of a sudden Puck was afraid. Saffron began to laugh from a badly torn throat.

At the same moment, Hamlet was anxiously climbing upwards in pursuit of the last rat. Thresh had somehow eluded them and was headed up again, scrabbling from shelf to shelf toward the vent opening and escape.

"Saffron?" Puck whispered, leaning close to her. Her eyes were glazed and unfocused, as if she were seeing not him but Something Else.

"*Still alive,*" she said, laughing that unnerving laugh. "He's still alive."

"Who is?"

"They buried him," Saffron continued, not hearing. "Buried him in The Boneyard. But they couldn't kill him. Wounded. That's all they could do."

"The Boneyard? Saffron, what are you saying? What about The Bone—" Puck cut off as Saffron suddenly grabbed his arm, gripping it with amazing strength. She stopped looking at Something Else and focused her gaze on him, and he tried to pull away, because what he saw in her eyes terrified him.

"Pandora's Box is going to open soon," she told him, not letting him go. "They trapped him, but he's going to get out. *He's going to get out.*" Her grip tightened until Puck felt sure his forearm would be crushed. "And once he's out, once he gets free, he's going to eat you all right up, *right up, RIGHT UP!*"

"Got you now, you son of a bitch," Hamlet said, steadying his aim. The rat was directly under the vent, and Hamlet was at last at a good angle. He fired, thinking to pierce it through the heart, but the rat moved at the same moment and was struck in the flank instead. It paused, half in and half out of the opening, then pushed itself in with one last great shove of its haunches. An instant later it was gone.

Saffron stiffened, tightening her grip still more for one excruciating moment. Then she faded, leaving Puck shaking beside a pile of dead leaves, the remains of her clothing.

Pandora's Box is going to open.

Soon.

Half a mile away, the Tower Chimes tolled midnight.

A KISS
IN THE DARK

The Fevre Dream Tavern took its name from a novel about vampires on the Mississippi, and its politics from somewhere about a thousand miles left of center. The most militantly liberal territory in already liberal Collegetown, it served as a natural haven for the Bohemians and the Blue Zebras on their nights out. The music was often live and the drinks usually half-price; they could ask no more.

Stephen George found himself in the 'Dream one night about two weeks into the semester, sipping a Slow Comfortable Screw that had been mixed by an expert hand, and feeling strangely elated. The featured band of the evening was Benny Profane and the V-necks, who specialized in mismatched covers; clad in a white alligator-hide vest that showed off his biceps to maximum effect, Benny opened the sholated. The featured band of the evening was Benny Profane and the V-necks, who specialized in mismatched covers; clad in a white alligator-hide vest that showed off his biceps to control on his amp up to maximum and burned off the Canadian national anthem in three-quarter time. This received a rousing round of applause.

To George's left, through an open archway, was the pool room. Here Preacher and Fantasy Dreadlock played Eight Ball against Ragnarok and Fujiko, under the learned kibitzing of half a dozen spectators. Fujiko and Ragnarok were up by one game, but this promised to change as Fuji got further along in a row of White Russians and lost more and more of her motor control. Meanwhile, back in the barroom proper, Myoko, Aphrodite (the Bohemian Minister of Love), and Panhandle (the Bohemian Minister of Unbridled Lust) gathered around a table to watch Lion-Heart play a game of Devil's Advocate with Woodstock. Technically, Z.Z. Top was also at the table, but he had slumped so far down in his chair as to become invisible.

" . . . now take this crap about the Space Defense Initiative," Woodstock was saying. "The Star Wars thing, with the laser satellites and all. That's scary shit. That dick's gonna get us all nuked, pushing it too far. . . ."

"Dick?" Lion-Heart asked innocently. Cinched around one arm was a cloth band adorned with pink elephants, the traditional symbol of the Advocate. "What dick?"

"*Reagan*, of course."

Lion-Heart smiled. "That dick, my friend," he pointed out, "is a publicly elected dick. Twice over. And last time around he got every state except Minnesota, which isn't exactly the voice of the nation, if you know what I mean. He must have had some brains to get all those people over on his side, don't you think?"

"Reagan has no brains," Woodstock insisted. "The man's senile."

"So you say. But what about the Democrats, eh? They're the ones who picked Walter Mondale to run against him. So they must be getting a little old in the head too, right?"

"Geraldine Ferraro wasn't a bad choice," Myoko offered.

Lion-Heart raised his eyebrows in mock horror, secretly squeezing her hand under the table. "She's from Queens."

"What the fuck does that have to do with anything?" demanded Woodstock.

"Maybe if we could have had some sort of guarantee," Aphrodite suggested, "that Mondale would drop dead right after he got elected, so Gerry would have taken over. . . ."

"Reagan's going to drop dead soon," Panhandle predicted cheerfully. "The Zero Factor'll kill his ass any day now. That's the real reason he got reelected: he hadn't died in office yet."

Myoko considered this. "Does it count as Zero Factor," she asked, "if Washington gets bombed before Air Force One can lift him out of there?"

"That's the Ground Zero Factor," replied Panhandle.

"Hey," said Woodstock, "Let's try to keep this discussion on a mature level, OK?"

Feeling a sudden thirst, Aphrodite got up from the table at this point and headed for the bar. Though the temperature inside the Fevre Dream was quite warm, she still wore her longcoat, a garment covered entirely in red Velcro—when Aphrodite hugged someone, they stayed hugged.

"Hey, storyteller," she said, taking the stool next to George and ordering a Bloody Mary from Stainless Marley, the bartender.

George smiled at her. "Long time no see. How goes it?"

"Oh, average. Panhandle's falling all over himself tonight trying to seduce me, as usual."

"Yeah? Planning to take him up on it?"

"Are you kidding? Look at what he wears, George." Panhandle's longcoat was transparent vinyl, slick as grease. "Nothing to grip," Aphrodite said, indicating her own Velcro-clad arms. "Think I'd trust a man like that?"

"You could always knit him a sweater."

"Hmm . . ." Her drink arrived and she took a long swallow. "And you?"

"Doing good," George said, bouncing a little on his stool, nervous energy in his legs. "I mean, I don't know, feels like something's in the wind. Can't really explain it, but these past couple weeks I've had the damnedest feeling of . . . of *waiting* for something." He shrugged. "I don't know."

"So what's this I hear," asked Aphrodite, "about you and a secret admirer?"

"What, has the Top been blabbing about that business with the rose?"

"Yes, but don't go hit him for it, he's too drunk to feel anything just now. Has she gotten in touch with you yet?"

"Don't know that it's a she, necessarily. Hell, I don't even know that it's not just a coincidence."

"No such thing," Aphrodite assured him. Then: "Oh my, looks like Lust is calling me."

"Huh?" George looked around. Benny Profane had retaken the mike and was belting out a punk rendition of "Heartbreak Hotel." Panhandle stood on the dance floor, sans longcoat, beckoning Aphrodite to come slam dance.

"Hmm, maybe there's hope for the boy yet," she said. She set what was left of her drink on the bar in front of George. "Be a dear and finish that for me, would you? We'll have to trade love stories the next time we bump into each other."

Giving his shoulder an affectionate squeeze, she headed off to dance.

George spent five minutes on the Bloody Mary; he had barely drained the last drops when all activity in the Tavern came to an abrupt halt. It was an odd moment, difficult to recall in detail later. Such is the nature of genuinely magical events—drunken, disjointed bits of time that could never survive if clearly remembered.

Seconds beforehand, Stainless Marley had come down to the end of the bar, bearing a pen in one hand and a copy of *The Knight of the White Roses* in the other.

"Hey George," Stainless began to say, "you got to do me a favor. I got this lady up in Dryden, and she doesn't believe—"

The front door of the Tavern swung open in silence, a silence so loud it drowned out every sound in the barroom. Stainless' words trailed off to nothing; Benny Profane cut off in the middle of shouting how he was so lonely he could die; Woodstock, caught in the heart of some clinching argument, shut up as if struck; other conversations died similarly, even in the pool room, and all eyes, all gazes were drawn to one spot.

Calliope moved in the doorway, more a vision than a person. She was wrapped in a diaphanous white gown that might have been cut and woven from a dream, and a breeze played through her long hair, holding it at just the perfect angle to the light, making it seem alive. Her lips were set just right; her skin glowed. The word beautiful, at that instant, would not have been sufficient to describe her.

"Jesus" Woodstock whispered. "*Look* at her."

Lion-Heart alone resisted the temptation; his lips were pressed firmly against Myoko's, and he clung to her for dear life. The other men and women in the Fevre Dream surrendered their hearts without a struggle; Stainless Marley swayed on his feet, and in the archway to the pool room Ragnarok and Fujiko had to lean against each other for support.

"George . . ." Stainless breathed. For the vision had locked her own gaze on someone. A perfectly formed hand let go the knob of the front door, which eased shut; Calliope began to glide across the room, weaving among tables where the frozen statues of bar patrons dared not reach out for her. And George, sure at the last that she came for him, stood to meet her, seeing finally what it was he had been waiting for.

Closer and closer, George stretched out a hand toward her, wondering if she would ever reach him, wondering if she did whether she would be real or a phantom that his fingers would pass through like smoke. But she did reach him, solid flesh and bone clasped his hand, she came closer still, and as he leaned in to kiss her it all seemed quite natural, quite ordinary, most wonderful. He was caught up in her magic, and when their lips met and every light in the Tavern went out simultaneously, that too seemed natural, as if it were just another stage direction in some script that had been written for this moment.

"What the fuck?" cried Z.Z. Top, rising from stupor and thinking himself blind. "What the fuck is happening here!?"

In George's perception, that one kiss in the dark stretched out for minutes, hours, days—an uncertain span of time in paradise. When at last Calliope drew back her head, she whispered three words to him, a promise of more to come. Then, somehow, before the lights came back on, she disentangled herself from him, vanished. Again, George was never certain later exactly how it had happened—it was so memorable, and yet so difficult to remember—but it might have been that she simply evaporated in his arms, just melted away. Though of course that was impossible.

"What the fuck?" the Top continued to shout. "*What the fuck?*"

MAKING
FLIPPY-FLOPPY

I.

One of the prevailing myths about Cornell and other liberal universities is that they contain no virgins, or an insignificant number. Of course an informal visual check—for an experienced observer can spot a virgin by the way he or she laces his/her shoes—will quickly demonstrate how inaccurate this assumption is. Even simple logic should be enough to disprove it, for if virginity were really so rare, why would there be so much concern about it? Yet despite the fact that Cornellians are supposed to be bursting with logic, on any given night at least thirty percent of the student body goes to bed convinced that everyone is getting laid but them.

Which is not to say that, as abstinence goes, Cornell can ever hope to hold a candle to Oral Roberts University. But a night on which a majority of the population had sex would be an unusual night indeed, and a night on which almost everybody did would be nothing short of miraculous.

These, then, are the mechanics of a miracle: even as George locked lips with Calliope in the Fevre Dream, two tanker trunks were colliding head-on on a highway just north of Ithaca. One of the trucks belonged to a scientific research group and contained a thousand gallons of an experimental human pheromone; the other was an industrial tanker carrying one of the primary chemical ingredients used in feminine hygiene spray. In the aftermath of the accident, fumes from both substances mixed to form an invisible cloud that was swept southward by the wind, lowering moral standards, raising erections, and hardening nipples wherever it went. At approximately eleven-thirty it passed over North Campus; by midnight the Entrepot student store had sold out every condom in stock, and those customers who had come too late were forced to improvise. Rubber gloves became a hot item about five minutes before closing time.

The wind kept up, and the cloud moved on through West Campus and down to Ithaca proper, sparking more sexual abandon. It was a providence-ordained night for making love or just fucking cheerfully, and more is the pity that no statistics were collected; Masters and Johnson would have paid handsomely for the data. Yet it must remain an irony that, while a full detailing of the night's adventures would fill volumes, the most intense encounter of the evening had nothing to do with the pheromone cloud. The honor fell to a certain fiction writer who lived alone in a gaudy yellow house on Stewart Avenue, and who, tonight, needed no help from stray chemicals in the atmosphere.

Stephen Titus George had finally lucked out.

II.

Home before midnight, George found himself contemplating, not surprisingly, lust, and more specifically the difficulties involved in writing about it. He had pushed all thoughts about the "Fevre Dream woman" to the back of his mind—but not really—deciding that it would be best to wait until she sought him out again. As he rooted around in his cupboards and refrigerator for a snack, he concentrated instead on the inadequacies of the English language. The particular problem he had in mind, which had cropped up in the first draft of an aborted novel called *Venus Envy*, was epitomized by the word *fuck*—bumpy, arrogant little four-letter bastard, impossible to use with any degree of subtlety or elegance (and the phrase *make love* came with its own problems, implying an emotion that was not always there). Things got even worse if you wanted to describe in detail what went on between two partners, for English also had a glut of stupid words for the sexual anatomy. *Breasts* was sort of OK-sounding, but just about everything else was either coldly scientific—*penis, clitoris, buttocks*—or straight out of a Brooklyn cab driver's mouth. Like *cock;* George had never understood how any author could write the word *cock* with a straight face. "But it's *supposed* to sound silly, didn't you know that?" Aphrodite had explained to him once. "It's one of the most ridiculous-looking things on God's earth." All fine and true, that, but George hadn't bothered to point out to her that there were about six million equally silly euphemisms for the female genitalia.

"Yes," George said to himself, cramming two cherry Pop-Tarts into the toaster, "yes, right, but I wonder what her name is."

Of course it's impossible to forget about a beautiful woman who has just recently kissed you in the dark, especially when she happens to be the most beautiful woman in the world. Calliope came crowding back to the fore of George's thoughts, despite all efforts. Anyway, who really cared if you couldn't write seriously about sex? *Venus Envy* had been laid aside unfinished, but he still had his other projects, no need to even think about *Venus*, and what the hell was her name? George was aching to find out, and not just about that.

He had taken a carton of milk out of the fridge and set it on the table. Nice half-gallon carton, with a grinning cow on the side. "I don't know what it is," George told the cow. "It's like I won the lottery somehow, only I don't remember signing up for it, and I never checked to see if my numbers took the jackpot, and I'm not even sure what's *in* the jackpot. All I know is that it's on its way."

He got himself a glass and filled it halfway with milk. Sipping anxiously, he began to pace up and down, and that was when he noticed the draft from the living room. He stopped pacing. Through the living room door, he could make out a figure standing in the dark by an open window, a window he had closed and locked not ten minutes ago.

George did not bother asking who was there, despite an enormous temptation; he knew well enough who it was. Hadn't he been expecting her? She began to move forward into the light, looking just as alluring as she had in the Fevre Dream, more so, because now she wore nothing except a funny silver whistle that hung between her breasts. Beautiful breasts, beautiful face. The other stuff was beautiful too.

With a click, the Pop-Tarts peeped up out of the toaster to see what was going on. George, his eyes riveted on Calliope, reached out to set his glass back on the table. He set it on thin air instead, and it fell to the floor and shattered, spraying milk everywhere; George didn't notice.

"So," he said (the last words out of his mouth before his tongue found other employment), "this is kind of interesting."

Then they were drawing together again, and once more George found himself wondering if they would ever reach each other, and also whether she would evaporate after the first kiss as she had in the Fevre Dream (for it *had* happened). And lastly he wondered what would come after the first kiss, if anything did.

They did reach each other.

Calliope remained solid in his arms.

What came after that was more magic.

III.

Puck lived in the high rafters of Barton Hall, in a connected series of hanging birdhouses that he and Cobweb had set in place some years earlier. A trapdoor no bigger than a playing card gave access to a concealed hangar on the roof. It was here that Zephyr found him, sitting in the moonlight at the edge of a narrow runway, staring off in the general direction of the Plantations. She landed her glider most carefully—other than the runway the roof was set at a treacherous slant—and having secured it in the hangar came out to sit beside Puck. For a long while they did not speak.

"The funerals were well done," Puck finally said, breaking the silence. "I liked Hobart's eulogy for Cobweb."

"He's given a lot of eulogies in his time," was all Zephyr could think to reply. "During the War against Rasferret, sprites were dying by the hundreds."

"But that was over a century ago." Puck spoke tonelessly, looking always into the distance. "He hasn't lost his touch."

Because sprites leave no body when they die, there is of course no burial, and funerals are solemn gatherings of the bereaved without the open or closed coffin found at human funerals. Custom also holds that except in time of great emergency, when other matters press for attention—such as during the War—each of the departed must be given an individual ceremony. Thus the gatherings in memory of Cobweb, Mustardseed, and Saffron Dey had been held consecutively rather than jointly, and by the end of the third funeral the nerves of all involved were frazzled. And when, as a parting remark, Saffron Dey's brother Laertes had commented insultingly about Puck's relationship to her, a duel had sprung up before anyone could intervene. Puck now had a scar on his cheek where Laertes' sword point had grazed it; Laertes himself would be limping for some time to come.

"You still mad at me?" Puck asked now. "About Saffron?"

Zephyr nodded, regretfully. "I don't want to be, especially after . . . after all that's happened, but I am. What you did to me hasn't changed."

Puck also nodded, still not looking at her. "I guess I can't blame you for that. But why are you here, then? Shouldn't you be following that George guy around or something?"

"George isn't any of my business anymore." It was Zephyr's turn to gaze into the distance. "He's kind of occupied tonight."

"Finally found himself a human lover, eh?"

"Maybe. There's something . . . something strange there. I haven't actually seen her."

"Then how do you know about it?"

"The wind. The wind's been whispering the news all night." She sniffed. "Something strange in the wind, too."

Silence descended and began to draw out again. Zephyr forced herself to go on with the business she had come here for.

"I've been talking to Hobart," she said.

"Really? What about?"

"Things. He told me a story, a story about what he and Grandma Zee did one time when they had their worst fight ever. This thing they did, it saved their marriage."

Puck nodded. "Tell me."

"Suppose," said Zephyr, "that there were these two sprites. Suppose that one of them was very angry at the other for something he'd done, and at the same time he was very depressed, upset, maybe a little angry in his own right. Not a very romantic couple, right?"

"No. Not very."

"But there might be a second couple, almost exactly like the first, really the same, only strangers."

At last he did look at her. "Strangers?"

"Strangers. Never met. And one of these strangers, she might decide to take a trip some night, climb into her glider, say, and fly someplace private—like one of the river banks down in Fall Creek Gorge. Now if the other stranger happened to go there too, purely by coincidence, and they bumped into each other, that could turn out to be romantic, don't you think? I mean, if they didn't know each other beforehand, she wouldn't have anything to be mad about. And if he was depressed, she might be able to cheer him up. They might even fall in love."

Puck digested this.

"It might work," he finally said.

"Oh, but there's one other thing," Zephyr added. "These two strangers—they'd have to be very careful to be faithful to one another. Not like those others. If one of them were to start cheating, it could be very bad luck."

"Bad luck," Puck repeated. "Right. But I don't think there'd be any problem with cheating."

"Of course not. Why would there be?"

"So." Puck finally glanced at her. "Fall Creek Gorge, did you say?"

Zephyr shook her head. "*I* didn't say anything. But those strangers . . ."

"Right. Those strangers . . . they'd better get flying."

A moment later they were both preparing for takeoff.

IV.

"So what do you say, Luther?" Skippy prodded. "You gonna come down and chase bitches with us? Huh? Huh?"

"Good times, Luther," Joshua added. "Don't want to miss it."

Luther lifted his hind leg and scratched his ear. "Maybe this time I'll stay behind," he said. "Thanks for the invitation, though."

Six of them stood at the crest of Libe Slope—Luther, Joshua, Skippy, a mongrel named Ellison, a Bull Terrier named Highpoint, and a black Puli—looking down on West Campus. The Puli was a strange dog, with hair that grew out corded like hanks of dark yarn. They called him Rover Too-Bad.

"I an' I t'ink you ought be comin' with us, Luther," Rover nudged him. "Lady Babylon, she be waitin' down below. She one rude sister, that Lady."

Lady Babylon had the most active heat cycle of any bitch in Ithaca. Nights she roamed outside the West Campus dorms, accompanied by others of her litter. On occasion their combined heat scent was strong enough to attract studs from a mile away; tonight the wind was blowing the wrong way to catch it on the Slope, but rumors alone were enough to send Skippy, for one, into a leaping frenzy.

"It's tempting . . ." Luther admitted.

"You know what Rover really be t'inkin', Luther? This 'Heaven' you want so bad—I an' I be t'inkin' maybe you find it. Down below. Lady Babylon, she show you Heaven."

"Not that kind of Heaven, Rover. Besides, it would be over too quickly to make me feel much better."

"Really?" said Highpoint. "I'd heard your kind can—"

He cut off abruptly as Luther turned on him, eyes narrowing. "My *kind?* What do you mean by that?"

"Nothing," the Bull Terrier replied, nervous. "I just . . . I . . ."

Luther looked to Joshua and Ellison for some kind of support, but they had already started down the Slope, led by an impatient Skippy. Highpoint began to follow them.

"Wait a minute!" Luther cried. "Wait a minute! *What did you mean by that?*"

"Nothing! Nothing at all!"

"Babylon's no Terrier, you know! You understand me? If you get her pregnant, the litter will be all mongrels! Understand? You're not so far from me! Understand?"

"I didn't mean anything like that!" Highpoint called back, a final protest. He broke and made for the bottom of the Slope at top speed.

"No," Luther said, whining. "No, it can't be . . ."

"What?" asked Rover, the only one to stay behind with him. "What 'can't?'"

"This is Heaven," Luther insisted, for perhaps the last time. "There can't be *mange*-thoughts here. We left all that behind when we got away from Dragon. So Highpoint can't have been thinking that . . . not even the littlest bit . . ."

He growled deep in his throat, angry at something beyond his reach, and began to snap at his own tail.

"Luther! Luther, you stop that an' listen to Rover! You want I an' I go get Blackjack for you?"

With an effort, Luther brought his rage under control. Disappointment rushed in to replace it.

"Blackjack's busy," he said. "Busy with Sable. Could you just leave me alone, Rover? Go down and visit Lady Babylon with the others. I'll be all right eventually."

"You sure, dahg?"

"I'm sure. Go on, now."

"OK fine good, Luther. But I an' I be checkin' you up after Babylon time. You be better."

"I'll try. Just get going."

"Jus' so. Jah love, Luther."

Rover moved off down the Slope. Luther waited until he had vanished beneath the arch between Lyon and McFaddin Halls, then set to grapple with the terrible realization that was at last forcing itself on him.

We left all that behind . . . with Dragon.

And so they had. But if Raaq's evil could even be here, in this place, no matter how much Luther wished to deny it . . .

The possibility was too much for him. He raised his head and howled, oldest of canine traditions, howling at the moon, though of course what you were really doing was howling at the sky. It was quite sensible; wherever you might be, there was always a lot of space in the sky, space enough for the loudest, most anguished howl to go up into. And of course it was very, very important for your anger and pain to have enough room as it was released outwards.

Otherwise it might fall back, and smother you.

V.

Elsewhere:

In one of the high bedrooms in Risley's central tower, Lion-Heart and Myoko made perfect love to each other. Their coupling was echoed in some form or other in almost every room in the dorm. The building, as a point of information, was constructed of steel-reinforced concrete, one of the first such structures ever designed, and triply sturdy; yet still, it vibrated that night—ever so slightly—from the energy contained within its walls. This vibration was picked up by the crickets and night creepers in the area, sending them into a frenzy of chirping that was deafening to hear.

It was a night for first times, as well as old times. In the early morning hours after last call at the Fevre Dream, Aphrodite at last consented to Panhandle, and the two of them coupled with no small gymnastic prowess in the lower branches of a maple behind Rockefeller Hall. The tree barely survived.

Blackjack and Sable mated in a tussle of claws and fur; Nattie Hollister of the Ithaca Police Force made love to her husband and then collapsed from exhaustion; back on The Hill, Fraternity Row bumped and ground. Everywhere the same, everywhere different, and it was not until very late indeed that the last bit of energy had been expended and an aura of peace settled over the town.

Even then, not everyone slept.

VI.

George stood naked at his bedroom window peering out into the dark, heedless of any passerby who might see him from the street. He had little ego as far as his body was concerned, and it never would have occurred to him that a peeping Tom (or Tom-ette) might be interested. Besides which, precious few peeping Toms were still out and about at this hour; the moon was almost down, dawn could be no more than an hour away, and most activity worth peeping on had ceased.

The house was a shambles. George and Calliope's lovemaking session—which would have set the readership of the *Penthouse* Forum on its collective ear, if written up and published—had ranged through every room in the place, leaving a trail of disorder and outright destruction. Furniture was moved or overturned; the love seat in the living room had collapsed on all four of its legs like a dead camel. The bathroom was awash in water, and the showerhead was still spraying full blast; in the hallway outside, a spiderweb of toilet paper hung from the overhead light. In the kitchen the refrigerator door hung open, various foodstuffs having been used for various interesting purposes; likewise the doors to the cupboards were thrown wide, and the bottle of Crisco Oil was empty. About the only thing undisturbed was George's typewriter, a casual observer in the eye of the storm.

How long? George wondered to himself. *How long were we at it?*

At best guess he could only say that it had been a very long time, longer than he could ever credit to his own natural stamina, even should he want to be vain about it. It was as if some outside force had lent support to him, allowing him to go on and on with her for hours without pause. George remembered the old expression, *I'll jump your bones.* He had not just jumped Calliope's bones; he had partied on them, and she on his.

He looked at her, stretched out on the bed, apparently asleep. At last. And though love was done for the night, she still appeared as beautiful as when he had first laid eyes on her.

No, not beautiful. Perfect.

Yes, perfect. And that was what frightened him. For didn't everyone, in some not-so-secret corner of their minds, have a fantasy of what the perfect physical type would look like? The fantasy was apt to change over time—before meeting his first Grey Lady, George's idea of the ultimate had been a pale redhead—and was not nearly so reliable a criterion as personality when judging a lover. But was there anyone who didn't quietly wish for both, good personality *and* the perfect type?

There was very little moonlight left, but George could see Calliope quite clearly. Every line, every detail, from the tone of her skin to the set of her mouth, was just right. Who had read his mind?

"Don't worry about it," Calliope advised him. By some strange trick she was no longer asleep on the bed, but behind him with her arms wrapped around his waist. "Just enjoy it."

George shook his head, and leaned heavily against the windowsill. "This isn't real."

"What isn't? Me?" She pressed tight against his back. "Tell me you don't feel that."

He did not respond, instead asking another question: "What's the price?"

"The price?"

"I think you know what I mean." He spoke softly, as of a matter that was of great importance but beyond his control. "You're too good to be true. When we finally get our clothes back on, is the conversation going to be perfect, too?"

She kissed his neck. "We don't have to get dressed for that."

"We've read all the same books, haven't we? And our likes and dislikes are almost exactly the same, just different enough to give us something to talk about. Somehow I know that's true. I know your name, too. But when did you tell it to me?"

Calliope was breathing softly into his ear now. It took an effort to keep speaking.

"Tell me what the price is!" George insisted, gripping the windowsill so tightly that his fingers nearly snapped from the strain. "You look perfect, you are perfect, and you came out of nowhere. So what's the bad news? Does Mephistopheles collect my soul in six months, or what?"

Calliope laughed. "You're already in love with me, George," she said to him, in a kindly tone and with no trace of vanity. "Why bother being so curious? Even if it meant your death, you couldn't help your feelings. You know that, don't you?"

"Yes," George whispered.

"But you still want to know more."

"*Will* it mean my death? Is that the cost?"

"It might," Calliope said seriously. "Oh, you won't die on my account, though you might prefer it. We'll be lovers for a time, and I'll teach you a few things, and set a few other things in motion. When my job is done I'll leave, without warning, and then you'll want to die, but he won't let you, not then."

"He?"

"You're caught, George. Caught in a Story, or a Daydream, you could say. Whether it ends happily or in a nightmare depends entirely on you."

"Wait," George said. "Wait, I don't understand this part."

"Don't worry yourself," Calliope told him, turning him around. "There'll be plenty of time for understanding. The Story goes on for a long time yet. In some ways it hasn't even really begun."

"What are you, then?" he asked. "The Prologue?"

Calliope smiled. "That's very close, George," she said. "Very close."

She drew him in, and together they brought in the sunrise.

TWO HOUSES

I.

On a bright morning some two weeks later, a Bohemian envoy composed of Lion-Heart, Myoko, and Z. Z. Top set out from Risley on a diplomatic mission up Fraternity Row. It was Sunday, and the members of the Society for Pre-Renaissance Mayhem were out on Risley's front lawn in full battle armor, whacking each other with wooden swords and clubs; Lion-Heart saluted them as he came out.

"Nice day," he said, saluting the sky as well.

"Great day to die," the Top added; not five yards away, a sword-swinger went down under the combined assault of three clubbers. "Bet Myoko could kick all their asses, though."

"Thank you, dear," replied the Queen Grey Lady. She took Lion-Heart's arm and they set off on their journey.

The nearest Greek House was of course Zeta Psi, just across the street. The Zetas' lawn boasted a rusty Civil War cannon, a token of former hostilities between Zeta Psi and Risley. Two years ago, however, after the Bohemians declared eternal war on Rho Alpha Tau, an unofficial Risley-Zeta peace treaty had been negotiated.

"Where're we going today, anyway?" asked the Top. "You got some beef to settle over at the Rat Frat?"

"There's always a beef to settle with them," Lion-Heart said darkly. "We've got other business today, though. This other frat wants to make us all honorary members."

"Honorary members? Hell, Li, Bohemia can't go Greek."

"That's what I thought at first. But this frat is special."

"How special? Greek is Greek."

"It's Tolkien House," said Lion-Heart.

Z. Z. Top did a double take. "*They* want us as brothers?"

"And sisters," Lion-Heart replied, clasping Myoko's hand. "I met one of their acting Presidents—they've got three instead of one—Friday night down at the New Wave. Fellow name of Shen Han. Interesting character; he was drinking a Tequila Sunset."

"Sunrise," Myoko corrected him.

"No, Sunset. Brandy instead of grenadine. Just offbeat enough, you know? I liked him."

"But why do they want us to link up with them?" asked the Top.

"That's what we're going to find out, Tasteless. Main reason I brought you along is because I figured you'd get a kick out of it. *Lord of the Rings* still your favorite story?"

"I just reread it for the twelfth time last week."

"Good, then. This should be fun."

Tolkien House, so named because it took as its inspiration J. R. R. Tolkien's fantasy world, was at once one of the most famous and least known of Cornell's fraternities. Located far off the beaten track, the House was not generally open to visitors. That the Bohemians had been invited to become members en masse could only mean that something big was afoot; Lion-Heart had an idea or two what the something might be, but kept quiet about it.

They followed Thurston Avenue to its end, then left street and sidewalk behind and turned onto a dirt path leading into a thickly wooded area. Each of them had a sense of stepping into another world; the trees were especially tall, forming a thick canopy overhead that blocked out most of the sky. Not for nothing was Tolkien House known as the only Elvish Greek House.

They came upon it suddenly. The path led inwards for perhaps forty yards and opened without warning into a clearing. The fraternity stood revealed before them like some great stone fortress out of time. It was huge, seeming to strain the boundaries of the clearing; in some places the surrounding trees crept within five feet of the House. At either end of the building, which was roughly rectangular in shape, sat a squat tower, the names chiseled into blocks in their foundations: MINAS ANOR on the right, MINAS ITHIL on the left.

"Too much," breathed the Top, finding it hard to take in.

"Funny, though," Myoko said, a little less dazzled. "There are no cars parked out front. Is it legal for a fraternity not to have cars?"

Lion-Heart smiled. "Maybe they have a stable."

The main entrance was a great arched doorway, the double doors made of iron-banded oak. TOLKIEN HOUSE, read the inscription on the keystone, GIFT OF A LADY. And below that, in some strange language: *Pedo mellon a minno.*

Myoko again: "Don't rich women usually endow sororities?"

"Maybe she was funky," Lion-Heart suggested. He turned to the Top. "What's that 'Pedo mellon' stuff?"

"It's Elvish," Z. Z. Top explained. "Tolkien invented a lot of fantasy languages, you see. He was what you call a philologist, and—"

Lion-Heart held up a hand to cut him off. "Can you translate it?"

"Sure. It's a password-type thing. 'Say "friend" and enter.'"

"Friend," said Lion-Heart, reaching for one of the heavy iron knockers. The doors swung inward before he could touch them, revealing a dim grey-stoned corridor within. No one waited inside; the doors had apparently opened themselves.

"Invisible butler," Lion-heart commented. "I like it."

They stepped inside, none of them being terribly surprised when the doors closed unaided behind them. They found themselves in a shallow alcove; a stuffed thrush eyed them from atop a coat rack. Left of the coat rack another door was set into the wall, and above it a plaque which read: ENTRY HALL AND MICHEL DELVING MATHOM-HOLE.

"Mathom-Hole?" Lion-Heart queried.

"It's a kind of museum," explained Z. Z. Top. "Run by hobbits."

"Hobbits?"

"Little people with hairy feet. They eat and smoke a lot, but they're cool."

Nodding, Lion-Heart reached for the doorknob, but again the door opened itself before he could touch it. Beyond was a large space. Shen Han's voice boomed from within.

"Welcome to Middle-earth," he said.

II.

The Presidents of Tolkien House were three: Shen Han, Amos Noldorin, and Lucius DeRond. Each had on a simple robe, and in token of their office each wore a ring set with a single gem: Shen Han's bore a ruby, Noldorin's a white opal, and Lucius' a sapphire. They awaited their guests in the west end of the "Mathom-Hole," which was actually a huge central hall with a great arched skylight. Sunlight from above reflected off dozens of display cases, each of them containing objects from Tolkien's epic. These objects were all meticulously labeled and their history given, with one exception: lying on a pedestal at the exact center of the hall was a seamless glass case, and within it a broad, shining spearhead. It was not identified.

"Thank you for coming," Shen Han greeted them, striding forward with the other two Presidents at his side. He shook hands with Lion-Heart and made introductions all around. "I hope before you leave we can convince you to throw in with us."

"We'll definitely have to see about that," Lion-Heart replied. He looked around the hall admiringly. "Impressive."

"It's nothing," Shen Han assured him. "There are other things in the House that you'll barely be able to believe. We'll have one of the brothers give you the Grand Tour later."

"Who built this?" asked Myoko, gazing in wonder at the skylight, which would have served well as the hull of a glass-bottomed frigate.

"The Lady built it," Noldorin answered.

"The Lady?"

"That's the only name we have for her," Shen Han explained. "The House Founder has always been anonymous. In a way it fits; magic dies with no mystery, and magic is what we're all about. All that's known for sure is that she loved Tolkien's work, favored the University . . . and had enough money to make dreams happen."

"How long ago was the House founded?" inquired the Top.

"They laid the first stones in thirty-six," Lucius responded. "But the finishing touches stretched on into the mid-Fifties."

"That can't be," Z. Z. insisted.

"Oh?"

"*The Lord of the Rings* wasn't published until nineteen fifty-five, and that was over in England . . . not even *The Hobbit* was in print until the late Thirties. How could your Lady model a House on a set of books that didn't exist yet?"

Shen Han only smiled. "Like I said: no mystery, no magic. Would any of you care for drinks?"

Sunlight flashed on silver as Noldorin raised his ring-hand. Somewhere near an unseen chime sounded; in answer, a chubby man no more than four feet tall came scurrying into view.

"Ori here is the House butler," Shen Han introduced him. "He'll take your orders."

Ori bowed low to the Bohemians, and Myoko had to suppress a giggle. The fellow wore a colorful pointed cap, and sported a well-kept beard of incredible length.

"I'll take some Midori," Lion-Heart told him. "In a shot glass."

"The same," said Myoko.

"Black Label Light," the Top requested, "with a twist of lemon."

"As you wish," Shen Han said. "The usual for us, Ori. And you can bring the drinks to . . . well, where shall we entertain our guests?"

"The Wood," Noldorin suggested.

"The Wood," Lucius echoed.

"Lothlórien," explained Shen Han, in answer to Myoko's curious expression. "In Tolkien it was a great Elven forest."

"Where is it?" Z. Z. Top asked. "Out back?"

"Oh no," Shen Han replied. "We do have a fairly extensive woodland surrounding the House—to make it seem more remote, you understand. But

it wouldn't do to have Lothlórien outside; it might rain when we wanted to
have a party."

"You're not saying it's *inside?*"

Again Shen Han smiled. While Ori hurried away to get the drinks, he
lifted a ring-adorned hand and pointed to a nearby door.

"The elevator," he told them, "is that way."

III.

Lion-Heart had seen a good many elevators in his day, with all manner of
interior decor, but this was his very first encounter with one that utilized
stone. The inside walls were sheathed in black, mirror-like obsidian, and the
door was a thick slab that slid open and shut God knew how. The control
buttons were translucent, genuine-looking jewels. Altogether it had a decidedly unelevator-like appearance, which he supposed made sense in this place.

The stone box carried them downwards, until Lion-Heart felt certain
they were deep underground. How there could be a *forest* . . . but he would
have to wait and see.

"Khazad-dûm sub-cellars," Shen Han announced as the elevator
smoothed to a halt and the slab-door slid open. He took an oil lantern from a
stand just outside and lit it; when the elevator door closed again behind them,
they found themselves in a pool of light surrounded by blackness. Smooth
stone floor stretched off as far as the eye could see in all directions, with no
sign of wall or ceiling; even the elevator shaft was no more than a square stone
column rising out of sight above them.

"This has ceased to be real," pronounced the Top, his mind imagining an
impossibly large space around them. One thing sure, this was no ordinary
basement.

Shen Han offered him another smile. "The cessation of reality has barely
begun. This way, please."

"How do you know what the right direction is?" Z. Z. Top asked, as
they were led into the darkness. "Shouldn't you get something more powerful
than that lamp? We don't want to get lost."

"We know the way," Noldorin assured him. "More light, less mystery."

"Mmm. I understand . . . if we could see better, it'd spoil the illusion."

"Or terrify you," Lucius suggested.

Even as he spoke, Lion-Heart drew in his breath. Before them the floor
abruptly dropped away, as into a chasm, and only a slender, railless bridge of
stone continued on.

"No way," the Top protested, his maximum level of suspension of
disbelief reached. The light of the lantern revealed no bottom to the gap in

front of them, but he knew that it was impossible—*impossible*—for an actual canyon to have been excavated down here. "What is it really, six feet deep?"

His question went unanswered. "Take care not to fall in," was all Shen Han would say, as he led them single file over the bridge. For the briefest of instants Z. Z. Top was tempted to make the ultimate test and leap over the side. There could be no real danger . . . but then Z. Z. heard a sound like wind moaning beneath him, and his courage faltered.

At the far end of the bridge they found a short corridor, and at the end of that a pair of stone doors that Shen Han thrust open with the help of Noldorin. The Bohemians passed through and found that they had just stepped out of a hillside into a wooded glade.

A light breeze was blowing, and above them hung a night sky full of stars.

IV.

"A dome," Lion-Heart said, penetrating this illusion immediately, though not through any flaw in its quality. "Like the Hayden Planetarium, underground and bigger." He turned to Shen Han. "How far can I walk down here before the sky touches the ground?"

"You could experiment and find out," Shen Han replied. "But why do it? It's a paradise here, if you let it be. We have complete control over the climate: we can make it colder, warmer, more or less windy, we can weave a fog, conjure up a meteor storm for a light show, even make it rain if the mood strikes us."

"Can you make a sunrise?"

"Starshine is more peaceful."

"I'll bet," put in the Top. "And a day sky wouldn't seem so realistic, would it? Where are the projectors at?"

"Do you really want to spend so much time asking unimportant questions?" came the reply.

Lion-Heart laid a hand on Z. Z. Top's shoulder. "No," he said for both of them. "You're right, a little mystery will be good for us."

Shen Han nodded respectfully, dousing the lantern at the same moment. Here there was no need for it; night sky or no, Lothlórien had enough light—light from unknown and best-left-unquestioned sources—to see one's surroundings. Real trees grew in the forest, beautiful trees with pale grey bark and golden flower blossoms among their leaves; how they were sustained in this odd witchlight was yet another mystery.

The Bohemians were given a brief tour. Lion-Heart guessed that this brevity was due in part to the fact that, whether or not Shen Han wanted to discuss it, the underground paradise had a fairly limited area; enough room for relaxation, but not enough for an extended hike. The three Presidents each pointed out their favorite features of the forest: a fountain formed of uncut stone, with a tiny brook leading away from it; a giant mushroom that would have been more at home with Lewis Carroll than Tolkien; an Enchanted Circle of bright stones. Through it all there was a sound of almost-singing in the air, as if a chorus were being hummed in the background by creatures that could not quite be seen.

At the last the tour group came into a clearing surrounded by a tall hedge. The brook from the fountain ran through here, and beside it stood a water-filled silver basin set into a low pedestal. The basin and pedestal were central to the clearing, and no doubt intended to be the main attraction, but most of the attention was stolen from them by a tall figure leaning against a hedge across the brook.

"What the hell is that?" the Top burst out.

"That," Shen Han replied, sounding sheepish for a change, "is the Rubbermaid. Our mascot, sort of."

"That thing is from Tolkien?" Myoko asked doubtfully.

"Not fucking likely," Z. Z. Top answered her. "Unless he wrote a porno novel that nobody knows about."

The Rubbermaid did look like something out of a blue novel or movie, not very Tolkienish at all. A tall, pale mannequin with dark hair and a frighteningly exaggerated bust-line, it was garbed in black leather in the manner of a dominatrix. Its plastic arms were outstretched, and gloved hands offered a bowl that contained something the Bohemians could not see from where they stood.

"Where'd you get this?" inquired the Top, hopping over the brook and approaching the mannequin. "And more important, why? I'd really like to know, unless it's another one of your mysteries."

"No mystery," Lucius responded. "Despite all our magic we're still a fraternity in the end, and we share a certain bond with the other Houses. Do you remember the controversy last year, with that group that called itself PUGS?"

"People for the Undermining of the Greek System," Myoko said. "I remember them."

"Then," Lucius continued, "you'll recall PUGS' main platform: they thought the evils of the fraternity-sorority system outweighed the good. One of the main charges against the fraternities was that they promoted sexism. . . ."

"And they do," Lion-Heart pointed out. "But then so does the rest of the world, more or less. No one's pure."

"Not even the Bohemians," Myoko suggested.

"Not even the Kennedys," the Top added, scratching his nose.

". . . Well," Lucius pushed onward, "be that as it may, maybe you can understand that we felt a bit left out. All the frats were getting blasted without any distinctions, but as far as we could tell Tolkien House didn't have so much as one nude pin-up on the walls. So to save face, we went and had the Rubbermaid custom-designed for us."

"Very Bohemian of you."

"But not Tolkienian," commented Z. Z. Top, taking something from the bowl the Rubbermaid offered. There was a tear of foil packaging and he shook out a lubricated latex tube with a grinning face inscribed at one end. "'Mr. Happy,'" Top quoted the advertising jingle, "'the only condom with a smile to call its own.' Tolkien would have *crucified* you guys."

Shen Han shrugged. "Eventually we'll get rid of it. For the time being, though, the Rubbermaid's become quite a conversation piece."

"This whole place is a conversation piece," Lion-Heart said. "And now that we've seen Lothlórien, how about telling us what you want?"

"We've told you already," said Shen Han, a touch nervously. "We want you as members . . ."

"If the rest of the House is anything like this forest, here," Lion-Heart replied, "there's no chance you'd be giving away a blanket membership to a group like the Bohemians. Not without some other string attached." He spread his arms, as if to gather in earth, greenery, and projected sky. "This is too pretty. Share it with the wrong people and they might ruin it. So what's the extra hook?"

Shen Han considered for a moment, then turned to Noldorin. "Show him," he said.

Nodding, Noldorin stepped up to the pedestal that held the silver basin. He gestured to the Bohemian King to come forward, and Lion-Heart did so. Staring into the water he saw that the bottom of the basin was dark, reflecting the stars above.

"Watch closely," Noldorin told him. "And be careful that you don't touch the water."

With that he gestured at the basin with his ring-hand. The stars in the basin vanished, to be replaced by various scenes of Ithaca and the Cornell campus. Though he knew them to be some sort of mechanical projection, Lion-Heart was still impressed, for unlike a series of slides, the images faded smoothly from one to the other. After a time Risley appeared in the water, and this image gave way to a face that Lion-Heart knew well. He burst out laughing; for the face was Fujiko's, and the reason behind the offer of membership suddenly clear.

"Which one of you is in love with her?" Lion-Heart asked. He looked at Noldorin, saw something in his expression. "You?"

Very slowly, Noldorin nodded. He tried not to blush; that would have been unbecoming for a fraternity President.

"Well, she's unattached," said Lion-Heart. "Not that I can promise you anything more than an introduction, and you can have that free if you want it. Are you sure you want to make such an uneven trade?"

"We're sure," Noldorin replied. "It's the spirit of it."

"All right then," said Lion-Heart. "I guess Bohemia's going to be honorary Greek—or whatever this place is."

Noldorin smiled broadly and reached out to shake Lion-Heart's hand. As he did, the image in the basin shifted yet again; now it showed an outside view of Tolkien House itself, a treetop-level view that looked beyond the surrounding wood tract and revealed, just barely, the rooftop of another nearby Greek House. It was really just a glimpse, but all the same Lion-Heart recognized that rooftop, and froze. His good humor of a moment ago drained away.

"What's wrong?" Noldorin asked, concerned.

Lion-Heart looked at him with a deadly seriousness. "You have neighbors."

"What?"

"We have two neighbors on adjoining property," Shen Han spoke up. "Carl Sagan and Rho Alpha Tau."

"Trust me," said the Top, "he's not talking about Carl."

"You're worried about our relationship with Rho Alpha Tau?" asked Noldorin of Lion-Heart. "Is that it?"

"Let's say I'm curious what you think about them."

Noldorin shrugged. "The distance between the two Houses could be wider," he said. "And if the ground opened up and swallowed them I don't suppose we'd hold a wake."

"What is it you want us to say?" Shen Han inquired. "The Rat Frat's reputation is an embarrassment for the whole system. No one loves them."

"No one but Tri-Pi sorority," Z. Z. Top corrected him. "Isn't that a fucking shame?"

"It's a shame, but we don't share Tri-Pi's enthusiasm," Noldorin insisted. "Do you want us to swear to that?"

Lion-Heart stared up at the stars in silence for a long moment before answering.

"Sometimes I speak too quickly," he said. "I have one more question I have to ask before we can seal the bargain. You may be insulted by it, but I need to know . . . and I'll be able to tell if you lie to me."

"Go ahead," Noldorin prompted him, nodding.

"Has there ever been a rape here?"

"A rape?" Shen Han exclaimed.

"Yes, a rape," Lion-Heart repeated. "It's this funny thing that happens at fraternity parties sometimes. A woman gets so drunk that she barely knows what's going on, and she winds up in bed with some brother who knows exactly what's going on. Maybe a string of brothers; maybe they planned it that way in the first place. Am I coming through clearly?"

"Any of our brothers," said Noldorin, "who were involved in something like that would be permanently expelled from the House. But it's never happened here, and we don't expect it to. Our brothers have never needed to get their partners drunk."

Lion-Heart studied his face carefully as he spoke, nodding at the conclusion; there was no dishonesty to be found in Noldorin's expression.

"Tell me," asked Lucius, who had said nothing for a long time, "did something happen to one of your people? Something involving Rho Alpha Tau?"

"Yes," the Bohemian King said softly. "Something happened to a very dear friend."

He looked over at the Rubbermaid, reconsidering it.

"Can you do me a favor?" he asked them. "Can you get rid of that thing before we have our first big party together? It ruins the atmosphere in here."

"It'll be done as you wish," Shen Han promised him.

"You'll join with us, then?" asked Noldorin.

Lion-Heart nodded. A moment later he managed a smile. "Well, where's that butler of yours? Might as well do this right and toast each other."

Ori the dwarf appeared as if on cue, bearing their drinks: Midori for Lion-Heart and Myoko, beer with lemon for Z. Z. Top, and Tequila Sunsets for the three Presidents. These were passed round, lengthy and eloquent toasts made, and friendships begun between the Bohemians and the Tolkienians. Yet through it all, Lion-Heart never stopped thinking about his archenemies, the brothers of the Rat Frat.

V.

Despite the jokes it had to endure at the hands of its many detractors, Rho Alpha Tau's name was not as foolishly chosen as might first seem. It must be pointed out that the Greek *rho* is written as *P*—thus the letters spelled *PAT*, not *RAT*. This being made clear, it should come as no surprise that one of the founders of the House was a not-very-modest Anglo-Saxon named Patrick Baron, whose father had made a small fortune in the coal mining industry. Rich and conservative in a bad way, Baron became the fraternity's first president and set the tone of the House leadership for decades to come.

Rho Alpha Tau came into being in the last days of the McCarthy Era; Red-baiting was a popular pastime for the early brothers. But it was the Sixties, decade of civil and social rights, that saw the first real tarnishes to Rho Alpha Tau's image. The bad word began to spread after a series of incidents in the latter half of the decade, including the infamous Martin Luther King party. The party, a very exclusive affair to which only verbal invitations were given, was held shortly after King's assassination. Guests were encouraged to bring chains, hubcaps, and other appropriate items to the celebration; the highlight of the evening was the Costume Contest, at which fraternity Vice-President Ted Pulaski appeared in blackface, wearing a blood-stained shirt. This proved too tasteless for a good many of the brothers; seven of them quit the House during the following week. Yet none of these seven would stand witness to what had happened, and though word did get out about the party, nothing was ever proven.

In spring of the following year, Cornell made national headlines when a group of militant black students staged a takeover of Willard Straight Hall during Parents' Weekend. The Straight Takeover of '69 was to become legendary, though it need not have been; in the beginning, at least, it was no more serious than numerous other takeovers that occurred throughout the Sixties and early Seventies.

The blacks moved in at 5:30 A.M. on Saturday morning, evicting those visiting parents who had been put up at the Straight for the Weekend. At 9:30 A.M., the course of history was changed when Ted Pulaski (now PAT President) led a commando force of twenty-five Rho Alpha Tau brothers into the Straight through a side window, intending to recapture the building. They were not successful; Pulaski was ejected bodily out the same window through which he had entered. Thereafter the Cornell Safety Division tightened security around the building, but rumors began to spread that members of several white fraternities, including the Rho Alphas, were planning a second assault, this time with rifles. The threat never materialized, but that night the blacks, no longer trusting the campus police (if they ever had), imported guns of their own into the Straight to protect themselves. Though the incident was resolved without bloodshed, this additional element of the guns assured nationwide media coverage, and helped the story pass on into local myth. Years later "the Straight Takeover" remained a campus catch-phrase, though not everyone knew the details of what had taken place; nor was Rho Alpha Tau's role in the events ever quite forgotten.

Certainly it was well remembered in the first few years after the Take-over. When the newly-christened Africana Center was gutted by fire in April 1970, many blacks suspected arson, and at least one carried his suspicions a step further. On a moonless night a few weeks later, Ray Avriel Stanner '72 crept up on Rho Alpha Tau after midnight with a ladder and a bucket of paint. Working quickly and quietly, he added an extra leg to the 'P' above the front porch of the House. Like the Rho Alpha's commando raid on the Straight, this simple act changed history.

Stanner was spotted by two brothers halfway down the ladder. They sounded a call to arms; Stanner ditched his paint and ran for it, pursued by an angry mob. Flying down Thurston Avenue he was saved by the timely appearance of a cocky young Ithacop named Samuel Doubleday. Doubleday, a white man with no college education, didn't know exactly what he thought of black people, but he did know that he didn't like lynchings on his beat. Not one for long speeches, he dispersed the angry brothers by emptying his revolver into the air. Stanner later faced charges for vandalism, but he graduated Cornell with honors, and Rho Alpha Tau was known ever after as "the Rat Frat." The nickname did not fade with time, for the House never ceased to deserve it.

And so it happened that, two years prior to the alliance between Tolkien House and the Bohemians, a Grey Lady named Pearl wound up drunk at a Rho Alpha Tau after-hours party. She didn't realize which fraternity she had come to; that night she had been at a dozen parties up and down the Row, looking for a Sigma Alpha Epsilon brother named Jim Richland. Instead she met Jack Baron, second son of Patrick Baron, who led her—already drunk—to the House bar, and with a well-practiced charm coaxed her through three Kamikazis. When Pearl woke up in the morning, crashed out on the Rho Alpha's back lawn with a paralyzing hangover, she could not remember who or how many of the brothers had been with her, but what memories she did have were almost more than she could live with.

Two weeks later Pearl left the Bohemians, and a week after that the University; Jim Richland, who would eventually take the name Panhandle, went looking for Jack Baron and got a black eye for his trouble; an investigation by the Inter-Fraternity Council into the events of the after-hours party turned up no witnesses; and Lion-Heart, infuriated by the Council's helplessness, swore an oath of vengeance against Jack Baron and the brothers of the Rat Frat.

For two years the Bohemian King had sought the overthrow of the House; yet in the end he played no part in the matter. The very same day that he toasted Shen Han, Noldorin, and Lucius in the garden of Lothlórien, the downfall of Rho Alpha Tau was set in motion. Ragnarok, not Lion-Heart, was its instrument, and it began, ironically enough, on the steps of Willard Straight Hall, shortly before midnight.

JINSEI AND THE
BLACK KNIGHT

I.

Evening came to that well-hilled part of the World, but in an even loftier place, in Mr. Sunshine's Library, it remained as bright and Saturday-after-noonish as always. The breeze still smelled pleasantly of laurel; the lowing of cattle and the distant lyre-chords continued to accompany the clacking of the Typewriters.

The Storyteller had shoved over one of the Monkeys again, taken its place at the Typewriter devoted to "Fool on The Hill." Calliope and George were already together; she had him well in hand. Now it was time to add another layer to the Tale, bring another Character to the fore.

Mr. Sunshine Typed:

Set Ragnarok up against Jack Baron.

Having Written this he paused briefly, then added:

Ragnarok's trial is not George's trial.

Almost immediately he shook his head at the redundancy. Obviously their trials were not the same. No need to waste Words—William Strunk, E. B. White, and the Chinese Emperor Shih Huang Ti had all been in agreement on that.

"I must be getting Old," said Mr. Sunshine to the Monkey. The Monkey had no comment.

Obviously their trials were not the same; they were very different Characters. Yet just as a classic heroic tale needs a Saint, an unabashedly White-Hatted and periodically naive champion of romantic love, so too it isn't quite complete without that other, more dubious, good guy: The Black Knight.

II.

The computer jockey's name was Lenny Chiu, and he stood just over five feet in his black dress shoes. He wore no tuxedo—Jinsei had convinced him to go for a less formal and more comfortable style—but he carried himself regally, like a prince on his way to the palace ball. He perhaps had reason to feel special, for Jinsei had fished him out of a sea of seemingly cloned Engineering students with matching steel-rimmed glasses, no-nonsense work shirts, and multi-function programmable calculators. They were not steadies in any sense of the word, just dating; but if Jinsei did not give much thought to the possible future of their relationship, Lenny certainly did, and this added an extra spring to his step.

Jinsei, dressed simply in a clean white jumpsuit that reflected the moonlight, thought only of having fun. Since the first week when Ginny Porterhouse had introduced her to the campus—an introduction that included Ragnarok and Preacher—her workload had been without respite. Tonight represented her first real chance to just relax and enjoy herself, and she planned to do so. Walking hand in hand with the wind ruffling her hair, Jinsei too felt a touch regal—though Princess was not quite the title she would have chosen. A Lady of the Court, perhaps.

The royal function she and Lenny had chosen to honor with their presence was the semi-annual Cornell Asian-Americans United (CAAU) Dance, which had got going at half past ten and was now in full swing. Inside Willard Straight Hall's Memorial Room, Adult Eastern—a good band, if no match for Benny Profane—played to an enthusiastic audience: Chinese, Japanese, Korean, Thai, Western Orientals in pressed tuxedos and long cotton dresses. The Bohemians were there too, of course, accompanying the Grey Ladies and making as much of a scene as possible. Lion-Heart and Myoko calmly ruled the dance floor; Z. Z. Top threw toast at the band; Preacher discussed Third World politics and any-world sex with a Taiwanese exchange student; Woodstock got drunker than a fish and made a general nuisance of himself.

Jinsei and her date walked up the steps of the Straight together, laughing, and at that same moment the front doors of the building swung outward. A cake-slice of music slipped through the opening, and with it three brothers of the Rat Frat, Rho Alpha President Jack Baron leading the pack. At his side was Bill Chaney, the House Treasurer, and directly behind him, Bobby Shelton, a lineman for the Big Red football team who weighed in the neighborhood of two hundred and thirty pounds. Shelton was in the process of demolishing an apple he'd smuggled out of Oakenshields late-night dining; so intent was the football player on this bit of food that he very nearly ignored the Asian couple and kept to his own business.

Then Jinsei's laugh drew Bobby's attention and almost as a reflex he launched the apple—now little more than a core—through the air with a flick of his wrist. It struck Lenny Chiu hard in the side of the head, stunning him and sending his glasses spinning away.

Even then a full-blown incident might have been avoided, if Lenny had done the sensible and unsatisfying thing and kept walking. But Jinsei's presence made that a hard choice, besides which Lenny Chiu had more courage in him than might be expected of a brain. He stooped down and sealed his own doom by retrieving the apple core instead of his glasses, turning on Shelton with an anger that his small frame could not quite hope to live up to.

"You apologize," he demanded. "Now."

Bobby Shelton chose his response with care.

"You go fuck yourself," came the reply. And as an afterthought: "Chink."

Lenny brought this arm up and winged the apple core back at Bobby. The return throw was not as strong, but just as accurate as the opener. The core flew on a direct bead for Shelton's face . . . and then the football player's right hand snatched it out of the air, no more than two inches from his nose. Pass intercepted.

And still events might have gone no further. As President of the House, Jack Baron maintained absolute authority over his brethren; a single word would have been sufficient to call Shelton off. Later he would wonder at length why he did not do this, what passing lunacy or compulsion kept him from giving the word of command that would bring Bobby Shelton to heel as effectively as a leash. Instead he watched in silence while the football player closed his fist around the apple core, crushing it. There was almost no flesh left on the fruit, yet so strong was his grip that juice ran from the cracks between his fingers. Lenny Chiu saw this and his courage wavered.

Smiling, Bobby Shelton glanced briefly at Jack, double-checking that he had free rein; Rho Alpha Tau's President made no motion to stop him. Shelton's attention returned to Lenny.

"You're all done," he said.

III.

"Did you say pool?" Ragnarok shouted above the din. Adult Eastern's lead guitarist was tearing through a high-volume solo, and what room she left for other noise was mostly filled by Z. Z. Top, arguing with the Dance Organizer about whether bringing his burro onto the dance floor constituted a safety hazard or not.

"Pool," Panhandle agreed, stepping closer around a press of Grey Ladies. He held up a shiny bit of metal. "Key to the game room upstairs. You look kind of bored, figure a rack or two of Eight Ball'd be just the thing."

"Dollar a game?"

"Sounds fair."

"You're my man," Ragnarok said.

They elbowed their way to the exit. After the clamor of the Memorial Room, the Straight Lobby seemed almost church-quiet.

"So tell me the truth," Panhandle asked, "How come you never dance at these things?"

"Just not my kind of excitement," the Black Knight told him. They turned right, toward the steps up to the game room, but all at once Ragnarok stopped and cocked his head. Adjusting his sunglasses on his head, he stared across the Lobby at the front door.

"What?" Panhandle said.

IV.

"This man is hurtin' for certain," Bill Chaney observed wryly.

Lenny Chiu was down on the ground, for the third, but unfortunately not last, time. Though hurt indeed, he didn't look that bad; Bobby Shelton had been careful to keep his punches below the neckline and above the waist, so the only visible damage was a scrape on the heel of Lenny's hand, where he had skinned himself falling. Now Jinsei leaned over him, trying to see how bad off he really was and at the same time convince him to stay down.

"Better listen to her," Shelton advised, as Lenny shrugged Jinsei's arm away and started struggling to his feet again. "Aren't you people supposed to be smart? Don't push your luck with me."

Lenny made it all the way up and launched himself at the football player, arms pinwheeling. One wild swing actually got through, a clip on the side of the Rat brother's head, and then Shelton lost control of his temper and hit Lenny three times. The computer jockey crumpled—this time for keeps—blood running from his lip and nose.

Now it was Jinsei's turn to run forward, shouting something like "Stop it! Stop it, you leave him alone you—"; Chaney caught her, holding her back easily, laughing, but still she managed to turn her head toward Jack Baron and scream "Stop it!" At last some of Jack's sense returned to him. He remembered where they were, how easy it would be for one or more of the revelers at the dance to step outside for some fresh air, how easy it would be for a *Sun* reporter to get downwind and escalate this into an Inter-Fraternity Council–sponsored nightmare. Things had already gotten ridiculously out of hand.

"Bobby," he said. But for once Shelton was not of a mind to rein in immediately.

"Son of bitch tagged me, Jack," Shelton replied, rubbing the side of his head, trying to shake off a buzzing noise that had settled in his left ear. He gave Lenny a not-too-gentle nudge with his foot. "Come on, asshole. Get up again. I want one more round with you."

"Bobby!" Jack Baron repeated impatiently. But then several things happened in rapid succession.

Shelton, still ignoring Jack's word of command, bent down and grabbed Lenny by the collar. As if aggravated by the motion, the buzzing in his ear grew louder, changing to a roar . . . and now he was not the only one who heard it. Jack Baron froze at the sound, his veins filling up with ice; Bill Chaney let go of Jinsei and turned toward the source of the noise. Jinsei took the chance to run once more to Lenny's aid, and that was when the doors of the Straight crashed open, vomiting forth a black-garbed demon on a motorcycle. With the bike's throttle wide open Ragnarok sideswiped Chaney, then flew off the edge of the steps, landing safely at the bottom on two wheels. He swung the cycle around in a controlled skid, braking and bringing it to a halt no more than ten feet from the locked doors of the Campus Store.

Eyes wide, Shelton stood back up, forgetting all about Lenny with the appearance of this new enemy. He spent a brief moment sizing Ragnarok up, the lesser evolved part of his brain clicking over twice and throwing all circuits into the red. Then he charged.

"Here I come!" he bellowed, springing down the steps and stampeding with more enthusiasm than he'd ever shown on a football field. Ragnarok dropped the motorcycle's kickstand and cut the engine in one motion. Perfectly calm, he stepped off the bike, removed the black mace from the side rack. Readied himself. Then Bobby Shelton was on him, eyes blazing, arms raised to deflect an overhead swing.

"Here you go," Ragnarok whispered, coming from below, driving the head of the mace end-on into Shelton's lower abdomen. The football player's stomach muscles were rock hard, but even rock will yield to the force of a jackhammer; he doubled over, all the air going out of him in a whoosh. Ragnarok disentangled his arm and stepped forward, aiming a wide-arc swing at the back of Bobby's right knee. Once, twice he struck, and on the second blow the leg gave and Shelton fell, crashing to earth with all the grace of a collapsing mountain.

Now Bill Chaney came on, easier meat by far. Ragnarok stood motionless and gave him two free swings, neither of which seemed to have any effect. Then the Bohemian Minister of Defense took his turn, not even bothering to use the mace; he decked Chaney with an old-fashioned right cross instead. Chaney did not go down like a collapsed mountain; he went down like a duck at a Coney Island shooting gallery, splat, flat, just like that.

Jack Baron had not moved. He remained on the front steps of the Straight—where Jinsei also still stood, looking at Ragnarok with complete shock on her face—mustering all the cool he had in him. There were two down, one to go, but the president of Rho Alpha Tau did not intend to be that one.

"Why don't you come over here, Jack?" Ragnarok called to him, his voice emotionless, almost dead. "Show me your best move."

"No," Jack said, forcing a cold smile. "I don't think so. You'd have a bit too much advantage with that club you're holding."

Ragnarok gestured at Lenny, who was sitting up, bloody. "How much advantage did Shelton have on him, Jack? How many pounds? Seventy-five? A hundred?"

"Yes, well, be that as it may, if you intend to beat me to death, you'll have to do it without provocation."

This brought a soft chuckle. "Oh, you're good Jack, you really are. Sound innocent even with your hand stuck in the cookie jar. Maybe that's why Lion-Heart never managed to get even for Pearl—it's not in him to fight down and dirty, even against a born dirty-fighter. But you've never really gone up against me before, have you?"

"I'm thrilled to finally see what I've been missing."

"Oh, you aren't thrilled," Ragnarok said seriously. "You're scared shitless. It's taking everything you've got not to shake. And the thing that's bothering you the most is that you can't read me at all." He adjusted his sunglasses. "The shades have got you going, too. You're wondering what the fuck's going on behind them, wondering how the fuck I can see. Most of all you're wondering exactly where I'm looking right now. That's got your balls up."

"And you said *I* was good," came the reply.

"You *are* good. I just laid out two of your brothers without a sweat, and inside that head of yours you're figuring I'm probably going to do the same to you, but you've managed not to panic."

"You're not that frightening."

Ragnarok pivoted suddenly, lashing out with a boot. Chaney gave a cry and flopped over, clutching his side.

"Might have sprung a rib there." mused Ragnarok. He turned back to Jack. "You sure you're not frightened?"

The Rho Alpha Tau President made no reply, but his cool was slipping away visibly. Next to him Jinsei made a strange sound in her throat.

"You should be frightened," Ragnarok continued, beginning to walk closer as he spoke. "My old man sold his soul to the Devil, you know that? Bet you didn't. Sold his soul, sold a good piece of mine in the bargain. You *ought* to be frightened, Jack. Because I know the Devil, and *I know where you live.*"

Jack's eyes narrowed. "What are you saying?"

"Gets dark up there at night, up around Fraternity Row," answered Ragnarok. He stood now at the foot of the Straight steps, smiling like a pallbearer. "They've got streetlamps and all, but streetlamps have a peculiar way of breaking. On a dark stretch of road, cloudy night, a white man dressed in black would be nearly invisible if he kept his head down. You might not ever see him coming.

"But it might not even be you he's coming for. Cars have a way of breaking down too, just like streetlamps—especially those fancy cars fraternity boys drive. Boom, one night your Porsche just won't start, no way to pick up your girlfriend, so she walks over to the House to meet you instead, and now *she's* on that dark stretch of road, all alone. . . ."

His voice was calm, matter-of-fact, full of genuine threat. Jack's cool drained off entirely.

"You shut up!" he told Ragnarok, trying to back his words with real fury, but terror undercut it. "You shut up with that talk! If anything ever happens to Alison. . ."

Ragnarok nodded sympathetically. "It's different, isn't it? When it's someone you know, maybe even care about, instead of just some drunk chick at a shagging. When it's you and yours on the block instead of a stranger up against someone twice his size. When you don't have control."

He set his foot on the lowest step, and Jack flinched, convinced now that Ragnarok meant to club him down, worse.

"Stay away from me! You stay away, there's people right inside there, some of them could come out any time now."

"No one's come out for a while," Ragnarok observed, rising another step. "Who knows, maybe they really like the band. Or maybe someone's detouring them."

"What about out here?" Jack countered, backing up. "It's not so late, people go by all the time. . . ."

"I know. Do you see them?"

He looked around, and he did see them, a small group, maybe four or five, watching from a safe distance.

"Hey!" he shouted, almost shrieked. "Hey, don't just stand there! Call Public Safety! Call Safety, goddamnit!"

"Twelve patrol cars loaded with Ithacops," Ragnarok assured him, "couldn't keep me from breaking your jaw if I moved fast enough."

Jinsei's voice, soft but urgent: "No. Stop."

Jack looked around at the swinging doors, too late to dive inside to safety, for Ragnarok had him backed up against the side of the building now. The mace came up slowly, head pressing firmly against Jack Baron's Adam's apple, pinning him.

"The big surprise," said Ragnarok. "is I'm not going to put a scratch on you. All I want is your jacket."

"My what?" Strained; he was having trouble breathing.

"A trade. Pride for pride. Your House jacket for his bruises."

Jinsei again, close at Ragnarok's side, imploring: "Lenny's hurt. This won't help him."

Ragnarok did not ease off. "Your jacket. Now."

"All right!" Jack caved in. "All right, fine, here, take it!" And he was struggling out of the Rho Alpha Tau blazer, Ragnarok drawing back the mace to let him do it.

"Good," the Bohemian said, when the blazer lay at his feet.

Shorn, a touch of bravado returned to Jack Baron: "Aren't you going to make me apologize now? Grovel?"

"Not worth the trouble. But when you get home and start thinking about all the ways you want to get even with me, remember how you felt a minute ago. You can feel that way again. With cause."

And Ragnarok stepped back, letting Jack hurry past, only sticking his foot out at the last moment. The Chief Rat tripped, stumbled, rolled down the steps, bruising an elbow and tearing up the sleeve of the silk shirt he was wearing.

"You bastard," he whispered, pulling himself up.

"That's just right," replied Ragnarok. "Now take your people and get the fuck out of here."

He did as he was told, levering Shelton to his feet, helping up Chaney. With the action over, the knot of spectators dissolved, going their various ways, but Ragnarok did not take his eyes off the Rat brothers, not when Jinsei laid a hand on his arm, not even when Z. Z. Top at last came out to see what was happening. In his heart of hearts, the Minister of Defense, the Black Knight of Bohemia, tended a flame of perfect hatred for the retreating trio.

But even more than that, he hated himself.

SLEEPTALKING

I.

In her high-security single in Balch Hall (nicknamed the Nunnery for its standing as one of the last all-female dorms on campus), Aurora Borealis Smith lay deep in dream. It was a pleasant vision, no trace of nightmare; in it, she lived the life of a tree spirit in the enchanted wood of Stephen George's book. She danced among oak and maple, flew up above the highest branches on invisible wings, watched the sun set over a long pond not unlike Beebe Lake . . . and on the far bank, a storybook knight in shining armor flew a kite in the evening breeze.

"Why not go over and introduce yourself to him?" suggested Walter Smith, who was a tall willow in the dream. "He looks like an open-minded sort of fellow. Not so stubborn as some."

"Oh, Daddy . . ." Aurora turned over in her sleep, unconsciously bumping the night table beside her bed. A torn envelope fluttered over the edge, and with it the folded card that had come inside. The card was silvery and imprinted on the outer cover were the words:

AN INVITATION . . .

These two words written in some odd flowing script, and so too the continuation on the inside:

The Lady of Tolkien House
Invites You to
A Hallowe'en Revel
Ten O'Clock, Hallowe'en Night
Dress Casual or
Come as Your Favorite Elf
+ + + + +
No RSVP Required;
Bring a Guest
An Enchantment Promised for All

153

At the bottom was an imprint of a white rose.

Earlier in the evening Aurora had shown the invitation to Brian, discussed it with him. He had been mostly negative, reminding her that the Cornell Christers would likely have a Halloween outing planned.

"Besides, I don't know that a fraternity party is the sort of thing we'd enjoy," Brian had told her.

"We have lots of friends in Houses," Aurora protested. "And anyway, Tolkien House is supposed to be something special. Didn't you ever hear of it?"

"I guess not. But 'The *Lady* of Tolkien House?' You sure this isn't some kind of joke? It is still a little bit early to be sending out Halloween invitations."

"I don't think it's a joke," said Aurora, studying the card. "Don't you think it's too pretty for a prank?"

"But who would have sent it? We don't know anyone in Tolkien House, do we? . . ."

So it had gone, back and forth for nearly half an hour. At the end Brian had stepped out of the argument by reminding her again that it was still a ways to go until Halloween, and they could decide what they were doing later. Aurora knew from experience that by the time "later" rolled around Brian would probably have made other plans for the both of them, but this time, she thought, she would insist on having her way no matter what.

An Enchantment Promised for All . . .

In the dream, the sun sank completely, vanishing behind a lone hill on the horizon. The knight began reeling in his kite.

"Yes ma'am," commented Walter the Willow, "fellow like that might know the rule of give and take. No sense fighting over little things."

"But who is he?" Aurora asked.

"Why don't you go ask him? Maybe he's waiting for someone to go ask him."

"Oh, Daddy . . ." Aurora repeated. But even as she spoke she was rising into the air, catching the wind and skimming above the surface of the pond, hurrying to catch up to the knight.

II.

Hobart was alone in the Clock Tower, drinking. He had gone down into the drop-shaft, where slowly descending weights had originally driven the gears of the Clock before its connection to an electric motor. Sitting on a ledge with his legs dangling over a dark gulf—a safety cord tied around his waist to prevent him from tumbling into oblivion in a stupor—he took long draughts from a thimble mug. The drink was a special mixture of alcohol, hash oil, and various magic herbs; used properly, in liberal amounts, it brought about visions, often visions of lost friends or loved ones. Hobart did not make a regular habit of it, considering himself too old for such artificial fancies, but once in a very long while he put aside his maturity and indulged.

Shortly after draining the mug, Hobart's head began to nod. His snore drowned out the sound of a thimble as it slipped from his grasp and fell into the gulf, striking the side of the drop-shaft twice before hitting bottom. Drifting into dream, he was filled with a pleasant expectation, thinking to see his wife Zee—who had met with a fatal accident some five years ago—or perhaps Jenny McGraw, shrunk down to sprite size through the magic of hallucination.

But this time, at first, there was no vision at all, only darkness, and the disembodied voice of his granddaughter Zephyr, asking: *What's so bad about the Boneyard? What's in there?*

His own voice, answering: *Nightmares. Old nightmares.*

Then the sounds of rain and thunder, a storm in full fury, and underneath a babble that was just barely intelligible. More voices, these from the distant past.

Rats! I see rats over behind those stones!

Get those crossbows reloaded! Mercutio, you others, start lowering the box!

Hobart! . . . Hobart, watch out, the seal is broken!

"No," Hobart whispered. Now a scene was materializing around him. He stood in The Boneyard, his back up against a tombstone. It was dark, raining, but for all that he could clearly see the second stone off to his left, a plain white marble square carved with a single word:

PANDORA

" 'Fraid I got some bad news for you, Hobart," said a long-deceased but well-remembered figure from Hobart's youth, stepping out of the gloom. "Got a warning for you, too."

"Julius," Hobart said, recognizing him. Then he shook his head. "No. You can't be here, Julius."

"Why not?" the figure inquired. "I'm dead, ain't I? Over a century now, longer than that Jenny McGraw, even. You wouldn't have been surprised to see her, would you?"

"Not here," insisted Hobart. "I don't want to talk to you in this place."

"This place. You just want to forget about the Boneyard, don't you? Fine. Only you can't, not yet. Maybe never."

"The War's ended, Julius. For a long time. There's nothing here that concerns me."

"So am I, ended," Julius replied. "Long time. But a little magic drink, and voom: I'm back, even if it's only in your head. Magic can bring back a lot of things, Hobart. Especially if they were never really gone to begin with."

Shaking his head: "No. No."

"We never killed him, Hobart."

"*No*, Julius."

"We put him in the ground, you and I and the others, but we never actually killed him."

"The *box*, Julius," Hobart hissed. "No air. No food. No water. After a century—"

"More than a century, Hobart. But the past doesn't always bury so easy. He still had a lot of power when we put him down the hole." Julius grinned in a way that made Hobart shiver. "I ought to know that better than anybody."

"He can *not* still be alive. I won't accept that."

"Then how is it you keep warning your granddaughter away from here, eh? 'Fraid a bad memory might get her?"

"There are rats . . ."

"Sure. But that ain't what scares you, Hobart, and you know it."

Hobart opened his mouth to protest, but at that moment the ground shook. There was a booming sound as if the earth had been struck from below. Heart skittering, hand drifting to his sword hilt, he turned and saw that the white square had tilted up some, the dirt beneath it bulging upward.

"He's going to get out," Julius continued. "He's going to be *let* out, *commissioned*, by a higher Power than you or I. And he hasn't forgotten you, Hobart."

"I'm old!" Hobart protested, still clutching his sword. "Isn't it enough that I faced him once when I was young? Why twice in one lifetime?"

"Why ask me?" Julius countered. "I never was one for answering the big questions, you know, and I surely never bent Fate's ear. I didn't even have the fortune to survive the first time around."

A twinge of guilt: "Julius. Please . . ."

"Beware the Ides of March, Hobart," said Julius, turning away. "And before. Even the Big People are going to suffer, this time."

He disappeared, swallowed once more by the gloom.

"Wait! Julius, wait!"

Hobart broke into a run, but there was no catching him, and when at last the sprite gave up the chase and looked around he had gone nowhere. The white marble square was still just off to his left, levered up further. Any moment now, Hobart told himself, it will flip over entirely, and a silver-bound box will burst up out of the earth. And then the box will open. . . .

The vision was a long time fading.

RAGNAROK'S
DREAM

I.

"How do I thank you?" Jinsei said later. They were on North Campus outside Low-Rise Eight, the International Living Center. Lenny Chiu, immensely shamed and unwilling to have himself checked out at Gannett Health Clinic, had already gone inside to clean up the blood.

"You don't want to thank me," Ragnarok told her. "What I did tonight doesn't deserve thanks."

"You saved Lenny from an even worse beating."

"By beating the shit out of two other people and terrorizing a third. Great rescue."

"But they *deserved* it," Jinsei argued. "They—"

"They ought to have been arrested," said Ragnarok. "All I did was give them a lesson in what real bullying is all about. Maybe in a way that's rough justice, but I'll tell you a secret: it wasn't justice I was thinking about when I dropped Shelton. I was thinking about how good it felt to make the son of a bitch's stomach cave in."

"Maybe," she suggested, "maybe it's not so bad to enjoy hurting those kind of people."

"Really? Except for the 'maybe,' I'll bet that's exactly what Bobby Shelton would say about what he did to your friend."

Silence. Ragnarok gave a little nod, raised his foot to kick-start the bike.

She stopped him with another question: "What did that mean, about your father selling his soul to the Devil?"

Ragnarok stared at the ground for a long moment. "It means," he replied, "that I've got no right to go feeling self-righteous about Jack Baron. Do you know what a Georgia bedsheet salesman is?"

Jinsei shook her head.

"It's not important," said Ragnarok, after another pause. "Listen, you want me to see you home?"

"This is home," she replied, nodding at the Living Center.

"You'd better go in, then. Your friend could probably use some company."

"I think Lenny wants to be alone. He must be really ashamed about what happened. You know . . . that someone else had to—"

Ragnarok nodded. "He's not going to call the cops, is he?"

"I'm not sure."

"Right," said Ragnarok. "It doesn't end then, you see? What I did to Jack and Shelton won't mean a thing by this time tomorrow. They're a hell of a lot more scared of being busted by the Inter-Fraternity Council than they are of me."

"I'll talk to Lenny about it," Jinsei promised.

"You do that."

He dropped his foot, kicked the engine to life; Jinsei touched his arm.

"Who cheers *you* up?" she asked him.

"What?" Ragnarok looked at her, and for the first time noticed that she was crying.

"You say Lenny could use some company," she said. "But don't tell me you don't feel bad about what happened tonight."

"I feel bad that I enjoyed it. But I wasn't shocked by what the Rats pulled, if that's what you mean; hell, don't get thinking you're safe from rednecks here just because they teach Marx over in the Government department."

Crying more heavily now, Jinsei made no reply, only lowered her head. Without thinking, Ragnarok reached out to brush her cheek. He caught himself in the middle of the gesture, but then to his great surprise Jinsei abruptly leaned forward; with Ragnarok sitting astride the motorcycle, his head was at the same level as hers, and his mouth.

"Hey—" Ragnarok said, as she drew in to him. Jinsei did not hesitate; her lips met his, and after a dazed moment he kissed back.

By the light of a scythe-blade moon, they embraced.

II.

He would not take her home with him.

When at last they disentangled from each other, Ragnarok insisted that Jinsei go back into the dorm, though she wanted badly to stay with him. He knew that she would not like the house he lived in—no one ever did—nor did he want to take her over to Risley, where he might have to face the Top or some other Bohemian who had heard about his run-in with the Rho Alphas. Besides which, he was unworthy of her company, or anyone else's, tonight. Only later, when he realized he had fallen in love with her, did Ragnarok regret not bringing Jinsei along.

Riding home, he took the motorcycle up to seventy-five and kept it there. Twice he nearly lost control of the bike; once he avoided a head-on collision with a van by mere inches. Each of these near misses left him more numb than shaken, and he would not slow down until his house was in sight.

Ragnarok lived in a ready-to-be-condemned Saltine box on University Avenue, just below The Boneyard. Being entirely self-supporting he could not afford the dorms—not Risley, in any case—and slumlord Denman Half-ast the Fourth had given him a rare bargain. This was not due to any latent generosity on Halfast's part, but reflected the fact that in the past five years, no other student had been willing to rent the place, what with its lack of hot water, substandard wiring and insulation, and thriving roach colony. In addition to the low rent—and here lay the main attraction—Ragnarok had gotten Halfast to agree to let him redecorate the house in any fashion he desired.

And so the house was black: walls, ceilings, floors, the few sticks of furniture, even the ancient commode, which had been stained a dark jet. Thick ebony drapes—scrounged from the Salvation Army downtown—shut out all external light, and the interior lamps were of low wattage, specially shaded to cast a yellowish-brown glow. All together, these redecorations created a style that Preacher had dubbed Early American Funeral Parlor; but more to the point, they created an atmosphere in which the only white thing was Ragnarok himself. With even his sheets and underclothes dyed black, there need be no worry that he would start awake some night, bleary-eyed, and imagine a phantom in the room with him.

There was a small shed beside the house made of rotting wooden boards, splintered and brown, and it was here that Ragnarok parked the motorcycle on returning from North Campus. He padlocked the shed door, glancing up at the silent Boneyard as he always did, then went around to the front of the house.

The lock on the front door was broken. Halfast had promised several times to have it fixed, but as Ragnarok had never once pressed him on the matter, he was taking his time about calling a locksmith. The present method for opening the door was to jiggle the knob furiously until it popped; Ragnarok did so now, passing within and closing the door again behind him. He kept the lights off, finding his way through the living room—which was also the bedroom and study—by memory. He did not even turn on the overhead in the bathroom, where he went to splash cold water on his face. Since he had removed the mirror on the medicine cabinet there was nothing to see anyway, other than the roaches.

After washing up, he went back to the living room/bedroom and un-dressed. A light at this point would have revealed two scars on Ragnarok's body: a thin line running all the way across his chest, and a more jagged indentation on his left shoulder. He stripped down quickly, then donned the dark, long-sleeved robe that served as his bedclothes. He lay down on the creaky bed, drawing covers like a swatch of starless midnight up to his chin.

People are going to think you're a vampire, Rag, Myoko had told him, the one time she'd paid a visit; Fujiko had thought the house too creepy to even enter. Ragnarok did not care what people thought of his living quarters, or of him, so long as he could keep his nightmares to a minimum.

Tonight the dreams would not stay away, though. He closed his eyes

and he is back in North Carolina, a young boy named Charlie, a carpenter's son living in the West End of Griffin's Rest township. It is his birthday, he is six and stands alone in the living room while his father clears dinner. In his hands is his last unopened present, a long narrow box wrapped in brown paper. He holds it up to his ear and shakes it, hears nothing but a thump, and dreaming thinks: dead serpents, dead serpents.

An eyeblink and the box is open, paper strewn on the floor, Charlie studying himself in the tall standing mirror that graces one corner of the room. The costume which is his present makes him look like a small ghost, a ghost with a peaked hood and a red circle above his heart, a red circle enclosing a red flame. His father Drew is beside him, a larger ghost; Drew lays a hand on the back of his neck, a dream-hand made of lead.

"Don't you go showing it to anybody unless I say it's OK, partner," his father warns him.

"All right, Daddy," he says.

"I love you, Charlie."

"I love you too, Daddy," he says

and he is running across the highway that leads north out of town, running to catch the dark boy who is just now vaulting the cemetery fence. Charlie is older; his friends Scott Noble and James Earl join him in the chase. Together they are fast, faster than the dark; they enter the cemetery themselves barely twenty strides behind him.

Charlie is fastest of all. He races ahead, leaping over graves. All the tombstones bear his mother's name. He runs, Scott and James Earl yell for him to slow down, wait, wait, but he is intent on the quarry and leaves them behind. Now it is a race of two instead of four.

The ground slopes down to a stream. The dark splashes halfway across and trips over a stone. Charlie cries his triumph: "Got you, partner, got you now!" He charges into the stream and the dark rises up, rises and turns, and Charlie ducks back easily to avoid the swinging fist. He laughs and sees the blade and victory turns to terror as he realizes it is not a swing, but a cut. Fire brands his chest

and he is in his father's study, watching Drew Hyatt at his desk from an impossible angle, a dream-perspective. The desk is stacked with a mountain of books and pamphlets; muttering to himself, Drew tends a gin bottle with one hand and a well-thumbed tract with the other. RAGNAROK IS COMING, *reads the title.* Being a comparison of the Norse Apocalypse and the decline of the Aryan races in modern North America, by Dr. Hiram Venable.

"It's here somewhere," Drew *says, clutching the tract.He sets down the bottle, makes a note with a hand that never quite stops shaking. The stack of notes is tall, almost as tall as the stack of pamphlets. The perspective swings around and it is possible to read what he has written on the top sheet, an endless repetition of one phrase:* "Her only tears are dry tears."

"It's here somewhere," Drew *repeats*

and now it is night, Charlie running again through a wide field, this time chasing not a dark boy but a girl with strawberry blond tresses. "Lisbeth," *he calls, and she laughs and keeps moving, but not so fast, she wants him to catch up. He smells the tobacco all around them, feels the wetness of the leaves as they brush against his legs. They have been hosed down just in case; you can't trust a fire after all, you have to be careful of stray sparks.*

"Lisbeth," he calls again, and as she stops and turns to face him he also sees, on the periphery of his vision, the cross flare light. The Ghouls in their white robes gather around it in a circle, their outlines flickering and indistinct.

"Here I am, Charlie," Lisbeth *says, smiling. Her cotton blouse is unbuttoned at the top, a locket shines against her throat. Charlie reaches out to touch her*

and razors cut his hands, the cross still burns on the horizon of his awareness but he is in the living room once more, the mirror stands shattered before him.

"You had it coming to you, partner." His father's voice, behind him. *"You were asking for it."*

Blood runs in his eye from another cut. His shoulder is the worst, though; a jagged shard of quicksilver has punched a hole in the muscle.

"You had it coming," his father repeats. *"Gordon-Small. A nigger lumber company. You shame me. You shame me."*

Charlie reaches up with his right hand, yanks the mirror shard from his shoulder. The pain is indescribable; little slivers remain in the wound, biting. Charlie stares at the shard in his hand, tiny reflecting dagger. Fury threatens to choke him, but still he speaks the words: "I love you, Daddy. I always loved you."

"You shame me," Drew Hyatt *says.*

The burning cross.

His father's blood, hot on his fists.

STEPHEN GEORGE
AND THE DRAGON

I.

Some three days later found George busy at his typewriter. He had a short story in the works, a story inspired by one of the tombstones he'd seen on that late August walk in The Boneyard, now nearly two months in the past. It was the tale of Harold Lazarus, a plumber who had died unrepentant. As punishment for his numerous sins, he had been transformed into the shape of a gargoyle and set to work fixing the leaky pipes in the darkest pits of Hell—a literally endless job, seeing as Hell was the sewage nexus of the universe. Lazarus' one consolation was the absence of his wife, the nagging nexus of the universe. Yet her death approached, and Lazarus' desperate attempts to scare her into accepting salvation—he tapped out warnings of the torments of Hell in Morse Code on the leaky pipes, which echoed all the way up to earth and the Lazarus family commode, and, incidentally, to billions of other commodes throughout creation—formed the basis of the story. The working title was *Porcelain Messiah;* George figured the *Harvard Lampoon* would take it, if no one else.

Calliope puttered around in the kitchen, out of sight but continually making just enough noise—or so it seemed—that she remained tantalizingly on the edge of George's thoughts. Not that he ever stopped thinking about her, anyway. Every night since that first when she'd appeared at the Fevre Dream had been filled with their lovemaking, and every day with his writing—except when he had to teach, a grudging chore now. He remembered once believing that requited love might spell the end of his creativity, but the truth was that Calliope inspired him more than loneliness ever had. Her origin, the reason for her coming to him, were still mysteries.

She had the radio on in the kitchen, and a squeaky-voiced announcer—no doubt an Ithaca College student on a work-study program—recited the major news items of the day: President Botha of South Africa had reiterated

that there would be no end to white minority rule; Nancy Reagan had bought
still another set of china for the White House; and at O'Hare Airport, FAA
investigators were unable to account for the appearance of a two-headed cow
which had wandered onto a runway and into the path of an accelerating 747.

As George finished a page and set a new sheet in the roller, Calliope
appeared at the kitchen door, cloaked in her silver-threaded robe and bearing
a big package wrapped in brown paper.

"This came in the mail today," she said, setting the package down on the
coffee table next to his typewriter. "And this." She handed him a cream-
colored envelope. George stared at it.

"The mailman hasn't been by yet this morning," he reminded her, not
really expecting any sort of explanation. He did not get one.

"Well," was all Calliope would say, and she shrugged, smiling. For
whether the mailman had been here yet or not, both packages were properly
stamped, postmarked only yesterday afternoon, and if that defied logic then
Calliope cared little. And while she smiled at him, looking more beautiful
than any metaphor could suitably describe, George discovered that he didn't
much care, either.

"Fine," he finally said. He opened the envelope first, drawing out a
silvery card identical to the one Aurora Smith had recently received.

An Enchantment Promised for All . . .

Like Aurora, George had to wonder who in Tolkien House would think
to invite him to a Halloween party, for though he had heard of the place, he
had never been there, or to any other fraternity for that matter, during his
entire time at Cornell. But there were a few other things about the card that
caught George's eye especially where Aurora would have noticed nothing
unusual, such as the imprint of the white rose, or the first few words of the
invitation itself. *The Lady of Tolkien House,* it said. This did not bother George,
as it had Brian Garroway, because of the notion of a woman sending invitations to a frat party, but rather because for some reason "Lady" made him
immediately think of Calliope.

"You . . ." he began awkwardly, glancing up at her.

"*I?*" Calliope queried, raising an eyebrow and smiling wider than before,
as if at some private amusement.

"It's stupid," said George, almost in warning. Then he stumbled on: "Do
you know any . . . any *other* people at Cornell? What I mean is, you haven't
been to Ithaca *before*, have you?"

"I've never come to The Hill for anyone's sake but yours, George,"
Calliope assured him. It took him a minute to realize that this did not answer
his question, but by that time the Lady had retreated to the kitchen. George
turned his attention to the big brown-paper-wrapped package; faintly he
heard a metallic clink and a hiss of igniting gas as Calliope set the tea kettle on
to boil.

He somehow did not expect to find a return address on the package; when he did, he was not surprised to see it had been badly smudged, so that only the city of origin—Chicago—could be made out. Glancing again at the date and the P.M. on the postmark, George thought that it must have been shipped express, and one hell of an express at that to get all the way from Illinois to New York ahead of even the mailman. The delivery address was similarly question-raising: TO THE PATRON SAINT OF DAYDREAMS, Ithaca, N.Y. 14850. No street number, but it had found him anyway, and though "Patron Saint of Daydreams" kicked modesty to hell and gone, George saw how it might be applied to him, by a fan if not by a critic. But how had the not-yet-arrived mailman known whom to deliver it to?

"Screw it," George muttered, deciding to work out the paradoxes later. He tore away the brown paper, and numerous layers of newspaper that he found beneath it. When the last sheet had been torn off and tossed carelessly to the floor, he was left holding a dark wooden box, with a silver latch and silver hinges and a single word inlaid in ivory letters on the box's lid:

PANDORA

"Right," said George. Not touching the latch, he held the box up by his ear and shook it. It made no sound; the contents either filled the box entirely or were well padded. He reread the word on the lid.

Pandora's Box, he thought. It seemed rather small to contain all the evils that plagued humankind. But no, even if it were the genuine article—which he was not ready to discount at this point, seeing the odd way it had come to him—according to the old Greek legend it had already been opened, the evils loosed, Hope the only thing remaining inside. Being optimistic enough in his own right—and having Calliope living with him—George didn't suppose he had much need for a box full of Hope. Perhaps he could give it to someone else who did, someone like Ragnarok, who'd been looking troubled just recently.

Inevitably thinking of the white marble square in the Boneyard—even the style of lettering on the box was the same—George sprung the latch and lifted the lid. Metal flashed within.

The figurine in the box did not look much like Hope, unless it were Hope as conceived by a chronic depressive: Hope with coiled body of silver, ivory fangs, jade scales inlaid on the wings and belly, eyes of what looked like sapphire. The only thing missing was a plume of flame to shoot out of its mouth.

A dragon. Someone had sent him a miniature wingéd dragon. He took it out of the box, surprised by its light weight, and set it on the coffee table. The thing must have been quite valuable, but this fact, as well as the craftsmanship that had gone into making it, was lost on George for the moment. For all its finery, it was also an ugly thing, as a monster ought to be, and those dark blue eyes held an undeniable malevolence. In fact it was as mean-looking as it could be, considering its size—barely a foot from tail to snout.

After trying to stare down the dragon for a full five minutes, George picked up Pandora's Box again and checked to see if there was anything else inside—a subsidiary Hope, perhaps, or a note containing even a *clue* as to why it had been sent to him. There was nothing more.

"What the hell is this?" George said bemusedly, studying the dragon again. Just then Calliope returned from the kitchen, balancing a cup and saucer neatly in the palm of one hand.

"Tea," the Lady announced.

"Hey," George looked up. "Check out what I got."

"Yes, I know," she said calmly, as if she had looked inside the package herself before giving it to him. She set the tea cup in front of him. "Drink this. It's not too hot."

George glanced at the cup, then back at her. "Who do we know in Chicago?" he asked, accenting the second pronoun carefully.

"Mayor Daley?" Calliope suggested. "Maybe he liked one of your books and wanted to send you a present."

"I don't think Mayor Daley does much reading these days," said George, and Calliope laughed and leaned across the coffee table to give him a quick kiss. He laughed too—what else could he do? He could not force a straight, sensible answer out of her if she didn't want to give it, that he'd long since learned.

"Drink your tea," Calliope repeated. George picked up the cup and sipped gingerly at it. She was right—it was not too hot.

"They couldn't really fly, you know," he said.

"What that?"

"Dragons. Aerodynamically unsound—a physics prof I know told me about it once."

"Bumblebees are aerodynamically unsound," Calliope pointed out. "And besides, the stories all say dragons could fly. Which would you rather believe?"

"Well . . ." He stroked the figurine. "A *metal* dragon couldn't, anyway."

"That might depend on what kind of wind he's got behind him."

Another sip; George felt suddenly light-headed, the taste of tea bitter on his tongue.

"Can you do magic?" he asked her next.

She smiled. "Magic? What makes you think of magic?"

"All this . . ." He tried to indicate dragon, box, party invitation and 'Patron Saint of Daydreams' with one gesture. "It's too weird, Calliope."

With a look of genuine compassion on her face, she reached out to stroke his cheek. "Poor George," she said. "You have no idea what that word really means yet. But as for magic . . . I can't do any more magic than you can."

"That answer doesn't say anything."

"It says everything," Calliope insisted. She gripped the hand that held the teacup, raising it to his lips and gently making him drink the rest down. When the last drop had been drained, cup was returned to saucer and pushed aside as Calliope locked gazes with him. There was an actual physical feeling of being held; George's head had now passed from lightness to a rising tumble, yet Calliope's eyes riveted him at the center of the spin.

"Tell me a story, storyteller," she said.

"What story?"

"About the first time you called the wind. When you were a boy."

"I was with my Uncle Erasmus," George recalled the day as if hypnotized. "He'd managed to sell one of his sculptures—one of his *real* sculptures, not the concrete animals I told you about—and we went out kite-flying to celebrate. Huge multi-colored box kites, those were Erasmus' favorite. We went out to Flushing Meadow Park, out by the big steel globe from the World's Fair, only the wind wouldn't blow. Hours we waited, from just before noon to near on dusk, talking about everything under the sun and then some. We wouldn't give up and try it another day—it was like a point of honor.

"Finally the sun was going down, still not a rumor of a breeze, and my Uncle said 'OK, George this wind isn't going to cooperate on its own so we're just going to have to figure out some way to twist its arm.' I asked what way was that and he rolled up his sleeves, sat back, and thought it over.

"Now when Erasmus sets his mind to a problem he comes up with these bizarre solutions that usually work. He watched the sky for few minutes and then said to me: 'You want to be a writer, right George?'

" 'More than anything,' I told him.

" 'Well,' he said, 'imagine you were writing a story about two fellows who'd just spent a whole day waiting for the wind to blow. How would you end it? Would they finally get what they wanted, you think?'

" 'Well sure,' I said (it was a couple years yet before the idea of a less-than-perfectly-happy ending even *began* to penetrate). 'Of course they would.'

" 'Just like that.'

" 'Well,' I said, 'I suppose if it were the whole *point* of the story . . .'

" 'Yes?' said Erasmus.

" '. . . then I guess maybe they'd have to do something first.'

" 'Like what, George?'

" 'Oh, I don't know . . . an Indian Wind Dance, maybe?' "

Calliope smiled. "An Indian Wind Dance?"

"Hey, I was twelve, OK?" He continued: "So right there Erasmus says 'Great, let's do it,' like I actually have some idea what this dance is like."

"What did you do?"

"What could I do? Made something up on the spot. Wasn't much—just turning in place really, with the kite held up in one hand, string in the other."

"What happened when you tried it?"

"Nothing." Now George smiled. "Not at first. We tried it, and there was still no wind, and so we tried it again, and again, and then . . ."

"And then?"

" . . . there was a crossover moment, a moment of *control*—who knows, maybe I just got dizzy—but it felt as if it really were a story, a story but still real life, and there was an ending to be chosen, and it seemed *right* that it should end with the wind blowing."

"And it did." A statement, not a question.

"It did," George agreed. "And ever since . . . I don't know, it's like—"

"Like writing without paper," Calliope suggested.

"Yes," said George. "Yes, that's just right."

"Do you suppose," she asked him now, "that it would work with something other than the wind?"

"I don't know. I've never tried." He shrugged. "Guess it might depend on the circumstances."

"Well then . . . what if your *life* depended on it, George?"

She blinked deliberately, releasing him, and George became aware once more of the room around him. His light-headedness had risen to a plane where the very color and dimension of the things around him had become malleable. The upholstery of the couch, originally brown, now wavered between dark red and fluorescent orange; the edges of the coffee table had become indistinct, as if it were no longer certain how much space it wanted to occupy. And as for the sunlight streaming in through the living room windows . . . God . . .

"You put something in my tea," George realized, paranoia pouncing like a tiger that had been creeping up through the brush all this time. "What did you put in my tea, Calliope?"

"Something to expand your mind a little," Calliope told him, herself remaining unchanged, distinct. "And to help you defend yourself."

"Defend my . . . oh—oh, hey, *no!*"

With a click of claws and teeth, the dragon figurine had begun to uncoil. It pulled itself out straight, wings flapping, sapphire eyes flickering with some ignited inner spark. George shied back from it.

"What the fuck, Calliope!" he cried out. "What—"

"I told you when I first came to you," she replied, calmly, "that I had a few things to teach you. Consider this a lesson."

"Thanks, but I don't think I want a lesson. Could you please—"

"Writing without paper, George. Just think about writing without paper and you'll be fine, probably."

She stood up.

"Wait a minute!" George commanded. "Don't you go anywhere!"

"I'm already gone," Calliope said. "See you after class." Her form blurred and faded out; her robe, empty, dropped to the floor.

George did not even bother to marvel at the vanishing trick, but merely accepted the fact that he was on his own and turned his attention to the dragon, which was now drawing air into its mouth and expanding like a balloon.

"Good God," George exclaimed, as the creature attained the size of a small dog and continued to grow. The dragon ceased to draw air and fixed its eyes on him with a hiss. It tensed as if to spring. George did not waste time gawking. Without thinking about it he brought his legs up hard against the underside of the coffee table, upending it. The dragon, the typewriter, and Pandora's Box were catapulted into the air to land with a crash by the far end of the sofa. The coffee table itself flipped over and shriveled up like a deflated rubber raft, cycling through three shades of indigo before it evaporated altogether.

A weapon. He needed to find a weapon, quickly. While the dragon untangled itself from the wreckage of the typewriter and the manuscript pages of *Porcelain Messiah* hovered near the ceiling like giant moths, George made a hurried scan of the room. He saw nothing that might serve as a club or mace, nothing sharp—once upon a time he had actually had a replica of a Viking battle-ax hanging on the wall, but that had long since been sent to rust in a Tompkins County junkyard. Desperate, George's eyes lighted on Calliope's fallen robe, and, vaguely remembering an old fairy tale where a prince had used a fair maiden's girdle to leash a monster, he dove for it.

The dragon came at him even as he snatched up the robe. George held the garment out to his side, waving it like a bullfighter's cape in the hope that the beast might be distracted. But the dragon, borne on a whisper of silver wings (it didn't seem to need a wind at its back after all) did not even hesitate; it ignored the robe and went straight for George's chest. Only at the last moment did the storyteller swing the robe around to use as a shield.

Ivory fangs and claws parted the material easily; the dragon's head poked through the hole in the robe, mouth open for a bite. George ducked back, at the same moment gripping the robe by the thick fold of the hem, using that as a garrote to wrap around the monster's neck. Incredibly, it seemed to work; all at once the dragon began flapping its wings in reverse, jerking its head around and hissing as if it were really short of breath. It even seemed to shrink a bit. Suddenly overconfident, George yanked harder on the ends of the hem, willing it to constrict still more and choke the beast.

"That's it! That's got you, you—" George's cry of victory was cut short as the dragon simultaneously spat smoke in his face and tore at his arm with one wildly swinging claw. Beneath the sudden pain the storyteller felt his grip loosen, and before he could lose it entirely he used the robe as a sling to hurl the monster into a corner. Then he staggered, eyes watering fiercely, arm bleeding from three deep gouges.

With a fresh whir of wings the dragon was up and moving again. George beat a hasty retreat into the kitchen, where multi-hued rays of sunlight streamed in through the window, every color in the spectrum being represented except the normal yellow-white of mid-morning. It would have been quite beautiful to stand and watch, really, had he the time.

"Oh burn in hell!" George cried, kicking open the refrigerator door and slamming the dragon a good one on the nose as it buzzed into the kitchen. The storyteller continued to back away, hurling utensils, spice jars, Hi-C cans—anything that came to hand—in his wake, none of it slowing the monster for more than a moment. Tossing one last juice can, George ducked into the rear hallway. Knowing he would never make it to the back door of the house (and not sure where he would run to if he got outside), George cut into the bedroom instead and tried to shut the door behind him. Close on his heels, the dragon got one claw and half a snout inside the room; two quick slams of the door convinced it to back off.

Door shut and latched—for whatever a two-bit latch was worth—George waited for the inevitable tear and splinter as the monster tried to claw through the very wood of the door itself. What he heard instead was even more ominous—a steady sucking noise as the dragon drew more air. It was expanding again. George suffered a sudden vision of a lion-sized dragon bursting through the door to drag him down with no further struggle possible.

Writing without paper. Think about writing without paper.

"All right!" cried George, abruptly angry. He pounded on the door himself a few times, for attention. "All right! You want to play, want to be a real live dragon, fine! I'm going to be the goddamned White Knight, we'll see how you like that!"

To himself he said: *This is a story, a fantasy; anything can happen. You will close your eyes. you will turn around, and you will open your eyes again. When you reopen them, there will be a sword on the bed.*

He closed his eyes. He turned, and opened his eyes again.

The bed was breathing. Charcoal-grey coverlets bulged in and out with a steady rhythm. Both pillows had flattened themselves out against the headboard as if terrified of something, but he could see no weapon.

"Damn it!" George said. "I asked for a sword."

His head felt light enough to float, but still he concentrated, growing more and more angry as the sword refused to appear. Then came a moment—a crossover moment—when all fear, all thought of the dragon vanished, leaving only a sharp fury at a story that was not turning out the way he wanted it to.

"There is a *sword*," George said definitively, "on the *bed*."

Wind gusted suddenly in the room. With a low ripping noise a seam opened in the coverlet, and a sword hilt—an ornate hilt with a white rose superimposed on a red cross on the pommel—forced its way up out of the mattress. It rose to a height of six inches above the surface of the bed, revealing a sharp blade beneath it, and stopped, waiting now to be drawn.

The dragon too stopped, stopped drawing air, and George did not wait any longer. With legs more muscular than those he had woken up with in the morning, he sprang onto the bed. Strong hands—warrior's hands—grabbed the sword by the hilt and drew it free. The four-and-a-half-foot blade cast its own glow, multi-hued like the sunlight.

"All right," George called, assuming a batter's stance. "You can come in now."

The bedroom door exploded off its hinges. The dragon, bigger than lion-size, came in trailing smoke like a locomotive. This time George stood firm when it tried to blind him, stood firm in the midst of the whirlwind that the monster's now-huge wings created. His fear was gone, he was in control of the story, and nothing need bother him if he didn't wish it to. He merely waited—not too long—as the dragon gathered itself for the attack.

"Come on," George whispered, and the dragon pounced, mouth gaping wide, claws extended and locked to tear him apart. Still he did not falter, weapon ready, waiting, waiting one more second.

The dragon came in, screaming triumph. Even as it did, Stephen George brought up the sword in a perfect arc, slicing the air in two, and lopping off the beast's head with an explosion of sparks that seemed to fill the world.

II.

He did not start awake. It was a calm awakening, with Calliope nestled in his arms, her eyes closed, her lips pursed in a smile and a gentle snore. Careful not to disturb her, George pulled free and got out of bed.

What had he been dreaming about? Already it was frustratingly vague, though the memory might jog free again in some future dream. Something about a Box . . . and being wounded. He glanced absently at his arm and noticed three white lines, like scratches that were nearly healed.

Shaking his head in confusion, George drew on his pants and went out to the kitchen to make breakfast. Through the door to the living room he caught a glimpse of his typewriter, sitting patiently on the coffee table. He had a story to finish today, he remembered, a story about a plumber in hell.

He was packing toast into the toaster when there came a knock at the front door. That did make him start; his arm jerked and sent a carton of orange juice tumbling to its doom.

Standing in a newly formed puddle, George shook his head once more, smiling, for of course there was nothing to get excited about. It was only the mailman, arrived at last.

THE HALLOWE'EN
PARTY

I.

The first Ministers and Grey Ladies arrived at the Tolkien House Hallowe'en Revel shortly after 10:00 P.M. Turning their mounts over to attendants the Bohemians hurried inside, glad to get out of the weather, which threatened rain before long. Within, a string of fairy lights lit a path through the "Mathom" hall and back to the elevator, for of course the party was being held in the underground Garden of Lothlórien, where the starry sky remained free of clouds.

By eleven o'clock the Revel was in full swing, good cheer and alcohol flowing freely. Then at eleven-thirty the party skipped a beat with the arrival of Stephen George and Calliope. They wore costumes designed by the Lady herself, Prince Valiant for him, Little Bo Peep for her; a good many Bohemians and House brothers went to bed later dreaming of sheep.

Then midnight. Precisely at twelve o'clock, after much coaxing and arguing with her boyfriend, Aurora Smith entered Tolkien House—and that was when the real Revel began.

II.

"It's just that I don't see the point in us going to a party where I don't know anybody," Brian Garroway said, as the obsidian-lined elevator descended to the cellars.

Aurora adjusted a picnic basket on her arm—for she had come as Little Red Riding Hood—and asked him: "Didn't you see those people who rode past us coming through the woods? Those were Bohemians."

"I don't know any Bohemians," Brian informed her. Perhaps one of the things making him so testy was the outfit Aurora had thrown together for him at the last minute. A set of blue drapes had been converted to a cape, and a loaf of French bread thrust under Brian's belt like a short sword. A hastily-scribbled tag pinned to his collar explained: I AM THE EARL OF SANDWICH.

"Well," said Aurora, "I can introduce you to a few. I met some in that course on Jonathan Swift I took last year."

"Swift. It figures."

In the sub-cellars, two dwarves waited just outside the elevator to receive them.

"Hi there!" Aurora beamed, stepping away from Brian. "Is this where . . ." She trailed off as she saw the zombie-like expressions on the dwarves' faces. Both stared off into the distance as if paralyzed by some recent vision. Yet even as Aurora was about to wave a hand in front of one of their faces, they spoke.

"Follow the lights," the first said, wistfully.

"Take care crossing the bridge," added the second. Neither of them looked at her.

"Um-hum," said Brian, examining each dwarf in turn. He had never touched drugs himself and never would, but he knew a heavy buzz when he saw one. "So what have you all been into?"

The first dwarf sighed a lover's sigh. "The Lady . . ." he whispered, and said no more.

"Aurora," Brian started in again, glancing sharply at her. "I'm really not sure—"

But she tugged impatiently at his arm, anxious to get to the party. "Come on," she insisted, and began following the line of lanterns that lit a path across the otherwise pitch-black cellars.

"Aurora!" His voice was stern but she kept right on moving, forcing him to run after her; in fact he didn't catch up until she had nearly reached the bridge.

"Aurora," he asked her when he had pulled even with her again, "are you really certain we should be going to a party where even the door checkers are stoned?"

She ignored the question. "What's this, now?" she said, as they came upon the chasm. The lanterns on the bridge were perched precariously to one side, leaving as much room for walking as possible.

"Aurora!" Brian grabbed her arm as she stepped onto the bridge. She turned on him suddenly, yanking her arm free and inadvertently kicking one of the fairy lamps into the gulf. It tumbled end over end, quickly blowing out, but not before they both saw it fall a frightening distance. If the unlit lantern struck bottom after that, they did not hear it.

"Jesus Christ," Brian Garroway—not one to casually break the second commandment—said, peering into the chasm. "What the heck is this?"

Aurora took advantage of his distraction and got moving again. Brian followed after her—stepping carefully, to be sure—this time not catching her until she was across the bridge and beyond. There even Brian had to shut up momentarily, stunned by his first glimpse of the wonder that was the Garden of Lothlórien, home of the Revel.

III.

A great pavilion, a long, open tent of leaf-green canvas on grey ash posts, had been erected in a clearing among the trees, and within it a fully stocked bar, wood-finished in such a way as to suggest that it had just sprouted up out of the ground. Though the bar came equipped with all the modern conveniences—and all the best labels—everything had been carefully camouflaged so as not to detract from the atmosphere of the Garden. Of course some anachronisms were inevitable; Z. Z. Top, dressed head to toe in combat gear, sat playing Beer Hunter with a six-pack of Schlitz, one can of which had been given a good shaking-up.

Outside the pavilion, Bohemians mingled with House brothers mingled with Grey Ladies mingled with other miscellaneous guests. Some danced to the music of an impromptu band that played a cross between medieval minstrel tunes and jazz fusion; some just drank and talked. Wrapped in a Roman senator's toga, Grey Lady Fujiko stood deep in conversation with Noldorin, the Tolkien House co-President who had granted an honorary House membership to all Bohemia in return for a chance to meet her. So far they seemed to be hitting it off pretty well, and throughout the Garden barely a couple could be seen who didn't look either happy or too blitzed to care.

While Aurora studied the faces, Brian turned his gaze to the sky above. Like Lion-Heart before him, Brian penetrated the illusion immediately.

"A dome," he said aloud, not unimpressed. "An underground dome."

Another House President, Shen Han, passed near just then and overheard Brian's words, but he did not respond, just as he had made little response to Lion-Heart's questions. What could he have said? Of course the stars shining above the Garden were a projection, and Shen Han knew well the secret controls that could make them dim or brighten, knew too how to moderate the rest of Lothlórien's climate: the wind, the fog—which now curled seductively around the guests' ankles—the temperature. What he did not know was the actual mechanism employed, for neither he nor any other Tolkien brother had ever seen so much as a single machine or projector, though some had searched; wherever and whatever they were, they must have been of marvelous construction, for they never seemed to need maintenance or repair. In fact the House had pretty much maintained itself from the time it was first built, according to legend. But that was not the sort of legend guests were likely to appreciate, or believe.

"George!" Aurora called, spotting a familiar figure. Brian returned to earth; Shen Han passed on his way.

"Hey, slugger," George greeted her, walking up. His Prince Valiant cape billowed behind him; unlike Brian's, it did not look as if it belonged in a window. "What brings you here?"

"I got an invitation in the mail," she explained. "From the Lady of Tolkien House."

"The Lady?" said George, an uneasy expression crossing his face.

"Yes, And of course we couldn't pass up a chance to see what this place is like." She glanced at Brian. "Could we?"

"No," Brian agreed. "No, of course not. How's your new girlfriend doing, George?"

George's expression went from uneasy to startled. "Where did you hear I had a girlfriend?"

"There was a paragraph on it in last Tuesday's *Sun*. Something about a mystery lady who none of the photography staff have managed to get a picture of."

"Really?" Aurora spoke up. "Can we meet her? Is she here?"

"She's here," said George, "Though at the moment she's disappeared on me."

"Disappeared?"

"It's kind of odd, unless you've known her for a while. The fog swirled up really high for just an instant when we came into the Garden, and then she was gone. Like the Shadow. I'm sure she'll turn up eventually, but in the meantime I guess it's at least a partial blessing. Calliope has a funny effect on people whenever we're out in public together."

"The dwarves by the elevator . . ." Brian mused. George nodded.

"Right, the dwarves, that's just what I'm talking about."

"Well," said Aurora, "we really *will* have to meet this . . . Calliope. If she shows up come find us. We'll be here for a while."

"Maybe not that long," Brian tried to amend, but Aurora had already added a farewell and moved off to get a closer look at something interesting she'd spied among the trees. Once again Brian went to pursue her, his exasperation peaking; yet he had barely taken the first few steps after her when a leg thrust out to trip him, bringing him tumbling to the ground.

A wild cackle rang in Brian's ears as he pushed himself up. Furious, he turned to look at the prone form of the Bohemian Woodstock, who lay beside him in the grass, a flagon of ale in one hand, a half-smoked joint in the other, both legs outstretched. Woodstock's head was tilted way back and it looked as though he might laugh himself into a stroke.

"Very funny," Brian said, rising to a crouch and brushing dirt off his pants. The word *asshole* rose to his lips but did not slip out. "You jerk," he added instead.

"Huh?" Woodstock brought his laughter under control and tried to focus on Brian, as if he'd only just noticed him. "Jerk?"

"Glad you enjoyed my fall. I could have broken my neck . . . or yours."

"Enjoyed?" Woodstock repeated. "You? . . . No." Giggling, he jabbed a finger at a bare patch of ground behind Brian. "Little man . . . only this high." He held his hands half a foot apart as a visual aid, spilling the contents of the flagon on himself. "Only this high, I swear."

"Of course," said Brian. And then, at the top of his lungs: "Aurora!"

She was nowhere to be seen. Leaving Woodstock behind in a fresh fit of laughter, Brian got up and headed down a path he thought she might have taken. Passing two House brothers and a trio of sorority sisters imported from Alpha Phi, he arrived in short order at the clearing that contained the Enchanted Circle, a wide ring of colored stones believed by the brothers to possess a special protective power. A woman lay within the ring, passed out from too much wine. A very pretty woman, Brian noted, but not his; nor was there anyone else in the clearing, conscious or unconscious, whom he could ask about Aurora. Nearly at his wit's end, he caught a flicker of red out of the corner of his eye. Peering into a place at the clearing's edge where the trees seemed to draw particularly close together, he saw it again, more clearly this time: a figure in a red cloak and hood, moving deeper into the wood. Brian called out but the figure did not turn.

Anxious not to lose her again, Brian padded across a thin carpet of fog and entered the trees. He did not pause to check his bearings, or keep track of landmarks; the idea of getting lost in an underground wood was ridiculous. But the trees grew closer together and before long the sky could no longer be seen through the branches. Ahead, the figure in red had all but vanished from Brian's sight, as the fog rose higher, obscuring the view.

"Aurora!" he shouted. "Aurora, stop! Wait for me!"

She did not stop; she walked on, into a thick band of fog that completely engulfed her. Suddenly afraid, Brian thought to turn back, back to the pavilion where he might find a brother to help him navigate these impossible woods. But when he looked around, all directions had become the same, fog growing thicker in all quarters, and he realized that he did not know the way out.

IV.

"Puck, stop teasing him! Let's go."

"Just another minute, Zeph . . ." The sprite made another face at Woodstock, watched him roar with laughter and pound his fist against the ground. Puck was fascinated; only rarely had he actually been seen by one of the Big People, and even then a reaction such as this was most unusual.

"This is silly, Puck," Zephyr reasoned with him from her hiding place behind a shrub. "What if he decides to step on you?"

"I'd be surprised if he could stand up," Puck replied. But he had tired of the game, and so with a final nose-thumbing, he bade farewell to the Bohemian and rejoined Zephyr. "Where to now?" he asked her.

"Let's go over to the Circle. Grandfather's supposed to be telling stories." Puck nodded agreement, and together they made their way along the same path that Brian Garroway had gone rushing down not long before. The two sprites were careful to keep well to the side of the trail, lest they be trampled by some other passing human. Little feet carried them at a slower pace, but in due course they came to the clearing and the ring of magic stones.

Aphrodite, the Bohemian Love-Minister, still lay unconscious within the Circle. Unafraid, a milling group of sprites clustered freely around her, some even using her as a giant sofa; one sprite stood calmly on Aphrodite's neck, trimming locks of her hair for later use in weaving.

Puck and Zephyr mingled with the crowd. Unlike the humans, sprites wore no costumes on this holiday, for why should invisible, magical creatures bother to dress up as spirits and hobgoblins? Sifting through the faces Puck spotted Hamlet, garbed in his regular oak-leaf garment, pinsword at his side; he was chatting leisurely with Jaquenetta, the animal-handler who had been with them on the night of Cobweb's and Saffron's deaths. Farther off, near the edge of the Circle, Zephyr's Grandfather Hobart and two other sprites were assembling a storyteller's chair, a construction of Popsicle sticks and tongue depressors that resembled a lifeguard station.

"Hobart looks pretty happy," Puck observed, watching the old sprite give orders to the younger two.

"This sort of thing always flatters him," said Zephyr. "He's Eldest, after all, and this gives him a chance to show off his history."

"What story are you going to ask for?"

"I'm not sure. Something with butterflies in it, maybe."

The last slat of the chair was set in place and Hobart hoisted up to his seat; hands were raised for silence. The crowd—grown quite large in number—quieted itself, all eyes turning to the storyteller.

"Ahem," Hobart began, clearing his throat, unable to restrain a certain swell of pride in his voice, "I imagine I don't need to introduce myself. You all know me, and I've met most of you at some time or other, though I might have a chore keeping certain names straight. As for this night—you will already have realized that my memory is less than perfect. Nevertheless I believe I can keep you entertained with that portion of the past that hasn't yet slipped away from me. My only request is that you don't ask for details of anything too personal." His smile broadened. "Unless, of course, the details are about someone other than myself."

This brought polite laughter. Hobart spread his hands and nodded in recognition.

"So . . ." he continued. "Let's begin. What would you all like to hear about?"

The crowd exploded with noise, every one of several hundred voices shouting out something different. Hobart listened intently, here and there actually managing to make out one of the requests.

"Tell us about the Bell Tower!"

"Let's have a Midsummer's Eve love story!"

"Butterflies!" cried Zephyr. Hobart heard her voice above all the others, and nodded once more.

"Enough!" he said; the crowd fell silent once more. "My granddaughter has just asked to hear a tale about butterflies. This happens to be an amazing coincidence, because I was just now thinking about a sprite named Falstaff, who earned the title Captain Caterpillar when he—"

"Hobart!" a voice called out. Heads turned at the sound; such an interruption was a horrible breach of manners. Puck, for one, was not surprised to see Laertes, Saffron Dey's brother, standing atop Aphrodite's rib cage with a hand on the hilt of his sword.

"I want a death story," Laertes said, heedless of the stares and whispered comments of the crowd.

"A death story?" Hobart replied, learning forward in his chair. "And what makes you think death is a more appropriate topic than butterflies?"

"I don't care about butterflies. I've lost family this past season, and not just me. Now winter is coming on; I'll wager death has a stronger hand then than anything that flies. Even the Big People"—he gestured at Aphrodite— "seem to realize that. Isn't that why they call this the Feast of the Dead?"

"I'm not sure they do call it that," said Hobart, "and we certainly don't. There are worse terrors than cold weather, Laertes."

"I don't care. I want a death story."

"You want a lesson in etiquette," Puck spoke up from the crowd. Laertes scowled at him, his hand tightened on his sword hilt. From his chair, Hobart saw the draw coming.

"None of that!" the old sprite commanded, before Puck and Laertes could rush at each other; Hobart had not forgotten their duel at Saffron's funeral. "You stop right now, or there'll be no tales of any kind!"

"You see?" Puck said to his opponent. "You ruin it for everybody!"

Laertes looked across at Hobart. "Do I get my story, or not?"

"Yes, yes, all right! If you insist on behaving like a spoiled child, I'll give you what you want to quiet you. Puck, put that weapon away!"

"Not just any death story," Laertes added, as Puck reluctantly sheathed his sword.

"You have a particular one in mind, do you?"

"Yes. I want to hear about the War."

Hobart paled. "The War . . ."

"Yes, why not?" said Laertes. "It's the worst death story of all, isn't it?

Exactly what I'm in the mood for. So tell us the tale, the tale of the Great War. Tell us the tale of Rasferret the Grub."

V.

Stephen George sat at the bar in the pavilion, sharing drinks with Lion-Heart and Shen Han.

"Sorry, George," the Bohemian King said, sipping his usual Midori in a shot glass, "I don't know what you're talking about."

"Neither do I," said the Tolkienian President.

Lion-Heart finished the shot and called for another. "Understand, we should have invited you, and of course you're welcome to stay now that you're here, but . . ."

"But you didn't send me the invitation," George finished for him.

"What did you say the wording was?" Shen Han asked. "'The Lady of Tolkien House?' Our standard invitation is from The Brothers of Tolkien House. We don't even know anything *about* the Lady, except that she built this place."

"I think I might know something about her," George muttered.

They lapsed into a puzzled silence. Lion-Heart downed another Midori and glanced over at Shen Han, remembering something.

"Hey," he said. "I wanted to thank you. I was over by Galadriel's Mirror a few minutes ago, and I noticed the Rubbermaid is gone. You got rid of it, eh?"

Shen Han blinked. "I should have . . . I'm sorry, it must have slipped my mind. One of the others must have taken care of it. Noldorin, maybe."

"No matter," said Lion-Heart. "So long as it's gone."

"The Rubbermaid?" George queried. "What's the Rubbermaid?"

"Just a bad joke," Lion-Heart told him. "It's not important. Tell us when you got this invitation."

"I don't know. Funny thing, but I can't remember actually receiving it. I just know it was sitting next to my typewriter for the past couple weeks. I can't—"

He stopped. Across the bar and out the other side of the pavilion, he saw a shepherdess' crook beckoning to him from behind a tree. He stood up.

"George?"

"You'll have to excuse me," George said. "I've got to go talk to some-body."

Shen Han looked around. "Who?"

"Little Bo Peep. Catch you guys later, OK?"

Nodding to both of them, George ducked around the bar and made for the tree. The crook vanished behind the trunk just before he reached it, reappearing from behind another tree some ten yards farther on.

"Right," George said. "Here we go again." He allowed himself to be led, following the elusive shepherdess on a merry chase. Where Brian Garroway had called out almost constantly for his lady to slow down, George did not even bother; Calliope knew what she was about, and never once had he seen her give up a game until she had finished it. No sense fighting the flow.

He blundered into an open glade, where the third House President, Lucius DeRond, sat astride an impossibly large mushroom, smoking a hookah. "This side of the 'shroom makes you grow shorter," Lucius intoned, blowing smoke rings at the sky, "and this side makes you grow longer." George asked him what the middle of the mushroom did, but did not wait for an answer; for the slender pink crook beckoned him anew.

Beyond the glade the trees grew denser, the fog thicker. Soon he was no longer following the crook at all, but rather the sound of soft footsteps that remained just ahead of him in the mist. Then even that faded. Lost in a world of swirling white—yet untroubled—George let his instinct guide him on-ward, confident that he had not been abandoned.

The trees parted once more, opening into another clearing. George sensed this rather than saw it; it had become impossible to see farther than the tip of his nose. He walked forward, feeling carefully ahead for any obstructions, and suddenly she was there. His hand brushed the back of what he took for Bo Peep's bonnet; his arms went out to embrace her as she turned. She too reached out, gripping the hem of his cape as if to reassure herself of his identity. Then they were kissing, silently, and as the Lady's fingers ran up and down his back in a deliriously wonderful way, it did not even occur to George to ask what had happened to her shepherdess' crook.

VI.

"Rasferret the Grub . . ." Hobart began, his face grave. "Known also as Rasferret the Evil One, Rasferret the Destroyer. Precious few names you'll find as feared as that one. Rasferret is our collective nightmare, our patron demon, still able to inspire terror after more than a century—though most of those who actually lived to see him did not live to tell about it. Just look at me, with the title of Eldest at an age that once would not have been considered remarkable. Back then, back when I was young and Julius was Eldest . . . in those days, old meant *old*. Rasferret's War left us decimated, and changed in more ways than one.

"And what was he, this demon? Some say he was the offspring of one of our own people who had mated with a rat, though I myself cannot imagine such a union; some say he was a true sprite, but evil, who having wandered long paths and years gradually took on the shape of his sins. Whatever his origin, his appearance is easily imagined from one of the names he came to be known by, 'The Grub': small, loathsome, twisted creature, eyes shining with the blue glow that is the hottest part of a flame. Pure malice his only motive, he came from some distant place to wage War against us—and mark you, Laertes, he came not during cold winter, but at the dawn of spring.

"Some might wonder on first hearing this tale what threat such a creature could pose, so small and alone. But of course he was never alone; he had the rats as his allies from the very beginning. Nor were they ordinary rats. For Rasferret also had magic to wield, magic I believe he must have stolen—I cannot see him creating his own—and through magic he changed the rats, made them to stand on two legs and bear swords, clubs, crossbows. With an army of perhaps five hundred he began a gradual assault on The Hill, meaning to annihilate us.

"The first engagements were sneak attacks, Rasferret's attempt to do as much harm as possible before being discovered. The rats would surround and surprise small groups of sprites in isolated areas, leaving no witnesses behind. My own brother was killed in just such a raid; for a long time we had no idea what had happened to him.

"Then came the day when Rasferret at last felt secure enough to operate in the open. A wedding was due to be held at twilight in a garden—not this Garden, of course, but one not distant from here—with over two hundred guests in attendance. No sooner had the last of them arrived and the cere-mony begun than the entire army of rats swept in, the sunset at their backs. Rasferret did not fight alongside them—a coward, he always hung back from battle—but nevertheless he made his presence known. Among the sprites was an exceptionally bright fellow by the name of Touchstone, an inventor and tinkerer by trade. He escaped the carnage on the back of a grey squirrel, riding with all speed to a great hollowed-out tree stump where he had housed his latest creation." Hobart's eyes lit briefly on Puck. "It was a vehicle, a land vehicle with wide treads for locomotion, only now in his moment of need Touchstone used it as a battle wagon, returning to the garden as quickly as possible and overrunning the marauders, killing some and panicking the others into a rout. But then Rasferret sent a bit of his own soul into the heart of the machine, and all at once the vehicle took on a life of its own, running down sprites now before ramming itself into a tree and killing its driver. And that was how we became acquainted with the most terrible of Rasferret's powers, the power of *animation*—"

VII.

The woman was not alive. Brian Garroway knew that even before he touched her, for the figure that stood facing him—the fog had thinned somewhat, and he could make out her contours if not her features—held far too rigid a posture to be flesh and blood. With open palm Brian reached out to touch her midriff, feeling first the textured springiness of leather and then a hardness beneath that could only be plastic. All at once the mystery was made clear.

He reached up to stroke the mannequin's cheek, touched her coarse hair, wondering all the while how she had gotten here, out in this boondock fringe of the Garden that Brian had decided must be intended for hazing House pledges. As he puzzled over the matter his hand traced the curve of a bare plastic shoulder, down along the arm, into the swell of her left palm.

"You haven't seen my girlfriend, have you?" Brian asked the Rubbermaid, part of him hoping there was no one around to hear him acting so foolishly. And that was when the mannequin's fingers closed over his hand.

He jumped back, jerking his hand free; the Rubbermaid swayed in place but did not fall over. Brian flattened against the trunk of a tree, eyes cranked wide open.

Did not, could not, *did not*—

"Aurora!" Not a shout this time; a shriek. Brian's feet found the good sense to run and he bolted away, braying a panic-stricken litany: "Aurora! Jesus! *Auro-o-o-ora . . .!*"

VIII.

"How many battles all told? That question has no answer. Three weeks the War lasted, and in all that time I doubt if a minute passed without some skirmish taking place somewhere on The Hill. Our losses mounted hourly, while Rasferret's army continued to grow in size; for there were always more rats to be recruited. New troops issued regularly from The Boneyard, where Rasferret had set up his main camp."

Zephyr nodded understanding, remembering her grandfather's many cautions about that place—nor had she forgotten the rats that had attacked her and Puck. Meanwhile Laertes, who had gradually moved up through the crowd to stand directly before Hobart's chair, asked impatiently: "But what about the Big People? Surely they must have noticed something unusual, with such a large conflict going on right beneath their noses."

"And why do you assume that?" Hobart responded. "Understand me, Laertes, I respect human beings and love them dearly, but I'm told that on occasion they don't even notice their own wars. Oh, it's true enough they were aware of some of the damage—their newspapers were full of vandalism stories—but for the most part I doubt their minds could have accepted the truth of what was going on. Therefore they didn't see it."

"But surely Rasferret saw them," Laertes protested. "And with an army of rats, and this animation power . . ."

"No," said Hobart, obviously troubled. "No, he never once directly attacked any of the Big People. Naturally I've wondered at that myself, but I can't claim to know the reason. Perhaps his magic wasn't strong enough, perhaps he simply feared to risk it . . . to be certain you would have to ask Rasferret personally, and I'm relieved to say that's not possible."

Laertes nodded. "His downfall . . . tell me about it."

"We got lucky," Hobart expained. "That is the simple truth of it. We had a plan, of course, but all plans, all but the most certain, have luck to thank for their success. The strategy was born in desperation; at the end of three weeks' fighting our numbers had sunk so low that we knew any more losses would finish us. Hecate, who was great-grandmother to Macduff, there"—Macduff nodded with grim pride—"led the larger of two contingents on an assault against The Boneyard. Her task was to stage a planned retreat at a given time in order to draw away as many of the rats as possible. Then a second, smaller group, led by Eldest Julius, would sneak in and attempt to kill Rasferret, in the hope that without their leader, the rats would return to their natural state and disband. Hecate did well for her part, achieving the desired goal with minimum casualties; but of that second group, I alone survive to tell the tale."

"You killed him, then?"

Hobart hesitated only the briefest instant. "Of course we killed him. You wouldn't be here, making such a nuisance of yourself, Laertes, if we hadn't."

"But how? How did Rasferret meet his end?"

Another, oh-so-brief hesitation. "Julius killed him. Ran him through with a magic sword." Hobart touched a place below his left breastbone. "Right here. The Grub crumbled to dust and blew away on the wind."

Laertes' eyes narrowed. "Julius struck the killing blow? But then how did he die? You said you were the only survivor."

"The rats killed him, obviously. Don't get the idea that Rasferret sent his entire army after Hecate. We still had a good fight on our hands."

"So the rats didn't disband, as you'd hoped."

"They did, but not immediately."

Laertes shook his head. "What about this business with the magic sword? And the crumbling to dust? I never heard that part of the story before. My Granduncle Claudius told me—"

"Claudius?" Hobart burst out, red-faced. "My dear fellow, Claudius was even younger than I at the time, he fought in Hecate's contingent, and further I don't recall ever giving him the details of what happened in The Boneyard. It's no wonder he's got his facts wrong."

Macduff had moved up to stand beside Laertes now. "Aye, laddie," he said to the young sprite, "and since ye've got it all straight at last, how's about movin' yerself over so as to make way for more cheerful tales? I'm sure Hobart's grown tired o' tellin' this one."

"Just one more thing," insisted Laertes, pushing his luck. "How do you know it won't happen again some day?"

"I imagine," Hobart told him, "that if Rasferret were capable of returning from the grave, he would have done so by now."

"But there might come another like him," Laertes suggested. "A second Grub, wandering in search of a War to wage."

"No," said Hobart firmly.

"Why not?"

"Because *I'm* Eldest now, and while I may not be half as old as Julius was, I'm over a hundred years your senior, with that much more experience. Which makes it my prerogative to be optimistic." He nodded dismissively at Laertes, then focused his eyes on the rest of the crowd.

"Now . . . I believe we were talking about butterflies. . . ."

IX.

"Auro-o-o-ra! . . ."

The shriek echoed through the clearing where the man and woman lay together in the grass. Like a broken enchantment the fog lifted all at once, and as the woman raised her head she saw clearly for the first time whom it was she embraced.

"George!?"

"Aurora? . . . What—"

"Oh my," she said, rebuttoning the top buttons of her blouse. "Oh my." She sprang to her feet and was gone into the woods, but not without a backward glance or two.

"What?" George repeated, sitting up. He heard a laugh behind him and turned to see Calliope reclining against a tree, shepherdess' crook held loosely in one hand. From the other she dangled a picnic basket.

"It's hers," Calliope said, setting the basket on the ground. "She dropped it in the fog just before the two of you bumped into each other."

"You saw us?"

Calliope nodded. "Very exciting. Another minute and you would have had her costume off. Now that would have been interesting."

"I thought she was you," George said. "I don't understand how I couldn't tell . . ."

"You were an English major, weren't you? Remember Chaucer's *Reeve's Tale?*"

"What?"

"Never mind."

George struggled slowly to his feet. "Are you angry about this?"

Ignoring the question, she reached out to stroke his chin. "Did you enjoy it, George?"

"I . . ."

"The truth. I'm honestly curious."

"I though she was you."

"Which means?"

"It was perfect. I mean . . . not that anything really happened."

"Oh, George, it's not how much you do, it's what you feel while you're doing it. You know that. But do you know the real truth?"

"No, What?"

"The real truth is that whoever you love will be just like me, and not just in the fog. Understand?"

"No."

"You will . . ." The Lady moved in closer. "She's really a very good person, that blond girl. A lot more to her than you'd first think."

"She's in love with someone else," George said. "So am I."

"Mmm . . . of course."

"You're going to leave me soon, aren't you?"

"Soon," Calliope agreed. "But not today, and not tomorrow—there's still a good number of things to be done." She began kissing his fingers, one by one, and with her foot lightly nudged the picnic basket. "Let's see what we can find to eat, shall we?"

THE ROMANCE
OF THE BONE

I.

The Revel began to break up a little over an hour before dawn. The sprites crept out through the secret exits that they had dug years ago, when Tolkien House was new. The Bohemians took the more conventional route, back over the Khazad-dûm bridge, where safety lines had been rigged to prevent anyone from pitching over the side in a drunken stupor.

Outside a thunderstorm was winding itself down. Z. Z. Top stepped out into a lightning flash that lit up the front lawn in flickering white; smiling, he turned face up into the rain and saluted the sky with his last Schlitz.

"Very nice," he said. "Very pretty."

Others drifted out: Lion-Heart, Myoko, Panhandle, a shorter-haired Aphrodite, many more. Aurora Smith and Brian Garroway had long since taken their leave, but George and Calliope did not come out till very near the end. A flash of lightning revealed the Lady's face for the barest instant, rooting three House brothers to the ground where they stood; they had to be literally dragged in out of the rain.

Last to go were Jinsei and Preacher, who walked out into the wet supporting Ragnarok between them. Preacher was costumed as an unlikely Miles Standish, Jinsei as a cat; her tiny cardboard ears wilted quickly in the rain.

Ragnarok, dressed only as himself, had gotten so deep into the bottle tonight that he'd nearly come out the other side, and on his way to the door he'd thrown up on his trenchcoat. They'd wrapped him in Preacher's long-coat now, which led to a bad moment when, during another lightning flash, Ragnarok looked down at himself and realized he was wearing white.

"Shit! Oh shit what the fuck—"

He fought them. Jinsei took a good elbowing to the side of the head and staggered away, nearly falling. Without her support Ragnarok slumped half-way to his knees, but Preacher caught him up, holding him in a bear hug from behind so that he could not turn and punch.

"You get off me!" Ragnarok bellowed, jerking like a fish in a net. "I'm not, *not*—"

"It's *me*, Rag," Preacher said softly, speaking right into his ear. The fish paused in his struggles.

"Huh? Whu—Preacher? Preach?"

"It's only my coat, Rag. You got that all right? It's only my coat."

"Whuh . . . this your coat, Preach?"

The fight went out of him like a departing spirit. He slumped all the way now, and as dead weight Preacher had a hard time keeping him from falling flat out in the mud. Fortunately Shen Han appeared at that moment, two brothers trailing at his heels.

"We'll take him," Shen Han offered. "We can put him up for the night in one of the spare rooms."

Preacher nodded, handing Ragnarok over to the brothers, who picked him up by his arms and legs and bore him back into the House. Preacher turned his attention to Jinsei, who was gingerly rubbing the side of her face.

"You hurt?" he asked.

"No," Jinsei replied, watching the retreating form of Ragnarok with something like pity. "No, not badly. Is he always like this?"

"Does he always get drunk at parties, you mean?"

"Does he always invite women to parties and then get drunk?"

Preacher shook his head. "Hardly ever seen him drink before. And as far as it goes, he talks a lot about women but it's a rare day he actually asks one out. He must like you."

"He barely said a word to me all night."

"Yeah, well, that figures, actually. See, Ragnarok's got this big disagreement problem with himself between what he wants and what he thinks he deserves. Has to do with where he comes from."

"Where is he from? I mean I know somewhere down South, but not what city, or anything like what his parents do."

"He didn't tell you about his growing up?"

"No. Not really."

"Then I don't know if I ought to." He was looking at her in the gloom between lightning flashes, trying to decide if something he'd seen in her expression was real or imagined. Hesitantly: "Hey listen, you need a lift home?"

Jinsei smiled, remembering a similar offer. "I think I'd rather go on foot than ride a motorcycle in this weather. Thanks anyway."

"Motorcycle, hell," said Preacher. He pointed off to their left, where one of the brothers was leading a white stallion around the corner of the House. "That's my transport. Name's Calvin, Calvin Coolidge."

"Are you sure he's safe with all the lightning?"

"Safe as walking, if we're careful." As if to demonstrate, another flash lit up the sky; Calvin did not twitch so much as an ear at it or the accompanying thunder. "You see? He's steady under fire."

Smiling broadly now, Jinsei said: "Maybe you should go and get your coat back. That Pilgrim outfit doesn't look very waterproof."

"Don't worry it. I don't get cold easy."

Her eyes narrowed. "You're not drunk too, are you?"

The Bohemian shook his head. "Don't touch alcohol," he said seriously. "Don't touch tobacco, either, or dope. And that, pretty lady, is why they call me Preacher."

He gave Jinsei a wink that brought her smile back; his hand brushed hers and in that moment he knew he had not been imagining things.

"All right then," Jinsei said, and Preacher took her home.

II.

Luther had not been idle these past weeks. Forced at last to admit that this place he and Blackjack had come to was something less than Heaven, he had decided to bury his regret in canine academia; he had taken on The Five Questions of Ultimate Wisdom. Choosing to start with the First—*What is the nature of the Divine?*—he had inquired after the canine philosopher assigned to the subject, the local God-expert.

There were two. Blackjack had come along to meet them, though the Manx soon lost his patience with the whole business. The philosophers were a Cocker Spaniel named Cashmere and a Greyhound named Estrogen. They were both chained to a dead tree on North Campus, beyond Fuertes Observatory; it was said a boy came to feed them every evening at dusk. They were quite insane.

"We're waiting for a fellow by the name of Dogot," Cashmere had said in greeting. "Have you seen him by any chance?" Thus began one of the most bizarre conversations Luther had ever been party to. Estrogen pointed out that nothing is better than complete happiness; but, he added, one must concede that even a dry milk bone is better than nothing, especially if you're hungry. It followed through transitivity that a dry milk bone is better than complete happiness, which served as conclusive proof of God's existence, for how could such an odd state of affairs arise purely by chance?

No wonder, really, that Blackjack had stomped off in disgust barely fifteen minutes after they first arrived.

This morning of November first, All Saints' Day, Luther figured he would give The Questions another chance. Alone this time, following directions given to him by Rover Too-Bad, he checked a number of possible locations in search of the canine philosopher in charge of the meaning of life. The philosopher was an Irish Setter, lanky and red-haired, and hence his name: Ruff. As the thunderstorm passed on to elsewhere and the sun peeked over the horizon, Luther caught Ruff's scent and tracked him to the face of Libe Slope.

He was perched midway down the Slope in a peculiar position: reared up on his hind legs, front paws in the air, nose tilted toward the clouds, long ears flapping in the breeze that meandered up from town, back warming in the rising sun. The Setter's eyes were closed, his attitude almost prayerful, and indeed, the litany of thoughts going through his head as Luther approached was very much like a prayer-chant: "Oh sun Oh sky Oh clouds Oh wind Oh grass Oh trees Oh hill Oh milkbone Oh bitch-in-heat Oh life is grand . . . Oh sun Oh sky Oh clouds . . ."

Luther came up to him slowly, not wanting to disturb him and a little afraid at the same time. Love, passionate love, as humans think of that emotion, is a rare occurrence among dogkind, yet Luther had heard that this Ruff had been in love not once but several times. One notorious incident, involving a Chow who had eventually run off with a Mastiff, had supposedly driven him a little mad . . . which left Luther to wonder if there were any sane philosophers on this Hill.

" . . . Oh trees Oh hill Oh milkbone Oh bitch-in-heat Oh—"

The Setter stopped abruptly as Luther came upwind of him. Ruff cracked an eyelid, studied the mongrel curiously.

"Name?" he asked, bluntly.

"I'm Luther," said Luther. "Are you—"

"Ruff!" Opening both eyes now, the Setter dropped to all fours and barked a cheerful greeting. "Well, well, Luther, so we finally meet."

"Finally?" Luther cocked his head. "You've heard of me?"

Another happy bark; Ruff would have laughed, if he could.

"Heard of you? *Heard* of you? Oh hell . . . I've been *telling* your damn story for the past month and a half."

III.

"I can't eat watermelon," Preacher said, tossing more wood into the fire. Outside the sun was coming up, but they were still damp and chill. "Nor fried chicken, either. Put me on a desert island with a watermelon patch and a chicken coop and I guess I'd starve to death."

"You're that afraid of the stereotype?" asked Jinsei.

"My *father* was afraid of the stereotype. Me, I'm afraid of what my father taught me to be afraid of."

Cowcliffes, one of three large rooms that opened off the main hallway of Risley's first floor, was deserted but for the two of them. They stretched out on sofa cushions around an open hearth; Calvin Coolidge had been hitched to a radiator out in the hall, where he made breakfast of the memos on the Risley Committee bulletin board.

"He's a wealthy man, my father," Preacher continued. "Nothing to hold a candle to Lion-Heart's folks, but still. And there are almost no role models for that situation. Even though he's not first generation—the money in the family goes back to a Madame C. J. Walker who made her fortune in hair care—he never really learned how to handle being rich and black at the same time. Books and movies aren't exactly full of helpful examples, know what I mean? So he's always been kind of offstep, and I inherited a lot from him."

Jinsei traced the lines of his palm with a finger. "How did you come to meet Ragnarok?"

"That—that was one of my Dad's 'notions.' We started taking in boarders—mostly white—around the time I was ten. Didn't need the extra income at all, you understand, my father just thought it was a great idea, giving shelter like that. Ragnarok was the last of them. He came up from North Carolina so broke he couldn't even pay what little rent we were asking, but my father didn't care, that made it even better, he took Rag in and practically adopted him. Even helped him get the scholarship to Cornell, and if you knew how Rag feels about charity, you'd understand how amazing that is."

"Why did he come up from North Carolina broke?" Jinsei pressed the subject gently. "Why didn't his own father help him pay for college?"

Preacher didn't answer, just stared at the fire. She tried another tack: "Did you hear what happened in front of the Straight the night of the CAAU party?"

"Can't say as I did."

She told him. Preacher looked grim but not surprised. "Jack Baron . . . that son of a bitch, he's got a very hard fall waiting for him one of these days. Almost too bad Ragnarok didn't let him have it."

"I know it's personal," Jinsei went on, "but I'd really like to know what Ragnarok meant about his father selling his soul to the Devil. He wouldn't tell me, just said something about a 'Georgia bedsheet salesman.' I thought about that, and it almost sounds as if he was saying . . . well, that he was saying his father was . . ."

"Klansman," Preacher finished for her, at the same time coming to a decision. "Klan Ghoul, rank and file member." He squeezed her hand. "It's all right, talking about the Klan isn't one of my taboos. Ku Klux, you know that's from the Greek word for circle?"

"But I thought the Klan didn't exist anymore."

"Oh hell, sure it does, Lady. They may not have a goddamn five-million-person membership like they did in the Twenties, but I'll be stone dead surprised if they ever totally disappear. You walk out of this dorm right now, a twenty-mile hike'd take you to the door of an active klavern."

"That's . . . very hard to believe."

"Lots of things are hard to believe, lady. . . ."

IV.

"Did you really come here in search of Heaven?" Ruff asked, making his way south along the face of the Slope. Luther kept pace with him.

"I know it must sound silly," the mongrel replied, "but I really hoped—"

"It doesn't sound silly at all," the Setter interrupted him. "Not to these shaggy ears. I think it's *marvelous*. It's got all the right ingredients for an epic: courage, determination, nobility, a strong sense of pathos—"

"An epic?"

"Hmm, well . . . the story about your travels going around now isn't quite of epic proportions, but give it time and some more embellishment and you'll be amazed. A dog scenting after Heaven! You're the stuff that legends are made of, Luther."

"Legends? But wait, I didn't come looking for Heaven so I could be famous."

"Doesn't matter. Most of the famous canines in history had no special wish for recognition. Rather, it was their desire, their obsession over something *other* than fame that made them famous. The tragic love of Rufus and Juliet; Spot driving the pack rats out of the temple; Dog Quixote tilting at fire hydrants; The Romance of the Bone . . ."

"I don't know any of those stories," Luther said. "What's the last one again?"

"The Romance of the Bone," Ruff repeated. "An epic's epic, really: in addition to standing well on its own it serves as an allegory for almost every story ever told."

"Can you tell it to me?"

"Not now. It's very long—it takes three days to tell from beginning to end, and because of that there's a ritual to the telling. It's an event, really. Who knows, maybe later in the year . . . but for today I can at least tell you something *about* it. The hero of the story is called Everydog, and he is in search of his lost love, the Bone—Wait! Hold up a second!"

They were at the far end of the Slope now, beneath Willard Straight Hall by the loading dock for Oakenshields Dining. A delivery truck with a chrome rooster for a hood ornament had backed up to the dock, and a fat man was offloading a stack of bloodstained white boxes. Even with the wind blowing in the wrong direction it was not hard to guess what they contained.

"Time for brunch," Ruff announced, licking his chops.

Luther looked at the fat man. "Will he give us scraps?"

Again, Ruff would have laughed if he could. Instead, leaving Luther to gape at his actions, the philosopher sprang forward, charging up to the dock. He took the trucker by surprise; barreling between the human's legs he caught him off balance, sending him sprawling, then hurled himself at the stack of boxes. The top one tottered free and broke open, spilling uncooked chicken halves across the dock.

"Jay-sus!" exclaimed that fat man, thinking at first that a low-flying whirlwind had struck him. It was only when Ruff had grabbed a chicken between his teeth and trampled back over the fellow—squashing a pudgy nose beneath a damp paw—that he realized what was afoot.

"Oh fowl," chanted the Setter as he raced back to Luther, while a steady gush of human profanities flooded the dock behind him. "Oh fearless chicken thief Oh thundering heart Oh drool Oh brunch Oh life is *so* grand—"

V.

Sitting in front of the fire while the sky brightened outside, Preacher told Jinsei what he knew about Ragnarok's childhood—not all that much, for Ragnarok had never been one to open himself up, even to the closest of friends. Preacher told her about Ragnarok's father, Drew Hyatt; about the loss of Drew's wife to bone cancer when his son was only two; about his slow descent into a lonely and hateful obsession as his son came of age. Most of all, he told her about the Klan, an organization that was dangerous not, as Jinsei had always thought, because of its embodiment of an almost mythological evil, but dangerous, rather, because the evil it embodied lay tooth and jowl with human nature.

"And Ragnarok was quite the little Klanster at first, when he was growing up. You figure it'd have to be like the Boy Scouts with a few extras tossed in. Cross-burning must beat hell out of merit badges, especially for a kid."

"How could he break out of that?" Jinsei asked. "Being raised that way. He *changed*, I know he changed, but how?"

"Don't really know." Preacher shrugged. "Could be something big happened to help shake him up, but knowing the way he is now, I always figured it was just like that old saying, you can't keep a good man down. Sooner or later I guess he was *bound* to shake it off, you know, unless it killed him first. 'Course he's still one of the most violent people I'm likely ever to know personally, but more than once I've been glad to have him on my side in a fight."

"You're not the only one."

"Right. You understand, though, that's one thing he's never made peace with himself on, and I suppose he'd go through torture before he ever admitted there was the least bit of good in him. Kind of a strange fellow to be best friends with sometimes, I have to admit."

Jinsei made no response to this.

"What're you thinking?" Preacher asked, after a moment.

In answer, she resumed tracing the lines of his palm with a finger.

"Problem," she said.

Preacher nodded, closing his hand over hers. "Problem," he agreed.

VI.

The Irish Setter tore into his purloined chicken. Luther looked on enviously but received no offer to join in; though a good dog, Ruff let nothing come between him and his food.

"The Romance of the Bone," he began, "is the epic tale of Everydog's search for his lost Bone. Not a dry bone, not a bleached bone, but a Bone"—he ripped the drumstick free of the chicken carcass—"meaty and brown, crunchy with marrow, delicious on the tongue."

Trying hard not to drool, Luther asked: "That's his *love*, a Bone?"

"Well, it's a symbol. Everything in The Romance of the Bone is symbolic: the Bone isn't actually a lover, it *symbolizes* love. Though of course if you wanted to, you could make it symbolize almost anything that a dog would desire enough to go on a quest for. It could be love; it could be knowledge; it could even be the glories of Heaven itself. Desire, *obsession*, that's what the Bone really symbolizes, beyond all else."

"And does Everydog find it in the end?"

"Eventually. First there are trials, of course, dozens of enemies trying to keep him from his goal, all of them allegorical: he faces other dogs named Doubt, Fear, and Indecision, for example, a swarm of hornets called Rabies, a wild boar named Distemper. But at the last Everydog reaches the Ivory Butcher Shop where his Bone awaits him. . . ."

"And they live happily ever after?"

"For a minute. He finds the Bone, picks it up, savors it, and then, having tasted its splendor, wakes to find that the entire quest has been a dream."

"What!?" said Luther. "But that's such a *cheat!*"

"Not at all," Ruff told him. "It's a wonderful story."

"I bet Everydog wouldn't think so. Going through all that trouble, finally getting the Bone, and then having to wake up. That must have been terrible for him."

"That would depend on how he looked at it. What about you and your quest to find Heaven? Do you feel terrible that you didn't find it?"

"Of course I do! All the miles we walked, nearly getting killed by a pack of Purebreds—no offense—and now it turns out that we didn't even get away from the prejudice—"

"You look at it the wrong way, then," Ruff told him. "*I* first heard your story from Denmark, and I thought to myself, what a shame, but also, how wonderful. I retold the tale to some other dogs who came to me for entertainment, and they were amused, or stunned, or saddened, but they *enjoyed* it, every one of them."

"But what does that have to do with *my* feelings about it? What do I care if some stranger enjoys hearing about me?"

"Luther, Luther . . . the lesson of Everydog . . . the meaning of life . . ."

"Is what?"

"*It's* all *a story,*" the Setter exclaimed. "The whole world: Oh sun Oh sky Oh wind Oh trees Oh dogs and cats, it's *all* a story, a grand entertainment."

"An entertainment for who?"

"For *God*, silly. For God, for His Kennel, for Raaq, maybe."

Luther's eyes narrowed. "*Raaq* is entertained by torture and death . . ."

"And you think God isn't? You think He can't appreciate tragedy and horror? Life, with all its miseries and joys, is a story—or rather a Story—with God as the listener, and we mortals as the plot. Doesn't it make sense? And doesn't it explain why we can't keep the Bone for more than a moment, why the dream has to end so another can begin? Who could enjoy a Story where everyone was perfectly happy?"

"Crazy," said Luther, after this speech. "I was right, you philosophers are *all* crazy. I pity you, if that's what you think of God."

For a third time, Ruff would have laughed if he could.

"Pity *me*?" he said, crunching a chicken bone contentedly. "No, don't waste pity on me. The lesson of Everydog, the meaning of life, whether you believe it or not . . . it holds me up, elevates me. In the most terrible of times, with everything turned against me, I can marvel at the knowledge that my struggle is part of the Story. And I still suffer, that's part of the Story too, but the suffering is balanced by wonder . . . and my times of happiness become even more wondrous.

"No, don't pity me. Pity those who can't understand The Romance of the Bone, can't see the purpose behind the up-and-down plot of their lives . . . pity yourself, if you can't, other dogs if they can't, or cats, or sparrows, or Oh the beasts of the field, or even the Masters.

"Yes . . . even the Masters."

VII.

"How bad is it," Jinsei asked, "if I'm attracted to you?"

"About as bad as if I'm attracted to you," said Preacher. "Not so bad for us. But for Rag . . ."

"You think he'd take it really badly."

"Well hell, I'm no Psychology major, never had the bullshit tolerance to handle Freud, but it wouldn't surprise me. Rag talks a blue streak about women sometimes. But with Rag, the real way you know he wants something bad is, some part of him takes over and busts ass to make sure he *doesn't* get it. With you, first he steps in and saves the day from Jack Baron and his Rat buddies, it gets looking like you're more than just a little grateful, then tonight—*last* night—he asks you out and then gets drunk for the first time in a year, goes out of his way to be an asshole—"

"But I don't want him," Jinsei said. "Not as more than a friend. Maybe I thought I wanted more, that night with Jack . . . but I think it was just needing somebody at the time. I was more upset that night than I'd ever been before about anything, and Ragnarok was there. Before that night, though, when I first met the two of you, that day with Ginny Porterhouse—*you're* the one I thought about afterwards, not Ragnarok."

Preacher grinned. "Well well . . ."

"Don't," Jinsei stopped him, when it sounded as if he might make a joke. "Please don't. I know he's a good friend, and I don't want to see him hurt either, so if you think this would be a bad idea then fine. But don't make light of it.

"Fair." The grin took a step back; Preacher appeared to think it over, but his fingers were already twining and untwining in her hair, long before he spoke. "Discretion," he finally said, "discretion, I'm not so bad at that game. How about you?"

She leaned forward and kissed him, lightly, trying it out. She had wiped most of the cat-makeup off her face a while ago, but the faint impression of felinity that remained had an effect that was, well, not very conducive to further rational discussion. Jinsei drew back a little and they shifted position, Preacher's hand dropping from her hair to her back, stroking, one of her hands coming up to touch his face.

It was during the second, longer kiss that they realized they were not alone. A Greek tragician with a demonic sense of timing could not have arranged it better: Jinsei's gasp as she noticed Ragnarok standing in the Cowcliffes' archway, the suitably guilty expression of shock on Preacher's face as he too looked around, Ragnarok's usual lack of any identifiable expression, dark lenses, as always, hiding his eyes. The Black Knight held Preacher's longcoat in one hand, half outstretched like an offering, the tightness with which he gripped it the only clue to his feelings.

That he should be up and about at all, rather than crashed out at Tolkien House with several unconscious hours and a bad hangover still ahead of him, was miracle enough. That he should have come and found them, and at just this particular moment, was almost too much to accept. Jinsei and Preacher were frozen in place, speechless, all too aware of their hands on each other. Ragnarok was likewise unmoving, though he did sway a little on his feet, his body's bout with the alcohol far from over. He stared at them, and they back at him, for what might have been a full minute or more.

Then a door slammed somewhere and the tableau was broken. Preacher's longcoat dropped to the floor; Ragnarok's fist, empty, opened and closed twice. Then he was gone down the hall, something out of sight of the two lovers making a tremendous crash as it was knocked over. The slam of the front door as it was thrust open, not quite hard enough to break the glass; the hiss as it eased closed again. The gunning of a motorcycle, which had somehow not been heard in its approach.

After that, silence.

ALL-NIGHTER

I.

November passed quickly. A busy month for a University—many long tales could be told about what transpired between All Saints' Day and Thanksgiving, but a summary should suffice: George and Calliope's love affair continued while Preacher and Jinsei's blossomed; Hobart the sprite grappled with constant nightmares about The Boneyard while Luther the mongrel struggled against despair; Blackjack ate well and was in general one of the most content individuals in Ithaca.

Ragnarok became the scarcest Bohemian on The Hill. Following the tableau in Cowcliffes, he spoke to no other Minister or Grey Lady for weeks; there were scattered sightings of him, brief glimpses of a black-clad figure dodging quickly through the between-class throngs, but no contact. Lion-Heart posted sentries at a number of auditoriums where Ragnarok was due to attend lecture, but he either came in disguise or skipped entirely. Preacher and Jinsei's efforts to see him were similarly in vain.

The last Thursday of the month drew on, and those Cornellians who could manage it departed for a holiday at home with family and friends. Among those who remained on The Hill, though, were two people who had pressing business with each other, though they did not know it.

Mr. Sunshine did a lot of spare Typing that Thanksgiving weekend.

II.

"But why can't I come with you?" George asked, as Calliope packed her duffel bag.

"Oh, George . . . don't look so frightened. This isn't it. I'll be back in two nights, and I'm sure you can survive that long without me."

"I just thought we'd spend Thanksgiving together, is all. Mashed potatoes, Cornish game hens. . . ."

She smiled. "No turkey?"

"I hate turkey. You know that. You know everything about me, and nine times out of ten you feel the same way. Look, how can I be sure . . . I mean, you said it would hurt me when you finally left, make me feel like dying, and if you were to just take off for keeps now after telling me you'd be back, I . . ."

"I swear to you, George, I will come back this time." She faced him, took the silver whistle from about her neck and pressed it into his hand. "Here, wear this. It's good luck, and you can be sure I wouldn't leave without it even if I were planning to sneak out on you."

George absorbed this, then slipped the chain over his head and clutched the whistle tight in his fist, a gesture that would become compulsive over the next few weeks. "All right," he said, "all right. But what am I going to do all by myself tomorrow night?"

"Oh, I'm sure you'll find something," Calliope said. She kissed him on the tip of his nose. "Or something will find you."

And that was how George came to be shopping alone in Egan's Suresave Grocers the next morning, where he bumped into Aurora Smith. Actually she spotted him first; it was the first she'd seen of him since Halloween night, and so embarrassing was the memory of what had happened that she very nearly snuck by without saying hello. But George was in rare form that Thanksgiving morn: with two jars of Vlassic pickles, a gallon jug of milk, an impulsively selected slab of feta cheese, and a huge frozen bird balanced in his arms—he had not thought to get a grocery cart for himself—he cut an amusing figure, and when one of the pickle jars slipped with a crash to the floor and George yelled "Shit!" Aurora could not help but laugh.

"Vinegar splashes all over my new sneakers," George said to her by way of greeting, "and you get cracking up over it. Thanks a lot."

"Sorry, but you're *hopeless*, George!" She held her sides and struggled to gain control of herself. "Why don't you get a cart for all that?"

"Too practical. How you be, lady?"

When a fresh wave of giggles had subsided, Aurora told him: "Pretty good, really. Say, that's a funny-looking turkey."

"It's a goose," George explained. "They were all out of Cornish game hens."

"Having a quiet Thanksgiving with your girlfriend?"

"Alone, actually, Calliope took off for a couple days. Some kind of private business to take care of."

"Well that's not right," Aurora said. She paused as if to consider, and just then the milk jug began to slip from George's grasp. "Here, I'll carry that," Aurora offered, and grabbed it, only to have the other Vlassic pickle jar tumble to earth and shatter.

Now they both got laughing. An obviously displeased grocery boy appeared from behind a stack of three-liter Coke bottles and gave them the evil eye; the fellow seemed so upset over the broken pickle jars that George took pity on him, offering him the feta. "Protein," the storyteller said. "You won't be so pale."

Later, outside in the parking lot, their respective purchases packed carefully in non-slip grocery bags, Aurora and George lingered and talked for a few moments.

"So how come you aren't back home in Montana for Thanksgiving?" George asked her.

"Wisconsin," she corrected. "I was supposed to go back yesterday, but when Brian and I got to the airport there'd been some sort of a computer mix-up. The reservation desk only had one ticket for us, and every flight between now and Sunday was booked solid. I made Brian go by himself."

"You miss going home?"

"Well . . . Christmas will be here soon enough. My father seemed kind of upset when I called to say I wouldn't be coming. He's been wanting to talk to me about something since August, but we've never gotten the chance. . . . Listen, would you like to come up to Balch tonight and have dinner with me? I can pick you up; I've got Brian's car."

"Can I bring my goose?" George asked. "Not to insult your turkey, or anything, but I wanted something greasy."

"Tell you what: you give me the goose, I'll put it in the oven right next to my turkey. We'll have leftovers for the next month."

"You've got a deal."

"Good then," she said. "You want a lift home right now?"

"Sure thing."

She led the way to Brian Garroway's car, which—though George did not recognize the make—was a very practical-looking vehicle; it was brown, and probably got great gas mileage. They stowed their groceries in the back trunk and Aurora had wandered around to the driver's side to let herself in when a thought seemed to strike her.

"Oh hey . . ." she told him, "we won't be eating alone tonight. My friend Cathy Reinigen stayed up too, so she'll be with us."

"Fine," said George. Aurora's tone was innocent enough, yet for some reason he was reminded for the first time of their intimacy in the Garden, and Calliope's question after: *Did you enjoy it?*

Hiding a sudden blush, he climbed into the car beside her and they drove off.

III.

Catherine Anne Reinigen turned out to be a real trip and a half, to use a Bohemian expression. They ate dinner in her room, a cavernous double with an immaculately clean white carpet. The door was plastered with a collection of tracts, Bible passages, and religious artifacts—George was frankly surprised not to see the finger bone of St. John taped up beside the memo board. Every inch of space on the wall above Catherine's bed was likewise filled, and featured a series of pen-and-ink drawings of the Holy Saviour. An amazing variety of representations was displayed: the traditional Western Jesus with long hair and beard, Jesus as a black man, Jesus in a three-piece suit handing out Bibles to stockbrokers on Wall Street, a hippie Jesus playing electric guitar alongside Jimi Hendrix, Jesus sitting in the backseat of a Brooklyn cab, Jesus' face framed by a television screen, an American Gothic–style portrait of Jesus standing in front of a farmhouse with a hoe in his hand and Mary Magdalene at his side, and—this one George found particularly interesting—Jesus as a Teamster.

"So where do you get your inspiration?" Cathy Reinigen asked him during dinner. This was a not untypical question for someone first meeting him, and George gave his not untypical response: he made something up on the spur of the moment.

"Roses," he told her. "Every morning I have a half dozen fresh-cut white roses brought to my house. Of course when I was younger I couldn't afford roses, so I kept a window box full of poppies instead, but I've moved up since then."

"Roses? What do you do with roses?"

"Sniff them, naturally. Your olfactory cortex—your smelling center—is located just off the Dinsmore lobe in the right hemisphere of your brain, which is where all creative thinking takes place. You studied this in Bio, didn't you? The idea is if you stimulate the old olfactory, it sort of gives a jump start to the Dinsmore lobe, and all at once you're coming up with story ideas faster than you can write them down. Now I know how strange that must sound, but it's documented fact; Hemingway did African violets three times a day, except when he was boxing."

"That's amazing."

"That's reality," said George, keeping a poker face. He took a side-glance at Aurora and saw from her smug expression that she wasn't buying any of it, but she seemed amused by the tale, which was just as good.

"So tell me," Cathy went on. "Your latest novel, *The Knight of the White Roses* . . . is that title an allusion to—"

George nodded. "Clever. You found me out."

"Well," Cathy smiled, feeling enlightened. "I guess that just shows how limited critical analysis really is. I never would have figured that out in a classroom."

"That's why I don't trust English teachers," George confided. "Did you read the book?"

"The *Knight*? Yes, that one I read. It's a shame my roommate isn't here—

she was going to eat with us, but she's out on a date—and she's in love with every one of your novels."

"What did you think of the one you read?"

"Me? . . . I . . . that is to say . . ." She hesitated, as if groping for a polite response.

"She thought it was great," Aurora spoke up. "She told me so. It got her Dunsmore lobe all excited."

"*Dinsmore*," George corrected.

"No, no," Aurora recorrected. "*Dunsmore*. That's the lobe in the left hemisphere that *enjoys* the story. You must have learned about it in Bio; it's due south of the optic cortex. If you stimulate it with enough good literature your nose starts to grow longer."

"Oh yeah," George said. "Now I remember."

"I *liked* your novel," Cathy inserted, glancing confusedly at the both of them. "It's just that I was sort of . . . disappointed in the way you handled a few of the characters."

"Like who?" George asked seriously.

"Well, for example, Abbot Mattachine."

"But the Abbot was a good Joe. I thought the way I had him save the Knight from the tax collectors was pretty nifty."

"There was that business with him and the choirboys, though . . ."

George shrugged. "Lots of abbots had business with choirboys. Even a fantasy novel has to touch base with reality once in a while."

Cathy Reinigen cleared her throat. "It's not that I'm a moralist-reconstructionalist," she said, borrowing a phrase from a long-ago freshman seminar. "And I certainly wouldn't want to infringe on your notions of realism by insisting that characters should always be properly punished; real people get away with crimes every day. It's just that to me, the very best stories are those where the author gets a strong moral message through no matter what actually happens to the characters in the end. Do you understand?"

George nodded. "The big problem with messages like that," he told her, "is that you can make them clear as a bell, in letters ten feet high, impossible to miss, and readers still don't get the point. Shakespeare was a kick-ass storyteller, but look what's happened to *Romeo and Juliet*. Almost everyone forgets that the play was a *tragedy*. Tragedy, that means Fate doesn't like you, but nine times out of ten it's you who makes the final screwup. These days we call a lovesick man a 'Romeo'; you'd have to be pretty sick, though, to really want to *be* Romeo. He was a punk kid; in the story he kills two people in a passion and he's directly responsible for the death of a third. In the last scene he kills himself over the loss of a woman who isn't even dead, and then she wakes up and follows his example. The double suicide is the unforgivable part; it's not touching, it's dumb. They gave up hope, and that means it's not even a love story, it's an immaturity story."

"Mature people despair," Aurora suggested.

"Never completely," George insisted. "Mature people make mistakes, they have breakdowns, they lose, but they never stop looking for the chink in the wall of Fate. The only time they suicide is to save another life; otherwise it's just quitting. That's a children's escape."

"But Romeo and Juliet loved each other so deeply—" Cathy began.

"If that were true," said George, "they both would have come out of the tomb alive. Even Juliet's real death wouldn't have broken Romeo permanently. Hell, do you think Abbot Mattachine would have cashed it in over the death of one choirboy, when there were so many others in the world?"

"Well now that," Cathy Reinigen said, beginning to look annoyed, "that is an entirely different case."

"Oh, but it *isn't*," George insisted. "That's the other thing you've got wrong . . ."

They argued back and forth about it for some minutes more without resolving anything until Aurora tactfully changed the subject. No matter, it had been enough; Mr. Sunshine must surely have overheard them, for what happened later in the evening seemed a most amazing coincidence, the ever-moving wall of Fate bending itself to get George and Aurora alone again, unchaperoned.

IV.

A thick fog—another reminiscence of Lothlórien, but cold and damp, as genuine November fogs tend to be—rose up to cover The Hill shortly after nightfall. Some time after that three figures emerged from a door beneath the Balch Arch. Following dessert Aurora had suggested, much to George's surprise, that they all go down to the Fevre Dream in Collegetown for a beer. Even more to his surprise, Cathy Reinigen agreed wholeheartedly with the idea, offering to pay for the pitcher.

They crossed Fall Creek Bridge and meandered through the Arts Quad where the statues of Ezra Cornell and Andrew White kept their vigil, patiently awaiting midnight when perchance a passing virgin would free them to take a brief stretch. George and the two women were several hours too early to make the test, but George saluted Ezra all the same.

Then they were passing between Olin and Uris Libraries, both dimmed for the holiday. There in the shadows beneath the great Clock Tower stood two figures, holding hands. The fog parted fortuitously just then, and a chance ray of moonlight revealed that the figures were, in fact, two men.

"That is *disgusting*," Cathy Reinigen pronounced, when they were safely out of earshot. Aurora remembered her mother's first, and only, visit to Cornell; George, usually a bear for argument, let the moment pass. Though it didn't, really.

As the trio drew nearer to Collegetown, an astonishing number of same-sex couples began materializing out of the fog, most of them extremely taken with each other. Aurora noted this with interest; George stared openly (for he always stared at everything); but Cathy Reinigen took it as a personal affront, as if the law of averages had conspired to set up a visual gauntlet for the express purpose of making her uncomfortable. Which was close enough.

"Maybe this wasn't such a good idea after all," Cathy said, as they reached the Fevre Dream and spied two women necking in the front seat of a parked van. It was the sixth lesbian couple they had come across in less than ten minutes. George admired them greatly, for they were content in and of themselves, but his contemplation of them was interrupted by a blurred form that came bursting out of the bar. It was the Bohemian Love-Minister Aphrodite, and she had Panhandle slung over her shoulder like a war bride.

"Evening, George," she greeted them, "everybody. Hey, hurry on in, drinks are seventy-five cents until nine o'clock."

That said, she spun on her heel and rushed off down the block, still carrying the unconscious Panhandle.

"Well thank God for *normal* people," said Cathy, morally vindicated. Still bracing herself against possible improprieties, she thrust open the front door of the Fevre Dream and stepped inside.

Smiling discreetly at each other, George and Aurora followed.

V.

Though the members of Ithaca's gay community never understood why, the hand of Fate pointed in their direction that night. The town rednecks stayed home and bloated themselves on turkey and football. Among the Community, connections were made; the weak found courage, the lonely found companionship, and one and all found good fortune.

Over on East Hill, a seventeen-year-old football prodigy admitted to his parents during dinner that his unseen steady girlfriend was actually the team's wide receiver, a fleet-footed beanpole named Johnathan. Now it so happened that the football prodigy's father was a devotee of Lyndon LaRouche, and thus his first thought—actually more of a reflex—was to beat the living hell out of his son. But even as he rose out of his chair, a spoon clenched in one chubby fist, he lost his balance and pitched face first into a bowl of lumpy mashed potatoes. Inexplicably struck blind, the old man was carted off raving in an ambulance, and spent three sightless days as a guest in Tompkins County Hospital. Finally, at sunrise of the third day, he awoke from a deep slumber crying, "All right, all right!" Instantly his sight was restored. He went home, embraced his son, and thereafter did good works.

Down by the shores of Cayuga Lake, three men who had been infected by the AIDS virus were walking in Stewart Park when they heard a hidden lyre playing a distinctly Greek variation of a Calvinist hymn. At the sound the disease fled their bodies, entering into a nearby pack of squirrels who went mad and cast themselves into Cayuga's waters. Likewise four thugs in pursuit of a lone lesbian had their bashing days brought to a premature end when a sewer gas explosion blew the roof off a (thankfully unoccupied) Kentucky Fried Chicken restaurant, showering the thugs with fire, brimstone, and extra-crispy wings.

This sort of thing went on throughout the night, and the only real disappointment came when a mysterious one-block power outage forced the early closing of Jenny's New Wave, the gay bar downtown. But the problem was easily solved; their spirits undimmed, the patrons relocated to The Hill— to the Fevre Dream. And the upshot of that was that Cathy Reinigen spent a good deal of time hiding out in a locked stall in the women's room, while George and Aurora, untroubled, took advantage of the bargain price on mixed drinks and got quietly trashed.

"Tell me why," Aurora asked over her third Tequila Sunset (she had tried one at the Halloween party and fallen in love with them), "you don't like Christians."

"What makes you think I don't like Christians?"

"Little things. They way you looked at the drawings on Cathy's wall."

"I loved those drawings," George said truthfully. "Wish I had a book of them."

"The way you act around Brian sometimes."

"Well now, with Brian Garroway you're talking about a two-way street. He's got a way of acting around *me*."

"I know."

"With me," George added, "what you're basically dealing with is the Baskin-Robbins theory of Christianity."

"The what?"

A low chuckle rumbled from an adjoining table, where a mountain of a man sat with five beer mugs arrayed in front of him like toy soldiers.

"The Baskin-Robbins theory," the mountain said, speaking in a rich bass. "Thirty-one Flavors. Disliking mint chip doesn't mean you boycott the entire store."

"Exactly," said George.

"Nonsense," replied the mountain. "You are a storyteller, George, and all storytellers are liars and prejudiced. In your case the prejudice happens to be for outcasts, which puts you in a natural opposition to any organized religion. You also have delusions of godhood and don't like anyone ridiculing your theories, most of which are romantic trash."

"This," George explained to Aurora, "is Rasputin."

"The Queen of Hearts," Rasputin added with a nod. "Tell me, has he fed you the one about Romeo and Juliet yet?"

Aurora smiled, charmed, as most people were, by Rasputin's unabashed rudeness. "Yes," she said, "he's mentioned them."

"No doubt you were discussing homosexuality. He has a writer's fixation about that. George, you see those two dykes over there?" He jerked his thumb at a pair of women in checked flannel shirts who sat at the bar arguing with Stainless Marley.

"I see them."

"Do you think they would make it out of your Shakespearean tomb alive?"

"Sure. Why not?"

"You see?" Rasputin looked triumphantly to Aurora. "He doesn't even know the ladies in question, and already he's granting them nobility and strength of character. What if I told you, George, that they were the two biggest neurotics in New York State, ready to fold their cards at the first sign of crisis?"

"Fuck that," said George. "I like the way they smile at each other."

"Naturally. Be truthful—you fantasized about lesbians in your adolescence. That's the real story."

"You've got me pegged, Raspy."

"Hmmph . . . liar."

"Christians can be outcasts," Aurora spoke up.

Rasputin cocked an ear. "Beg pardon, my dear?"

"I said Christians can be outcasts, just as much as anybody else." She fished beneath the collar of her blouse and brought out a tiny golden cross on a chain. "Do you have any idea how some people react when they see this? Unless you're obviously wearing it just for fashion they get nervous; mention God as more than a concept and the conversation ends like someone pulled a plug."

This brought another low chuckle. "That's the spirit! Well spoken—take it from Rasputin, my dear, you keep talking like that and you'll have him eating out of your hand in no time."

With a final nod, Rasputin dismissed them and left the conversation as abruptly as he had entered it. Focusing his attention back on the rest of the room, he raised a beefy hand; at this signal five lithe choirboys in silk shirts appeared from various corners of the bar and replaced his beer mugs with slopping-full champagne glasses. It was strange.

"You have a point, you know," George told Aurora, looking at the little cross. "But I promise I won't pull the plug if you start talking more than concept. It's just that I have a hard time believing God only wrote one Book. Hell, I've got three novels under my belt and I'm not even especially hot shit."

"Oh, I'd say you're at least warm shit," Aurora said seriously (and seriously not intending any insult, no matter how it sounded). "As for God, I don't claim to know if the Bible is all She wrote or not. In fact, there are a lot of things I don't claim to know."

"Then you're not mint chip," George pronounced, "and I can deal." He raised his glass in a toast, then paused. "Did you say 'She?'"

Aurora twitched her nose mischievously and sipped her Tequila Sunset. "Maybe," she said. "Will you put me in one of your stories?"

"What kind of story?"

"A fantasy, like *The Knight*. You remember the woman in the enchanted forest?"

"The one who turned into a grizzly bear when the moon rose?"

"Yes," Aurora said, "but never mind the grizzly bear part. That's the kind of character I'd want, sort of off the beaten track."

"Sort of outcast?"

"Maybe." She toyed with her cross.

"You should keep wearing that," George told her. He let one of his own hands stray to Calliope's whistle.

"Who knows?" said Aurora. "I might get a bigger one."

"Good. Can I ask you a personal question?"

She twitched her nose again. "If you promise to put me in a story."

"It's a deal."

"OK, shoot."

"How did you fall in love with Brian Garroway?" George asked. "He's mint chip to the core, or at least he seems to be. I don't see the attraction."

Aurora first laughed, then fell silent, searching for words. It promised to be a long and difficult explanation, but she was spared by Rasputin, who chose that precise moment to vent a remarkable gout of wind. Big men as a rule cut big farts, but if flatulence were visible he would have literally been enveloped in a vapor cloud. Embarrassed, he tried to cover up his *faux pas* as best he could.

"*Hmmph!*" he grunted, pretending it had just been a noisy throat-clearing. "*Hmmph!*"

Holding her nose and grinning, Aurora glanced at him and then past him, her eyes fixing by chance on yet another pair of women at the bar. She gasped, and not from Rasputin's scent.

"My God," she whispered.

"My God what?"

"There." George looked where Aurora pointed, recognizing Bijou, a female guitarist who had once played with Benny Profane, and with her a dark-haired woman he did not know.

"That's Bijou," he said. "Rock musician. I know her, if you want to be introduced."

"No, no, not her. The other girl."

"Bijou's steady, probably. What about her?"

"That's Cathy's roommate."

"Cathy *Reinigen's* roommate?"

Aurora nodded. And then, out of nowhere, a smile bloomed on her face, stretched wide but not quite making it to a laugh.

"What?" said George.

"Oh my . . . I just realized."

"Just realized what?"

"Her name," Aurora said. She seemed to have trouble getting the words out, as if she actually were laughing.

"I don't know her name," said George.

"*I* know it."

"You know it?"

"Yes."

"Well, what is it?"

The smile stretched so wide George feared it might snap and hit him in the eye. Aurora's cheeks dimpled.

"Juliet," she finally managed to say. "Her name is Juliet."

"Hmmph!" grunted Rasputin.

VI.

Cathy Reinigen never did return from the bathroom. At some point she had simply evaporated; and it was funny, but George and Aurora felt no real compulsion to go looking for her. Instead, when Bijou and a few other free hands got up an impromptu rock jam at ten o'clock, they danced, and drank some more, and did not leave the bar until nearly closing time.

Outside the fog had tightened like a corset, and they were completely isolated as they walked back onto campus. It did not really surprise either of them when a horse trotted by out front of the Straight, for by that time they were past the point where anything could seem very odd. The filly walked right up to George, nuzzling his neck like an old acquaintance.

"She's beautiful," Aurora said, entranced. "Do you know her?"

"No, I don't think we've met." George's first thought was that she must belong to one of the Bohemians, but she wore no saddle—and he did not recognize her coloring, grey-olive coat with a midnight-black mane.

"We should go for a ride," Aurora suggested.

"Hmmm?" The storyteller was momentarily distracted; he had reached up to stroke the horse's head and discovered the mane had an unsettlingly familiar feel to it.

"We should go for a ride," repeated Aurora. She stepped up and patted the horse firmly. "That'd be all right with you, wouldn't it, girl?"

The horse whinnied in what Aurora took to be the affirmative; George struggled to catch up.

"Did you say take a ride?" he asked.

"Sure did." Aurora took a step back and then swung herself effortlessly onto the horse's bare back.

"But this horse's got no saddle," George protested.

"It's all right—I'll show you how to bounce."

"You'll show me . . . you're saying you know how to drive this animal?"

"Oh, come on, George," said Aurora. "I'm from *Wisconsin*, for God's sake."

That seemed to settle things. She offered him a hand and he reached up to grab it, a few of the black mane-hairs still tangled between his fingers. As their palms contacted George felt a jolt, and like magic he was behind her on the horse, his arms locked around her waist.

The ride that followed seemed to take both forever and no time at all. They ranged far, perhaps as far as the eastern reaches of the Cornell Plantations and back, and George discovered through the rhythm of the horse and the woman that bareback was not such a terrible deal at all. They seemed to flow through the night, caught up in an enchantment that bore them along on hooves of ivory . . . it was a pleasant journey. More is the pity, then, that George could never remember later—nor could Aurora—just when and where they finished their ride and turned the horse loose again.

Nor could either of them remember—and this was the real mystery—how they came to be in the top of the Clock Tower. When the Chimesmaster shook them awake at quarter to seven the next morning they had no recollection of climbing the long stair (How had they gotten through the locked door at the bottom?). They *did* remember being there in the open belfry, the high point of a pinnacle that rose above a world wrapped in gauzy white. They remembered talking for what seemed an eternity, talking about love, and dream, and Christianity, and Abbot Mattachine, and a dozen other scattered topics. They even remembered things that could not have been, such as a little old man (truly little—he stood no more than six inches high) who seemed to watch them for a long time before being startled away when Aurora tried to speak to him.

And what else happened?

Did they kiss? Perhaps. Perhaps the fog rose up in the deepest part of the night, scaling the walls of the Tower, turning back the hands of the Clock to the last night in October. Perhaps they did kiss, reenacting the scene in the Garden, each knowing (and not knowing) that their arms held the wrong (and the right) partner.

Did they love? No, probably not . . . not yet. George's heart still belonged to Calliope, and Aurora's (however mismatched it might seem) to Brian Garroway. But even where there is not true love there can still be the possibility of love, and that possibility, the knowledge of it, lingers long.

How long did they embrace? Who could say? Time has little meaning in the fog, and even less in enchantment. All that is certain is that they talked for a time, and held each other for a time, and then a woman was shaking them awake with musician's hands, to blink uncomfortably into the early sunlight.

The day after Thanksgiving had dawned clear and cold; autumn was rapidly approaching its end.

WINTER
DRAWS NEAR

Calliope returned, as promised, and for a brief while longer George's life resumed its normal pattern, however normal that might be. But in his heart of hearts he felt his time with her drawing short, and he loved her all the more intensely for that, knowing neither the day nor the hour when she would be taken away from him, and worse still, not knowing what would happen afterwards. Mornings he awoke to find a chill wind blowing across The Hill from the west, rattling windowpanes and hinting at the approach of something unpleasant.

Vanguard conservative William F. Buckley blew in on that wind one cloudy day. With a cold in his chest and a substantial lecturer's fee in his pocket, he took the stage at Bailey Hall before a packed audience to give a two-hour talk. Naturally certain campus elements could not pass up this opportunity to infringe on the right of free speech; the front rows of the auditorium were packed with Cornell Marxists, and as Buckley approached the podium they set up a cry of "Fascist swine! Oink! Oink! Oink!" in no less than seven East Bloc languages. Bohemian King Lion-Heart was infuriated by this; he had paid good capitalist money for the privilege of hearing Buckley out and then disagreeing with him. He raised his fist in defiance, and the Bohemains, Grey Ladies, and Blue Zebras began a counter-chant: "Bill! Bill! Bill!" The Young Republicans and reporters for the right-wing Cornell *Review* chimed in, perhaps not realizing, in their own fury, just who they were jumping into bed with. After a rousing chorus of "God Bless America," the Communists were at last cowed into quietude. Looking dazed but not unhappy, Buckley launched into a long address concerning the death of liberalism, the rise of the new right, and the tattooing of AIDS victims.

Wandering about the parking lot of Bailey after the end of the speech, Lion-Heart chanced to see Ragnarok driving off on his motorcycle. The King of Bohemia leaped to his horse and raced off in pursuit, nearly trampling Buckley, who stood among a press of admirers signing autographs. The chase was close at first—Ragnarok drove slowly, not noticing that he was being followed. Turning right on Tower Road, however, the Bohemian Minister of Defense glanced back over his shoulder, saw a purple-maned horse coming up fast, and gunned his throttle. Traffic forced him to slow up a moment later, but he made good his escape by doing a stunt-ride down the long stair that led behind and between Uris and Ives Halls. Lion-Heart tried to urge his horse into a full-gallop pursuit and wound up getting thrown for his trouble.

William Buckley wasn't the only thing blowing in the wind as far as politics were concerned. Fueled by fresh bad news from Pretoria, the Blue Zebra Hooter Patrol stepped up protests against University stock holdings in companies doing business with South Africa. On the last day of classes they gathered what allies they could and met out front of the Straight to build a symbolic House of Cards. They hoped to attract as many spectators as they could, but there were two attendees they never counted on.

One was a seller of lightning rods with a Master's Degree in Physics.

The other was Stephen Titus George, storyteller, kite-flyer, Patron Saint of Daydreams, and friend to the wind, who was about to earn his Master's Degree in the art of Writing without Paper.

THE FOOL, THE WIND
AND THE
LIGHTNING ROD SELLER

I.

Of course a certain number of scientists have to go mad, just to keep the tradition alive.

He was working on his Doctorate and he had a room of his own, which is an important thing for a man to have. Several levels beneath Clark Hall, the room was small, roughly cubical, and private. The door had three locks on it. Once upon a time he had been in ROTC, but even though he had quit the program the Army still loved him. The Army always loves Physics Majors; they build things.

He had built something, all right. He sat in a swivel chair in the late hours of the morning spinning slowly around, looking at the things in his room, especially *the* thing. Nearest the door, a yellow rain slicker hung on a plain wooden coatrack. Then there was his desk, and on top of it a number of interesting items: a computer that helped him count; a clutch of stuffed animals; his lightning rods, black iron straight and true; a leather satchel to carry them in; and, in a plastic bottle that might have once contained aspirin, his Gobstoppers.

He did not know where the Gobstoppers had come from, that memory had been misfiled somehow, though he suspected they were the gift of some woman, some Lady. He did know that they were wonderful. The Gobstoppers gave him dreams, wonderful dreams, and ideas; and they made him laugh, sometimes for very long periods. An irreplaceable treasure, he did not worry about running out of them, for the bottle never seemed to grow empty. He took them, and laughed, and had no fear.

He took one now. A smile bloomed on his lips and he reached out to pet one of the animals.

"Tigger," he said, lifting the rag-stuffed toy out from between Pooh and Piglet. "Tigger, Tigger, Tigger."

Holding it, still petting it, he spun round again in his chair, focusing on the red wagon, the child's wagon, that occupied one bare corner of the room. Bolted onto the back of the wagon was a crude tail of twisted hemp; painted on its side in white paint was the one word "Eeyore." Sitting inside the wagon was the thing he had built.

What the thing was exactly was hard to tell because it had been almost entirely covered by yellow and black stickers reading DANGER—RADIATION with the nuclear symbol stamped below the words. The thing was lumpy, halfway between a cylinder and a sphere, squat like a frog. A digital timer poked out of the sea of radiation stickers near the top.

"Tigger," the Doctoral Candidate—who had visions of being a lightning rod salesman as well as a Physicist—said, putting Tigger in the wagon too. Then he put Piglet next to Tigger, but left Pooh on his desk, looking forlorn. He bent to the digital timer, fiddled with it.

Andy Warhol had said that there would come a day when everyone in America would be famous for fifteen minutes. But a Doctoral Candidate surely deserves more than the average mortal, so he gave himself a full hour, pressed a button to start the countdown.

He put on his rain slicker and a pair of yellow boots produced from a drawer, double-checked a flyer (RALLY OUTSIDE THE STRAIGHT, 11:30 A.M.) and gave Pooh a parting pat on the head.

"Gonna make it rain, Winnie" he said. Then he slung his satchel full of lightning rods over his shoulder and, pulling the red wagon behind him, he walked out, not even bothering to lock the door as he marched off to collect his share of celebrity.

II.

The weather outside was cold, snow promised but not yet delivered. Actually, with the air still as a whisper it was not a bad day for an outdoor rally, though only a fool would think of kite-flying on such a morning.

The Blue Zebras had secured the main door of the Straight and set up a podium and microphone on the steps. They had put together an impressive selection of speakers and hoped to draw a respectable crowd even with final exams so close (like it or not, political consciousness on campus always tended to drop during the end-of-semester squeeze). But what most likely drew the largest number of semi-interested bystanders was not the list of speakers, or the informative pamphlets passed around before the start of the rally, but rather the House of Cards.

The Cards were oversized, three-foot-long playing cards cut from stout cardboard, and because of what they symbolized they were all black Aces or Eights, the Dead Man's Hand. One of the Zebras who had done time in the

Architecture School had designed the House to look shaky without actually being so. About eight feet high overall, it was topped by an extra-large ace of spades on which had been set a scale-model conference table surrounded by figures representing the Cornell Trustees voting on a stock resolution. Below the neck the figures were normal, but their heads had been replaced by various fruits and vegetables. A cabbage head led the vote.

"CORNELL'S INVESTMENT POLICY" read a cardboard plaque at the foot of the House. Higher up a small banner strung between two Eights shouted "DIVEST NOW!" Passersby both nodded and shook their heads at the structure, but most were intrigued enough to stay. A bipartisan crowd of nearly a hundred had gathered by the time eleven-thirty rolled around and Fantasy Dreadlock stepped to the mike. She studied the assembly, pleased at the variety she saw.

She opened her mouth to speak, but it was precisely then that the Doctoral Candidate trundled into view with his wagon, clutching a lightning rod in one hand and screaming that he was going to make it rain.

III.

At ten to noon George was once again on the Arts Quad between the two statues, assembling a kite, the same kite, in fact, that he had first flown on a late day in August while a St. Bernard watched him. The Bernard was nowhere to be seen this morning; Calliope was at George's shoulder, though, and he wouldn't have noticed the dog anyway.

They had risen early, Calliope announcing over breakfast that she wanted to see how George called the wind. And so they had climbed The Hill, first taking a long walk downtown, a rare event for the usually house-bound couple. Calliope's silver-threaded cloak had somehow sprouted a hood, partially hiding her face, though once she had caught the gaze of a passing biker. The fellow had gasped in awe and gone down in a crashing tumble of arms, legs, and Schwinn.

"Now like I said," George told her, fitting the crosspieces into place, "the kites Uncle Erasmus and I had weren't diamonds, they were box kites, huge rectangular things with tie-dyed cloth stretched on the frames. Erasmus said he loved box kites best because they looked like something that oughtn't be able to fly at all. . . ."

He went on, assembling and talking, caught up in the story of that childhood day, and he'd actually got the kite all together before realizing that Calliope was no longer beside him. Startled, he looked around, called her name, and found his gaze being drawn toward a press of people at the southwest corner of the Quad. Though it was the middle of a class period, a large body of frightened-looking people were outside and on the move, appearing along the asphalt between Olin and Uris Libraries, entering the Quad and crossing it to put some distance between themselves and whatever it was they left behind. An equally sizable group—curious rather than scared—moved in the opposite direction, trying to get a glimpse of what was up. Where the two groups came together they bottlenecked, became one struggling mob.

Calliope stood just at the fringe of the bottleneck. She allowed George to see her, smiled at him, winked, and melted into the mass of people.

"Hey," George said. "Hey."

He dropped the kite and went after her, hurrying but still catching a few bits and pieces from the refugees who streamed past him. Two men in Zeta Psi blazers blipped in and out of earshot, one insisting to the other: ". . . there's no way, it can't be, don't worry . . . there's no way. . . ."

Into the press of the crowd, shouting her name now, while others around shouted to know what was going on, someone had a *what* in front of the Straight? The storyteller was buffeted back and forth, turning, disoriented, until all at once two things happened.

The first was that he broke through the bottleneck,found himself at the top of the slope looking down at the Straight, and more specifically at the Doctoral Candidate, who stood alone with his wagon inside a police cordon, while outside the cordon a diverse crowd of Cornellians tried to decide whether to run for the valleys or stay and watch.

The second was that Calliope was behind him, laying her hands lightly on his shoulders, making him start.

"God," George said. "God, don't ever do that."

"Relax, George." She touched his neck in a way he liked and he did relax, leaning back into her, one hand clutching the whistle around his neck. Her breath in his ear.

"What the hell, Calliope." He watched the scene out front of the Straight, some part of his mind trying to understand it. "What the hell, I thought you said you wanted to see how I called the wind."

"I do," she assured him. She reached around from behind him, pressed an object into his hands. The kite. "I do, but here's something more interesting."

People continued to struggle in both directions, but now no one bumped into them. No one blocked their view, either. George kept looking down the slope.

"What's happening here?" he asked.

In answer she produced another object, set it on his head. Cowboy hat. "Looks like trouble in Dodge City," Calliope said. "Town needs saving."

"What . . ."

"Writing without paper," she whispered, and kissed him twice. The first kiss was on the side of his neck, soft, electric. For the second he turned, caught it full on the lips, and after that he would have jumped from the Bell Tower if she'd asked him to.

Would it work . . .

I never tried. Depends on the circumstances.

"Writing without paper," she whispered again, releasing him. "A *lot* of lives might depend on it, George." She pointed down to the Straight, down at the Doctoral Candidate. "Trouble," she said. "Fix it."

"Sure." He clutched the whistle in sudden fear. "You will wait here, won't you? I mean . . ."

"I'll be watching," Calliope promised, truthfully. "Now you go on."

A third kiss to send him on his way, just like that. And it did not seem at all absurd or surprising, not after living for months with this strangest and most beautiful Lady, to go trooping down into some sort of confrontation of which he knew nothing, looking and feeling like Wild Bill Hickock with a dragon kite in his hands. He held the kite in front of him like a shield, Calliope's last kiss still playing on his lips, and people got out of his way, the taste of her on his tongue, hands of the Tower Clock inching toward high noon.

Writing without paper, George thought. *Sure. Easy.*

A few pebbles rattled beneath the soles of his sneakers, reminding him of spurs.

IV.

The police cordon gave the Doctoral Candidate and his red wagon a fifty-foot circle of breathing room so he wouldn't get nervous. At the edge of this circle stood an assortment of Cornell Safety and Ithaca City Police, thirteen in all. There was also a police psychologist—whom the Doctoral Candidate refused to notice—but requests for a bomb specialist and a Special Weapons team had so far gone unanswered.

Despite the fact that the digital timer was clearly visible—00:20:22, it now read—and despite the obvious implication of the radiation stickers the Doctoral Candidate had plastered all over his invention, a surprising number of people had decided to hang out and see what happened. The Bohemians had gone so far as to throw together an Apocalypse Picnic on the grassy knoll above the Campus Store. Lion-Heart watched the action through a pair of opera glasses, sipped Midori from a shot glass, and arranged a chain bet as to whether they'd all be vaporized or not. Each Bohemian made one bet that they would, and another that they wouldn't, the individual bets forming a chain. If they were all still alive in twenty-one minutes, they would pass a five-dollar bill around in a circle.

"Gonna make it rain!" the Doctoral Candidate screamed, shaking the lightning rod. "Make it rain *fire*, see if I don't!"

He had been saying more or less the same thing, with little variation, for the past thirty minutes. He strutted about, sometimes getting a good distance away from his wagon and his digital toy, but in the hand that did not hold the lightning rod he clutched what looked suspiciously like a remote control transmitter, the button on it a traditional panic red. It was just a guess, since he had not bothered to explain his device or his motives, but it seemed likely that pressing the button would end the countdown prematurely, clicking the timer right to zero.

"We can't just shoot him," Doubleday said, sounding disappointed.

"Can't reason with him, either," sniffed the police psychologist. "Not if he won't even *listen* to me."

"God, God . . ." Nattie Hollister stood with them too. The Chief of Police and a member of the University administration made it a quintet. "What are the odds," asked the Chief, "that it's a real nuke?"

"Please," the University official pooh-poohed, "this is an *Ivy League* institution. We don't *do* nuclear weapons here."

"Be hard to get the plutonium," suggested Nattie Hollister. "Unless they've got some in one of the labs up here. But even without real atomics, a Bomb's still got a high-explosive trigger,and hell, I'm sure the chemistry labs up here have the ingredients for—"

"But he's Physics, not Chemistry, right?" said the Chief. He glanced at the University official. "That's what *you* said."

"Still . . ." said Hollister.

". . . we might not have a nuclear explosion," Doubleday concluded for her, "but we could still have a *high* explosion. Which would be bad."

"Nineteen minutes." The Chief of Police rubbed his palms together lightly. "Got to do something."

"Cordon's not far enough back," Hollister observed. "If it's *any* kind of explosive . . ."

"Where's the damn Bomb Squad?" Doubleday wanted to know.

" 'Scuse me."

"Huh?"

They all turned; a sixth fellow had joined them. He wore the uniform of Cornell ROTC and had peach fuzz on his chin.

"I can do this guy for you," the ROTC offered.

The Chief of Police narrowed his eyes. "What's that?"

The ROTC fingered a pin on his uniform. "Rifle team. Get me a gun and I can do this guy. Ever see Robert DeNiro in *The Deer Hunter?*"

"Go home, bedwetter," the Chief dismissed him. To the others he began: "Now I . . . hey! Hey, wait a minute!"

Someone had broken through the cordon. No, not broken through— George had simply *walked* through, while the Safety officers nearest him happened to be looking the wrong way. By the time they noticed him he was well into the circle and headed for the Doctoral Candidate.

"I'll get him," Doubleday said, fondling his nightstick.

"No," ordered the Chief, feeling a sudden compulsion. "No, hold on. . ."

George kept walking, oddly confident, still feeling Calliope's kiss. He no longer held the kite in front of him; he held it at his side, like a six-gun. Seeing the storyteller coming, the Doctoral Candidate broke off in mid-shout and turned to face him down.

"Howdy," George said, feeling not the least foolish, somehow, as he adjusted his cowboy hat. "Where're you from, stranger? Originally, I mean."

The Doctoral Candidate flared his rain slicker and shook the tip of the lightning rod threateningly at George . . . but he did answer his question.

"Chicago," he said. Piglet and Tigger watched from the wagon. "Illinois."

The digital timer clicked over from **00:18:32** to **00:18:31**. And the Tower Clock began to chime.

High noon.

V.

Lion-Heart adjusted his opera glasses, watching the play with interest. "What the hell are you up to, George?"

"Ten bucks says it's interesting," offered the Top.

"What's your name?" George asked the Doctoral Candidate. The Candidate flared his rain slicker again.

"Christopher Robin," he said.

George nodded, indicating the stuffed animals. "Where's Pooh?"

"Pooh is home in bed," Christopher Robin replied, beginning to sound impatient. "He has a social disease."

"Sure he does. And what's that thing you're holding?"

The impatience backed off a bit. "It's a lightning rod." He shook the satchel. "I'm a *seller* of lightning rods."

"Oh, *Je*-sus," cried the police psychologist. "He's read Bradbury! I *hate* it when they've read Bradbury!" The Chief of Police gave him a look.

"So what's your name?" Christopher Robin asked George jabbing the lightning rod at him. "Eh?"

George smiled in sudden inspiration. "What if I told you I was A. A. Milne? You being Christopher Robin, you'd have to do what I said. I'd have written you."

"No, you didn't write me." Sounding disturbed at the prospect.

"Are you sure? Would you bet everything you had on it . . . Christopher?"

"I don't like you," Christopher Robin warned. "And you're no cowboy, either."

"True enough. Maybe you're not Christopher Robin, either."

"Hey, you watch it!" Angry, and also afraid. This time it was the remote control box he shook threateningly. "Don't mess, I'm nuclear, buddy!"

"Of course," said George. "And you're going to make it rain, right."

To himself he thought: *I am being glib, I am actually being glib with a potentially dangerous human being. And enjoying it. Maybe I'm as crazy as he is.*

But he did not feel crazy, or afraid, what he felt was Calliope's kiss, a lightness in his head, and a strong sense of control. Very much like the control he'd felt on the day of the box kites when he was a boy; not quite as strong a control as he had over a written story, but close, and getting closer.

Calliope, kissing him.

The timer, ticking over: **00:15:09.**

Trouble. Fix it.

"Tell you what I am," George continued. He had spied the House of Cards out the corner of his eye and his mind toyed with the possibilities of it. "What I am, Christopher, is a professional kite-flyer. Yes, it's true. And if you don't simmer down and start behaving right now, well, I'm just going to have to fly this kite of mine."

"No." A sliver of real panic.

"Yes."

"You can't."

"Yes I can."

"There's no wind!" Jabbing, jabbing with the lightning rod. "You can't fly a kite with no wind, that's a rule!"

George looked sideways at the sky. Holding the kite in one hand and the spool of twine in the other, he turned in place. Once.

"The kite'll fly," he promised. "If you can make it rain, I can make the wind blow. Fair is fair." He turned in place again.

"I hope someone's videotaping this," Lion-Heart said.

"Don't you do it!" Christopher Robin's thumb hovered over the red button on the box. "Don't you *dare* fly that kite!"

"So what if he flies it?" Doubleday shook his head. "Can we please do something, Chief?"

And George turned in place a third time. "Put the box down," he said.

"Oooooo, gonna make it rain, rain, *rain*—"

"Oh shit!" said Doubleday.

"Come on," said George, and the wind did. It started as a whisper but immediately began to rise. One second, and the touch of the breeze caught the Doctoral Candidate's breath in his throat, froze him with sudden fear, two seconds, stacks of undistributed Blue Zebra pamphlets began to scatter, three, the House of Cards shuddered, four, George's cowboy hat tipped up, considered flying off, five, it did, six, the kite was straining against its string, seven, the wind was halfway to a gale.

"Magic!" Z.Z. Top shouted, laughing. "Fucking magic, George!"

"RAIN!" Christopher Robin bellowed. His thumb descended on the button; George gave the House of Cards an encouraging glance.

A Card near the top bent under the wind force, causing the mock Trustee meeting to keel over. The cabbage head rolled free of its body, dropped four feet to where the **DIVEST NOW!** banner snapped forward like a slingshot.

The cabbage flew, spinning, on a collision course.

It struck the Doctoral Candidate on the wrist.

The remote control box flew out of his hand, broke apart on the ground.

The timer continued to count, **00:13:59** to **00:13:58.**

"No no no!" Christopher Robin cried, looking at the wreckage of his box. He felt a tug on his other hand; George had wrapped the kite string three full winds around the lightning rod and released it. The kite yanked it away, carried the metal rod up and over the top of the Campus Store, where it landed without injury among the Bohemians.

"Damn you!" said Christopher Robin, "You're ruining it! You're ruining my celebrity time!" He drew another lightning rod from the satchel, this one sharp at the end and bearing an uncomfortable similarity to a shish kebab skewer. "Ruining it!"

"Hey," George said, and a gigantic Ace of Spades slapped the Doctoral Candidate in the head. He regained his balance and went for George with murder in his eye. But now the banner hit him, wrapped around his face, blinding him, turning him. With a last cry of "Ruining it!" he thrust forward with the lightning rod and impaled not George, but the thing in the wagon.

"Oh shit!" Doubleday had time to say again inaudible beneath the wind, but there was no explosion, only the puncturing of radiation stickers and the crumbling of papier-mâché. The lightning rod went in with silken smooth-ness, and as the top poked out the far side it dislodged the digital timer. Attached to nothing except itself, the timer tumbled to the ground, knocking itself silly. **OH:PO:OH,** it began flashing steadily.

The wind slacked off as Christopher Robin slid to the ground, bawling, "Ruined it," he sobbed. "Ruined it." The holes in his invention bled what appeared to be little amber beads; Piglet and Tigger were being buried.

Jelly beans, George thought, as three Safety officers pounced on Christopher Robin. *No danger after all, just jelly beans.* He tasted one. Hunny.

The Bohemians were on their feet and cheering; Z.Z. Top and Wood-stock wrestled for possession of the lightning rod. The police, in particular the Chief, were eyeing George as if they wanted to arrest him or at least talk to him, but were afraid to try. Somewhere close a black-and-white mongrel dog was barking ecstatically. Everyone else, from the Blue Zebras to the police psychologist, looked as if someone had struck them over the head with a large board. Loaves and fishes would not have astounded them more.

"Well," George said, feeling tired. He rescued Piglet from the jelly beans, then took Tigger too; no one interfered with him. Giving Christopher Robin a parting nod he turned and gazed back up the slope to where he had left Calliope. Among all the people he could not spot her.

"No problem." He felt a little tickle of fear but that was all. He still had her reassurance, after all.

You can be sure I wouldn't leave without it even if I were planning to sneak out on you . . .

Still searching for her, he reached up to his throat to touch the silver whistle she had given him.

His hand closed on empty air.

CALLIOPE EXITS

She did not even go back to the house to collect her things. Her duffel bag lay packed and ready at the foot of Ezra Cornell's statue. The wind screamed as she slung the bag over her shoulder, but it did not touch so much as a single hair on her head.

"Poor George," she whispered, crossing the Quad. "Poor George."

By now he had discovered her disappearance; the Hurt was beginning. As always she felt a certain regret at this, but causing the Hurt was after all a large part of her Purpose. A long (but not infinite) string of broken hearts stretched out behind her, a similar (probably not infinite) string waited just ahead, that was the road on which she traveled, and her name was Lady Calliope.

One more thing to be done before she resigned this town to memory. Moving rapidly under a darkening sky, she passed through North Campus and up Fraternity Row, coming in no time to the fortress-like Tolkien House. She did not wish to be seen and was not; none of the brothers were in sight of the front entrance as the Lady swept in, doors swinging open before her.

She entered the Michel Delving Mathom-Hole, the great hall in which the House artifacts were stored. Neat rows of glass cases, each containing a weapon or some other item, all taken from Tolkien's *Rings* trilogy. All but one. The odd-man-out was dead center in the hall, its case seamless and unlabeled.

It was a spearhead, some ten inches long and six wide, with a square socket for a shaft at its base. It had a long and mythic history, one that had never been chronicled by Tolkien or any other storyteller; for the past half century it had lain here, surrounded by a House that was itself drawn from myth.

Etched on the flat of the spearhead was a red-tinged cross, and beneath it the inscription:

FRACTOR DRACONIS.

220

The glass case sprang open at her touch. She grasped the spearhead incautiously; its edge defined sharpness, but it could not cut her unless she desired it to. She slipped it into the folds of her cloak and left the hall.

Down a corridor and into the obsidian elevator; she descended to the cellars. Not bothering to light a lamp, she made a beeline toward Lothlórien. Upon reaching the chasm she allowed herself a frivolity; breathing into her whistle, she scorned the stone bridge and treaded thin air across the gulf.

Through the stone doors, into the deserted Garden. A jeweled night sky glittered prettily above, but she headed for the part of the Garden where the trees grew thick and the sky could not be seen. Here she paused briefly to regard the Rubbermaid, which bided time beneath the branches of a dark oak.

"Soon," Calliope told the mannequin. "Soon."

She walked on, trees growing thicker and thicker, till all at once reality buckled. The trees thinned out again dramatically and she was no longer in the Garden at all but outside, halfway down The Hill, in The Boneyard. A few short yards ahead of her a plain white marble square lay flat against the ground, carved with a single word:

PANDORA

Selecting another oak tree, she brought out FRACTOR DRACONIS and threw it with a flick of her wrist, burying all but an inch of it in the wood. There it would remain until being drawn forth on the eve of the Ides of March.

The wind had died down a good deal. Snowflakes were falling now from a sky of leaden grey, but Calliope ignored them. For only a moment more she paused, looking up at the crest of The Hill, giving a final thought to the Fool whose real trial had not even begun.

"Best of luck, George," she said, and blew town.

GEORGE IN HELL

I.

"No, no, *no!*"

George made his way through a yielding crowd, the wind easing off, easing off. Luther ran up to him barking and leaping on his leg; at first George ignored him.

How could she have retrieved the whistle from him? But no, that was a foolish question even for a fool. The real question was, could he still catch up with her? He did not think he could convince her to stay, if she had decided time had come round to leave, but maybe, if he could only catch her, he could still manage some sort of decent good-bye.

Thinking this, George ceased ignoring the dog and sought to enlist its aid. "I need to track somebody," he explained to it. "A woman. A beautiful woman. She was up there by the Tower just a few moments ago. Do you understand?"

Luther did not, as a matter of fact, understand at all, though he realized through empathy that George wanted something from him, wanted it rather desperately. Literally overwhelmed by the miracle of the wind-summoning, Luther was all too willing to please, but uncertain what was required of him. He saw George gesturing urgently in the direction of the Clock Tower and concluded that the man wanted him to go that way.

"Good boy!" George cried, as the dog took off at a run. He did not know as he followed that the tracking job was an impossible task, for as with most other things, leaving a scent was optional with Calliope. In fact at that moment the last traces of her presence were being erased: back at the house the bed regained some of its springiness, forgetting the extra weight of the past few months; the bathroom mirror lost all memory of the Lady's perfect image; no longer did the walls and ceilings recall the echo of her laughter, nor the floors the tread of her delicate feet. Her entire stay was, in sum, Removed.

Wholly unaware of this, George chased the dog up to the spot where

222

Calliope had last stood—receiving more scattered applause and awed looks until he had got some distance from the Straight—and Luther, glancing back and seeing the hopeful determination on the man's face, kept running on a more or less random course. For nearly half an hour they raced about in this way—it began to snow around the fifteen-minute mark—until somewhere in the vicinity of the Veterinary College Luther stumbled across, of all things, an abandoned soup bone, which he affectionately presented to George.

"*WHAT!?*" the storyteller cried, realizing his folly. "You brought me to a *bone?* You think I'm *hungry?*"

Luther was hurt by the venom of this reaction, but his distress could not match the Hurt that swelled in George. The enormity of his loss struck him like a hammer blow, driving him first to his knees and then flat out against the cold earth. Still not understanding but wanting to help, Luther came forward to lick George's ear, which did nothing at all to ease the pounding of blood in the storyteller's temples.

When my job is done I'll leave, without warning, and then you'll want to die . . .

That was just right; that was exactly right. In this weakest of moments George broke his own rule and despaired, though as Calliope had also foretold, he was not going to be allowed to surrender.

He went back to his house—yelling at the dog when it tried to follow him—and broke a large amount of furniture. This was no random act of destruction; George could sense Calliope's Absence, and punished the chairs, tables, and other furnishings as conspirators. He took a special lingering delight in trashing the mirror in the bathroom, but did not touch the bed, surmising that he would have enough trouble trying to sleep tonight without tearing up the mattress.

When there was more debris than he could stand he went out again, neglecting to take a coat although an inch of snow now lay on the ground and more was coming down every minute. In a well of self-pity he descended The Hill to The Ithaca Commons, thinking he would never recover from this.

Yet George's despair did not remain pure for very long. Even in Hell, common sense and optimism sometimes find a voice. As he entered The Commons he saw that the outdoor clock/thermometer read 25°, and a small rational segment of his addled brain spoke up. *Not wise to be out in this wearing just a shirt*, it said. *All chest-beating aside, you don't really want to die, do you?* The rest of his brain ignored the question, but he had barely gone ten yards when his body was racked with chills—Aha! You *can* feel physical discomfort—that nearly doubled him over.

A poor man who happened to be gazing wistfully through a store window took note of George's plight and went to help him. The poor man had on three overcoats one atop the other, all ragged, and he offered the outermost coat to George. The storyteller thought to run away at first, not wanting this act of kindness which infringed on his sense of abandonment, but the shivers were so bad he could barely stand up straight, much less run. Before he knew what was happening the poor man had draped the coat over his shoulders, saying: "There, there you go. Merry Christmas early, OK?"

The coat stank but it was warm, and at the feel of that warmth George's hands betrayed him. He reached into his pockets, taking out all his money— better than three hundred dollars—and giving it to the poor man in a crumpled ball. His lips betrayed him, too. "Merry Christmas early," they said.

The poor man's face lit up like a sunburst, much to George's chagrin.

"Oh Jesus," he said, counting the bills. "Oh Jesus, are you *sure?*"

"I'm sure," George muttered. Finding he had strength to move, he did so.

"Hey!" the poor man called after him. "Hey, can I at least buy you a beer or something?"

"No thanks!" George called back, desperate to escape.

"Well hey, you take care, OK? Can't thank you enough for this . . . Merry Christmas!"

The last thing George heard him say was "Holy shit, Oral Roberts was right," and then he rounded a corner and was free. But the poor man's generosity had done its damage—try as he might, George could not return to his state of despair. Instead he paused by a plate glass window and was berated by his own reflection.

"You ass," his reflection said. "What do you think you're doing out here in the snow? Go home, have some tea. Break a few more things if you can't help yourself. But cut the crap; frozen you'll look even dumber than Romeo did."

His sense of self-preservation restored, George could not ignore this advice. He remained more depressed than he had ever been in his life, but with a reluctant surge of optimism he began to suspect that he might learn to cope, after all.

Drawing the ratty, smelly coat tightly around himself, he headed back up The Hill to his house.

By way of The Boneyard.

II.

It was to see the stone that he went that way, the stone hand-hewn in memory of an infant child who had entered and left the world on the same day.

HERE LIES ALMA RENAT JESSOP
BORN APRIL 23, 1887
DIED APRIL 23, 1887
HER FATHER LOVED HER

What possessed him to come stand in ankle-deep snow and stare at this rock he could not say, not at first. Certainly Alma Jessop's father must have suffered a great deal of pain, but it was not really analogous to George's torment; one did not mourn a dead child and grieve over the loss of a lover in the same way. Although both might lead one down the path of despair. . . .

April, she had died. April could still be a very cold month in Ithaca, though it was certainly not the best month for dying of exposure. A depressed person would have a better bet walking along the edge of one of the gorges and "accidentally" falling in. Of course the man Jessop had done neither; hand-making his daughter's tombstone had probably kept him too occupied to even consider suicide.

Yes. That was it; that was the key. An act of creation in the face of loss. George was no carver of tombstones, but he could channel the Hurt into a story. Yes, how simple: A story about the perfect woman . . . and the Fool who fell in love with her. He could start writing as soon as he got home; like the bed, he had been careful not to harm his typewriter during the furniture-smashing rampage. Now it no longer mattered if he could not sleep tonight; he would write until plain exhaustion took him.

Heart aching but excited as well now, he turned from Alma Renat Jessop with new purpose. A book, another book, that was it: to ease the Hurt.

He meant to go straight home now, but his feet led him to the far north end of The Boneyard by force of habit. So preoccupied was he with thoughts of this Calliope-novel that he did not notice he was going the wrong way until he had gotten there, to a place where all the tombstones sagged or leaned away from a central point, like the petals of a grey flower.

"Ah, Pandora!" he exclaimed, after a moment's disorientation. He called himself a dunce and a few other things, though now that he was here he could not resist taking a look at the stone. He bent down and brushed aside the snow where he thought it should be, but uncovered only bare earth. He straightened up, took a step back, and his foot found the stone, skidding on the surface of the slippery marble square. George's balance went right out from under him, and after some half-hearted pinwheeling of his arms he fell over backwards.

Typical, he thought on the way down. Then his head struck the side of one of the sagging tombstones and he blacked out, his coat hanging open in front, snow continuing to fall on his prone form like ash.

Uncovered, the white marble square flashed its single word at the sky:

PANDORA

Beneath the frozen earth, something chuckled.

DEUS EX MACHINA

I.

Once again Mr. Sunshine sat at a Typewriter. There was still chaos in Chicago, but it was getting a little dull; time, maybe, to hand that Manuscript over to the Monkeys and move "Fool on The Hill" to his Desk. Right now, though, he was going to have to think quickly if he wanted the Fool's Story to continue at all.

"George, George, George . . ." Mr. Sunshine shook his head. "What *is* your problem? I give you an extra shot of optimism to make sure you don't get suicidal and instead you have an accident. Are you trying to ruin my Story?"

A sudden thought . . . Mr. Sunshine glanced suspiciously at the Monkey standing beside him. It did not glance back.

"I'll deal with *you* later," Mr. Sunshine promised. "But for the moment . . . we need a fast save here. Hades, Hades, Hades, what am I going to do?"

He started with what he knew best, reviewed the other major Plots in the Story, checked where the Characters were. And smiled.

"Of course," he said. "Of course. Man—and Fool's—best friend. Simple. I like that."

Luther . . .

he began to Type.

II.

"I'm telling you, Blackjack, he made the wind blow, and I guess you could say the storm is his, too."

"Luther, I am *drowning* in a *snowbank*. Stop talking nonsense and help me out."

226

"It isn't nonsense, Blackjack. It really happened. Oh, I wish you could have been there to help me understand what he was saying, afterwards. He seemed very disappointed in me."

"I don't care, Luther," said the Manx, struggling against the white drift that lay piled up around him. "Help me."

"Sure, Blackjack, I'll help you. I just wish—"

A sudden gust of wind.

"Luther?"

"Oh no," the mongrel cried. "No, that mustn't happen."

"What mustn't happen?"

"He's in trouble, Blackjack. I've got to go help him before it's too late."

"Help *who?* Luther, I'm in trouble too, remember?"

"You'll get out all right, Blackjack. If you don't I'll be back to help you. But I've got to go, he's *freezing.*"

"Luther! *Luther!*"

III.

George knew that he must be dead, or dying, for he floated in a formless void, and there before him rose the image of the woman he loved, the woman he had thought forever lost. If death meant being reunited with her, he decided, he would not resist its embrace.

"No," Calliope said, reading his mind as she had always read his mind. "You can't give up, George. Dying won't get you what you want, or what you think you want."

"I want you," George told her, speaking through lips of ice. "I want to be with you."

"But I'm not even real. I'm only a dream you had."

"You *are* real. I touched you with my own hands. I made love to you."

"You made love to a dream. Have I ever lied to you, George? Then remember what I told you: *Whoever you love will be just like me.* Any woman seen through love's eyes is as perfect as you thought me to be."

"No," George said. "There's no one like you."

"They're all like me, George, if you see with your heart. But some of them stay."

"Why . . . why are you leaving me?"

"I told you, I'm a dream. Dreams have to end eventually."

"Why did you come in the first place?"

"More reasons than you can know. In the end it's all for the Story. That's what you should be worrying about. Not about me, not about love. Love is just part of the Plot."

Many more questions he had for her, and a good-bye to say, but now she began to drift toward him, arms outstretched.

One last kiss, he thought, blissfully. but it was a harsh kiss, alien and sloppy; the void turned over twice, depositing him in a cold graveyard with a dog licking his face.

"Whuh—" He tried to sit up, snow sliding off his coat, and pain shot him through. A good sign, perhaps, for pain signifies that flesh and bone are still hanging in there, fighting. His feet, though, he could not feel his feet, and the same was true of his fingers, though when he tried to flex them they moved, the knuckles giving a slight twinge.

"Warm," George mumbled, his tongue not cooperating. "Need warm." Luther actually understood this—or maybe it was only a lucky coincidence— and offered to share his own body warmth by leaping on George's chest. The dog felt warm, all right, but even his slight weight was enough to push the storyteller back down, nearly smacking his head against the tombstone a second time.

My head . . . his skull throbbed; he felt the back of his scalp with the heel of his hand and discovered a crusty mess that must have been dried or frozen blood. Not good. Could he have suffered a concussion? The mere thought made him dangerously weary, and he realized he had to get out of this place quickly or remain until the spring thaw. He shoved the dog off him as gently as possible and somehow managed to stand, the muscles in his ankles giving a satisfactory scream.

Walking uphill out of The Boneyard was one of the hardest things George ever did. He seemed to stumble as often as take a step, and the tombstones arranged themselves in an obstacle course, conspiring to trip him up. On the positive side, however, the snow had stopped falling, while the wind came up behind him, helping him along. Luther helped him as well; twice George slipped and fell, and twice the dog nipped, butted, and barked at him until he struggled back to his feet and got going again.

A small eternity later he emerged onto the sidewalk on Stewart Avenue, head reeling. He heard a voice calling his name from the other side of the street and looked up, expecting to see yet another vision of Calliope. Instead he saw a blond Christian Princess, tiny cross clasped to her throat, her right hand resting briefly on the hood of a snow-covered Volkswagen. Concern creased her brow and she was very beautiful.

"Borealis," George greeted her, finding her simpler first name too much of a chore to pronounce.

"George, are you all right?" she asked him. He looked like death. Noticing that he was swaying like a giddy flagpole, she stepped off the curb and began crossing over to help him; Luther, barking excitedly, rushed out to meet her in the middle of the street.

The silver Rolls came barreling at them from the left. The Greek behind the wheel—a frat boy but not a Rat boy—was more than a little wasted, driving on bald tires, and lacked the basic skill necessary to make an emergency stop even under better conditions. It should have ended in a manslaughter, but George saw the car bearing down out of the corner of his eye. In the brief second when he realized what was about to happen, he felt a surge of indignation and the same sense of control that he had had in front of the Straight.

"Uh-uh," George said, and a whirlwind exploded up around the woman and the dog, obscuring them and the offending Rolls in a funnel of snow and ice. When this cleared, Aurora and Luther remained untouched where they had stood, but the Rolls lay on its roof some ten yards farther on, its driver scrunched upside-down and looking more than a bit startled.

A good trick, but it robbed George of the last of his strength. With a smile he collapsed once more, felt soft hands touch the back of his neck, and slept in darkness until the doctors over at Gannett Health Clinic thawed him out.

IV.

"Good," said Mr. Sunshine, relaxing a bit. "Better, at any rate. If he can handle himself as well as he handles the air around him, there might be a decent Climax in this after all."

He stood up, letting the Story carry itself for a while. Mr. Sunshine was decided—he *would* move this Manuscript to his Writing Desk in place of "Absolute Chaos." But first he had to get something.

SETTING THINGS UP

I.

The nearest available vehicle, an Ithaca Sunshine Cab, took George up to Gannett. Though he came in as an unconscious human Popsicle, they soon revived him, and in no time at all he had regained sufficient strength to argue with his doctor. For in New York City, where George had grown up, a patient is discharged from the hospital as soon as he can walk, often within an hour or two of admittance; at Gannett, even though a head X-ray showed no skull fracture, they wanted to keep him overnight for observation. This was kind, thoughtful, and probably proper procedure as well, but in George's present frame of mind it only seemed stupid.

"So you think it's stupid, do you?" The doctor held up the tattered coat George had gotten from the poor man. "Is this all you were wearing in twenty-degree weather?"

Under a strong light the coat looked pitifully thin, and George got the point: he was not in a position to judge stupidity. Unfortunately, he was also not in a mood to spend a night in Gannett. He had as a roommate a pneumonia-struck graduate student who did nothing but stare catatonically at the latest *Soldier of Fortune* magazine, which made George decidedly nervous and got him wondering if he might just slip out through some window and escape.

About an hour after nightfall, however, his spirits took a sudden lift. Aurora Smith had entered the room, and though George did not recognize it as the source of his relief, for half an instant the sight of her made him forget Calliope. Oh, there was more to it than that, to be sure: she had ridden up with him in the patrol car, cradling his wounded head in her lap, and though he did not remember this some part of him did; knowledge of the gentleness in her, that too helped him smile.

"Hello," he greeted her, sitting up in bed. George was careful of his head, though in fact all pain had departed now, leaving not so much as a twinge. Likewise his frostbitten joints seemed miraculously renewed.

"Hello," she said back, then hovered for a moment as she looked for a place to sit down. George gestured to the foot of the bed and Aurora settled there. "I've been waiting to see you for a while," she told him. "They only just let me in."

"Mmm," George nodded. "I think they know about my money. If I die of unexpected complications I won't be able to endow the University in my old age."

"Oh George."

"Say, you wouldn't happen to have a hacksaw, would you? Or a getaway car?"

Aurora smiled and shook her head. "Neither one. Sorry. But are you sure you're all right? You look—"

"Peachy." He studied her. "You look like there's something heavy on your mind."

"There is," she admitted, becoming more serious. "I'm afraid if I tell you, though, you might laugh at me . . . or you might not. I'm not sure which would be worse."

"Guess we'll have to see. Go ahead, I'm listening."

Aurora struggled to get the words out: "I think . . . I think that we've been set up, George."

"Set up? Set up how?" Despite his remarkable physical recovery, he felt emotionally drained and would not have thought it possible for anything else to shock him after the day's events. He would have been wrong. What Aurora said next surprised him beyond all conception.

"I'm in love with you," she told him. "And I think, very soon, it's going to be mutual."

II.

Mr. Sunshine walked down a long and cavernous hallway. He did not like this part of the Library; the Others were here, seated along the windowless walls, ancient figures that might have been carved of stone, but were not. A well-muscled blacksmith with lightning bolts rusting at his feet; a goat man bearing two horns on his head and a third in his hands for winding; a beardless patriarch and his wife; eight younger women with an empty ninth chair in their midst; many more. They were not Dead but they were not Alive, either, and Mr. Sunshine would have far preferred to watch an eclipse than to spend any unnecessary time in their company.

Unfortunately, the Refrigerator was here too, and Mr. Sunshine had never got around to moving it to a more congenial location. It stood at the far end of the hall, and upon reaching it and opening it Mr. Sunshine wondered, as always, whether the little light inside shined on in his absence or doused itself when the door was closed. He barely glanced at the contents of the cooler racks—Milk, Ambrosia, the Primordial Feta—going straight for the Ice Box. It was there that he found what he needed, a Toy he had kept frozen here for quite a long time.

The thing was a bird, a fierce white bird formed of ice and snow. Cold crystal rimed its wings, curved icicles served as talons; Mr. Sunshine brought it out, put life into it with a breath.

"Hello there," he greeted it, as it perched on his hand, studying him with blank eyes. "Now listen carefully, I'm going to have you be a Messenger for me. . . ."

Mr. Sunshine shut the Refrigerator door and got walking, bearing the Messenger away to another part of the Library where there was a window that opened on the World. On the way he taught it what he needed it to tell; he gave it a Message, and a job.

III.

"Brian Garroway asked me to marry him last night," Aurora explained, sitting closer now; the grad student on the other bed remained catatonic. "I've always known he would ask me eventually; I was never sure what my answer would be."

"You told him no," George guessed.

"I thought to tell him no. And I will. Last night I chickened out, told him I needed time to think it over. It didn't help any; he got upset that I even hesitated."

"He was expecting a prompt yes."

"He's always expected it," Aurora agreed. "I can't say I ever gave him reason not to expect it. I think it may break his heart when I turn him down."

"Too many broken hearts around," George said. "I broke mine today, along with nearly breaking my head."

"I know."

"You know? How do you know?"

Aurora bit her lip. "Calliope told me."

He sprang like a trap, gripped her arm. "You saw her?"

"In a *dream!*" she protested. "Only in a dream!"

"A dream?"

"I had two dreams," Aurora told him. "One last night and one this afternoon, although I guess the second one was more like a vision. I don't remember lying down to take a nap.

"Last night's dream, that was just about you. You and I. I dreamed about the Halloween party, about Thanksgiving night, other times we've been together. And times we haven't been: I kept seeing us eating breakfast back in my house in Wisconsin. My father was there too, laughing."

"But what about Calliope?" George said, insistent.

"The vision . . . I don't quite know how to describe it. I talked with her. She told me some things."

"*NO!*" He practically exploded.

"George, I swear to you—"

"I mean *no*, there is absolutely no way I am ever going to go through that again. Calliope nearly drove me crazy with her secrets, with all the things she knew that I didn't understand. And if she passed that on to you . . ."

"No, George, it's not like that. I don't understand most of what she said either, all this stuff about Stories, and Plots . . . only one thing I got clear. You have what I want, what Brian could never give me."

"And what might that be?"

"Magic. I heard what happened in front of the Straight today. And just a while ago, in the street . . . your magic, George, your daydreams. I want a stake in that. And love."

"But it doesn't work that way," George protested. "I'm flattered, but how can I just agree to fall in love with you?"

"Calliope said you'd ask that. But maybe it's not a matter of agreement. Tell me, honestly, what are your feelings for me?"

"Well, I—" It seemed a simple enough question, but as George seriously examined his own heart, he got another big surprise.

"You see?" said Aurora, watching his eyes widen. "We've been set up. *She* did it, tangled us up somehow without letting us catch on."

"All the more reason to reject it. Do you have any idea what she's already done to me? I nearly let myself die today."

"I don't want to push you into love, George." Aurora pleaded. "She . . she told me . . . "

"Go ahead, say it."

"She told me to ask you if you could even remember what she looked like."

"What she looked like? Don't be ridiculous, of course I—"

Another shock, the third and last, making the circuit complete. *Four months.* Calliope's face had hovered within inches of his own, above, below, all around, until it seemed etched forever into memory. But now . . . now that he tried to recall it, the memory blurred like a running watercolor. Of course he had a general impression of her, could have described her easily enough. But as far as summoning up a distinct image of her in his mind—this he could not do, and it shook him.

"Her picture!" he cried suddenly. "I have her picture in my wallet. Over there!" He pointed to the closet where his clothes had been stored after his transfer into a white hospital robe. "Quick, check my left front pants pocket!"

Aurora did as he requested, retrieving the wallet and handing it to him. He searched through it frantically and came up with a photograph . . . of a sunlit tree.

"No!" George nearly screamed; the grad student stirred at last from his catatonia to glance over at the raving madman. "No, no, that's not right at all! She was standing right there, right in front . . . ah, shit!" He tore the photo in half and hurled the pieces to the floor, disgusted. "Great! Just great! First I lose her, then my memory goes. What's next?"

"Come home with me," Aurora suggested, softly.

"To Balch?"

"To Wisconsin."

"*Wisconsin?*"

"Brian was supposed to drive me home," she explained, "but now I don't suppose he'll want to. I know you don't own a car, but you could rent one pretty easily. Come home with me; we'll have breakfast together, just like in my dream."

"That's crazy."

Aurora nodded. "Scary, too. Especially since I don't know what happens after. But she said it would be the right thing to do, and for some reason I trust her . . . even if she's only a dream."

George shook his head and moaned. "Oh man, oh man, when did I start living inside one of my own stories? Crazy, crazy, crazy . . ."

"It's crazy, George. But will you do it?"

His answer was a long time coming, but this time neither of them were at all surprised.

"I'll come. Do you really think I have a choice?"

IV.

The clouds had departed, and the air lay still once more. The Messenger came to a rough but not ungraceful landing in The Boneyard. It had flown a terribly long way in a terribly short time, but it had not tired; tired was not something it could be.

It came to earth in the center of the ring of leaning tombstones. And, having come to rest, bent immediately to tap its glacial beak against the ground, once, twice.

The earth tremor traveled outward from The Boneyard to a radius of about one mile, causing buildings to shudder, panicking animals, and making small objects dance with false life. Sneaking out of Gannett through a side exit, George and Aurora clutched each other in fear feeling personally threatened; nor were they just being paranoid.

It did not last long. Indeed, the earthquake ceased almost as quickly as it had begun. Collecting themselves, the man and woman stepped outside arm in arm and walked beneath the stars, filled with a new foreboding.

BEFORE THE STORM

I.

Ragnarok dropped by Risley on the twenty-first of December, the first true day of winter (and the last day of final exams). The campus had been emptying steadily over the past week, becoming almost completely deserted by now, and as the Bohemian Minister of Defense drove up to the dorm unannounced he would not have been surprised to find everyone gone. But it so happened that the Queen of the Grey Ladies had had a particularly late neuro-bio final, and she and Lion-Heart were out on the front lawn just saddling up to leave.

"Ragnarok!" Myoko cried happily as he drove into view.

Lion-Heart, remembering a certain tumble down a flight of steps, took a more restrained tone: "So, you're back, eh?"

"Had some thinking to do," Ragnarok said, killing the bike's engine and dismounting.

"Had some moping to do, you mean," Lion-Heart responded. "Almost two months' worth, by my count. You could have at least dropped word once in a while that you were still alive."

Ragnarok tried to shrug off this dig. "I could have, but I didn't. So are you guys all that's left, or is somebody else still around?"

"Now who might you be wondering about?" mused the Bohemian King. "The Top left days ago. Panhandle, Aphrodite, and Woodstock are gone too; I think they were going to check out Atlantic City. And Fujiko's over at Tolkien House for the duration. That what you wanted to know?"

"Stop it," Myoko warned. Then to Ragnarok she said: "Preacher moved downtown almost a week ago. He'll be in Ithaca housewatching for a professor for most of vacation."

"Is Jinsei staying with him?"

"I don't know. I suppose she might be."

Ragnarok nodded. "You have an address, or a phone number?"

"No," said Myoko. "I'm really sorry. If you'd only come by a few days sooner . . . "

"Right." He turned back toward his bike. "Guess I'll have to do some searching around downtown."

The Grey Queen caught his arm. "Wait," she said. "Why don't you come with us, instead? Lion-Heart and I rented a chalet up the Lake a bit, and I'm sure we'd both love to have you spend Christmas with us. Wouldn't we, Li?"

"It'd be a trip and a half, I'm sure," said Lion-Heart. "What the hell, Rag, she's probably got a point. There's bound to be tension at least for a while even if you do find Preacher. The chalet's only about ten miles away; you come along and have a good Christmas, and Preacher'll have a good Christmas, and then if you can't wait you can always drive down and look for him after New Year's."

"I don't know if I can wait even that long," Ragnarok told him seriously. "I've been having these nightmares . . . "

"Doesn't surprise me," said Myoko, reaching out to stoke his hair, like a mother with a son. "You need some of Lion-Heart's special eggnog. You'll sleep just fine then, you'll see."

"No. No, I—"

"Look, Rag," Lion-Heart interjected, "I don't know if you heard the latest weather report, but the queen bitch of snowstorms is on its way down from Maine, right this minute. New Hampshire and Vermont are already getting buried, and the first dusting is due in Tompkins County in about twelve hours. Which is why we've really got to move it, because once the heavy stuff starts the roads are going to be locked up tight. You catch that? By sundown it won't matter whether you're in Ithaca or not, because if Preacher's smart he won't be leaving his house for days."

"I've still got twelve hours . . . "

"Don't be silly!" Myoko exclaimed. "If you don't find him, then what? That place you live in doesn't even have hot water, does it? Now how am *I* supposed to have a merry Christmas, knowing that one of my friends is freezing himself to death?"

By steady degrees they wore him down—Myoko's arguments were the most convincing, because she kept stroking his hair—and at last he gave in, against his better judgment. Ragnarok's dreams over the past week had left him with a very bad feeling.

"Don't worry yourself so," Myoko chided him. "You'll see Preacher again soon enough, I promise."

In a literal sense, of course, that was absolutely right.

II.

George hired a gleaming white Eldorado for the trip, and Aurora drove, as the storyteller had never troubled himself to get a license. They did not leave immediately, but having packed their things into the trunk took a leisurely cruise around The Hill. They ranged from one end of the campus to the other, marveling at familiar and unfamiliar sights alike, enjoying each other's company throughout. Aurora switched on the radio as they were tooling along the fringes of the Cornell Plantations, and that was how they happened to catch the weather report.

"Oops," Aurora said. "We're going to have to move it if we don't want to get caught in that."

"No rush," George assured her. "The storm won't bother us."

She looked at him, and he smiled. "You're positive about that?" she asked.

"As sure as kites can fly," he promised.

Just to play it safe, they struck west immediately, making one last pass through the heart of the campus. As they turned onto East Avenue, George laid a hand on Aurora's shoulder.

"Stop the car," he said.

She braked and brought the Eldorado to a halt right in front of Day Hall. "What is it?"

"Just want to wish a buddy of mine Merry Christmas. Over there." He pointed. "That's the dog that got me out of The Boneyard."

Luther turned at the sound of the car door opening, and recognized the storyteller's scent even before he saw his face. George intended only a meager offering of gratitude, but from the dog's point of view it was quite a moment, for to him the Eldorado seemed nothing less than a chariot of white fire, reeking with the hills-and-rain smell of Heaven.

"Hey, hey, good to see you too!" George said, as the dog ran up to him, barking. He stepped out of the car and swept Luther up into his arms, at which point the mongrel nearly drowned him with sloppy licks.

"You're right," Aurora observed. "He *is* your buddy."

An idea struck him, "Hey," George asked, "do you think your parents would mind if we brought home an extra guest?"

"If they don't mind you they won't mind him. But what about his owner?"

"I don't think he's got one," George said. "There's no collar on him, and besides, he doesn't act like he has an owner. Know what I mean?"

"No." Aurora smiled. "But then I'm not a storyteller, so I'll trust you. Go ahead, bring him along if he wants to come."

George tapped Luther's nose with a finger. "What about it, dude?" he asked. "Want to come to Wisconsin? It's a long ride, but when you get there you'll get to see about six billion cows."

Once again Luther relied on empathy rather than actual comprehension, but this time the message was easy enough to fathom: the saint in whose arms he rested was offering to take him up to Heaven in the white chariot. Perhaps it would even be the real Heaven this time. Luther was acutely aware that he might be in for another disappointment, but he also remembered the summoning of the winds. If anyone could take Luther to Heaven, this man could.

Yet he could not forget about Blackjack. The Manx had been furious enough at being left to struggle out of that snowbank alone, nor had he believed Luther's explanation later. To just take off now without at least saying good-bye would be terrible, but Luther knew he had no time to waste. Chariots of fire wait for no one—you must ride, or not.

"What do you say, guy?" George asked, setting Luther down on the ground. "My lady and I have to get going."

In a quick decision that he later regretted—but all hard choices bring some regret—Luther leaped aboard the chariot and was suffused by the Heaven scent. George climbed in as well, slammed the door, and they were off.

Oh Blackjack, Blackjack, I hope you can forgive me. . . .

But wait, there was something: As the car slowed to turn another corner, Luther spied a familiar Beagle through the Eldorado's rear window.

"Skippy!" Luther called out mentally. "Skippy, look over here!"

"Hi, Luther!" Skippy replied, turning and racing alongside the car. "Hey, what are you doing in that thing? Huh? Huh?"

"Listen to me!" the mongrel said urgently. "I need you to take a message to Blackjack."

"Why can't you take it to him? You going somewhere, Luther? Huh? Huh? Where are you going? Huh? H—"

Running at top speed to keep pace with the car, Skippy suffered an abrupt face-first encounter with a mailbox. A resounding *whap!* marked the interruption of his curiosity.

"Listen to me!" Luther called back to the dazed Beagle as he receded into the distance. "Please get this! Tell Blackjack that I got invited to Heaven. Tell him I'll come back. Tell him I promise to come back. Have you got that?"

But Skippy was too far and too befuddled to answer, if indeed he'd gotten it. Luther settled down in the back seat, already wondering if he'd made the wrong choice.

I'll come back and see you, Blackjack. I promise.

III.

But of course reunions are notoriously chancy things. Often it seems as if the most likely meetings are those least desired; the unwelcome guest always comes back for seconds.

The storm struck Ithaca that night at quarter past ten, bringing misfortune as well as snow and ice. The Messenger found a perch in the high branches of a dark oak, the same oak into which a fair Lady's hand had hurled an ancient spearhead.

Strengthened by the cold, the Messenger kept a tireless watch on a hole that the recent earth tremor had opened in the ground. The white marble square, unmoved for more than a century, had fallen into this hole and lay in pieces at the bottom, beside another long-undisturbed object.

The object was a box, a cube no more than half a foot to a side, composed of black iron. Once the box might have been used to safe-keep jewelry, coins, any number of harmless things. But someone had shut it up tight, sealing its seams and cracks most carefully, wrapping the whole with a special silver band that remained untarnished after decade upon decade of burial.

The packed soil had served as an effective warden for many years. Now the earth had opened, exposing Pandora's Box to any and all who might happen by. The whirling snow would re-cover it, briefly, but all that really remained to be done was for some unlucky soul to break the seals and lift the hinged lid, unleashing the real storm.

It wasn't long before someone did just that.

Book Three

PANDORA'S BOX

1866—INSIDE THE BONE ORCHARD

It is in the north end of The Bone Orchard that the Plot really begins to come together for Mr. Sunshine. He crouches over the site of Ithaca's only live burial, a spot marked only by a ring of seven round white stones—enchanted stones, he senses. The other, more conventional markers surrounding the site lean away like the petals of a budding grey flower, but their lean is not nearly so pronounced as it will be a century from now.

Mr. Sunshine places his palm against the damp earth, understanding what it is that lies beneath. Its presence here is wholly fortuitous, nothing to do with any of his previous Meddlings on Earth, but—as much an opportunist as an originator, like all storytellers—he immediately sees its potential uses for the Plot he is weaving.

"Animation," he says. "Animation, that's wonderful, I can have some good times with that. And if . . . "

He trails off thinking: Stephen Titus George. St. George. And animation. Hmmm . . .

Standing behind him like an impatient valet, Ezra Cornell clears his throat several times.

"Getting a bit late," Cornell hints, wondering what in hell he is doing here in the first place. "Getting a bit cold, too."

"Hold this," Mr. Sunshine says, handing him the lantern. Cornell takes it obediently and waits while the Greek Original bends low over the site and does something Meddlesome with his hands.

"Better," Mr. Sunshine says a moment later, standing and taking the lantern again. "More appropriate, considering."

"Heh-em," Cornell throat-clears once more. "I really think . . . "

"Onward and upward," Mr. Sunshine interrupts him. He pats Ezra on the shoulder companionably. "You like climbing The Hill, I know

*you do. Good for the circulation, good for the lungs. I'd wager your
middle name is Sisyphus, you love climbing so much."*

"Yes," Cornell agrees, eyes glazing for a moment. "Yes, I love it."

"Good." Mr. Sunshine nods. "Double-time, then."

"Double-time. Yes . . . "

*They move off, and now the scene has changed. The center of the
budding grey flower is no longer a ring of stones, but a solitary, still-
enchanted marker. A white marble square bearing a single, appropriate
word:*

PANDORA

HOBART VISITS
THE BONEYARD

I.

The hangar doors slid open silently, moved by a set of rollers and counter-
weights finer than anything human hands could have designed. Snow whipped into the hangar as if seeking targets, yet Hobart stood right at the
opening, enduring the cold, looking down from the very pinnacle of the
Tower. Outside chaos reigned: with the setting of the sun visibility had
dropped almost to zero, and now the air currents goaded each other to greater
feats of abandon. Foolish to tempt Fate by venturing out on such a night, but
out he must go. Hobart's nightmares had gotten progressively worse, and he
could no longer suppress the feeling that something terrible had happened in
The Boneyard.

He walked back to the rear of the hangar where the gossamer glider
waited and climbed into the sling-seat. His pinsword was in his belt, but he
did not bother arming himself with a crossbow, for if he ran into trouble he
doubted it would be much use to him. Instead he had gone to a secret place in
the lower part of the Tower and obtained a tiny sackful of a very special dust.
The dust was silver, a special alloy also beyond the ability of human craft;
precious and rare, it might prove his only salvation in a true emergency.

Hobart gave the command, and the glider arose and hurled itself out into
the storm. Once past the hangar doors, Hobart's trip took on a decidedly
different character than Zephyr's months-ago chase after George: far from a
smooth glide, the first turbulence threatened to break the aircraft in two, and
at one point it seemed to actually be bouncing up and down rather than
moving forward. Hobart petitioned the wind to be gentler, after which it
eased off some—but a human being would still have compared the glide down
the Slope to a roller coaster ride, without the usual reassurance of a safe stop
at the end of the trip.

Hobart was frightened by the violence of the storm, yet he hoped very
shortly to be made even more afraid. He would pass perilously low over The

Boneyard, to check whether a particular ring of seven white stones was still intact—a ring specially enchanted to discourage overly curious animals and sprites from disturbing what lay beneath it. He could not possibly hope to see the stones what with all the snow, but if they were there he would feel it, feel the dread and desire to flee that they would project into him. And if, in flying over the old burial site, Hobart felt no fear except that which he brought with him . . . well, in that case, fear itself would hardly be enough.

II.

The glider made an almost reluctant dip as it passed over the chain-link fence that enclosed the upper 'Yard. Where up to this point a scattering of streetlamps like lesser stars had cast a feeble glow over the sprite's route, darkness now conspired with the snow to obscure even the most obvious landmarks. Hobart was forced to fly by instinct alone, instinct augmented by memory.

Memory proved a surprisingly sharp ally, and a bitter one as well. Though frost and night covered all, the hidden earth seemed to cry out to him, speaking of another fearsome eve when rain had crashed down in a deluge to hamper the advance of a sprite army traveling on foot rather than in the air. *Here Rosencrantz and three others slipped into a mud runnel and drowned,* Memory whispered beneath the howl of the wind. *The great unseen mass just ahead is the tree where Rasferret the Grub's troops waited in ambush. Directly below lies the tombstone beside which Miranda and Ariel were slaughtered, fighting back to back against an unrelenting enemy.*

He thought of the story he had told at the Halloween party, the death story that Laertes had been so anxious to hear: *Hecate led the larger of two contingents on an assault against The Boneyard. A second, smaller group, led by Eldest Julius, would sneak in and attempt to kill Rasferret . . . of that second group, I alone survive to tell the tale. . . .*

There was another story, an extremely ancient folktale in the sprite canon, that concerned a certain Robin Goodfellow, a rascal and Lothario of very much the same timber as Zephyr's love-errant Puck. Robin Goodfellow actually figured in a number of folktales, but the most popular by far told of his battle with the great Wildebeest of Rangoon. The Wildebeest, a ravenous monster with horribly sharp teeth, could not be killed because of a strong enchantment laid upon it. Despite this, Robin managed to defeat it through trickery, making it catch its head inside a stout earthen pot; unable to bite, it was thus rendered harmless, but did not die. Hobart recited the story of Robin Goodfellow and the Wildebeest more often than any other tale. He seemed truly fascinated by it.

You killed him, then?

Of course we killed him, Laertes.

Memory whispered to him once more as he neared the burial site, whispered of the death of a dear friend done in by a weapon that had come to life in his own hands: *Hobart, your crossbow!*

Was it a tear or merely a snowflake that caused Hobart's eyes to sting? He swiped at them with the back of his hand, briefly letting go of one of the glider's guide-threads. The wind allowed the nose of the craft to make another unexpected dip, and this saved Hobart's life.

The frost-feathered Messenger, roused by Hobart's intrusion into The Boneyard, shot past like an airborne scythe, talons extended to rip and tear . . . but it had not counted on this last second's maneuvering. Just the tip of a single claw drew a slit in the gossamer of the glider, which was not immediately disastrous; more damaging, a batting wing of ice twisted the frame of the craft and sent it spiraling downward.

Caught in a plummeting spin, Hobart didn't know what had hit him, only that he was in trouble. The wind helped level him out before he struck a snowbank—the glider would likely have buried itself to a depth of several feet—but luck must have lent a hand too, to keep him from smashing up against some obstacle as he hurtled through the darkness barely a breath's height from the ground.

Straining his ears for a telltale sound, Hobart began coaxing the glider back up to a safer altitude. A subtle shift in the shrieking of the wind warned him of the Messenger's second attack as the ice bird swooped in behind him. With no time to think, he raced his craft up toward the creaking tangleweb that was the upper branch-lattice of a dead maple. Straight for it he flew, at the final instant jerking the nose of the glider still higher, pointing at the crown of the sky. Once again the Messenger, with too much momentum for its own good, barely missed the target, passing just beneath to punch a splintering, jattering path through the maple branches.

"I'm *leaving*," Hobart announced, as if to appease his foe, but in the cold dark the Messenger was already wheeling around for yet another run. Banking above the level of the trees now, the sprite set a course for the all-too-distant lights of West Campus and the Slope. He freed one hand from the guide-threads and clutched at the pouch hanging from his belt.

The Messenger, seeing with magical eyes what would have been invisible to most natural creatures, homed in on the glider and readied itself for a final strike. As it drew closer in the glider's wake, it prepared to counter any further evasive action: it would dive if Hobart dived, climb if he climbed, chase him in circles if necessary. He would not escape.

Hobart tugged at the pouch. Against an ordinary predator—a hungry winter owl, say—it would have been useless, but the sprite had already guessed that his pursuer was anything but ordinary. Indeed, Hobart had guessed a great many things in the past few moments, and he had no response to these guesses, save one.

The pouch did not want to leave his belt. It hung there, the leather cord which held it unwilling to loosen in the midst of the rush and the storm. Desperate, Hobart jammed a finger into the neck of the bag, forcing it open. Directly behind him, ready for the kill, the Messenger let out a screech; Hobart jerked about and the bag came loose from his belt all at once, falling out of his grasp. The wind caught it, held it open, turned it inside out, and silver dust shot out and back like seed from a rainmaker's airplane.

It was only dust, but magical, and to the Messenger it was like a brick wall, an invisible fist swinging from nowhere. The bird stopped dead in mid-air, wings flailing, talons splayed. Then, paralyzed, it was thrown down from the sky; it fell and did not rise again that night. But it did not die, either, for evil things are difficult to kill.

Hobart, delivered only barely from his own death, retreated in a near panic back up The Hill, the winds that bore him no more gentle than those which had carried him down. The tear in the gossamer began to widen, the glider frame warped drastically, and only an extra whim of good fortune permitted a safe landing back in the Tower pinnacle.

He disembarked from the damaged glider, closed the hangar doors, then hurried down the secret staircase, through the open and wind-swept belfry, into the shelter of the drop-shaft where liquor waited. Some time later, deep in stupor, Hobart found himself looking once again into the face of the departed Julius.

"Why?" Hobart asked him. "Why twice in one lifetime? What could we have done to deserve it?"

"Justice is a funny thing, old friend," Julius replied. "It isn't always a matter of what you deserve, just what they decide to give you."

"I'm afraid."

Julius raised an eyebrow.

"You ought to be," he said. "You ought to be."

NORTHERN LIGHTS

I.

Two days it took them to drive to Wisconsin, two days, both a long and a short time. An outstretched arm of the "queen bitch of snowstorms" (meteorologists used a slightly less colorful phrase) delayed their progress, though at George's polite request the tempest quickly slacked off and fell behind them.

Both nights of the journey they spent in roadside motels, lying together in a double bed, Luther curled up contentedly at the foot. They did not make love on these nights; in fact, despite their earlier intimacy in the Garden of Lothlórien and whatever may or may not have happened on Thanksgiving, they hardly thought to touch each other. Instead they talked, and talked; in a novel you would say they "poured out their souls to one another," although the words they spoke did not pour or gush, they wafted. In calm but earnest tones George escorted Aurora through the vast library he had built up in his mind, shelf upon shelf of unwritten volumes, an army of stories waiting their turn to be told. His greatest fear was that in death he would take some of the best of these stories with him, never having had the time to commit them all to paper; yet this was also his greatest joy, for he knew his work would never be finished, knew the well would not run dry even if he outlived Methuselah. And Aurora—she had no library to reveal, but her dreams, like finely crafted antiques, would have more than filled the rooms of a tall mansion. Long past midnight she whispered to him—as she had never whispered to anyone—of knights and sorcerers, boisterous but cunning dragons, obsidian roads like frozen black rivers. Slowly George came to understand that her desire was not just to think or read about such things, but that she honestly desired to *experience* a fairy tale.

This was both more courageous and more difficult an ambition than simple storytelling: yet not so difficult, George realized, as he might once have believed.

By the time they crossed the Wisconsin border George had fulfilled Aurora's prediction and fallen as deeply in love with her as she had with him. Somehow the span of two days seemed hardly enough for this to have happened, and afterwards George thought that here he had glimpsed the essence of magic: changes that should take eons, changes that should never happen at all, coming about with a startling suddenness. Back in Ithaca he had first recognized opportunity in Aurora, yet Ached for Calliope; now the Hurt was lost somewhere behind him on the road, and Aurora had eclipsed his recollection of Calliope almost completely. For again, as predicted, the more George loved Aurora the more perfect she became in his sight, and when he tried to think back to that other perfect woman he saw only fair hair and pale skin. All that remained of the dark-eyed Asian was a wrinkle in the memory of his heart, which one day yet might find its way into a story . . . maybe, if he had the time.

At the moment he was fully occupied getting to know this new perfect woman sitting beside him in the car, beside him in the bed. And her parents, especially her father. It turned out that Walter Smith took an instant liking to George, and why shouldn't he? George was, after all, the answer to a desperate prayer.

II.

They arrived late afternoon on the twenty-third. Walter was waiting out on the front porch as the car drove up. He had a big smile on his face, and it wasn't just from what he'd been smoking.

"Hi, Daddy," Aurora waved, bringing them around and parking. Walter Smith waved back, looking not the least bit surprised at the appearance of the rental car or at George. In fact as they stepped out, it was the dog that Walter most seemed to raise an eyebrow about.

"Hello there," Walter said, as Luther ran up and barked at him. "This is George, Daddy." Aurora made a nervous introduction. She was unsure how her father would react to her bringing home a total stranger, although actually she hadn't.

"Stephen Titus George," Walter Smith said, nodding. "I've just finished reading your books. Good stuff."

"I'm in love with your daughter," George blurted out.

Walter nodded again. "Good stuff," he repeated. "We'll have something to talk about after dinner." He turned to Aurora. "Your mother won't be home till tomorrow. She had to rush down to Madison; seems your Uncle Bryce backed his Chevy into a pine tree. Totaled the car, then broke his leg trying to climb out the window when the door wouldn't open."

"That's awful."

Walter shrugged. "At least he won't be such a bother to his wife while he's in traction. She might even have a nice Christmas."

"*Daddy!*"

"Well it's true. He's always been a trial to her. Oh, by the way, Brian Garroway came by a few days ago."

"He did?" Aurora grew apprehensive. "What did he want?"

"To drive me deaf with all his talking. Told me you'd lost your mind and been abducted by Satanists, that sort of thing. I let him ramble on for a piece about how we had to save you, then sent him home."

"Oh my . . . "

"He'll get over it," Walter added quickly, fighting back a grin. "Trust me. So what do you say we eat before you folks unpack?"

They did just that.

Dinner was a wonderfully inappropriate combination of roast beef, cucumber sandwiches, and warm white wine. The roast was blood red and attracted the immediate attention of Luther, who leaped up onto the dinner table. Rather than shoo him off, Walter Smith set out an extra plate for the dog. "Don't tell your mother about this," he cautioned Aurora.

They talked a great deal over dinner, and during the course of the conversation it was revealed that Brian Garroway had somehow fingered George as the reason for his sudden loss of girlfriend (Aurora had told him nothing; at the moment of the breakup Brian had become so self-righteously angry that she had not even bothered trying to explain the why behind her decision).

"He said he only suspected," Walter told them, "but he said it was a strong suspicion, and terrible if it turned out to be true. Made you out to be a real corrupt character, George, a no-account purveyor of filth trying to destroy the morals of every literate soul in America. Just like that James Joyce. Of course after an introduction like that I couldn't wait to read your books. Town library didn't have them, and neither did the five and dime, so I took a drive down to Milwaukee."

"Milwaukee?" said George. "But that must be fifty miles south of here."

"Fifty-three," Walter corrected. "And worth every minute of the trip. Marvelous writing . . . I haven't been so entertained since I discovered Bel Kaufman back in seventy-five."

George was deeply flattered by this, though he hadn't the slightest idea who Bel Kaufman was or what she had written. Aurora, wondering what precisely had gotten into her father, fell silent and gobbled down an abundance of cucumber sandwiches, which gave rise to a loud burping fit during dessert. She excused herself and rushed off to the bathroom.

No sooner had Aurora departed than Walter also got up from the table.

"Come on," he said to George, gesturing.

"Come on?"

"Get your coat," said Walter. "We'll go out for a walk. There are a few things I want to talk over with you."

"All right." Leaving his dessert unfinished, George stood and followed Walter outside. Left unsupervised, Luther set about methodically devouring every remaining morsel on the table.

The two men walked parallel to the sunset, coming eventually to the great cow pasture that bordered the Smiths' property. Snow lay only sparsely on the ground, but it made a pleasant crunch beneath their feet, adding a cadence to the conversation.

"I'm going to use an old-fashioned expression," Walter warned, and then did: "You consider yourself a suitor for my daughter's hand?"

"Do I plan to marry her, you mean?" asked George. He thought this over a moment and laughed. "Talking marriage already, man oh man . . . well hell, who knows, I suppose that might be in the cards."

"Never mind supposes and never mind the cards, son. You've got a will of your own, don't you? Do you want to marry her, or not marry her, or some other option?"

"I love your daughter," George said earnestly, "and for all that it's come out of nowhere I have a feeling I'm going to stay in love with her, which means, to my way of thinking, that we'll eventually get married unless her feeling for me changes. But . . . I want you to understand that I consider myself a strong-willed person, Mr. Smith, but Fate doesn't always listen to will, and lately I've gotten especially nervous about Fate. Even if I did decide to marry your daughter, you never know, a flash flood might come sweeping through tomorrow morning and carry her off someplace where I can't find her, or an earthquake . . . "

"We'll put you down as a tentative suitor," Walter decided. "And as a concerned potential father-in-law, of course, I get to ask you some personal questions to make sure you're the right sort of fellow. I expect total honesty, now—I got sharp eyes, I'll know if you're lying to me." He began to rattle off a long list of queries, which George answered as best he could: "Are you in any way peculiar?"

"Yes sir, I guess I am."

"Praise the Lord. Ever been convicted of a felony?"

"No sir."

"Ever commit a felony and not get caught?"

"Not that I know of."

"Ever want to commit a felony?"

"Like what, Mr. Smith?"

"Oh, I don't know . . . something interesting like train robbery or vandalizing a national monument."

"I could think about it if you'd like me to."

"Fine—I'm going to hold you to that. Ever been a member of a subversive organization?"

"The Writers' Guild of America."

"Not good enough."

"I went on a Unitarian Church picnic once."

"You're my man. Have any homosexual tendencies?"

"Not unless they're lesbian tendencies."

"Pity. You a drinking man, George?"

"Occasionally. I've toned it down since my undergrad days."

"Better for your liver that way. Take any drugs?"

"Well . . . it's more or less traditional to experiment in college, you know, and at Cornell—"

"Smoke any pot?"

George nodded, tentatively. "Been known to. But not often—I can't write worth shit with a buzz on."

"You write every day, do you?"

"I ought to. Sometimes it doesn't work out that way."

"I know how that is. Plan on doing any writing tonight?"

"Tonight? No, this is my vacation time."

"Well then." Abruptly, and with a suddenness that belied his years, Walter Smith turned and vaulted the fence in a single bound. Once on the far side he spun himself around several times, laughing like a schoolboy.

"Mr. Smith?" George inquired, fearing a brain tumor.

"George," Walter replied, stopping his spin. "George, you'll be happy to know that I've decided to give my full blessing to you and Aurora, whatever you may want to do with each other. Now how about we say screw formality and go get stoned over by that tree stump yonder?"

There are some offers which a wise man does not even consider rejecting. In any case, the sight of this senior citizen producing a joint from his breast pocket—and not just an ordinary joint, either, but a six-inch Bob Marley Memorial—so stunned George that he could not help but comply. Nodding, he too vaulted the fence and followed Walter down to the old tree stump, where they talked about their respective unorthodoxies for as long as conversation was still possible.

A long time they were out there, smoking by the stump; the sun finished setting, the stars flickered into life, and a cold breeze blew, bothering them not at all. They only went back to the house when Aurora came and got them—her eyes wide at the sight of the two men capering beneath the moon like mad priests—and long before that they were visited by the original aurora borealis, the glimmering Northern Lights. Caught up by that unearthly glow, a spectacle sent from a higher place, Walter Smith at last found peace, for now he knew, whether it ended well or poorly, his daughter's life would not be average. George, never at peace—for storytellers and saints are not afforded such a luxury in this world—nevertheless appreciated the Lights as much as Walter did, for in that glow he could sense the soul of creation itself, and creation always made him smile.

SURPRISE PACKAGES

I.

Breakfast the next morning was almost exactly as it had been in Aurora's dreams. They had fresh eggs specially purchased for the occasion, bacon, toast, butter, milk, and orange juice. Very traditional, but at the same time not, for once again Luther was up on the table partaking alongside them. The dog was the one element she had not dreamed in advance, but all else was the same: she and George smiling at each other across the bacon plate, her father laughing from the corner at some joke or other. Both men were red-eyed from the previous night's smoking activity, but Aurora tactfully did not mention this.

When the last bit of egg had vanished from their plates, Aurora stood up and led George out of the house in much the same way as Walter had last evening. George did not even ask where they were going, for he had decided overnight that anything this family did after a meal was bound to be enjoyable. While Walter saw to the dishes, Aurora took George on a long, meandering journey through the surrounding countryside, stopping here and there to show him the memory-places of her childhood. Once they knelt to drink with cupped palms from a partly frozen stream, and she asked if this wouldn't be a good site for destiny to bring two lovers together. George said he thought it would, and Aurora grasped his hand and pulled him to his feet, making him run upstream with her to an open field where a farm had once been. The field was heavily overgrown now, the only outbuilding left standing being a dark and weather-stained barn. The barn looked less than inviting—it looked haunted, in fact, perhaps with the spirits of long-departed milk cows—but it was to this very place that Aurora gestured.

"Inside," she told him.

"What's in there?"

She grinned and kissed his mouth. "It's a surprise."

254

II.

Many miles east, a snowball fight had whipped up on The Ithaca Commons. Two teenagers had started it, but it had rapidly spread to their friends and then to a group of younger children from the local elementary school, let loose for the holidays. Preacher and Jinsei—out to take advantage of the sunny Christmas Eve day—got caught somewhere in the middle of the fray and, laughing, began to pelt each other with armloads of snow.

About this same time, a particularly juicy slushball winged out of control and knocked off the hat of a beefy Ithacop who was just stepping out of McDonald's. The cop grunted and fixed a baleful stare on the eight-year-old pipsqueak who had thrown the slusher.

"Hey, *cop!*" piped the pipsqueak, who last evening had snuck into his parents' bedroom to watch *Blackboard Jungle* on late-night TV. "What's ya name, cop?"

"Doubleday," the cop roared. "Sam Doubleday."

"*Ooooooh!*" replied the pipsqueak, matching bellow for bellow. "Ooooooh, *Double*-day!" And he winged another slushball, hitting dead center on the chest this time.

Doubleday, murder in his eye, unhooked his nightstick from his belt and did a lumbering buffalo's charge at the pipsqueak. The pipsqueak, immature but not stupid, made an immediate run for it. What followed was an uneven chase, for Doubleday, with his considerable bulk, was restricted to the paths an early plow had cleared on The Commons, while his small tormentor scrambled easily over the highest snowbanks.

It was into one of these snowbanks that Preacher and Jinsei had collapsed in a tight embrace. Both of them would have been content to remain locked together until the spring thaw, but the passing of the pipsqueak (the bellowing Doubleday remarkably close on his heels) disturbed their intimacy. Preacher raised his head to glance around at the commotion, receiving a severe shock from what turned out to be an optical illusion. His eyes at a low angle, he spied a nearby pair of black boots, black pants, the hem of a black trenchcoat . . .

"Rag!" he blurted out, an instant before realizing that the head sticking up above the collar of the trenchcoat was that of a jaundiced woman with coke-spoon earrings. The woman made no attempt at recognition but walked onward in search of leather goods, leaving the two lovers to their business in the snow. Jinsei reached up to the touch Preacher's face; he shied back, the mood ruined.

He had long since given up feeling guilty, of course; guilt is a difficult emotion to maintain when you know you have done nothing wrong. But the loss of a best friend—you can agonize over that forever, even if, again, you rest assured of your innocence. Ragnarok had done a heroic job of avoidance over the last two months, yet while Preacher had not seen him personally he kept encountering reminders of him, which were no less upsetting.

"Let's walk," Jinsei said, forcing him to stand. Down at one end of The Commons, Doubleday had successfully chased the pipsqueak up a traffic signal pole and was shouting the most dire threats at him; they turned and headed the other way. Speaking in soft tones, Jinsei tried to lull Preacher back to pleasanter thoughts, only to be thwarted by the appearance of another figure garbed in black. This fellow, a mime, wore a bulky robe rather than a trenchcoat, but his face was painted an obscene pale white and he stood within an inch of Ragnarok's height.

The mime was handing out flyers; Jinsei and Preacher moved to avoid him but he sidestepped even as they did, thrusting a paper in Preacher's hand and then whirling away with a wink.

"What does it say?" Jinsei asked him. Preacher shrugged and handed her the flyer, which read:

THE NEWLY FORMED BARDIC TROUPE OF ITHACA
gives advance announcement
of a wondrous Shakespearean event
Coming in March
ROMEO AND JULIET
"A tale of star-cross'd lovers . . . "
and
JULIUS CAESAR
watch for further details
in the coming weeks

Jinsei looked at Preacher and smiled.

" 'Star-cross'd lovers,' " she said, squeezing his hand. "I like the sound of that, don't you?"

III.

The hayloft was high above the barn floor, the ladder leading to it rickety enough that you were quite content just to make it safely to the top, though there was precious little to see. The last bales of hay had long since been removed, and all that remained on the hard wooden platform were some rusting farm implements, a scattering of chaff, and a pair of plaid quilts that were a little moldy but good for sitting on. It was warm in the loft, surprisingly so; a draft whined somewhere off in the rafters but did not disturb them.

"So what do we do?" George asked when they had got themselves settled. "Enjoy the view?"

"The view's exciting," Aurora said seriously, glancing down at the distant barn floor, "but I had something else in mind."

She lifted a loose plank near the corner of the platform, and in what seemed to George an act of pure magic, produced a bottle of red wine and two crystal goblets from the space beneath.

"How did that get up here?" he gasped. "What did you do, sneak out in the middle of the night?"

"No, silly," Aurora laughed, wiping the goblets with the sleeve of her coat. "These have been here since I was twelve."

"Since you were twelve?"

"Yep. This was my secret hideout when I was little. All of the other kids were afraid of it because there were supposed to be monsters inside, but I had a great time playing here. This loft makes a great pretend balcony for a Princess to address her loyal subjects."

George nodded, smiling. "But what about the wine and the cups? Where'd you get them in the first place?"

"A man gave them to me."

"What man?"

Aurora shrugged. "I don't know. A stranger who was standing outside in the field one day. Southern European looking, Spanish or maybe Greek. Friendly eyes. Maybe I should have been afraid of him but I wasn't. He said he had a present for me, something I should save until the time was right." She handed George the wine, and a silver corkscrew. "Here, you do the honors."

George studied the bottle in his hand.

"Interesting label," he said. "'*Leidenschaft von Heiliger* . . .'"

"'Doctor Faustus Vineyards,'" Aurora finished for him. "'Vintage 1749.'"

"Sounds like a joke," George decided. "And there's no way it could be that old. I'll bet it's just grape juice laced with codeine—that stranger was probably a drug pusher out to get you hooked."

"I took codeine once," she said. "For an ear infection. It's not all that terrible."

"Might be poisoned, too."

She shook her head. "It's not poisoned."

"How do you know?"

"The same way I know it's time to open it. I just do."

Nodding, George argued no further but broke the wax seal on the bottle and inserted the corkscrew. The cork came out with a pleasant ease; the wine murmured comfortably as he poured it.

"Tell me about the monsters," George said, when they had toasted each other.

"Hmm?"

"The monsters that were supposed to be inside the barn when you were little."

"Oh, that." She shrugged. "Plain old ghosts, I suppose . . . whose I don't even know. I guess I couldn't bring myself to be scared over what was dead and buried. It was nice, really, having a private place where nobody else would bother me."

"Nice," George agreed, his tongue already heavy though his goblet was not yet half empty. Heady stuff.

"You know I'm still a virgin," Aurora said next, and the wine must have affected him, for the sudden change of topic did not, as it normally would have, cause him to choke, drop his cup, or otherwise lose control of his bodily functions.

"Ever read Fariña?"

"Fariña?"

"Richard Fariña. Went to Cornell in the late Fifties and raised some hell with this dude Kirkpatrick Sale from the *Sun;* the two of them would have made prime Bohemians. After graduation Fariña married Joan Baez's sister and wrote this wild novel about college and hell-raising in general. Motorcycle accident killed him two days after the book was published."

"Perfect timing."

"Really. I should be so lucky. Anyway, the novel's protagonist is a very Fariña-type guy named Gnossos Popoudopolos, and Gnossos has this theory about virginity being spiritual. . . ."

"Is this like your theory about the nobility of gay people?"

"Hey, Fariña knew that of which he spoke. The idea, see, is that you can screw every man and woman in the jolly United States of America and still be a virgin. The membrane only breaks when you make love."

"But you've made love, haven't you?" Aurora asked. "With Calliope?"

"That's true."

"And I've never even screwed anybody."

"That's true."

"So how is Fariña's theory possibly relevant to our situation?"

"Well, it isn't," George said, swallowing a long draught of *Leidenschaft von Heiliger.* "But it's bad luck to pass up any chance at a literary reference. Beside, it's a great damn book."

"Sure it is," said Aurora. "Finish that drink and teach me how to seduce you."

IV.

"I don't know if it's such a good idea to go through the graveyard." It had been Jinsei's idea to climb The Hill in a show of pure defiance against the snow, but now, at the lower entrance to The Boneyard, she balked. "Look, the plow hasn't even been through there," she pointed out. "And I'll bet the drifts are pretty deep."

"At least we won't have to dodge cars," Preacher replied. They had been walking in the road, for the plow that had cleared University Avenue had inadvertently erected a scale rendition of the Alps above the only sidewalk.

"We'll get our boots wet," Jinsei countered.

"No matter. Look, Jin, that snow's virgin. Don't you want to be the first to walk on it?"

"I don't know . . ."

"You scared of what's buried under?"

She shrugged. "Maybe a little. Aren't you?"

"No point to it. Dead body's like a waxwork, lady. Might as well get uptight over a scarecrow or a dresser's dummy."

This did not seem to comfort her a great deal; smiling gently, Preacher clasped her hand and took a step toward the cemetery gates.

"Come on, Jin," he said. "Let me tell you another secret: as long as you walk in under your own steam there's nothing to fear. When they hire six guys to *carry* you in, that's the time to wig out."

He tugged lightly on her arm and she relented, following him through the gates. Just beyond, a group of snowbound mausoleums jutted out of the side of a slope, like a great townhouse for the dead. Jinsei spied this with more than a little apprehension, but of course it was not the dead she ought to have been afraid of. Not at all.

Kicking up small clouds of snow, they turned left when they could, and headed unwittingly toward the north end of The 'Yard.

V.

George undid the last button on Aurora's blouse and slipped it back, revealing the warm pale shoulders beneath. He thought to himself that that was an odd word, *pale*—a word that could be positive or negative depending on the context, one that could describe everything from death to the forehead of a medieval princess.

Ah, literary to the last. He bent his head and began kissing her breasts. Time went away for a while, like a tactful fade in a romance novel; when it came back they were both naked, lay pressed together on the quilts. They had kissed and touched and explored one another and now the Moment was upon them.

"This might hurt some." George warned her. "Since you've never done it before."

Beneath him, Aurora smiled. "Did you read that in some book, too?"

"Read it in a lot of books. Had a few friends describe the pain to me, too. In detail."

"Same here." Her lips parted to kiss his shoulder. "But right now," she said, "right now I feel very . . . relaxed. I don't know if I could hurt, feeling like this. Maybe that's what the wine was for."

"Maybe," George agreed. There was nothing more to say; he went into her with a kind and dreamy gentleness. There was no pain.

VI.

"Jesus!"

Preacher took a step and suddenly sank waist deep in snow. Jinsei immediately gripped his arm with both hands and prepared for a struggle, for it seemed almost as if something had grabbed Preacher from below in an attempt to drag him under.

"It's all right," Preacher assured her. "Just stepped in a hole. I'm OK."

"Can we *please* get out of this place?" Jinsei pleaded, still gripping his arm.

"Sure, right up . . ." Preacher started to pull himself up when his foot caught on something. "Wait. Hang out a second."

He pulled his arm loose of her, then turned and stepped full into the hole, knocking out some more space for himself. He bent down and dug.

"Preacher, what—"

"Something here . . ." He gave a hard tug, freeing something from the earth. He held it up triumphantly.

Jinsei blanched, thinking at first that Preacher had somehow dredged up a piece of corpse, though on closer inspection she saw that the object was actually a box—a black iron box, a cube no more than half a foot to a side, wrapped with a single silver band.

VII.

Approaching the pinnacle, the two lovers abandoned the quilts and rolled precipitously close to the edge of the hayloft, groaning in comfortable uncomfortableness at the feel of the uneven wood planking. George found himself once again in a state of awe, for where making love to Calliope had been smooth and perfect, this present coupling was marvelously amateurish and sloppy—and all the better for that. He reveled in the reality of it.

Very near the summit now, somebody's arm or leg struck the bottle of *Leidenschaft von Heiliger*, sending it flying. It did a bombs away and sprayed red wine all the way down, smashing to bits on the floor below. Neither of the lovers even noticed.

VIII.

"Preacher, I really wish we could go somewhere else to open that. . . ."

"Hang out," Preacher responded.

Paper thin, the silver band tore easily. He unwound it from the box, offering it to Jinsei. She would not take it; shrugging, Preacher folded it and placed it in the pocket of his longcoat.

"Preacher, I think . . ."

But he did not hear her, so fascinated was he with the riddle of the box. All the seams had been carefully sealed with some sort of solder, but the solder was brittle with time and chipped away easily enough. Using his thumbnail, Preacher cleaned off most of it, then began to raise the lid of the box.

Even as he did, something with wings and talons of ice struck him on the side of the head and sent him sprawling.

IX.

George and Aurora cried out together, as did the wind, ever George's ally. Shrieking, it took hold of the barn and shook it like a toy.

"Again," Aurora whispered, when the earth had stopped moving.

X.

"What *is* it?"

Preacher pushed himself up on one hand, using the other to touch his bloodied forehead. The box had been knocked away and had landed on its side in the snow a few yards beyond him, open just a crack. It was not the box that held his or Jinsei's attention anymore, however, but rather the strange bone-pale bird that had settled on top of it.

"Sweet Jesus," Preacher said, as Jinsei knelt beside him and pressed a handkerchief on his wound. The bird had to be the most unnatural-looking creature he had ever laid eyes on, like a crystalline statue somehow animated to life.

The Messenger steadied itself on the tilted surface of the box. It watched the man and woman warily; it had been watching them ever since they had first entered The Boneyard. Preacher had been permitted to pick up the box and break the Seals, but now that that was accomplished the Messenger would kill him—kill both of them—to protect the contents.

"Let's get *out* of here!" Jinsei hissed. Preacher nodded, took her hand, and together they backed away, turning to run as soon as they had gotten a reasonable lead. The Messenger made no move to follow them but did not take its eyes off them, either; it studied their retreat most attentively.

From within Pandora's Box, another creature studied them as well.

MESSAGES,
AND A PARLIAMENT
OF VERMIN

I.

"All right," Mr. Sunshine said, eager at his Writing Desk. "All right, George has his Princess, the Princess has her George, and the box is open. Now, what's next . . . " He riffled his Notes. "The dog! That's right, the dog!"

Searching inside his Desk for a piece of Stationery (not, of course, ordinary stationery), he scrawled a quick Message. Then, folding it twice, he wended his way through the Monkeys to a dim corner where a Mail Chute waited with open mouth. The Chute bore this symbol: ☿ and the legend: UNDERWORLD CORRESPONDENCE ONLY.

"Not quite like the old days," Mr. Sunshine said wistfully, as his Message made an uncertain descent down the dark Chute. "But still, that takes care of that. Now . . . "

II.

Just after dusk on that same Christmas Eve, Mrs. Smith called from Madison to announce that she would not be home for another day at least, though she felt terribly about missing the holiday with her family and gave all her love to Aurora. Sensing a golden opportunity, Walter and George built a cozy fire in the hearth and conspired to introduce Aurora to what Lion-Heart had always called the Dubious Art of Getting Stoned; after the briefest hesitation, she turned out to be an excellent pupil. The three of them were soon giggling like cheerful idiots, hugging one another, and tossing off non sequiturs a mile a minute. Even Luther managed to join in the fun. He could not puff a joint, of course, but he stuck close to Walter—of whom he had grown quite fond, thinking him an archangel—who obligingly exhaled in his direction.

Luther had at last found contentment: more food than he had ever seen before, warmth, dry shelter, and kind Masters. Surely he must, finally, be in

Heaven. True, he had encountered no other dogs here, nor had he seen any during the entire chariot ride up, but for the time being he was so overwhelmed by comfort that he asked no questions. He had even ceased to worry about Blackjack, though he knew he must soon find a way to get a message to him.

Now, as his shaggy head tingled strangely in response to the smoke, Luther felt the divine power of Heaven close in around him. The room grew bright; Luther's eyes were drawn to the space right before the fireplace, where, as casual as you please, an aging mongrel materialized out of thin air. It was a dog he knew well, a dog who had protected him and given him love when he was only a pup. A dog he had initially set out for Heaven to find.

"*Moses!*" Luther cried, his deepest hopes realized. "Moses, I found you!"

Moses did not speak, but turned almost immediately and began walking out. Luther followed him, leaving the humans to their laughter.

"Moses, Moses, where have you been? I missed you more than anything! I—"

Moses led him down a short hall into the kitchen, where a gust of wind blew open the back door. The older dog marched straight outside, unmindful of the cold. Luther stayed close on the heels of his sire. Long minutes they walked, deep into the night, until the Smith house became a mere twinkle of distant warmth and light. Only then did Moses stop and turn once more.

"Oh, Moses!" said Luther, who had kept up a joyous babble the whole time. "Moses, it's so good to be here with you."

The old mongrel looked at him with deepest regret.

"You gotta leave this place, Luther," he said.

III.

The creature crept out of the iron box shortly after nightfall. Small, twisted, utterly loathsome in appearance, it was no wonder his enemies had called him Grub. At last released, his first thought was to vent his anger on the prison that had confined him for so long. Yet to his great fury he discovered that he could do nothing to the box; the act of sustaining himself for more than a century had drained him of his magic, and he was now powerless.

Hateful, hateful, hateful! How could he wreak his revenge, without magic? To be free and still helpless was even greater torture than confinement. . . .

Rasferret.

The Messenger waited patiently on the snow behind him, wings folded.

Rasferret, a bargain for you.

The Grub quailed at the sight of the ice bird, for he was a coward at heart, and without magic he could no more defend himself than he could attack. Only the mention of a bargain kept him from fleeing, whatever good that might have done.

And so in that cold place of the dead, the Messenger passed on the Word that Mr. Sunshine had given it, communicating in a silent tongue. Rasferret listened, growing bolder as he heard the terms of the offered bargain. Was it revenge he craved? He would have it. Did he need fresh magic to accomplish that revenge? That too would be his, in greater amount than he had ever known before—and with it he could slay and destroy to his heart's content. Only one catch was placed on the deal: that an opponent would be raised up against him, not a sprite but one of the Big People, a man with great power and will of his own. The Grub would have magic to fight him, but to keep it he must win the battle. If he failed, he would forever after be powerless.

The strength of magic began flowing back into Rasferret's body even before the Messenger concluded, and having tasted of it the Grub could not refuse the deal, no matter what the eventual consequences. He flexed his newfound power by warping the prison-box into an unidentifiable wreck of metal, making the lid-hinges pop like breaking bones.

Well, well. In the blink of an eye he had shed his helplessness. But his power was not yet complete—he was made to understand that the magic would accrue gradually, peaking some two and a half months from now on the Ides of March, when the crucial battle would take place. Between then and now there was much work to be done. He had never killed a human before; he would have to practice.

IV.

"Leave?" Luther protested. "But I just got here!"

"Don't you give me that look, Luther. It's not my fault. You got a part to play, back on that Hill you came here from. Not a big part, but it's what's wanted."

Luther glanced back toward the distant house. "But *they* brought me here. I can't make the trip alone."

"Why not? You already did it once. Only difference is you won't have the cat with you this time, but you'll manage fine enough without him. I'm not saying it won't be a trial to you, mind—the Road's got longer, and you can be sure Raaq is still angry at you for getting away from him. But like I say, you'll manage."

"But do I have to leave right now?"

"What'd I always teach you? Did it ever pay for a dog to put off a hard task?"

"No," Luther replied despondently. "But—"

"You've gone and used one 'but' too many already, Luther. Now—"

"*Listen to me!*" Luther insisted, with an abrupt burst of anger that was completely unlike him. "This whole thing—the reason I left home in the first place—was to find you again. And after all I've gone through you show up just to tell me how I have to leave a place where I'm finally happy."

"Spirit," Moses observed, showing the first bit of good humor since his sudden appearance. "You changed, Luther. You're not the innocent little pup I left behind me. I wager it's the Road that changed you—could be it'll change you more before it's done with you. But any way you look at it, you don't need me anymore."

"I *want* to be with you. Will you walk with me?"

"I'll show you where to pick up the scent. Beside that . . . well, I'm a ghost, Luther. What you want to spend time with me for?"

"I told you . . ."

"That's a kind thing," Moses said. "You missing me so much. But it makes no difference, you see, 'cause you were wrong. You can't walk to Heaven, Luther. It may come to *you*, sometime, but—"

"You mean this isn't Heaven, either?"

"Guess you ain't lost all of your innocence. *Course* it ain't Heaven. Heaven's like nothing you could ever expect, Luther. Neither is death, come to that. And a wise dog, he don't waste his time looking for either one."

"One of the philosophers I met told me it was good to waste time doing things like that . . . following obsessions. Especially when I don't know what else to do."

"Well . . . when you don't know what else to do. But I just told you what you ought to be about, didn't I?"

"You did," Luther admitted.

"Just so. Come on now and I'll show you where to start."

V.

Even as Luther was engaged in the curious reunion with his sire, many hundred miles to the east Rasferret the Grub was busy setting up a little reunion of his own. Reunion, of course, is not quite the right word; recreation would be more accurate.

Riding on the back of the Messenger, the Grub relocated to a different part of The Boneyard, away from the place where he had been so long entrapped. As the moon rose in a cold arc above the horizon, he used his magic for a Summoning. Some hours later, near midnight (Luther had by this time bade a regretful farewell to Moses and set out on his new journey), Rasferret had himself set down atop a jutting stone rectangle that bore the words:

DEDICATED TO THE LOVING MEMORY
OF HAROLD LAZARUS
1912–1957
BY HIS ADORING WIFE
GOD GRANT HIM REST

This tombstone, as mentioned before, was capped by a gargoyle figurine. It was onto the shoulders of this figurine that Rasferret settled himself, and to say whether gargoyle or Grub had the more horrendous countenance would be difficult. The Messenger set down nearby, perching in a lower place. When all was ready Rasferret brought his Parliament to order with a silent command.

In excess of fifty rats had gathered on the snow surrounding the tombstone, like dark castings left by a passing beast. They had come in answer to Rasferret's summons, some creeping out of deep tunnels in the earth, others from cellars and dank sewers, all bringing bits and pieces of junk as tribute—shiny scraps of metal, snips of wire, beads, small bones. Having taken their places they waited to be made over, the tiny white plumes of their breath mimicking a ground mist.

Rasferret did not speak so much as a single word; instead, eyes glowing bright blue—the blue that is the hottest part of a flame—he lifted his misshapen arms, in the manner of a preacher bidding his congregation to rise. And rise they did, or tried to. Each rat, spine crackling in metamorphosis, struggled to stand straight on its hind feet. Some succeeded; others, less fortunate, got halfway up only to collapse, crippled beyond repair. Most of these did not live long.

The metamorphosis concluded. Of the fifty or some rats who had come to the Parliament, perhaps twenty survived the transformation and became Rats, bipedal soldiers in Rasferret's new army. They were already armed, for the objects they had brought with them had also been transformed, bits of metal becoming crude swords, wire and bone knitting together to form crossbows.

The Grub reviewed his troops. Twenty was not a large number, but there would be many more as his power increased. Even the magic he had already been granted would have been sufficient for quite a few more transformations, but he was conserving, saving his energy for a special bit of business several nights hence. Rasferret grinned obscenely in anticipation of his first murderous acts in more than a hundred years.

As he grinned, one of his troops broke ranks. The Rat was a large one, the largest of the twenty actually, and carried both a crossbow and a long blade. It limped, but Rasferret sensed that the limp was the result of a previous injury, not an accident in metamorphosis. Curious, Rasferret met the Rat's gaze, saw the anger and love of destruction within it. There passed a moment of perfect communication between the two of them during which, again, not a word was spoken.

At last the Grub nodded in assent, receiving a clumsy bow in return. And that is how Thresh the Rat, the slayer of Cobweb, became a General in the army of vermin, second in command only to Rasferret himself.

THE KILLING HOUR

I.

Wind the clock for a killing hour, then. Let it begin just before the turn of years, at 11:15 on the night of December thirty-first, with the snapping of a branch. Let it conclude fifty-eight minutes later, at thirteen past midnight, with a sound like fingernails on a coffin. And set it up just so:

On the morning after Christmas, Preacher looked into the bathroom mirror to find his head wound almost healed. Noon of the same day, Jinsei received a phone call from the supervisor at Uris Library, where she had been working since October. Over the winter break the Library was doing an extensive reorganization of its card-file system, and those few student workers who remained in Ithaca were urgently needed. The roads had been cleared sufficiently of snow by now that travel up The Hill was no longer a great odyssey, and after a short conversation, Jinsei agreed to come in that afternoon. In fact, Jinsei worked at the Library almost every afternoon that week, up to and including the thirty-first, often staying until late in the night.

Late in the night on the twenty-seventh, Rasferret moved his camp from The Boneyard to the crown of The Hill. Riding on the back of the Messenger, he soared unseen to the belfry of McGraw Hall, the central of the three grey boxes that had been the first buildings erected on the campus. A century ago the belfry had housed Jenny McGraw's famous chimes, but now only dust resided there—dust, and Rasferret the Grub. His Rats traveled on foot over snow-encrusted ground to join him, and together they set up a discreet base of operations, within sight of the Clock Tower where Hobart dreamed fearsome dreams.

The twenty-eighth and twenty-ninth were days of watching and waiting, with precious little incident, but a number of important things happened on the thirtieth. Preacher got in touch with Fujiko, who was having a wonderfully carnal vacation over at Tolkien House; they agreed to have a small get-together to celebrate New Year's Eve, with Preacher bringing Jinsei up to the House after she got off work. The sprites, too, had a New Year's celebration

268

in the works, an HO-scale gala with skating on the frozen surface of Beebe Lake. One of Rasferret's Rats managed to overhear a group of sprites talking about this, and while the creature did not understand much of what was said, it got the gist: that tomorrow night, the majority of the Little People would be off away from the center of campus, out of ear and eyeshot of whatever might go on there. Rasferret had at last been provided with a striking date; he spent most of that night laying his final plans. Barely twenty miles away, in a chalet along cold Cayuga's shore, Ragnarok spoke a prophecy. From a deep slumber he uttered a single sentence: "My God, her eyes are glowing." Myoko and Lion-Heart, locked together in their own room, did not hear this, nor would they have understood it if they had.

December thirty-first dawned bleak and cold, with a promise of fresh snow. Jinsei and Preacher made love one last time before she went up The Hill to work. Love left them joyful and unaware.

Night came all too quickly.

II.

Preacher tramped up the front steps of Uris Library shortly after eleven o'clock on New Year's Eve, bearing a gift for his Lady. Snow came down in light swirls, enough to dust the ground and obscure the glowing faces of the Clock Tower in a fine reflected haze. He stepped right up to the glass doors, which were locked, and rapped loudly with a white-gloved fist. Jinsei appeared a moment later, a long-stemmed rose wrapped and tucked delicately into the crook of one arm. She fumbled with an enormous ring of keys and managed to unlock the doors.

"Hey," Preacher said, leaning in out of the cold to kiss her. "Where's your coat?"

"Um . . ." Jinsei replied, kissing him back. "Mrs. Woolf wants me to stay on another hour."

"Does she?" he said, sounding unimpressed. "It's New Year's, Jin. Fujiko, her dude, and midnight are all waiting on us. Can't you work an extra hour some other time?"

"I could, but . . . well . . ." She held up her hand, the thumb and forefinger a bare centimeter apart. "We're *that* close to finishing with the letter R."

"Oh," said Preacher, and they both got laughing. He laid a ginger hand on the wrapped flower under her arm. "What's this?"

She shrugged, handing it to him. "Something I picked up for you on the way to work. It's probably wilted by now."

"Mmm." He bent and kissed her again, lingering a bit longer at her mouth. "I brought you something, too."

"Oh?" She traced the line of his jaw with a finger. "What?"

He drew back, grinning. Wind rushed in the open doorspace and shuffled the dark strands of her hair.

"Tell you what," Preacher said. "I'll give it to you when we get to Tolkien House."

"Mean." Jinsei tried for a pout but couldn't quite handle it. "I gave you your flower already, didn't I? But honestly, Preacher, Mrs. Woolf really wants me to stay that extra hour. I think it'll make her New Year for her."

"If you finish the letter R?"

"If we finish the letter R."

"That's going to make her life better?"

"Old librarians are easy to please."

"Hmm," He kissed her a third time, lingering, lingering. "What about young librarians?"

"Oh, they come along eventually," she told him. "Why don't you go ahead, tell Fujiko and Noldorin that I'll be a little late. I'll probably miss midnight, but I'll be there as soon after as I can."

Preacher opened his mouth to speak and she caught him in yet another kiss, putting the brakes on any further argument. When they broke for air he was nodding, a smile practically etched onto his face.

"All right," he conceded. "Can't disagree with that kind of reasoning. You just be careful walking up to the House, hear me?"

"I'll be careful," she promised.

"All right. And here." Clutching the rose affectionately, Preacher fished in his coat pocket with his free hand and brought out a small white box.

"What is it?"

"I forget," Preacher shrugged. "You'll have to open it and see."

She did. The bracelet in the box was dark-stained wood, girdled with a band of bright silver that shimmered prettily in the arc-light above the library door.

"It's beautiful!" Jinsei gasped, then remembered a bone-pale bird and a sealed iron box. "Oh no. This isn't—"

Preacher nodded. "I had it in my pocket when we ran. Got it in my head yesterday to go see a friend on Buffalo Street who makes jewelry. Waste not, want not, I figure." That was not all of it—there was more to his odd compulsion to do something with the silver band than simple economy—but it was all he could find words to say.

"Oh, Preacher," said Jinsei haltingly, "Preacher, it's beautiful, but . . . I never want to go into that graveyard again, and I'm not sure I can keep something that will remind me what happened there."

"What *did* happen there, Jin? A little scare, a little scratch. My head's all better now." He looked at her, caught her with something in his gaze. "It's a pretty thing," he said. "And I don't know, maybe it'll bring you luck sometime. They say silver's good for that."

It was her turn to argue no further. A strange feeling seemed to charge the air around them, a feeling of . . . well, momentousness. Something big, something serious about to happen. Jinsei took the silvered bracelet and set it upon her wrist; in that moment her love for Preacher was as strong as it ever had been, ever would be.

"You be careful too," she said, catching his hands in her own. "Walking."

Preacher grinned. "I'm always careful, Lady."

They drew together for one last kiss before he set off, but the kiss multiplied into a long series of kisses, and for a precious grain of time they stood necking in the doorway, card-files and Rhetta Woolf waiting within for Jinsei, snow and darkness waiting without for Preacher, the dance of lips and tongue obliterating all but each other.

III.

Rasferret the Grub was alone in his hideaway, his Rats since dispatched on various dark errands, the Messenger set to circling above the Arts Quad, a warden against unforeseen intrusions in the hunt. Not that Rasferret was entirely blind, shut up in the belfry. He had a Sense, a magically enhanced feel for the surrounding territory; he knew where his troops were, and his targets.

He crouched in a tight wooden crawlspace littered with the scraps of careless meals, concentrating on his first animation in over a hundred years. A long time it had been, but he was fresh with power, and he had not forgotten the trick. It lay in a drawing together of the mind, a focusing, a willful push. A portion of Rasferret's being—soul, spirit, *ka*, call it what you will—twisted free, coalescing in front of him, little more than a sparkling shimmer in the air, really, a gossamer of gossamers. He concentrated still further, marveling at the ease of it despite his lack of practice, and sent the essence outward into the night, searching for a host to animate, not knowing that one had already been selected and prepared for him by the Storyteller.

Rasferret's *ka* shot northward with dizzying speed and purpose, drawn magnetically toward Fraternity Row, toward Tolkien House, where a pale mannequin stood waiting like an expectant bride. In that hidden part of Lothlórien where the trees grew thickest, Rasferret's spirit entered into the Rubbermaid, giving life to plastic limbs, igniting glass eyes with blue fire. Looking out through those eyes, Rasferret sampled his new shape, flexing the hands, swinging the arms, breaking a branch underfoot as he took his first step forward.

It was 11:15, and the killing hour had begun.

IV.

Tolkien House co-president Amos Noldorin and his Lady Fujiko—naked as Adam and Lilith in Eden—lay together on a white silk sheet in the clearing by Lothlórien's entrance. Just above them was the door in the hillside that led to the Khazad-dûm sub-cellars and the elevator.

The stars winked prettily in the skydome, with the brief flicker of an occasional meteor adding variety. The air in the Garden was pleasantly warm, not too humid, a faint breeze bringing a scent of exotic flowers— African violets, perhaps, or *mallorn* blossoms. With this environment-controlled Paradise serving as a backdrop, the lovers argued good-naturedly about what they ought to do in the next fifteen minutes or so. Noldorin insisted that they should get dressed and go upstairs to await Preacher and Jinsei, who were due to arrive at any time now. Fujiko, her Bohemian libido in full ascendancy, made her own desires known by running her tongue briskly up and down behind his left ear.

"Now wait," Noldorin protested—not too strongly—as she pushed his back down flat against the sheet and endeavored to climb on top of him. "Just wait, they're going to be here any minute."

"Is the front door locked?" asked Fujiko, her small form above his large one now, kissing his chest.

"No," Noldorin admitted, weakening.

"What of it, then?"

"I'll tell you what of it . . . I'll . . . look, *look*, what if they walk in and find us like this?"

"Let them get their own sheet," Fujiko suggested, her hands at work. "Or they can use the grass."

"Don't you think—" Noldorin paused briefly to gasp. "—don't you think that would be just a little breach of good manners?"

"Never preach etiquette to a Risleyite," replied Fujiko, and that was when someone pulled the switch, changed sensual daydream to ice-veined nightmare. Her hands on Noldorin's body grew rigid. His budding erection wilted like a cut flower, and gooseflesh arose on both their skins.

"*Jesus*," Fujiko exclaimed fearfully, and Noldorin, still flat on his back, did not have to ask what was the matter.

The skydome had gone black. Utterly. But that was not the worst thing. The breeze had dropped to nothing, yet somehow all the warmth seemed to have been sucked out of the air with its passing. Steam wisped from the bodies of the two lovers; the temperature plummet was that sudden, that instantaneous. But that was not the worst thing, either, nor was the fog that began to materialize around them, threatening to nullify what little illumination remained from the hidden groundlights. The worst thing was the sound, the not-so-stealthy approach-sound of something that echoed toward them from a nearby bank of trees.

"Jesus, oh Jesus, we're not alone," Fujiko cried, shivering. In another place and time—an eternally distant time—she had gone into battle against an angry motorcycle gang without a qualm, but now a supernatural dread entered her, filled her head with terrible storybook images: the Big Bad Wolf out for Little Red Riding Hood's blood, Hansel and Gretel's Witch, hungry for gingerbread.

Noldorin rose to a crouch, drawing the sheet about him and Fujiko to keep away the cold, hiding their nakedness. He too felt the dread, but not only dread. He felt strangely dizzy: dizzy from the sudden change in temperature, dizzy from lying on his back, dizzy from the wine he had drunk earlier. Head swimming, he studied the ring on his right hand, a silver band set with a white opal. It was intended as a replica of one of Tolkien's three Great Elvish Rings. Magic. Oddly or not so oddly, with his head in a spin and terror crawling beneath his flesh, Noldorin found the concept of magic more interesting than ever before in his life. More crucial.

"The elevator," Fujiko was saying, tugging at him. "Come on, we've got to run to the elevator, get upstairs—"

"No," Noldorin said with sudden certainty. "We won't make it that way. Not the elevator—the Circle."

"What?"

"The Enchanted Circle." He was on his feet, pulling her with him. "Hurry, it might be our only chance!"

Too panic-stricken to argue, she followed him, racing barefoot along the path to the ring of magic stones, the same ring within which Eldest sprite Hobart had, at the Hallowe'en revel, shared the tale of Rasferret the Grub with his fellow Little People.

Noldorin sought no stories, only sanctuary. He hauled Fujiko along as fast as she could go; the thing among the trees drew nearer, hearing them run, pursuing them. Almost at the Circle they lost the white silk sheet. It snagged on a branch, and rather than stop to retrieve it they sprinted the last ten yards naked, diving into the Circle, clutching each other protectively.

Sounds. Wolf, witch, whatever, the thing was still coming, very close now.

"It's all right," Noldorin said, holding Fujiko tight to him. "It's all right." Not stopping to think, he raised his ring hand and called out with as much surety he could muster: "Listen to me! We're in the Circle! Do you hear? We're in the Circle, and you can't come in!"

Fujiko gasped. "Look," The stones forming the Circle had begun to glow, a strong witchlight that cut easily through the gathering fog. Noldorin's ring glowed as well; all at once the air did not feel nearly as cold.

The sounds of approach had stopped.

"That's right!" Noldorin shouted, his voice firmer. "You can't have us! We're safe in the Circle, and you can't come in! There's nothing for you here!"

He waited, and Fujiko with him, wondering if the thing would leave now that it had been thwarted. For a long moment there was silence. Then a loud rustling began, very near them. It was the white sheet being pulled free of the undergrowth where it had fallen. Though both strained their eyes to see, only Fujiko caught a glimpse of the creature, and a vague one at that: a dark shape with two blue sparks where eyes might have been.

Approach-sounds were now departure-sounds; it was leaving them, crashing back through the trees as if remembering an important date elsewhere. Noldorin relaxed, slumping limply back against Fujiko, his relief a thing almost too great for expression.

"What . . . what was that?" he stammered. He rested his head on Fujiko's shoulder, shaking. Around them the ring of stones began to dim, their magic no longer needed.

"I don't know," Fujiko answered, a tear running down her cheek. "I don't know, but Preacher and Jinsei are going to be walking right into it."

V.

The white sheet had become animate at a touch, and now, as the obsidian-walled elevator rose swiftly up to the main floor, it wrapped itself around the Rubbermaid like a living shroud. The sheet was a spur-of-the-moment thing, a casual addition; the Rubbermaid's search for a weapon was more deliberate.

On the first floor, seeking an exit, the mannequin discovered the Michel Delving Mathom-Hole. The Rubbermaid surveyed its collection of relics, each marked with its own label: THIS IS THE HORN OF BOROMIR; HERE IS ANDURIL, THE SWORD THAT WAS BROKEN. In one case that drew the 'Maid's particular attention lay a long black mace shod with iron. The label pronounced THIS WEAPON WAS WIELDED BY THE LORD OF THE NAZGÛL, THE WITCH-KING OF ANGMAR.

Glass shattered as the Rubbermaid thrust plastic hands into the display case like a weasel puncturing an eggshell, groping for the treasure within. The mace was solid, with a good heft. The Rubbermaid swung it once as a test, sending another glass case crashing to the floor, then hurried out into the night in search of prey.

VI.

Preacher actually spent a good long time necking in the front doorway of the Library before finally disentangling himself from Jinsei. The beckoning voice of the head librarian interrupted their reverie, and with a last peck Preacher turned and set out across the Arts Quad. It was 11:22.

He might have gone down the Slope, crossing Fall Creek Gorge along Stewart Avenue and so coming to Tolkien House that way; instead he chose to cross the Gorge on the suspension bridge. Ultimately it made little difference. Preacher's movements as soon as he left the Library were tracked most closely, and compensated for.

Oblivious to his own peril, he half walked, half floated past McGraw Hall, whistling some or other love song that he'd heard that morning on the radio, snow swirling blithely around him. He cut left between White and Tjaden Halls, laughing out loud when he slipped on a patch of ice and almost fell. In front of the Johnson Art Museum he paused to listen to the wind chimes. In the cold winter air they made a flat, haunted sound, but Preacher found them cheerful. He found damn near everything cheerful tonight.

The bleak—but cheerful, oh so cheerful—glow of one of the campus Blue Light Emergency Phones marked the way down to the suspension bridge. The Phones had been installed several years ago after a series of at-gunpoint rapes. That had been a nervous time, back then; the rapist had been black, and Preacher, who was often abroad at night, had been stopped on no less than four occasions by Campus Safety. In the end the best efforts of the police had done nothing but drive the criminal to other hunting grounds, which turned out to be enough. Near the end of Preacher's freshman year the rapist attacked one Donna Winchell of Cayuga Heights. Like her assailant, Donna Winchell carried a handgun, and in the crunch she turned out to be a hell of a lot faster on the draw than he was.

But Preacher did not think of any of this as he descended the metal-and-timber stair into the Gorge. He gave only a glance to the second Blue Light Phone at the bottom of the steps, with its instruction sticker: PHONE IS NOT DEAD. TIME DELAY. PLEASE WAIT FOR ANSWER.

Still over a hundred feet from the floor of the Gorge, the suspension bridge hung elegantly, spanning the gulf with a quiet grace. The twin support cables were ice-encrusted and stretched away in perspective like beams of frozen light. A fresh layer of snow lay unblemished on the walkway, pure and white, the few random patches swept bare by the wind glittering with imbedded quartz. Preacher took a step onto that virgin layer, and remembered something his Orientation Counselor had told him during his first week here: *They say you're not a true Cornellian until you've kissed and been kissed on the suspension bridge.* This Preacher had never done; he would have to bring Jinsei down here sometime, perhaps tomorrow on the way back from Tolkien House.

He took a second step, felt the vibration of the bridge under his weight . . . and another, much fainter vibration in answer. If he ever felt so much as a tickle of fear it was then, as he peered through the falling snow and caught his first glimpse of the white-sheeted shape coming toward him from the far end of the bridge. But the shape was alluring as well as unsettling. The white wrap moved hypnotically, as if dancing not at the mercy of the wind but with its own will. Preacher could not help but wonder what sort of person was hidden within, so strangely garbed.

"Good evening to you," Preacher said in greeting, as they met near the middle of the span. "Happy New Year."

The shape paused, turned toward him as if to speak. The sheet flew open with a snap, revealing the Rubbermaid all bedecked in black leather, and Preacher's last coherent thought was *My God, her eyes are glowing*. Then the Nazgûl mace swung up with deadly force, striking him full on the side of the head, blasting thought and balance to fragments. Preacher was felled like a tree, the flower Jinsei had given him flying out of his grasp. The Rubbermaid stepped over his prone form and readied the mace for a second swing, but none was needed.

The blow had spun Preacher completely around. Lying flat out against the snow, he saw through one unfocused eye the distant gleam of the Blue Light Phone. He no longer comprehended what it was for, but tried to crawl for it anyway. He got all of three feet before the Rubbermaid reached down, grabbing him by the collar and the belt, lifting him up, above the safety-fencing of the bridge.

"Gunnh," Preacher mumbled from a broken jaw, vaguely sensing the long drop beneath him. One randomly flailing hand found and gripped a hank of the Rubbermaid's hair, which was long and silky. *Jinsei*, he thought lovingly.

Jinsei, his mind repeated, and the Rubbermaid hurled him into the void, *Jinsei*, he was falling, tumbling, it felt like flying, the wind rushing past him, *Jinsei I lov*— and a final shock as he plunged into the icy waters of Fall Creek, sharp rocks beneath the water, and beneath the rocks darkness, and long sleep.

The Rubbermaid did not even wait for Preacher to strike bottom. Mace in hand, it headed for Uris Library in search of Jinsei, Rasferret's second practice victim. It was 11:35.

VII.

Fairy lanterns illuminated the frozen surface of Beebe Lake, where the full company of The Hill's sprites skated, danced, and cavorted, laughing and making merry as they anticipated the New Year. Only one remained aloof from the festivities: Hobart, who seemed to have aged tremendously since Halloween. Well wrapped in furs, he stayed near the edge of the lights, muttering to himself. Despite frequent requests he would tell no stories this night, though there was one tale he needed to tell.

Puck was matching riddles with Hamlet when Zephyr came to find him.

"What's the matter?" Puck asked, seeing the concern in her eyes. She said nothing, only pointed off to where Hobart stood alone, half-shivering. Even from a distance the pallor of his face was frightful. "Is he sick?" asked Puck. "I don't know," Zephyr told him. "He hasn't been sleeping well, I think." She caught his hand. "He says he want to speak to you. Alone."

For no good reason at all Puck felt the first twinges of a growing unease at the base of his spine. "He wants to speak to me alone? What about?"

"He wouldn't tell me. It has something to do with a favor he wants from you."

"A favor . . ." Puck licked his lips nervously. He could not refuse, of course—in addition to being Zephyr's grandfather, Hobart was, of course, Eldest, and you did not withhold a favor from the Eldest.

"All right," he said, after a long hesitation. He excused himself to Hamlet, gave Zephyr's hand a squeeze, and moved deliberately over to Hobart's shivering form.

"You called for me, Hobart?" Puck greeted him. At first the old sprite, staring into the heart of one of the lanterns, did not seem to notice his presence. Only when Puck touched him gently on the shoulder did he look up.

"Good," Hobart said to him, speaking barely above the level of a whisper. "Good."

"Zephyr—" Puck began, that unease rising another notch. "Zephyr said you had a favor to ask of me."

"A favor." Hobart nodded. "I need an ear."

"Beg pardon?"

"A listening ear. I have something I need to pass on, to an ear I can trust. One who can help me decide what needs to be done." He drew a long breath, and coughed deep in his chest.

"Are you all right, Hobart?"

"Not in the least. So little sleep lately. Nightmares . . . you think they can get no worse, and then they do. Your plane carries two passengers, doesn't it?"

"My biplane? You know it does. I brought Zephyr here in it."

"Good. Good." Hobart straightened up, seeming to regain a bit of his former strength. "I want you to fly me back to the Tower. We'll have a drink, and a long talk. And then we'll see if either of us can sleep."

VIII.

At Uris Library, the letter R was at long last finished and done with. Rhetta Woolf had gone up into the stacks to take care of some last-minute business, leaving Jinsei to tidy up behind the circulation desk. Jinsei did this effortlessly, whistling to herself, thinking how she would soon be with Preacher.

Loud noises are always startling in a library, ordinarily a storehouse of soft whispers, and when the crash came, it was startling indeed. It jibbered in a splintering echo from the direction of the lobby, suggesting cataclysmic images: Superman hurling a glassed-in phone booth out a third-story window, an angry rhino taking issue with a chandelier. A silence followed which was not so silent as before.

"Mrs. Woolf?" called Jinsei, who had jolted upright at the sound, dropping a pack of borrowers' cards to the floor. Her hand strayed to a convenient telephone; the number of Campus Safety was taped right on the back of the receiver. Then curiousity got the better of her, and, moving gingerly, she slipped out to the lobby to see for herself what had happened.

Apparently nothing had, at first glance. The lobby was multi-leveled; from where Jinsei stood, wide steps led down to the checkout desk; to the right of the checkout, the main doors remained shut and undamaged. Off to Jinsei's left, a narrower stair climbed upwards, giving access on one landing to the Andrew D. White Reading Library.

The door to the White Library rattled in its frame, as if some prankster had hold of the knob on the other side.

"Who's there?" Jinsei called, feeling foolish. Like the main doors, the entry to the White Library was made of glass, and she could see without moving that there was no one touching it within. Still . . .

She ascended the stair to the landing, drawn as if by a magic spell. The door continued to rattle; standing before it, she peered inside, straining, for the lights were out and it was difficult to see. Even so, enough light filtered in from the lobby and the outer windows for Jinsei to make out an amazing fact: it was snowing in there, actually snowing! And of course what had happened should have been obvious at that point, but for an instant she was completely taken by the illusion, it truly looked as if it were snowing indoors, and then the Tower Clock began to chime midnight.

"Magic," Jinsei whispered, hardly realizing she had said it. As the New Year became reality, she laid her hand on the knob and pushed the door inward. A blast of cold air greeted her as she stepped inside.

IX.

As the Clock chimed its twelfth chime, Puck angled the biplane in for a final approach, a single wing-light his only aid in targeting the hangar entrance. "You did leave the doors open, didn't you?" Puck asked, but Hobart made no response; he had been silent throughout the flight.

In fact Hobart did say one thing, as they swept in toward the Tower pinnacle and the beam of the wing-light confirmed that the hangar doors were open. He said: Something is not right here." It was a mutter only, and Puck never heard it.

Then with a single bump they were landed inside, braking to a stop. The wing-light pierced the darkness, picking out the wreckage of Hobart's glider at the rear of the hangar.

"Jesus, Troilus, and Cressida," Puck muttered. "What did you do to that, Hobart?"

One again Hobart made no answer. The Eldest was otherwise occupied, sniffing the air. The hangar was crisp and cold, smelling principally of fresh snow, but beneath that there was another smell, far less pleasant.

"Hobart?" asked Puck, for he too had caught the underscent. "What is—"

"The Fates!" Hobart swore, coming suddenly to life. "Get us out of here! Get us out of here right now!"

"What—" Puck began to say, and then the first Rat leapt up on the biplane's left wing, sword drawn to kill. Puck did not balk at the absurdity—a Rat on two legs, wielding a weapon—he merely brought up his own sword, which lay unsheathed on the floor of the cockpit, and caught the Rat coming in, piercing it through the breastbone. It twisted away into the darkness with a squeal, wrenching Puck's sword out of his hands.

Now from all around them in the dark shadows of the hangar came the sounds of swords being drawn, crossbows being cocked. The full complement of Rasferret's Rats had been waiting here for over an hour, in the hope that the master of the Tower might return alone, or in such scant company as to be an easy mark. Fate had handed them a splendid opportunity.

"Turn us around!" Hobart was shouting, his own sword out, ready to defend. Puck, unarmed, *was* turning the plane, praying that the creatures would not think to shut the hangar doors. As long as the escape route remained open there was a chance, no matter how outnumbered they were; the biplane had a couple of good surprises in it.

Crossbow bolts struck the wings and fuselage of the plane as it swung around. One lucky shot smashed the wing-light; now the only illumination, what there was of it, came through the hangar doors. Emboldened, the Rats pressed forward. Some came at the sides of the plane, and Hobart fought wildly with these, finding strength in panic. A good many others moved to block the exit; as the plane completed its turn, Puck could see them, silhouetted against the opening.

As Hobart struggled behind him, crying out as he was wounded, the younger sprite reached low in the cockpit to find an almost forgotten switch—the switch connecting to the mini-cannons. *You'll probably blow your own wings off,* he remembered Zephyr saying about them. *And maybe I will,* he thought now.

"Happy New Year, you bastards." He flipped the switch and the biplane jumped. Fire licked from beneath the lower wings, the blast resounding like a great cymbal crash. Eleven Rats were killed instantly, ripped apart by flying buckshot; a twelfth was blown clean out of the hangar.

Puck saw his chance. Keeping one eye on a nasty web of cracks in the lower right wing assembly, he throttled the biplane forward. But at least one of the Rats had some intelligence after all—the hangar doors were sliding rapidly closed, pulled by hidden counterweights. Already the opening seemed too narrow. Refusing to be trapped inside, Puck shoved the throttle to full and went for it anyway.

Both wing assemblies sheared clean off.

X.

The door snicked shut behind her. Jinsei stood on the green-carpeted floor of the White Library, staring at the gaping ruin of the north bay window. Here was the source of the crash: a man-sized hole had been punched through the glass. Wind and snow funneled in through the breach, dusting the Library. So it was no magic trick, after all. But there *was* magic here, of a darker sort.

Tap, tap, tap.

Cast-iron gantried bookstacks rose up two tiers high along the Library walls. It was from the upper tier, hidden in darkness, that the sound came.

Tap, tap, tap.

Jinsei should have been frightened, then. She should have asked herself just what precisely had punched such a large hole through the north window, should have turned, should have run. Instead, her earlier fear dissipated and, careful not to step on any broken glass, she made her way to the northwest corner of the room, where a circular stair led up to the tiers.

Tap—

Foot on the first step, face trance-like, some deep part of her trying to warn her to flee, her body paying no heed to the warning.

—tap—

Passing the lower tier, halfway up, climbing faster and faster.

—tap.

And now she had reached the top, stepped out onto the high tier. A few more brisk paces and she had come to a catwalk that reached from the west wall of the room to the east. Here she paused.

At the far end of the catwalk—which was not far at all, for the White Library is long but narrow—a pale sheet, ghostly in the darkness, stretched between two bookshelves like a shower-curtain. The sheet swung back and forth, beckoning her. Hidden behind it was the source of the sound, a rapping of metal against metal.

Tap, tap, tap.

Three long strides and Jinsei stood directly before the curtain. Again she paused, that inner voice screaming, shrieking at her. Unmindful, her left hand rose to pull aside the sheet. Her fingers brushed the fabric, which seemed almost alive.

From somewhere higher came another sound, like a muffled gunshot. Jinsei's hand faltered.

The sheet swept aside anyway. The Rubbermaid uncoiled from behind it, swinging the mace upwards in a diagonal arc. If Jinsei had hesitated in the slightest—if she had taken time to scream, for example—the police might well have found her body lying beside the broken window, snow-frosted, head dashed open.

She did not hesitate; she threw herself backward with the blessed speed of reflex. Even so the first swing might have finished her, had her feet not chosen that same moment to tangle beneath her. She fell flat on her back on the catwalk, the mace stroke whipping past her as she tumbled, the tip of the weapon brushing the tip of her nose like a lover's caress.

Undaunted, the Rubbermaid stepped forward, raising the mace high for another shot. As the weapon reached the height of its arc, Jinsei looked directly into the blue glow of the mannequin's eyes. In that instant she knew everything that had happened on the suspension bridge; she knew Preacher was dead, and how.

Maybe it'll bring you luck sometime.

Fury empowered her. Even as the mace started down Jinsei sprang up, aiming a blow of her own. She swung not her left arm but her right, leading with the edge of her wrist, on which the silver-banded bracelet now burned with green fire. It struck the Rubbermaid full on the side of the head.

With a crack like a rifle shot, the bracelet burst into a dozen pieces. The mannequin's own swing went wide, striking the catwalk railing; the mace jolted free and spun away into the darkness. The Rubbermaid itself was hurled back, as if jerked by a cable, to smash jarringly into the bookstack behind it. In a shower of books it collapsed, falling in a heap. But the glow in its eyes did not go out.

"Oh God," Jinsei croaked. Fury washed out of her as quickly as it had entered, to be replaced by an unbearable sense of loss. She staggered against the railing, blinking back tears while the white sheet whispered seductively against the bookshelves. "Oh God, Prea—"

The Rubbermaid straightened an arm. It sat up, scattering more books.

Once again, Jinsei acted reflexively. Both her wrists now bare, she gripped the catwalk railing tightly and swung herself over the side. The Rubbermaid sprang forward to grab her but did not quite make it; plastic fingers half-snagged a pants cuff and then let it slip free.

It was a long drop to the floor.

XI.

It was a long drop from the pinnacle of the Tower to the Library roof. The biplane, little more than a propellered pipe without its wings, dangled over the void at a paralyzingly steep angle. The closing hangar doors had caught the tail of the plane like a pincer, and right now were the only things keeping it from a fatal plummet.

Puck, one arm thrust into a shoulder strap of his emergency parachute, was trying desperately to get Hobart's attention.

"The wind, Hobart!" he shouted, snowflakes whipping past his face. "You have to talk to the wind and get it to help us! I don't know if my parachute can hold two!"

Hobart had slumped forward in his seat, bleeding from a scratch across his scalp and a far more serious sword puncture in his shoulder. He seemed in shock, oblivious to his surroundings or his peril.

"Hobart, please!" Puck screamed. "You've got to hear me! Hob—"

Another voice, heard only in the mind: *Ho-bart.*

Now Hobart stirred, raising his head sluggishly. "Wind . . ." he whispered, through dry lips.

Above, the General of the Rats stood just within the hangar doors, staring down the length of the plane at them. Yellowed teeth formed something that might have been a grin.

Ho-bart, the Rat General thought at them. *Thresh ends you, Ho-bart.*

Deeper within the hangar, another Rat pulled a lever. The doors began to shunt open again; the nose of the biplane dipped like a descending pendulum. "The wind!" cried Puck, attempting to grab Hobart and finish putting on his parachute at the same time. "The wind!"

Thresh ends you.

The biplane dropped, tumbling end over end and dashing to pieces on the Library roof below. Yet what of the occupants? A sudden furious blast of wind drove Thresh back from the doors, hiding their fate from him; likewise the Messenger, soaring high, was all at once so buffeted that it lost concern with anything but its own flight.

And as for the Grub, his attention was presently focused elsewhere.

XII.

In one sense Jinsei was extremely lucky: a long study table stretched directly beneath the catwalk and it would have been quite easy for her to land half on and half off it, breaking her back or worse. Instead she hit feet first on a strip of carpet little more than a yard wide. Her left leg took most of the shock; she felt her ankle scream in protest as she collapsed full out on the floor.

She would have liked to just lie there and cry out her pain, but Jinsei understood on a most fundamental level that she had no time. There was movement on the catwalk above, and any second the thing, whatever it was, would be down after her. Too much to hope that it would hurt *its* ankle.

What was it? She had no time for that question, either, no time to think how impossible this was, how this simply could not be happening. All her effort she concentrated on one thing, escape. She stood up, ignoring the complaint from her ankle as best she could, and half-hopped to the door.

A fluttering behind her as she set her hand on the knob. Jinsei did not look back, but if she had she would have seen the Rubbermaid descending through the air in slow motion, white sheet trailing behind like the cape of some vampiric Zorro. Jinsei yanked the door open, stumbled through. The wind coming in through the window slammed it shut after her with a roar.

Jinsei rushed down the stairs as quickly as her wounded ankle would allow, nearly falling headlong twice. She thought briefly of Mrs. Woolf and knew that the librarian was on her own; there was no way to warn her. As she staggered down the last steps to the main doors, she tried to recall the location of the nearest Blue Light Phone. She also wondered where she might go to hide.

With a crash louder than the original window-breaking, the Rubbermaid plowed right through the White Library door, snapping the wooden frame, shivering the glass to bits. Once out, however, it did not race to catch up or engage in any more leaping; it descended the stairs with a self-assured ease, as if confident that Jinsei could not escape.

Jinsei, confident of nothing but her own mortality, loped past the checkout desk. She was in luck; she had forgotten to relock the main doors after saying goodbye to Preacher.

Preacher, oh Preacher I—

She thrust the thought away, shoved through the doors, ankle throbbing now. Outside the wind seemed almost angry; it tore at her clothes, whipped her hair around. She did not bother locking the doors behind her, knowing her pursuer would not be deterred.

No Blue Light was immediately visible. Jinsei lost her balance on the Library's front steps, found it again, and limped toward the Arts Quad. On her right a sculpture rose up, The Song of the Vowels. Flash of a memory: a November night, cold but not as cold as this and without snow, she and Preacher sitting at the base of that sculpture, hugging for warmth. They had just come from a movie . . .

Stop it!

There: across the Quad between Goldwin-Smith and Lincoln Halls, looking terribly distant, the glow of a Blue Light. Moving as swiftly as possible, Jinsei set out on a diagonal for that cold spark of hope, not wanting to consider her chances. A hidden ice patch sent her sprawling before she had gotten ten feet.

The wind had quieted enough that she could hear the crunch of leather boots on snow, the flutter of the white sheet . . . she scrambled back to her feet, shouting now, though she knew there was no one to hear: *"HELP ME! SOMEBODY! SOMEBODY!"*

Her voice echoed back flat and dead from the Quad buildings. The statues of Ezra and Andrew stood mute. No help there

Jinsei stumbled forward a few more paces before falling again. Fresh pain shot her ankle; she feared this time she had broken it. She tried to push herself back up anyway, and plastic hands caressed her shoulder blades.

Jinsei screamed, putting all her strength into it. She screamed as the hands like steel pincers gripped her upper arms, screamed as they turned her over, screamed as she looked up into the face of the Rubbermaid, eyes blue death, lips stretched into a grin.

The scream choked off abruptly as the mannequin's hands found her throat.

XIII.

The patrol car reeked of vomit. Both windows were rolled down despite the cold, but this was not enough for Sam Doubleday; he had lit a cigar, El Topo or something equally foul, to further kill the smell. As far as Nattie Hollister was concerned the smoke just made things worse, but she bore it in silence, steering south on Thurston Avenue, passing Risley on the right.

They had just come from a house party up on Triphammer Road, where a very drunken individual had gotten it into his head to climb a tree on the front lawn. After fifteen minutes of coaxing they'd managed to get him back down, at which point he'd thrown up a great glurt of alcohol and half-digested junk food on Doubleday's trousers. Doubleday had wanted to arrest the drunk. Hell, he'd wanted to beat him senseless, even if that were a bit redundant. In the end Hollister's cooler head had prevailed; they'd seen to it the fellow was put to bed and taken off in a hurry. Now another call had come in, a domestic dispute over on State Street. *Bet they're going to love us,* Hollister thought, as the car cruised over the East Avenue Bridge.

"What I don't understand," Doubleday was complaining, "is why they can't find somebody else to take care of this."

"Busy night," Hollister reminded him. Rand Hall drifted by on the right. "Half the town's crocked."

"Screw in hell with that," replied Doubleday. "I just want to change these damn—"

(" . . . help me . . . ")

"—pants."

"Did you hear that?" Hollister said, suddenly alert.

The second scream came a heartbeat later. Hollister braked and swung a hard right, driving down the sidewalk between Goldwin-Smith and Lincoln Halls; Doubleday's hand dropped to the butt of his nightstick.

"Eyes sharp," said Hollister, as they passed the Blue Light Phone and entered the Quad, headlights cutting a swath across the snow. The scream had cut off, and they could not be sure where it had come from.

"There!" Doubleday shouted, pointing. "Go left!"

In the southwest corner of the Quad, two figures lay one atop the other, partially covered by some sort of white sheet. They might almost have been lovers, but Doubleday saw differently. Beating the crap out of a rapist, he thought as they drew near, would just about even out his night.

The rapist seemed unperturbed by the patrol car's approach. Ignoring the siren, the top figure bent lower, flexing arms that seemed unnaturally pale.

"My God, is it a woman?" said Hollister.

"Couldn't be," replied Doubleday. He was out of the car first, nightstick in hand, bellowing as he ran forward: "Hey! Hey, you son of a bitch!"

The Rubbermaid looked up and froze Doubleday in his tracks.

Sweet Jesus those eyes—

Doubleday dropped his nightstick in the snow. He took out his service revolver. Grinning, the Rubbermaid released Jinsei—who drew a ragged, painful breath—and stood up.

"Don't you move!" Doubleday demanded shakily, leveling the gun. "Don't you dare!"

The Rubbermaid took a step; Doubleday emptied the revolver into it. The bullets punched six neat holes in the mannequin's leather bodice, exiting out the back. Unaffected, the 'Maid kept coming, catching Doubleday by the wrist and collar, hoisting him into the air like a bale of hay.

"Jesus shit!" cried Doubleday, airborne. The Rubbermaid tossed him playfully back in the direction of the patrol car. He landed hard on the hood, his right arm connecting with the front windshield breaking both. He rolled free, dropped onto the ground in a heap, and lay still.

Nattie Hollister had not been idle. She stood at the rear of the car, struggling to get the trunk open. The key stuck in the lock, refusing to turn. Grin still firmly in place, the Rubbermaid came forward as if to help her, hands flexing.

"Bastard!" Hollister swore. Thus rebuked, the key gave in and turned; the trunk lid sprang open. Hollister groped inside, flicking the safety off the shotgun as she drew it out. *No need to worry,* she thought. *If this baby isn't loaded, the city'll pay for your funeral.*

She raised the gun. Aimed. Pulled the trigger.

It was empty.

The Rubbermaid plucked the weapon gingerly out of her grasp and threw it aside. Hollister tried to duck away but the mannequin had her by the neck. They danced, the white sheet whipping around them both.

Then with a rocking thump Hollister found herself pinned up against the side of the patrol car, a single hand at her throat holding her motionless. With her own hands the Ithacop beat at her assailant, but she might just as well have struck at a stone wall. The Rubbermaid drew back its free arm, making its intention plain by forking two fingers.

Hollister, who had once had the misfortune to see a man blinded with the jagged neck of a beer bottle, first widened her eyes in alarm and then shut them tightly. She drove both fists into the mannequin's midsection, succeeding only in badly bruising her knuckles. The Rubbermaid held her steady for the finger thrust; Hollister struggled to the last, wondering how it would feel.

And at his Writing Desk Mr. Sunshine, who had done nothing but watch for the past fifty-seven minutes now shook his head, said "No, the fat cop maybe but not this one, too good a Character to lose just yet," and Wrote,

and Rasferret the Grub shuddered as a great weariness came upon him, his present limit reached, his magic exhausted by the night's activities.

The Rubbermaid's eyes dimmed, its iron strength weakened.

"Gah!" Hollister gasped, jerking to the side with a last effort. The Rubbermaid's arm shot forward, punching a hole in the patrol car passenger window just inches to the right of Hollister's head. And there the mannequin froze, all life going out of it, its eyes dull glass once more. The white sheet caught in the wind and flew away down the Quad.

Her mind a reel, Hollister withdrew fully from the Rubbermaid's now rigid embrace, giving it a good stout kick with her boot. The 'Maid fell over easily, the forked fingers trailing against the side of the car, making a sound like nails scratching at the side of a coffin, begging to be let out once more.

Near silence followed, broken only by the moan of the wind and Hollister's own shivering as she tried to cope with her shock. The New Year was thirteen minutes old; the killing hour was over.

THE NEXT DAY

I.

The Ithaca Police had a pretty depressing New Year's Day. Beyond the actual prevention of crime, what are the meat and bones of law enforcement if not the apprehension and conviction of a perpetrator? And how is any sane cop supposed to cope when everything is provided as easily as a gift—witnesses, physical evidence, the "perpetrator" safely in custody—yet still there can be no conviction, no closing of the case, because the facts add up to an impossible occurrence?

Exhibit A was the Rubbermaid itself, shown by a preliminary lab examination to be nothing more or less than a life-size plastic doll, no regular store-window dummy but custom-made, yet lacking any internal or external mechanism that would allow it to move under its own power. Its eyes, glass beads embedded in the plastic of its face, might reflect light but could not glow on their own. Its legs and arms, though attached to the torso with ball swivels that allowed it to be posed somewhat, could not, again, move on their own, and in any case its fingers were rigid and unjointed—they could not grasp objects. Most certainly the Rubbermaid could not wield a weapon, much less commit murder.

Other evidence—and there was a lot of it—said differently. Just for starters, no less than five witnesses, two of them patrol officers, had either seen or heard the Rubbermaid in action, doing just those things, like walking and wielding, that it couldn't do, that were impossible for it to do.

Then there was the physical evidence, a trail of hearty demolition that began with the shattered glass cases in the Tolkien House Mathom-Hole and ended with the battered patrol car and Doubleday's broken arm. In between were a fair number of identifiable bootprints in snow and earth, as well as the extensive damage to the White Library. The north bay window had been knocked inward, leading to the logical question of exactly how the perpetrator had reached it from outside, as it was not readily accessible from the

287

ground, at least not to your typical human vandal. Likewise, the destruction of the White Library door—in a single blow, apparently—would seem to have required superhuman ability. And though broken glass lay everywhere, not a single drop of blood or skin scraping could be found, though there were a few shavings of plastic, a few shreds of white silk.

The bruise-marks on Jinsei Chung's neck, sustained during her near-strangling were of the proper size and shape to have come from the mannequin's hands, if a mannequin were capable of attempted strangulation (which of course the Rubbermaid was not). And when, acting on the last babbled words of the Chung girl before she was put under sedation, police searched Fall Creek Gorge and dredged up the body of one Miles Elijah Walker, alias Preacher, they discovered several black hair strands clutched in the frozen hand of the corpse. Not human hair. Synthetic. Walker's cause of death was determined, not surprisingly, to be injuries sustained during a fall from the suspension bridge, but someone had given him a fair working over before he plummeted. The coroner's report would indicate that the instrument involved in these earlier injuries might well have been the iron-shod mace found lying on the floor of the White Library, wielded with considerable force.

Oh, it was a headache of a day, all right. Hollister and Doubleday—he with his freshly-set arm in a sling—filed their reports on the incident, took care of a few other related matters, and then slipped away to a bar to see how much scotch they could put down before passing out. Quite a lot, it so happened.

The story that appeared in the papers was a patchwork meld of fact and fiction: an unknown assailant of considerable strength (the police press release did not specify, but most of the newspapers assumed the assailant to be male) had gone amuck on the almost deserted Cornell campus, murdering one person and hospitalizing another; the names of the victims had not yet been released. (One name that did make the news was that of Rhetta Woolf, the head librarian at Uris, who had by a lucky fortune been down in the lower stacks and out of harm's way when the intruder came through; she claimed to be quite shocked by the whole thing.) Two city police officers had chanced upon the scene of the second assault. In an attempt to apprehend the attacker one of the officers was injured; the attacker escaped. End of story. There was no mention of the Rubbermaid, wrapped up neatly in a large baggie and stored in the basement of the station house along with the other evidence, evidence which indicated against all logic that there was nothing more to be done. Not unless the laws of the state were changed to allow a mannequin to stand trial.

Just as well, though, that the community believe the killer to be still at large. Undoubtedly there would be pressures on the department to solve the case as soon as possible, but the news might also make people more careful. A positive side effect indeed, since if logic and rationality could be suspended once, there was no reason why they shouldn't be suspended again, and soon.

II.

Hobart was alive.

Two sprites riding squirrelback from the Beebe Lake celebration to their homes had discovered him by chance, half-buried in a snowbank and frozen just as near to death as one can get without passing over. Neither magic nor medicine had been able to revive him; taken to a warm healing warren within the walls of the Straight, he slept in coma.

The wreckage of Puck's biplane was discovered at first light. The surviving Rats, following Rasferret's orders, had disposed of the bodies of their fallen comrades, and the sprites were left to conclude that the crash had come about through simple misadventure. A more careful examination of the hangar, the biplane, or the wound in Hobart's shoulder might have suggested another possibility, but the Little People are not given to detective work.

Hobart's survival was considered a miracle. Puck's chances were thought to be slim indeed, and of course if he had faded there would be no corpse. In accordance with custom, then, a search of seven days would be conducted, and if he had not been located by the end of that time he would be officially given up as dead. Unofficially, in the minds of those closest to him, he might remain alive a good deal longer; loved ones of the deceased had been known to keep hoping for years, even decades. Such was the burden of a race whose bodies did not remain to rot.

Zephyr divided her time evenly that day between search duty and attending Hobart's bedside. She kept remarkable control of herself throughout the morning and afternoon, but broke down shortly after sundown, laying her head across her Grandfather's chest in a sudden outburst of sobs. The intensity of her emotion seemed to reach him, and he stirred the slightest bit, uttering one word before drifting back into comatose slumber.

"What Hobart?" Zephyr half begged of him. "What did you say?"

She thought the word on his lips had been *eyes*, whatever that might mean, but she was wrong. Hobart, or whatever prophecy spoke through him, had referred to a time.

Ides, he had said. *Ides*.

AN EYE TO THE IDES

The three Architects, vacationing Cornellians all, met to conspire in a Greenwich Village café on the sixth of January. The name of the place was Fischer's Angry Serpent, only too appropriate since the Architects were conspiring about this year's Green Dragon Parade, more specifically the Parade's main attraction, the Dragon itself. Larretta Stodges, the Mastermind, held in her hand the August *Sun* editorial mocking last year's Dragon, which had collapsed miserably not ten yards from its starting point. Larretta eyed her companions solemnly.

"This year," Larretta said to them, "this March, we're going to blow their plebian journalist minds. Our class is going to have the best, most exciting, most talked-about Dragon in the history of the event."

"History?" queried Curlowski, the lowly one. "Who cares about history?"

"Think about it," Larretta appealed to him. "The greatest success following on the heels of the greatest failure. Redemption for the College, immortality for us. We'll be like gods. Just think about it."

Curlowski thought about it; it still did not impress him. This was only to be expected, for Curlowski was very much like a tack, sharp but not terribly deep. Concepts on the level of immortality and godhood were beyond him, though when it came to calculating the stress on load-bearing members, he had no peer.

Modine, the third Architect, was not like a tack. He was, like, a total sex maniac. Beneath the table he had a hand on Larretta's thigh, stroking. She let the hand stay but rapped it sharply across the knuckles with a steel T-square any time it strayed too close to an erogenous zone. It was all right; Modine had extremely resilient finger joints.

"So . . ." Modine said, after a particularly nasty knuckle-rap. "What this *uber*-Dragon going to be like, 'Retta baby?"

290

"Call me that again and you die," answered Larretta. "Now I figure first off we want a big Dragon, huge, hulking, blot-out-the-sun kind of big . . ."

"On no," Curlowski interrupted. "Size was one of the major factors in last year's fiasco; they built it too big, and that threw off the balance."

"Which is exactly why we have to have an even bigger Dragon," she explained to him. "Your job is going to be to see to it that the suspension and balance are just right this time, while still giving us the maximum size possible. That's how you impress people, Curlowski, by succeeding and superseding where others have failed miserably."

"All right, I get the picture. What else are you planning to include in the structural design?"

"Wings," said Larretta, raising her arms. "Huge green wings that really move instead of just hanging there."

"No, wings are a bad idea. Wings catch the wind, that rocks the whole structure, and you've got another balance problem on your hands."

"You'll deal with it, Curlowski."

"I'll deal with it. Right."

"One more thing, the most important of all: our Dragon is going to breathe fire."

Curlowski dropped his glasses: *"Fire?"*

"Fire?" echoed Modine, actually withdrawing his hand. "Just a minute, isn't the fire bit supposed to wait until the end of the Parade, when they torch the whole monster?"

"It'll be great," said Larretta. "The Dragon will be rolling along East Avenue toward the Engineering Quad, engineers all lined up to throw snowballs or mudballs, and all of a sudden, *foom!*"

"I think *foom!* violates the Campus Code of Conduct," Modine warned.

"Not to mention the rules of practicality," added Curlowski. "You're talking about a construct of wood, canvas, and papier-mâché. How is that supposed to breathe fire without igniting itself?"

Larretta Stodges shrugged. "Gentlemen," she said, "I really don't know. But we have until mid-March to figure it out . . . right?"

Modine nodded, looking a little nervous. After a brief hesitation, so did Curlowski.

In the end, they figured it out just fine.

BOHEMIAN
REQUIEM

I.

Preacher's body was flown back to Brooklyn for burial. Of the Bohemians, only Lion-Heart, Myoko, and Ragnarok were in attendance at the funeral. They had gotten a phone call at the lakeside chalet and come down, the two men looking stiff and uncomfortable in rented suits. After the ceremony Ragnarok gave his condolences to Preacher's parents, the closest thing to a family he had had since his exodus from the South. But there was little enough he could say, and he was haunted throughout by the vague memory of some dream he'd had, blue sparks glowing against a field of darkness.

The tombstone was a ghastly irony, though there was no one who could have made the connection. Rather than purchase a huge, extravagant monolith, Preacher's father opted in this one instance for simplicity, almost humility. The stone lay flat against the ground, and bore only a name, date of birth, date of death, and simple epitaph *("Here will I set up my everlasting rest")*. It was square, without decoration, and carved of white marble.

Ragnarok, who watched the burial crew bring the stone to the graveside, did not much care for the color.

II.

George and Aurora heard the news five days before their scheduled departure from Wisconsin; Lion-Heart got the Smiths' number after some poking around and phoned long-distance from SoHo. He told them as much as he knew—which was still not very much—about what had happened on New Year's Eve, and then, speaking to George, made a formal request on behalf of Bohemia: he hoped that the storyteller would come to Preacher's wake, which would be held on the twenty-second, and read something.

Now a wake traditionally involves the body of the deceased, and takes place before the funeral, not after, but that the Bohemians would break tradition especially where a friend was concerned came as no surprise. George gave his word that he would attend, and promised to start work on a story for the occasion as soon as possible.

It made a crashing end to what had started out as the best Christmas vacation that either Aurora or George had ever known. Things had begun to go downhill with the disappearance of Luther. They had spent days searching, but whether he had been run down in some lonely place or simply run off, they found no sign. George in particular felt badly, for it had been his idea to take the dog from The Hill in the first place; he could only hope that the animal would make out well, whatever happened to it.

Between Luther's exit and Lion-Heart's phone call, Brian Garroway had done his own little bit to undermine the holiday mood. Twice he left long letters for Aurora, and three times came by to yell at her in person; Walter Smith was secretly quite pleased to act as bouncer on these occasions. Finally, though, Aurora took herself over to Brian's, and after a discussion/argument that lasted hours, managed to form a shaky peace and an understanding between the two of them. The effort wearied her, though; George could see it on her face when she at last came home.

The last half-week of vacation George divided his time evenly between Aurora and Preacher's wake-story, which came to be titled "The Crossing." The tale came easily to him; if there was one thing that served better as inspiration than unrequited love, it was death.

III.

The wake was held in the Risley Dining Hall, in design the closest thing to a medieval feast hall that The Hill had to offer. Starlight and a bright moon shone in through windows set high up along the walls, for outside the sky was clear, the air frozen. Within, warmth was provided by an open hearth, and, more mundanely, by the basement furnace. Rectangular tables arranged in two rows ran the length of the Hall. A Head Table had been set up perpendicular to the rows, and at it sat Lion-Heart, Myoko, Jinsei, and Ragnarok. A fifth, empty chair was set up in honor of Preacher. The other Bohemians and Grey Ladies took places at the long tables, and with them select members of Tolkien House and the Blue Zebras. George was given a seat of honor very near the Head Table, and Aurora beside him; she looked every inch the Princess that night.

Lion-Heart clapped his hands and the wake began. Food was brought out (Panhandle and Aphrodite had commandeered the Risley kitchen): a clutch of roast chickens, fresh baked bread, pears, apples, an assortment of cheeses, and a hot spiced drink that took ginger brandy as its main ingredient. They feasted in desperate fashion, the drink disappearing as quickly as it could be mixed. Some of those assembled blinked back tears, some grew angrily drunk, and some emptied their plates and began to dance frenziedly as though their own lives might depend on it.

Ragnarok sat in an uncomfortable silence beside Jinsei. Since his return to Ithaca they had exchanged words but not actually talked; that event seemed to be waiting on a catalyst, one which had not shown its face yet. He ate sparingly and drank heavily, and midway through the meal got up to stand by the hearth. There he remained for a good long time, jabbing at the fire with a metal poker that was not really a poker at all, but Christopher Robin's lost lightning rod.

The food lasted a good two hours, and this against surprisingly fierce appetites. When the pace began to flag, Lion-Heart clapped his hands again. The music was shut off; the dancers and other drifters returned to their seats, except for Ragnarok, who kept his vigil by the hearth. Lion-Heart nodded to George, who advanced to the center of the hall, story in hand. The assembled mourners grew still; Ragnarok poked at the coals; George cleared his throat.

"There was once a fisherman," he began unsteadily, "who left home and family to make a long journey across the sea. He had no choice in the matter; it was not his decision to leave, but another's. . . ."

IV.

A great white bird of ice cut the air above The Hill in its flight. Rasferret the Grub, his magic and his Rat troops more than replenished in the three weeks since the New Year, sat safe in his hideaway, his face set in a semi-trance; he saw through the eyes of the Messenger as it flew alone across Fall Creek Gorge toward Risley.

Tonight was a momentous occasion. Tonight Rasferret would finally get a glimpse of his opponent, the human he was obliged to defeat if he was to keep his newfound power. The Messenger knew just where and when to go; with its own vision it would show him what he needed to be shown. Now the wide brick-faced building, so much like a castle, grew larger in the Messenger's sight, and Rasferret was suddenly afraid, for he had not ceased to be a coward in his heart. What might this enemy look like? he wondered. A giant, huge even among the Big People, who were gigantic enough to begin with? Or something more subtly terrifying? The Grub's imagination played havoc with him in the brief time it had.

Then the Messenger landed on a ledge outside one of the high-set windows of the dining hall. It swept the room with its gaze, and Rasferret's fright trebled at the sight of the Bohemians, some of whom might easily have been sorcerers. But when the bird fixed on George, all fear dissipated.

The Grub, quite frankly, was not impressed. Compared to some of the others in the hall, this human appeared positively harmless. He certainly didn't seem magical. Physically George was not all that impressive either; most assuredly he was no giant.

He is weak, the Grub told himself. *Yes, weak.*

With that thought came an inspiration, an idea born of opportunity but also of lingering cowardice. Standing alone at the hall's center, George looked, more than anything else, vulnerable. The Messenger's angle of view only added to this perception. And so it occurred to Rasferret that he might save himself a good deal of effort—and perhaps personal risk—if he ended the thing now.

From his distant hiding place, from his comfort and safety, the Grub sent out a mental command: *Kill him.*

"What!?" Mr. Sunshine exclaimed at his Writing Desk, and the Messenger hesitated. "What's this? Not till the Ides, that's the deal, you were told, you don't touch him until the Ides!"

And the Messenger tried to warn Rasferret: *Not yet, not yet.*

Kill him, the Grub repeated, already obsessed with his own notion of how the deed should be done. Still the Messenger held back, and Mr. Sunshine could have changed Rasferret's mind as easily as a mortal writer changes a sentence, but he was fuming at the mutiny.

"You arrogant little bastard," he said. "After I dig you up, let you have magic, free rein except for this *one* thing . . . ought to give you ass's ears just to teach you, but it'd probably be an improvement. But OK, fine, I know just what to do. . . ."

KILL HIM, the Grub insisted, all too impatient. And the Messenger, suddenly freed from hesitancy, gathered itself up and propelled itself through the window in a cacophony of shattering glass.

V.

George had them spellbound.

If the storyteller seemed unmagical-looking from outside, then those gathered in the hall took quite a different view. Whether natural or enhanced by the emotion of the moment, his delivery and tone of voice were perfect, drawing. But it was the tale itself that truly captivated them: a proper tale for the occasion, well crafted, it did what all good stories should do, made its audience forget that they were hearing a story at all. They heard instead the rush of wind and water and the flapping of sails that George described to them.

"Now when I talk about the swell of the waves," intoned the storyteller, "you don't really understand me, because we who spend our lives on land think only of waves' ending, a crash of white foam against the coastline or against the bow of some great ship. But to the fisherman, so far on his journey that the coastline was a dream forgotten long ago, his boat not large enough to make even a scratch on the skin of the sea, these waves were like smooth hills, rising and falling on a plain of dark glass, and if some of them did peak and foam then it was of their own volition; no ship bled them. And the water's depths were black.

"Utterly alone on this shifting seascape, the fisherman remembered those he had left behind, and wondered if they sometimes still thought of him. Dozing, he imagined he saw his friends and loved ones coming across the waves toward him, but when he raised his head their images dissolved; they were only gulls, wheeling above the surface of the water, crying aloud in what seemed almost human voices. Then the gulls were gone too, vanished back among the hills of the sea, and he was once again alone. . . ."

The Bohemians and their guests were absolutely silent; even Ragnarok had ceased to stir the fire and set aside the lightening rod to listen. The allegory made its point; rather than dwell on their own loss the mourners now considered Preacher's journey beyond death, even those who did not ordinarily believe in such journeys. And here was the real magic: some of them forgot their grief, if only for a brief span of time.

Even when the Messenger exploded into the hall in a burst of glass and winter air, they did not immediately jolt out of their reverie. They looked up and saw the white bird, so much like one of the fisherman's gulls. For a moment it seemed as though the intruder might simply fly the length of the hall and exit, a heartbeat later, out into the cold night again, and if it had, George's story might very well have continued uninterrupted. But it didn't. The Messenger banked and dove at George with its wings swept back and its crystalline beak extended like the tip of a spear; it meant to run clean through him, and very nearly succeeded.

The bird was quick, but love was quicker. All at once Aurora was at George's side, shoving him to the floor while he was still caught up in his own tale. She had reacted instinctively—or so it seemed—and only barely in time; the Messenger missed clipping one of them by mere inches. Momentum carried it to the Head Table, where it crash-landed noisily in Lion-Heart's plate, knocking bread crusts and chicken bones into the Bohemian King's lap. Jinsei recognized it from The Boneyard and began to shriek, yet underneath her shock she was furious. She snatched up a mug of the ginger brandied drink and hurled it.

The drink was scalding hot; steam rose from the Messenger's wings and chest as it backpedaled. Its own shriek was like a gale whistling through a crack; it toppled backwards off the table, spraying melted bits of itself all over the floor.

George was struggling to his feet. The Messenger oriented on him and came again, flying a good deal less steadily than before. George had the pages of his story in hand, and he hurled them at the approaching bird. The sheets sprayed in a perfect blinding pattern; once more the Messenger narrowly missed its target, skidding onto the surface of one of the side tables this time.

"Give me that!" Aurora shouted, looking to Ragnarok. The Black Knight did not have to ask what she meant; he snatched up the lightning rod and tossed it underhand to her. Aurora reached up and caught it one-handed, even as the Messenger flew again at George. She turned and thrust, sizzling a hole through the ice bird's throat, catching it, drawing not blood but water.

The Messenger's wings beat the air ferociously but it could not unskewer itself, and now George's hands joined Aurora's in gripping the lightning rod. Together they began to turn in place, swinging the rod around as if in some odd courtship dance. Three times they turned, and then, screaming for everybody to get out of the way, get out of the way, Aurora's arms flexed, George's arms flexed, and they hurled both bird and iron at the blazing hearth. For one instant it seemed as if the retreating bird glared at them with two pairs of eyes, one inside the other; then the Messenger plunged into the fire and vanished in a cloud of steam. The fire guttered out; frost settled on the coals. The bird was gone.

"That'll teach you," said Mr. Sunshine. "See how you manage without it."

Another silence descended over the dining hall, this one very much like the silence on the Arts Quad some twenty-two days earlier, just after the Rubbermaid had slid to the ground. The parallel was apt; a good many of the Bohemians looked like mannequins as they gaped at the blackened hearth. A chill draft crept in through the window the Messenger had broken.

Ragnarok was the first to break the paralysis. With careful, trance-like motions he picked up the fallen pages of George's tale, setting them in order.

"Finish it," he said, handing the story back to the teller.

BLACKJACK'S LAMENT

The Bohemians were not the only ones on The Hill to have suffered a recent loss, but they certainly took it better than some: the day after Preacher's wake found Blackjack crouched in the slush at the base of Ezra Cornell's statue, consumed with self-pity. On the Arts Quad before him, a good half dozen dogs chased and frolicked in the snow, obscenely cheerful; if the sky had fallen in on the lot of them, the Manx would have rejoiced.

Stupid mutts, he grumbled to himself. In particular his anger focused on Skippy, the ludicrous, hyperactive excuse of a Beagle who had brought him the news of his abandonment.

"He was in this big car, with two Masters sitting up front, and he wanted you to know that he'd be back."

"Be back? What do you mean, be back? Where was he going?"

"Well I'm not sure, exactly—I got a litle dizzy just then. I thought he said he was going to Heaven, but of course that's silly, you can't go there while you're still alive. It's funny how you get things wrong when you're a little dizzy, isn't it Blackjack? Huh? Huh? Isn't it funny?"

"It's a betrayal," Blackjack said now, claws extended. Oh, for a deserving muzzle to slash. . . . Yet even after being deserted he could not bring himself to hate Luther. He missed the mongrel son of a bitch, that was the problem, and it just added to his anger, made him wish all the more that some other dog or cat would pick a fight. Not that he expected any of these damned University animals to have the guts to try it.

His emotions had run embarrassingly out of control since Luther's disappearance. Denied the release of aggression, he had chosen another outlet for his feelings: at the moment, there were no less than five pregnant pusses roaming The Hill, all with Blackjack to thank for their condition. Sable, whom he had mated back in August, had already littered half a dozen young; now the Manx threatened to be overrun by progeny. The irony of it was that Blackjack could not stand kittens, and was only too thankful that he had no responsibility toward their upbringing.

298

Luther, where are you ? How far did you go this time? Once or twice he had considered trying to pick up a scent, searching for his lost friend. But if Luther had been in a car, there was no telling how far he might have been taken, or whether he would stay in one place. And all impracticality aside, Blackjack did not want to face the open road again. He had seen enough of it.

Sorry, Luther. You left without telling me, this time you're on your own. Unless the loneliness became more than he could bear. But until then he would keep to The Hill with its cold winds and snows, where Luther's beloved Heaven scent was now suffused with another smell, like the smell of rat but far less tasty. For a stray, Ithaca was no paradise in winter, but the Bronx had been just as cold and food even harder to find. Yes, it was definitely preferable to the road.

"You listen, caht," the Puli Rover Too-Bad had said to him yesterday. "I an' I got premonition 'bout your Luther."

"Premonition?" Blackjack asked skeptically. He respected intuition even less than kittens.

"Jus' so. You don't worry 'bout him; that dahg, he come home wit' Lady Spring." After a hesitation he added: "If spring come."

"*If?*" The Manx was amused for the first time in weeks. "You mean that here in Heaven, even the seasons are optional?"

"No joke, Blackjack, I an' I jus' want t'say you ought worry less 'bout Luther, more 'bout you. Don't you smell it? Raaq—Raaq in the air. Bad time comin' to this place."

"Bad time? Well, Jah love and all, Rover, but I don't imagine a little stench in the wind is going to get me frightened, and as for your Devil, since I'm in the mood for a scrap it might be the best thing if he found me."

Before long the Puli had passed on, annoyed, leaving Blackjack much entertained . . . at least while he remained awake. But cats do not remember their dreams, and in the dark world of nightmare premonition becomes more than possible. That night in sleep the Manx was pursued relentlessly by a sharp-toothed monster that he knew all too well, that he had thought left behind but which now gained on him with the same implacable determination that drew Luther back toward Ithaca from the west. And when Blackjack awoke, he too was awaiting the black tidings of the Ides of March, though he did not realize it.

Meanwhile, Rasferret decided to amuse himself by having another go at the young Asian who had escaped him on New Year's Eve. The clock wound itself for another killing hour.

RASFERRET
AND THE
BLACK KNIGHT

I.

Carl Sagan's house perched on the rim of the Gorge, inviting speculation, as always, about what it might be like inside. Outside it looked more like a concrete bunker than anything else, proof against any meteorites or gamma rays that might pass by. Rumors about the interior, however, told of such wonders as a laser-lit jacuzzi, fully automated wet bar with robot butler, and a custom-made holograph room in which one could sit and watch the movements of billions and billions of computer-generated stars.

"So what did Preacher tell you?" the Black Knight asked. "About me?"

"What he could. No much. I wanted to understand your . . . attitude."

After an evening of studied procrastination in which almost no meaningful words passed between them, Raganork and Jinsei had gone out into the winter night, Rag guiding his motorcycle carefully around the patches of ice that littered the road. Now, parked on the northern side of the Cayuga Heights Bridge overlooking Fall Creek (downgorge from the suspension bridge), it seemed that the silence was finally breaking. The lights of northern Ithaca, stretching off to the west, reflected off Ragnarok's glasses as he peered over the side. Below, the Creek tumbled over a waterfall, whispering loudly in the darkness.

"My attitude." Ragnarok laughed. "You mean my *emotional problem*, don't you?"

"Whatever you want to call it," said Jinsei. "It scares me. It scares the hell out of me. I'm just sorry if you think Preacher was wrong to say anything."

"Wrong? No, that's not it, I never swore him to secrecy on it. It's just . . . as far as understanding goes, I'm not sure if you can.

"Violence. That's my first reaction when I'm angry, or upset, or scared, extreme violence, and I'm *good* at it, Jinsei, but I can't control it. The only other reaction I know is running away, and I don't do that enough, and always at the wrong times."

"I don't know," Jinsei said. "Maybe it makes you feel guilty, but I'm still glad, that night in front of the Straight, that there was someone there who was more violent than those fraternity brothers, and on my side. And then that morning in Risley after the Halloween Party—whatever you were feeling, if you couldn't stay and talk to us about it, I'd much rather have had you run away than take a swing at Preacher. I think you acted as well as you could both times."

"For the wrong reasons!" Ragnarok insisted. "I wasn't being your knight in shining armor when I put the fear into Jack Baron that night. That was Klancraft, terrorism in action. Only thing missing was the hood. You know who taught me the Craft, my father, and you can bet he didn't have the best interests of the Asian-American community in mind when he did it."

"Forget what *he* had in mind, what about *you*, Rag? You were just a boy, you cared about your father, and how could you help but believe what you were taught, at least at first. I'm still amazed that you managed to break away from it at all, from—"

"I didn't break away far enough! Not far enough, not soon enough. You're right, I did care about my father, I was Drew Hyatt's boy for sure. I hated the darks like he taught me—darks, what's what I was supposed to call them, never niggers—and when I realized they weren't the real enemy, I still had plenty of hate to go around. That's the inheritance he gave me, violence and hatred, and I'll never be rid of it. Don't you see that?"

"But . . ." Jinsei interjected.

"But what?"

"Just one question."

"What?"

"Did you kill him?" Jinsei said. "Preacher knew you and your father had some sort of big fight at the end, right before you came north, and it was very bad, worse than Preacher thought he wanted to hear about. Did you kill him, Ragnarok? Is that what happened?"

He looked at her, as if wondering where she found the gall or the courage to ask such a thing . . . and then nearly laughed again.

"*Kill* him? Huh. No. No, I didn't kill him." The Bohemian turned again to stare out at the city lights. "The son of a bitch. But I wanted to. More than anything else in the world, I wanted to."

II.

The trucker's name was Galatea Handel, and her eighteen-wheel rig, though not designed for livestock transport, was nonetheless loaded with a herd of pigs about ten hours overdue for an appointment with a Cortland County butcher. Engine trouble and navigation trouble had caused the extreme delay, and at this hour there was likely to be no one left to take delivery, but Galatea was damned if she'd keep charge of the animals any longer than absolutely necessary. Galatea's rig had begun to stink to high heaven—or at least low heaven—and the choir of pig-voices became less and less bearable with each passing mile.

She drove into Ithaca from the south on Route 13, took a wrong turn onto Seneca Street, and further improved her own temper by cruising aimlessly around downtown Ithaca for the next fifteen minutes. Several doublings back and misguided turns later she found herself at the base of The Hill, and, deciding higher was better, began following University Avenue upslope.

The Boneyard was above her on her right when the rig's engine gave out. Unlike earlier in the day, this time it went quietly, without clamor or smoke, just a sudden stall. The truck rolled to a swift halt and Galatea threw on the brakes before it had a chance to think about backing up.

The pigs, seemingly impatient for their own slaughter, set up a squealing ruckus in protest of the delay. Galatea ignored them and climbed out of the cab, bringing a flashlight. Tensing at the chill in the air, she attempted to raise the cab for a look at the engine; it wouldn't go up.

"What the Christ . . ."

Genuinely pissed off now, she made one more try, but the lift mechanism refused to cooperate.

"I ought to bury you," Galatea chastised the truck, conscious of the cemetery above her and not very comfortable about it. "You and the damn pigs."

Instead of whipping out a shovel, she crossed the road and went up to the nearest house, which was really more of a shack. There were no lights on in the place but that was all right—if Galatea had to have a crappy night she saw no reason not to share the feeling.

"Hello in there!" she shouted, rapping loudly on the front door. "Hey, wake—"

The door shook under the force of her knock. The lock jiggered, clicked, and all at once the door swung inward. It was black inside the house. Very black.

"What a creepy fuckin' place," Galatea observed. She pushed the door all the way open and took a step inside. "Hello, anybody home? I—"

The house having been officially pronounced creepy, Galatea would not have been altogether surprised if something had come leaping out of the darkness at her. The soft rattle and thump of her truck leaving without her, though—that came as a shock.

"Hey!" she shouted, spinning around. "Hey, *hey who the f*—"

There was no who, not that could be seen. In the dark the cab looked empty, though of course that could not be. Stranger still, the unseen driver had somehow gotten the truck moving uphill without actually restarting it, for the engine made no sound. This was apparent even though the pigs were making an incredible racket, not just squealing but *screaming*, as if they had arrived at the butcher's and hung upside down before the knife, at last comprehending their fate.

The rig accelerated faster than would have been possible even with the engine running, yet Galatea raced after it, catching up with the cab before it could make good its escape. She threw herself up the side, grasping the driver's door handle and struggling for a toehold. For a very brief moment she rode with the truck—just long enough to look in and verify that yes, there was no one behind the wheel. Then a jolt of the cab threw her off; her right foot shot beneath the truck trailer and was crushed by six of eighteen wheels.

The rig drove on up The Hill, leaving her that way, and in her pain Galatea did not fully appreciate how lucky she was that it had not bothered to stop and reverse over her a few times. From her vantage point on the ground she could see right under the receding trailer, under the cab, to where the glow from the headlights splashed against the icy surface of the road.

Blue, Galatea thought, beginning to scream. *What the Christ, they're shining blue . . .*

III.

"It was over a batch of shingles, that's what brought on the final blowup," Ragnarok told her. "Preacher told you my Dad was a carpenter, right? From the time I was fifteen I was sort of a junior partner in the business, helped him out when I wasn't in school. When I was nineteen, Lisbeth Folkers' father decided to have his roof redone. I was in charge of buying the materials. I got the shingles from Gordon-Small lumber out of Durham."

"A black-owned lumber company?" Jinsei asked.

"Gordon was black. Small was a Jew." He smiled. "It was time, *past* time, for me to do something like that. Daddy was furious when he found out, of course, but it was too late to send the shingles back—they were already nailed up. Who knows, if Pa Folkers had got wind of it he might have had them torn up and replaced anyway, but my father didn't go out of his way to tell him.

"So we had our fight. Started out as a lot of yelling, but I said all the wrong things and he just snapped, pushed me . . . we had a mirror, a wood-framed standing mirror that had been in the living room as long as I could remember, he pushed me right into it. Cut myself in about a dozen places. After that it wasn't shouting anymore."

Ragnarok swallowed drily. "I had a piece of glass in my hand, sliver from the mirror, like a knife. I thought I'd cut his throat with it. Almost. Almost . . ."

"But you didn't," Jinsei said.

"I dropped it. When I went for him it just wasn't in my hand anymore, so I punched him instead. More times than I had to. Then he fell down, started crying. You know the only thing worse than hearing your father cry is hearing him cry and knowing you did it to him. . . ." He trailed off. Shrugged. "Anyway, that was that. I walked out of the house, just kept walking. Starved off and on for a while on the road, least until I met Preacher's family, but I never went back home again. I couldn't; next time we had a fight it would have ended a lot worse."

"OK then," said Jinsei. "So why don't you give yourself a break, give it a rest?"

"What do you mean?"

"You scare me," she told him. "You scare me a lot. I think you scare yourself even more. You've got this image of yourself as a . . . I don't know what, a storm trooper waiting to happen, maybe. And you may be too violent for your own good, that's true, but I still don't see the lack of control you're so worried about. You beat up Bobby Shelton, you probably wanted to break Jack Baron's neck, but you didn't. God knows what you first had in mind to do when you saw me together with Preacher, but you didn't. And your father—I don't know what it must take to turn against nineteen years of . . . that sort of upbringing, but it doesn't surprise me that you'd have to be angry, very angry, to do it. Angry enough to want to kill him. But you *didn't*, Ragnarok."

"You weren't there. You didn't see—"

"I don't have to see. Try to be less violent, that's fine. I'll rest easier. But it's OK to forgive yourself, too."

"No. No, it isn't, you *don't* understand. Too much of the Klancraft . . . if I let myself off the hook, ease up once, then the next time I face down somebody like Jack I'll be patting myself on the back, good job. And then . . . then don't you see what would happen? I'll *never* be anyone's knight in shining armor. I'm like *them;* I don't have the stuff for it. Too much of my father in me."

Jinsei, looking unconvinced, touched the left temple of his sunglasses with a finger. "Could you please take these things off?" she said, then did it herself before he could reply. "That's better. You have pretty eyes, you shouldn't hide them.

"Listen, Rag, no one's asking you to be a knight or a saint. You can leave that job to somebody else. What I need you for . . . well, I'd like to have you as a friend. I need one now, especially with Preacher gone. I need somebody I can talk to about what happened on New Year's Eve. But it won't be much use if that somebody is eating themselves up inside."

"I'm not as good a person," Ragnarok insisted, "as you seem to think I am."

And at this she laughed, and caught him completely by surprise by punching him playfully in the arm. "You *bullshitter*," she said. "You must be from the Carolinas, I've never heard such crap from anyone up North."

"Huh," was all he could reply to this. "Huh."

"So listen, I'm getting cold, what do you say we hop back on your bike and . . ."

"Jinsei?"

"Oh my God," she said, not looking at him now, looking beyond him, to the road at the far side of the bridge. He turned to see, and there at the second curve, the one that vanished around The Hill, a corona like the glow from approaching headlights was filtering through the trees—but blue, the glow was blue. Like the color of the hottest part of a flame.

"That's strange," Ragnarok commented. He was about to say something more but the truck came into view around the curve, blue headlights and all, and suddenly Jinsei was doing the talking.

"Get on the bike," she told him. "Get your bike started, come on, come on, let's *go!*"

"What's the matter? Wh—"

"*Come on!*" Ragnarok found himself in motion; Jinsei astounded him again by grabbing him and half-shoving, half-dragging him to the parked motorcycle. Catching her urgency, he threw a leg over it, felt her climb on behind him. He gave the kick-start a try and got only a weak sputter.

The truck rounded the near curve, turning onto the bridge. Ragnarok looked into the oncoming headlights, less than forty feet away, and froze, hypnotized. "Eyes," he said. "They look like eyes. . . ."

"*It killed Preacher!*" Jinsei shouted into his ear. "*Go!*"

She raised a hand and pinched his neck, hard. He came alive, realizing their peril, and with the truck bearing down for the kill hit the starter again. Another sputter. Furious, Ragnarok bent the bike to his will and gave it a third kick, third to pay for all. This time the engine caught with a bellow. He twisted the throttle and they shot forward, skidding on a patch of ice, not quite losing control, making a giddy assault on Fall Creek Drive.

"All right," Ragnarok said, when the bike had steadied somewhat. "All right, all right." The road was slick and eager to spin them out, but even at a careful pace they were in the clear now. The Drive started out on an incline, and even at low speed there was no eighteen-wheeler running that could keep up with a motorcycle.

"*Faster!*" Jinsei commanded. He checked the rear-view mirror and saw that, possible or not, the truck hadn't dropped behind yet. It took the incline without a grumble—without any engine-noise at all, as a matter of fact—and gained ground rather than losing it.

"Jesus. Jesus, that's not a Mack, that's a trout!" He told the road ice to go screw and burned the throttle again, making the bike fly. The truck kept pace, drawing on, no more than fifteen feet behind now.

The Drive was narrow, with the gorge on one side and a row of houses on the other. There was barely enough room for one vehicle, and it occurred to Ragnarok that if a car were to come along moving the other way, the rig would be forced to stop . . . unless it drove right through it.

"It's still gaining!"

"It can't be!" said Ragnarok, although it was. The motorcycle hovered up near sixty now, the suspension bridge shot by on the right and was gone like a bad memory. Just ahead the Drive curved, and the Bohemian said a quick prayer that it wouldn't be too slippery.

Almost . . . the motorcycle started to slide and Ragnarok gave it an extra goose, his left boot kissing off leather against the ground. The bike hung on, but now an intersection loomed ahead, no choice other than to slow down a little and hope a sharp right might shake the pursuit.

The truck nearly had them there, coming around the curve itself with minimum skidding, hugging the road in defiance of momentum. It should have jackknifed, slammed sideways into the tennis courts that now lined the right side of the road, but the trailer stayed obediently with the cab. The wheels labored against the ice and asphalt, the engine remaining eerily silent; it was the pigs, the screaming of the pigs, that proved loudest.

The intersection: Ragnarok took it at forty, again only barely avoiding a fatal slide. He made it tight and reaccelerated as soon as they were out of it. The rig, not bothering to slow, swung a much wider turn. This time the trailer fishtailed out, caving in the side of a parked car, knocking a NO PARKING AT ANY TIME sign clear off its post and sending it wickering through the window of a house.

They were on Thurston Avenue now, North Campus, the road was a flat-out run with Risley, the East Avenue Bridge, and Central Campus dead ahead. Cashing in the last of his luck, Ragnarok took the bike up as high as it would go, sixty, seventy, eighty . . . Risley was past before he even had a chance to think of pulling in there.

"Still coming!" Jinsei shouted. There were no other vehicles on the road, not a one, though the hour was not so late. Too convenient . . . it was an open dragstrip, with a few nighthawk pedestrians to watch the unlikely sight of a jet black motorcycle being gradually overtaken by a motorless truck. The screaming of the pigs had become a demon-chorus now, the name of this rig is Legion. . . .

"Haven't got us yet, partner!" Ragnarok cried. They were across the East Avenue Bridge in a twinkling, the truck only ten yards back now, seven . . . "Hang on, Jin!"

He cut right, riding the sidewalk down between Rand and Lincoln Halls, certain to lose control and kill them both, keeping the bike upright despite this certainty. The truck followed them, zigzagging impossibly, scraping off paint and metal but not crashing, not jackknifing. And Ragnarok did the impossible as well, kept just ahead.

Down and onto the Arts Quad, snow under the tires now, snow tinged blue by headlights that were far too close. The rig surged forward but Ragnarok would not let it catch them, he willed a last bit of speed out of the motorcycle even though the throttle was as far open as it could go. Running out of options, he cut a beeline for the opening between McGraw and White Halls, while a trio of undergraduates scattered before the approach of the hunt.

"The Slope," Ragnarok whispered, beneath the screaming of the pigs. "Let's see how you like the Slope, partner."

It came on, closing the gap, two yards, one. The truck's front grille was weeping with snow kicked up by the motorcycle's rear wheel when they broke between the two grey buildings and all at once faced the drop-off of Libe Slope. Coming right up to the edge, Ragnarok simultaneously released the throttle and made a hard turn. The bike refused the maneuver; Jinsei cried out as it threw them both, ground falling away, wind and sky rushing around them.

The truck did not even try to save itself. Pursuing them to the last, it hurtled suicidally over the lip of the Slope, knocking the riderless motorcycle out of its way before losing all control. At last it jacknifed, throwing up great gouts of snow and turf as it cracked over on its side. The horn gave a blast as it slid down the Slope, momentum carrying it all the way down to West Avenue, where it came to a battered rest beside Baker Hall. Windows began to open all over the dorm; and as the startled residents looked out at the wreckage, the squealing of the pigs could still be clearly heard.

As Jinsei's senses came back to her she felt the cold comfort of a snowbank on her limbs. Her hands flew automatically to her throat, but no, that had been another night. Opening her eyes carefully, she strove to sit up . . . not a bone broken, somehow.

Ragnarok was already on his feet. Limping badly, he lurched across the face of the Slope to the twisted wreck of his motorcycle. It was not the vehicle he wanted, but the black mace still held in the tube rack on its side. He yanked this free and turned toward the dead truck.

"No . . ." Jinsei tried to warn him. She had no voice, the strength had gone out of it. Filled with the old fury, drawing his own power from that, Ragnarok tumbled and slid down to the Avenue. The blue was fading from the truck's headlights as he approached it—they phased to a more normal yellow-white and then went out completely.

"I don't know who you are, partner," the Bohemian shouted, hefting the mace, "but if you're not already dead you're going to be very sorry. . . ."

His leg twisted under him but he refused to let it give, he dragged himself forward on his good leg. Reaching the toppled cab, he circle the front grille, ready to dash out what was left of the windshield and get at whatever remained of the driver . . . and what he saw very neatly made him drop his weapon.

There was no one in the cab.

No one at all.

He shuddered with a sudden chill, and then his leg *did* give, spilling him to the ground, cold and hard and far more real than what he was seeing in front of him.

One of the back doors of the trailer fell off with a crash. Pigs flooded out. Now it sounded as if they were laughing.

HAMLET SEES
A GHOST

I.

The Hill's sprites had, by this time, begun to realize that something was wrong. A pattern of disappearances had begun in January, when two of the Little People out searching for Puck had vanished. Winter had devoured them, seemingly; a second search had provided no hint as to their fate, though it did create four more missing. By early February no less than thirty-five sprites were unaccounted for, an average of one per day since New Year's. Eldest Hobart, who alone could have given full explanation for the disappearances, still lay in feverish slumber within the walls of the Straight.

That his army remained a secret, its number now swollen to many times the original twenty Rats, pleased Rasferret to no end. If the Big People were proving resourceful, at least his original enemies remained as blind and unsuspecting as they had been a century ago. Oh, they sensed their peril, there was no doubting that, but by the time they realized the source of the danger it would be too late. Until that final confrontation, death would continue to stalk them stealthily, taking one or two at a time, leaving no trace.

Death came calling for Hamlet just past dusk on the sixth of February. It found him home.

II.

Snow was falling again, dusting the frozen surface of Beebe Lake, dusting the roof of the tiny hut at the tip of Hamlet's island. It stood alone, a far call from any other sprite habitation. More than a few concerned friends—Zephyr among them—had suggested that it might not be wise to remain in a place so isolated while sprites continued to vanish on a daily basis. Hamlet had only smiled; he liked his solitude, and should some bogie with sharp teeth wish to disturb him, it would face a loaded crossbow wielded by an extremely good shot.

But Hamlet was not carrying his crossbow that evening as he stepped out of his hut; he left it inside along with his sword. Holding a fairy lantern in either hand, he braced himself against the cold and walked the short distance to where his model battleship, the *Prospero*, hulked out of the ice. Puck had once asked him what he would do with the ship during winter, and Hamlet's answer was that he might just put it on runners, making an iceboat out of it. So he had; but the latest freeze had caught him by surprise, and the runners were now locked firmly beneath the lake surface until the next thaw. Unable to free it, Hamlet checked often to make sure that neither damp nor frost got at the engines, which he had assembled using parts purloined with great difficulty from the Cornell physics labs.

A twine ladder hung down the side amidships. Hamlet took the lanterns up one at a time, clipping the first onto a line halfway to the bow. It cast a green glow over the deck, which was slick with frost and canted slightly to starboard; Hamlet was forced to step carefully.

He took the second lantern and went below decks. The battleship was hollow, the interior one long hold that contained both the engines and the retracting catapult. Hamlet found a hook for the lantern near the stern and had a look at the engine turbines. They were actually quite well protected against the elements, thickly oiled and wrapped in scavenged strips of plumbing insulation. But here . . . something had been at the insulation since his last visit, tearing it to get at the greased machinery beneath. He bent closer, noticing no immediate damage to the turbines; the vandal, probably an animal of some sort, must have been scared off.

A Rat detached itself from the darkness of the forward hold while Hamlet was occupied. In silence it crept toward him, sword already drawn, meaning to run him through the back. If it had been alone, it might well have succeeded. But already a host of other Rats, having found Hamlet's hut deserted, were scrambling up the sides of the battleship, scrabbling across the deck. Hamlet heard the patter of gnarled feet, heard the crash as one of them slipped and fell, and shot a look upwards. Out of the corner of his eye he saw the gleam of approaching steel.

The Rat lunged at him, but he had already sidestepped, snatching for the lantern on the wall. As the Rat stumbled past, Hamlet swung the fairy lamp, shattering it across the vermin's snout. Green witchfire poured out over its eyes, igniting the fur on its head into a blazing green mane. Blind and in agony it spun about, and with a quick reversing maneuver Hamlet impaled it on its own sword.

The Rat landed dead beside the engine turbines, but its fellows were at the deck hatch and starting to descend into the hold. As the fairy fire from the broken lantern spread, licking at the grease and insulation, Hamlet yanked at the engine start cord. All the power the turbines could produce would not lift the *Prospero* out of the ice—nor would that do him any good even if it were possible—but he did not have it in mind to move the whole ship, only a part of it.

The engines started on the second try. The insulation had lit and was burning most cheerfully; racing flame and foes, Hamlet ran the length of the smoky hold, bowling over the first Rat down the ladder. Leaping onto the catapult platform he thumbed a switch; a section of the bow deck swung open above him—sending a trio of unsuspecting Rats over the sides—and the platform began to rise.

Rats filled the hold, confused in the smoke. Some edged warily toward the fire, some hesitated at the base of the ladder, some surged up to the bow in search of Hamlet. They were too late; the platform had already risen out of their reach. Then a cable burned through and the engines died, sputtering. The platform stopped, three-quarters of the way to the open deck. Hamlet climbed the catapult arm but found himself trapped; Rats swarmed around the opening in the deck. One leveled a crossbow at him.

Fire reached the *Prospero's* fuel tank. The explosion was a small one, but it did blow a hole in the stern of the ship and incinerate a number of Rats. It also triggered the catapult firing mechanism. Hamlet was abruptly airborne. He made a poor projectile, describing a most peculiar arc as he tumbled head over heels through the air.

These events happened so suddenly and in such rapid succession that, when Hamlet landed unhurt in a thatch of dead reeds on the far end of his island, he very nearly convinced himself that he'd been sleepwalking. Smoke drifting on the wind and a flickering glow from the direction of the *Prospero* spoke against this notion, however, and he got to his feet carefully, terrified that his bones might realize their error and break in retrospect. If he had landed on the ice . . .

Moving shakily, he dropped down onto the lake surface and made a beeline for the northern shore, counting on the snow to cover his passage. If the Rats had not thought to post scouts, he might just make it, catching a ride with a passing squirrel upslope to Helen-Newman Hall, where a few of his cousins lived.

The Rats *had* posted scouts. Two of them lay dead at the edge of the bank, stabbed from behind. A ghost stood over them, cleaning his sword.

"Evening, Hamlet," the ghost greeted him. "Good to see you're still in one piece."

For the second time in a very short period, Hamlet wondered if he might be dreaming. "You're dead," he informed the ghost. "Or at least, you're supposed to be."

"Well so are you, eh?" The ghost nudged one of the Rat corpses. "I've been keeping an eye on them, but by the time I figured out what they were after it was too late to warn you. Good thing you still had some luck coming to you."

Sounds reached them, footfalls from across the ice. The surviving Rats had abandoned the *Prospero* and were renewing their search for Hamlet.

"Come on, old friend," the ghost said, sheathing his sword. "It's time we went someplace a little safer. Hurry, now!"

Confused to a point where he could hardly think straight, Hamlet gave up thought altogether, shrugged, and followed the ghost into the night. Behind them the snow swirled, the *Prospero* burned, and the Rats raged, furious over the loss of their prey, and fearful, too, of the punishment that was sure to result from their failure. Thresh was not a forgiving General.

III.

Twenty minutes later Hamlet and the ghost lay in relative safety in a chipmunk burrow, sandwiched between the hibernating occupants for warmth. The burrow was dark and more than a little stuffy, but better by far than the exposed lake surface.

"Pity about the *Prospero*," Hamlet lamented. "That damn boat took a lot to put together."

"Boat?" the ghost snorted. "What about my biplane?"

"I always told you you'd wind up crashing it."

"And I always told *you* that my parachute would get me out of anything. Lucky for me I was right—surprised myself, how fast I could finish putting it on when I had to. But Hobart . . ."

"Hobart is alive," Hamlet said. In the darkness he could see how startled the ghost was at this news. "Nobody's really sure what saved him."

"Has he told everyone what happened to us?"

"He hasn't spoken a word of sense since he was found. Brain fever."

"And Zephyr? Is she all right?"

"Besides being in mourning for a certain undead friend of mine, and worried about Hobart's health . . . yes, she's doing well. When she sees you she'll be even better. Now I figure tomorrow morning, if we try cutting across the lake just before dawn—"

"No," the ghost told him.

"No?"

"You think I've been playing dead this past month just for fun? I've been trying to figure out what's happening. Somebody's killing sprites, and it looks like that same somebody is gearing up for a major war, but I don't know who or why yet. If you and I rush out to sound the alarm, it might just force the enemy to attack ahead of schedule, before we even know what we're up against. Safer to stay dead a while longer, keep our eyes open."

"If we wait too long . . ."

"We'll try not to."

A silence.

"So, Puck," Hamlet continued. "What were those things back at the ship? That's the first time I ever met a rat who could fence."

"Mmm," Puck agreed. "Sounds like something out of one of Hobart's stories. About the Great War."

Hamlet shook his head. "Couldn't be. Rasferret's dead, you know that."

"Mmm. But we're dead too, aren't we? Funny thing, I never realized until just recently how much a corpse can do."

ON THE ROAD

I.

Far west of Ithaca, in the uncharted wasteland of rural Ohio, Luther was talking to the Devil.

A full chronicle of the mongrel's travels from the Wisconsin outback would make a book in itself. Suffice it to say that the weather, the great distance, and the lack of companionship had made it a much harsher journey than his and Blackjack's initial Heaven-trek. Not the least of the obstacles in Luther's path had been Lake Michigan, which had balked him for over a week. Then one night a beautiful woman with a voice like music and a silver whistle on a chain around her throat had led him onto a ship in Milwaukee Harbor; he had crossed to the far shore in a cargo hold laden with case upon case of Meisterbrau, a ready wet dream if only Z.Z. Top could have been there. He had scavenged his way through Michigan and down to the Buckeye State, where this morning a quick-handed dairy farmer had tried to indoctrinate him into the ranks of the domesticated. The fellow had actually got a rope leash around Luther's neck when the dog broke and ran, charging across frost-covered pasture while a shadowy groundhog looked on in alarm. A quarter mile flew by and then Luther, rope still trailing behind him, leapt through a stand of bushes and discovered—surprise!—a low, steep bank and a slow-moving river beyond. He had plunged toward the water, only to be jerked back when the end of the makeshift leash caught on a bush.

Luther did not know what sort of swimmer he would have made, but at the moment it was the leash that was the greatest threat to him. The river bank turned out to be crumbly and unclimbable; unable to go up or down, Luther perched precariously near the water's edge and fought to keep his balance. The wind came, cajoling the bush into lifting its branches, drawing the leash noose-tight.

Beginning to' choke, Luther gazed into the depths of the river as if he expected it to rise up out of its bed and untie him. The river's only response was to show him a picture of a silly little dog with a rope around its throat. Luther turned away and tried to scramble up the bank. The bank tumbled him over, slid him right back down; now he was nose to nose with the other dog, and the leash had pulled so tight that neither of them could breathe at all.

As he watched, the image in the water rippled and began to change. It grew; no longer was it a tousled mongrel, but a Purebred, large, white, and sharp of tooth. Luther tried to back away but could not. His old nemesis addressed him in tones of brash fury, bold and triumphant.

Mange! he cried.

"Dragon . . ." Luther's legs seemed to flow out from under him. "No."

Did you think I forgot you, mange? I didn't. You're all I think about. And I'm coming for you.

"You can't. The 'catchers took you . . ."

They took me, Dragon agreed. *They took me and put me in a cage, and there was a mange there just like you, and what do you suppose I did to him? I'm in another cage now, but I'll get out. I'm almost out already.*

"No. You'll never find me, even if you do get out."

Of course I'll find you. We're both going to the same place, but I'm closer. I'll kill the cat first, and when you get to The Hill I'll be waiting there with his corpse. . . .

A sudden gust of wind drew the rope so tight that Luther became convinced his head had separated from the rest of his body. Tears filled his eyes, and as darkness drew down around him he found himself facing another apparition, infinitely large, a feral hound composed entirely of light and shadow. Its eyes were the color of mortality.

You know who I am, don't you, dog child? the Hound thought into him. Terror and wonder warred for Luther's attention.

"Raaq," he answered. "You're Raaq, you're the Deceiver, you're the Devil."

I am Raaq, the Hound agreed. *The Ender of Life. When should I end your life, dog child? Today? Now?*

"No," Luther pleaded. "I have to get back—back to Heaven."

The Hound made a sound like human laughter. *Heaven. And what will you do there, when your enemy comes? Will you fight to save your life? Kill, if necessary?*

"I'll never kill another dog. Whatever it costs me. I won't let you into my heart."

It's not your heart I'm after . . . how little you understand me. But as for this place you think of as Heaven, what makes you think you deserve to return there? You were given Questions, I believe. . . .

"Questions?"

Surely you remember. Five Questions they gave you. How many answers have you found, dog child? Do you know the nature of the Divine? The meanings of life and love?

Luther had no answers. His mind, his self, was dwindling down to a point, a candle flame which must soon be snuffed out.

What about the Fourth Question, dog child?

"Fourth . . . ?"

The Fourth Question. Answer me, dog child: Which is the superior breed of canine?

"Superior breed?" Old anger flared, giving Luther a last surge of strength. His reply was swift and indignant: "The superior breed of canine is the breed that admits it can't answer the Fourth Question, because there is no answer and it's a bad Question in the first place. Which must make me the superior breed."

And what breed are you, dog child?

Dwindling: "No breed at all."

Again, the sound like human laughter.

Live a little longer, then.

Somewhere Else, a rope loosed itself from a branch; Luther plunged head first into the river. For a moment all was struggling and water, and next he was lying on the far bank, the leash gone from around his neck.

The mongrel's senses came back slowly. When they did, his first thought was not of the Devil, but of the Purebred.

I'll kill the cat first.

"Blackjack."

Luther was back on the Road as soon as he could walk.

II.

Tyson Riddle, a Class Two animal handler at the Adams Research Station, had once dated a vegetarian for a period lasting about two weeks. Actually, he tended to think of it as simple fucking rather than something more fancy, for he was damned if he'd ever held the slightest shred of respect for the woman. Busty, yes, but more than a little too educated for Riddle's taste, and when she said she wasn't a meat-eater, she meant it in every way possible. Their fling had ended in a scuffle during lunch one afternoon—he'd been stewing a clam, she slicing a cucumber—when Riddle pointed out testily that the average meat source could at least put up a token defense, scream or whatever when you went to kill it, whereas a typical fruit or vegetable didn't have such options. Exasperated with the bargain-basement I.Q. she'd been sharing a bed with, the vegetarian set her pacifist ideals aside for a moment and became violent. After a brief exchange of kitchen utensils and other not-nailed-down objects, the two sweethearts slapped each other good-bye and went their separate ways.

Now, sipping coffee in the Research Station's receiving office and licking his lips over this month's "lesbian" pictorial in *Penthouse*, Tyson Riddle was reminded of the long-lost Lady Meatless by a coincidental birthmark, and felt a certain warmth from the knowledge that at this very institution, animals were tortured daily in the name of science, many of them quite unnecessarily.

He leaned back and put his feet up on a desk, kicking a stack of battered paperbacks. On top was a dog-eared edition of *Old Yeller* (fully illustrated); beneath that, and more to the point, a copy of the helpful AMA booklet, *Save the Head: A Guide to Handling Rabid Animals*. Riddle was in charge of the Station's dog kennels. He hated dogs.

A truck had parked out front of receiving and a deliverer named Abby Rasmussen was unloading stock from Boston Surgical Supply. Riddle put down the lesbians for a moment and watched her through the window. Rasmussen did not remind him at all of the vegetarian—she had long blond hair, for one thing, while Meatless had been a coal-hole brunette—and despite a lack of major cleavage, Riddle thought she was pretty damn sexy. When she came in to have him sign for the shipment, he told her as much.

"So how about it, Rasmussen?" he said. "You ever get lonely, out on the road all day?"

Rasmussen, who had spent a summer doing recruitment for the C.I.A. and found Riddle about as attractive as a Sandinista with an anal fixation, sucked reflectively on a Tootsie Pop.

"Well I'll tell you," she replied. "The way I see it, there's three states of being: there's lonely, there's desperate, and there's the point where you might as well save your self-respect and become a nun. Catch my drift, Tyson?"

After she had driven away, Riddle sat back down and got his stiletto out of the bottom drawer of the desk. The weapon sported an eight-inch blade and had come ready to assemble from a mail order company down South. Riddle clicked it open and used the point to doodle on the Penthouse pictorials. He stopped himself after five minutes, though; he was only a lukewarm misogynist.

He was brewing a fresh cup of coffee and considering whether he should notify someone about the delivery—or even get back to work himself—when the phone rang.

"Receiving. What do you want?"

The voice on the other end of the line sounded vaguely foreign.

"There's a dog loose in the kennels," it said.

"Huh? Who is this?"

"You've been sleeping on the job, Mr. Riddle. The door to one of the dog pens is standing wide open. I'm Looking at it right now. *Big* dog, too . . ."

"You can't be looking at it," responded Riddle, who had no patience for pranks. "There's no phone over there. Now who the fuck is this?"

"Ah, such sweet language. But do have a sunny day, Mr. Riddle."

The caller hung up. Riddle slammed the phone down, then went to the window and looked out. The shed housing the kennels was at the far end of the Station complex. It was a small building, relatively; Adams' main volume was in rabbits and smaller rodents.

"Shit . . ." Well, he had to go out there anyway and clean some of the pens. Foregoing the second cup of coffee, Riddle grabbed his jacket, slipped the stiletto absentmindedly into his back pocket, and started across the compound. He dragged a personal dark cloud of ill temper along with him, and did not care or find it strange when he met not so much as a single co-worker on the way to the kennels. On another day, he might have noticed that the Station had suddenly taken on the deserted air of a ghost town.

The kennels weren't deserted, that was for sure. As he stepped into the shed, Riddle was greeted by a chorus of barks and yaps and the just-trying-to-be-friendly smell of dogshit. He flicked on the lights and yelled at his charges to shut the fuck up, which did very little good.

The shed was long and narrow, divided into two aisles, both lined with pens on either side. Looking down the first aisle Riddle saw nothing out of the ordinary, no dogs wandering around loose. The open pen was in the second aisle, on the left at the far end. The door was indeed standing wide, but still there was no sign of the occupant.

"Well, well," Riddle muttered. "Guess I owe you one, whoever you are."

Of course he wasn't in a good mood to begin with, yet of all the pens that could have been open there was no other that would have displeased him more. Unless his memory was on vacation—and in this instance it wasn't—the resident of that pen was a fully grown male Irish Wolfhound, acquired just recently from a shelter in Eastern New York State and not yet slated for any experiments. In other words, not injected with anything or operated upon in any way that might slow it down if it decided to go for him. And the Wolfhound was a mean motherfucker, Riddle knew that well enough from having to feed it twice a day.

He went into the maintenance closet and unscrewed a mop handle. Holding it like a spear, Riddle advanced on the Wolfhound's pen. He was halfway down the aisle when the lights went out.

There was no dying flicker, no flash of a bulb burning out; the light simply shut off. The only remaining illumination came from a high-set window near the peak of the roof that let in a few feeble rays of sunlight. Riddle froze for a good half a minute, and then, ignoring the basic lesson that every horror film tries to teach us, he continued down the aisle.

That the Wolfhound was still in its pen there could be no doubt—the shed had been locked, and dogs have a notoriously hard time with dead-bolts—and Riddle could simply have used the mop handle to shut the open door. Because the Wolfhound's pen was silent, however, and because all the other dogs persisted in making a racket, Riddle *did* doubt. Standing directly in front of the pen, he half-crouched, still holding the mop handle at the ready. He saw no movement in the dark interior of the pen. Laying the mop handle aside, he bent down all the way to have a closer look. Somewhere near, the shade of Alfred Hitchcock shook his head in despair.

Riddle was on his hands and knees with his head inside the pen when the growling started. The animal handler's eyes finally decided to adjust to the dark, and a huge white shape materialized before him as if by magic. The Wolfhound was poised to spring.

"Oh whore," Riddle said. He remembered the knife in his back pocket and went for it.

Didn't make it.

"Very nice," Mr. Sunshine said. "Very *graphic*."

FINAL PREPARATIONS:
FEBRUARY
TO MARCH

I.

February became March, and The Hill entered a period of waiting.

Rasferret the Grub had suffered more than a little over the loss of the Messenger. Not only did it deny him a flying pair of eyes, but his occasional trips to The Boneyard to create more troops had become much more difficult and dangerous without a handy pair of wings. To further keep him in his place Mr. Sunshine put a blind spot in the Grub's magic Sense, to make sure he wouldn't go looking for George until he was damn well supposed to. Paranoia did the rest; unable to tell where his human opponent was, he became too cautious to make further moves against the sprites, even when his Rat Army grew large enough to have a fair chance warring openly.

Hamlet and Puck, who might also have triggered the War prematurely, kept finding new reasons to play dead. Every time they were on the verge of deciding to come in and warn their fellows, Mr. Sunshine fed them second thoughts. Hobart, meanwhile, slept on in coma, uttering no more prophecies.

Waiting for the Ides to arrive, Mr. Sunshine concentrated his attention in the final week on George, Aurora, Ragnarok, and the brothers of Rho Alpha Tau.

II.

On Monday, the eleventh of March, Aurora Smith woke to the sound of exploding glassware. She rushed out to George's kitchen and found the storyteller sweeping up the remnants of a McDonaldland drinking glass; bits and pieces of the Hamburglar were everywhere, and fresh coffee puddled on the linoleum.

"My Uncle Erasmus told me never to put hot liquids in anything but a mug," George commented as she came in. "Now I remember why."

Two plates of pancakes and plumped Ball Park franks sat unobstrusively on the stove. Aurora raised an eyebrow.

"George," she admonished him. "You aren't supposed to cook breakfast."

"Oh no? What century were you raised in?"

"The Twentieth—the one where people are supposed to take turns. You made breakfast yesterday morning, and the day before. . . ."

"So I'm selfish." He dumped the glass shards into the kitchen wastebasket and mopped at the spilled coffee with a dishrag. "I like watching you sleep. You're a beautiful sleeper, you know that? Watched you for half an hour after I woke up, was going to watch you some more if the smell of pancakes didn't get you."

George looked up and she was blushing, holding a terrycloth bathrobe closed around her throat with one slender hand. After over two months they were still new enough to each other that Aurora could be shy at times, and her shyness never failed to move him.

"You make me feel safe," he told her, standing up and tossing the dishrag into the sink. "It's like writing a long novel, you know? Most people figure the really satisfying part is finishing the novel, getting a good piece of work done, but starting it can be just as fine, even better. When you start, you have an idea what the future's going to be like, what you're going to be doing; and you know it's what you were meant to do. . . ."

She blushed a shade darker, and he touched her cheek, and she touched his, and she opened her mouth, no doubt to say something equally romantic in turn, and the romantic thing that came out was: "Hot dogs for breakfast, though? Do you want to vomit?"

"Why vomit? Hot dogs are God."

"For breakfast?"

"Why not for breakfast?"

"You generally have bacon with pancakes. Or eggs. Or both."

"Well, what's bacon except meat? Hot dogs are meat too, so you're talking about the same concept, basically. And if you want to get picky they've got chicken franks now, too, which of course are disgusting, but if you want to talk technicalities instead of taste, what's chicken except an egg that got left alone long enough? So there you are, same concept twice over."

"You're sick, George."

"Naturally I'm sick. Why do you think your father gave us his blessing?"

The fruit basket was on the kitchen table, patient as a snake. Aurora first noticed it after George had kissed her and picked up the dishrag again; there was some coffee staining the side of the stove that he hadn't gotten yet.

"And what's this?" Aurora asked, giving the basket a closer look. Wicker, with a ribbon and card attached to the carry-handle.

"Found it on the porch when I got up. You don't happen to know anyone who works on a cruise ship, do you?"

" 'Bon voyage,' " she read from the card. " 'From the Ferryman.' Is this some kind of prank?"

"Search me, Lady. You understand, I've more or less given up trying to figure out mysterious packages; it's not worth the effort. Have an apple."

The apple, he might have said; there was only one. Nestled atop a cradle of spotty bananas and sour-looking grapes, its own skin polished, flawless, and red, it was by far the most appetizing piece of fruit of the lot. Aurora picked it up, felt it cold against her palm, and a dozen old fairy tales sprang to mind. She smiled.

"Of course it's probably poisoned," George warned her.

"Like the wine in the barn?"

"Yes, just like that."

"Mmm . . . I could stand to be poisoned a second time that way."

"Bite in, then," George suggested. He discarded the dishrag once again and returned to the pancakes and franks. What happened next did not feel terribly dramatic, though perhaps it was supposed to.

George heard a crunch as Aurora took a bit of the apple; a moment later, a thud, as the fruit dropped from her hand.

"Oh my," she said.

"Aurora?" George turned and found her tottering.

"Oh my," Aurora repeated. For of course it *was* a Poisoned Apple. Yet it was also an Apple of Knowledge, and on the brink of collapse, Aurora's eyes were filled with that knowing. "The Sleeping Princess. *He* just loves the Brothers Grimm."

George caught her halfway to the floor.

III.

Two days later, the thirteenth, Ragnarok and Jinsei begged off from their morning classes and walked into Collegetown for a pair of sundaes at Cravings Ice Cream Shoppe. Since their race with the truck they had spent more time in each other's company than out. Ragnarok had never been close friends with a woman before, and once might have thought it possible; yet here were all the symptoms of intimate friendship, while his dwindling love interest, like a true Southern gent, seemed to be politely bowing out. It would be wrong to say that Jinsei had replaced Preacher for him—no one, man or woman, could have done that—but she certainly had come to occupy a similar place in his heart. Many nights they stayed up talking for long hours, helping each other, as good friends will, to grapple with old tragedies and more recent ones. They surely had a lot to talk about.

That Monday morning, Jinsei helped avert another tragedy by stopping a fight before it could begin.

"Well now, look who we have here!" Jack Baron, still reigning President of the ever-popular Rho Alpha Tau, stepped around his Porsche to confront Ragnarok and Jinsei as they left the ice cream shop. He was not alone: Bobby Shelton and Bill Chaney piled out of the passenger side of the car. "How's life in Bohemia?" Jack asked cheerfully. "And the Orient?"

"Don't," said Jinsei, grabbing Ragnarok's arm automatically. Two parking spaces down, Ithacop Samuel Doubleday rested his not inconsiderable weight against the side of his cruiser; Nattie Hollister had ducked across the street for bagels and coffee. If Jinsei thought that Jack Baron hadn't noticed the policeman, she was wrong. If she thought the policeman's presence would act as a restraint to the Rat Brothers, she was wrong again.

"Seriously." When Ragnarok made no reply, only glowered, Baron pressed right on. "Seriously, how have things been with you?" His lips curled up in a smile: "How's old Preacher?"

"Oh, Jack!" Bobby Shelton's expression collapsed in a perfect parody of shock. "Jack, you shouldn't have asked that. Haven't you heard the news?"

"Why no, Bobby." Jack looked properly mystified. "What news?"

"About our old friend Preacher," Bill Chaney put in. "The man succumbed."

"Succumbed to what? Academic pressure?"

"Gravity," Chaney answered, and then it was only by interposing her whole body that Jinsei was able to hold Ragnarok back. "NO!" she shouted at him, the same way one might shout at an attack dog, as he clenched both fists and tried to swing.

"That's right," Baron egged him on, not making a move to defend himself. "That's right, belt me right in front of that cop, I swear to God I'll have you crucified for assault. Come on!"

He almost did; Jinsei alone prevented him, more through force of will than physical strength. At last Ragnarok calmed down sufficiently that she did not have to hold him.

"That's right," Baron repeated, still needling. "You just take it easy, Bohemian. You just—"

Jinsei whirled on him.

"*Fuck* you," she said. An ancient and far-too-often-used expression, but coming out of her mouth it stung like new. Jack Baron was stunned into silence. Shelton, the football player, stepped in to retrieve the ball.

"Why don't you watch your mouth?" he threatened. In height and weight he had her hopelessly overmatched, yet Jinsei was unintimidated. Once Shelton had frightened her, but that had been before the Rubbermaid.

"No," she countered. "You watch it. One more insult, one more word and I'll go for you myself. And if you have to have me arrested for assault, I'm telling the cops you threatened to rape me."

"Rape you? Give me a break, who's going to believe we tried to rape you in broad day—"

"Go ahead and take the chance if you want to," Jinsei cut him off. "I know about your House; we'll see who believes what about rape. But one thing's sure, the best lawyer money can buy isn't going to get the scars off your face."

She hooked her fingers like claws; her nails were long, long enough, anyway. Shelton readied a snappy retort, but faltered, seeing something unexpected and dangerous in her expression. He stepped back.

"Don't bother us again," Jinsei warned them all. When it seemed even Baron took her seriously, she reached behind her for Ragnarok. Her hand closing around his was as gentle as she had been hard toward the Brothers. "Let's go, Charlie."

Ragnarok, every bit as stunned as the Rho Alphas, allowed himself to be led. The Brothers gave them room, but Bill Chaney was a bit slow about it; Jinsei shoved past him with such force that he lost his balance and went ass-down into the gutter.

"Hey!" Bobby Shelton shouted in Doubleday's direction. "Hey, did you see that?"

The patrolman, who was badly in need of a handkerchief, hurriedly took his finger out of his nose and glanced around in embarrassment. "Huh?" he sputtered.

"Never mind," Jack Baron said. He watched the Grey Lady and Bohemian disappear down the street, hand in hand. "This isn't over yet."

IV.

The final mechanical test before the assembly of the Green Dragon took place late that night, in secret. The main workroom in the Foundry, a shed-like structure on the edge of Fall Creek Gorge opposite Risley Hall, had been cleared of flammable objects. Lookouts had been posted along the road outside, on the chance that Public Safety might happen by and decide that laws were being broken; within, a cadre of six Architects stood ready with fire extinguishers. Two of the six were Modine and Curlowski, the designers of the beast.

Larretta Stodges, the Mastermind, crouched beside the disembodied head of the Dragon (the rest of it was in ready-to-assemble sections across the street at Sibley Hall). The head was over a yard high and some five feet from the tip of the nose to the back of the neck. The lower jaw was hinged, the teeth sharp and menacing; cradled within was a properly diabolical device of tanks and jet hoses to which Larretta was even now making last adjustments. The whole head was fireproof, or so they hoped.

"All set," Larretta told the others, wiping her palms. "Take your positions, and make sure you're not anywhere near the line of fire." She unhooked a second, not-quite-diabolical-but-still-ominous device from her belt—once it might have been a walkie-talkie, but it had been redesigned, painted bright green except for a single red (naturally) button on its side. "This is history in the making, gentlemen. Does anyone have a good quote?"

"Krakatoa or bust," Curlowski suggested.

"Sydney or the bush!" cried Modine.

Grimacing, Larretta pressed the button.

The Dragon's lower jaw dropped open.

Fire shot from the mouth in an eight-foot stream, blistering the far wall and nearly torching Modine, who of course had chosen the wrong place to stand despite the warning. He retaliated with his fire extinguisher, spraying CO_2 everywhere. Larretta released the button and the fire-stream cut off, the Dragon's jaw snapping shut again.

"Gentlemen," she announced, as Modine's extinguisher continued to spout, "I think we're ready to roll."

THE DARK RAIN

I.

March fourteenth, Eve of the Ides, the end of the Tale almost close enough to taste. Mr. Sunshine sat on the sill of his Window on the World, sipping retsina and watching yet another squadron of rainclouds gather over Ithaca as evening neared. Such depressing weather . . . but if Mr. Sunshine had been dead set against precipitation, he never would have bothered with The Hill in the first place.

His golden lyre, which he had not played in some time, sat on his knee; at his side was a tightly lidded pot. He had a last bid of Meddling to take care of before the big finish tomorrow. First, however, he indulged himself with a few melodies on the lyre, alternating, as was his habit, between improvisation and the faithful rendition of old themes. Throughout the playing he kept one eye on Ithica, laughing at the frantic antics of Stephen George, poor George with his apple-poisoned Princess lying in enchanted slumber in Tompkins County General.

"We'll wrap up our business soon enough, George, don't worry," Mr. Sunshine said, when his music was done. "There's only a few more things to be done. Just remember what a virtue patience is supposed to be."

He set down the lyre, took another swig of retsina, a bite of feta. What he had in mind to do now was, in one sense, extreme overkill, using an artillery barrage for what a few sentences on a Typewriter would just as easily accomplish. But over long centuries as a Storyteller Mr. Sunshine had come to love mayhem even more than he loved the Brothers Grimm, and if a few innocent sparrows happened to drop dead on the sidelines—out of the way of his main Plot—well, that just added to the fun, didn't it?

And so, taking care not to breathe the escaping steam, he lifted the lid from the pot, revealing the noisome stew within: a soup of surplus nightmares, brewed from dark arrowheads Mr. Sunshine had clipped from the quiver of one of the Others, seasoned with still nastier things that he had scrounged from various corners of the Library. Open to the air it began to bubble furiously, and Mr. Sunshine fanned the resulting cloud, an angry black cumulus, out into the stratosphere, where it found itself a seat among the other rainmakers.

The World turned beneath it like a free-floating globe, targeting.

II.

There are many kinds of rains: cold spring rains, warm rains of summer, rains that bring flood, golden rains that turn into gods, rains of frogs or other odd objects that leave scientists puzzled. But the rain Mr. Sunshine had chosen to advance his Plot was none of these; it was a Dark Rain, the sort of rain that brings madness like the rays of a full moon.

It fell in a wide radius that included the whole of Ithaca and much of the surrounding county. In the main it was quite ordinary, but here and there a drop would fall that was something more. These drops landed on powerlines, causing overloads and fires; wet exposed machinery which then failed, often in some cataclysmic way; splashed into the open eyes or onto the tongues of individuals needing only a push to set them to violence.

On patrol, Nattie Hollister and Sam Doubleday cruised along Tioga Street, listening to a babble of emergency calls on the police band. Like snowflakes in a shaken glass globe, every lunatic in Tompkins County seemed to have picked today to go over the edge. Hollister and Doubleday were on the lookout for a red Ford pickup that had been plowing through mailboxes all over the downtown area. "We're not sure if it's got a driver or not," the dispatcher had quipped; Doubleday, who had spent all of January with his arm in a sling, did not find that in any way funny. He'd read the official report on the "Hilltop Moto-Chase," as some Dexter at the *Journal* had dubbed it, and several of the details were too familiar for comfort.

"And today," he said now, while the dispatcher continued to jabber, "today is getting to be as wacked-out psychotic as—"

His sentence was interrupted by a brief explosion, off in the direction of The Commons.

"—as New Year's," he finished.

III.

It was raining steadily at twilight, when Ragnarok came home from an early dinner with Jinsei. He walked rather than rode because his motorcycle was still a week or so from being street-ready again. Forced by lack of funds to make his own repairs he had taken his time, enjoying, meanwhile, the leisure of traveling on foot, over dirt trails and through alleyways too narrow for any large vehicle to follow him.

Soaked but not unhappy about it, he came upon his house and jiggered the front door. The first hint of something wrong was the smell, though that was quickly followed by readily visible damage. A step inside the door Ragnarok could see, without turning on the lights, that someone had been redecorating with a pile-driver while he was out. Holes had been knocked in the walls, white plaster dust streaked the black paint. His few sticks of furniture had met a similar fate, and he guessed easily enough what the smell was.

The toilet. The son of a bitch must have taken the plumbing apart.

He didn't look in the bathroom just yet, for another thought struck him—*the shed . . .* —and he stepped back outside, his temper surprisingly even, at least for the next few seconds.

He went to the parking shed where his motorcycle was convalescing. The shed's padlock lay twisted and bent on the ground; the door hung ajar. Ragnarok reached out to swing it wide, and that was when the raindrop slipped under his shades and entered his eye, stinging, burning. The world went away for a minute and when it came back he was inside the shed, fists clenched, staring at the scrap metal that had once been his bike. It had been battered into its basic components and then battered some more, until only memory made it recognizable for what it once was.

Ragnarok shook with fury, wanting to lash out but impotent, as with the driverless truck, for lack of a target. He might simply have pounded the sides of the shed in anger, but then his gaze lighted on the one thing the vandal had missed: his mace, lying dark and unbroken beside a shattering of glass from the headlight.

It was his own weapon, not a tool or clue left behind carelessly, yet seeing it was like a revelation. All at once Ragnarok knew, he *knew* who had been there.

"Of course," he said, bending down to trip the mace in a gloved fist. "Of course. Jack, partner, *Jack Baron*, I *warned* you not to cross me again."

He extended his arm, spinning in place, once, twice, three times, swinging the mace. It connected with the wall of the shed, with a loud *crack!* sending a broken piece of siding spinning to the ground outside. Rain pattered down, wetting it.

"Here I come, Jack," Ragnarok said.

IV.

"There you go," Mr. Sunshine agreed, sitting back at his Desk to Watch. "But not as fast as you think." He sipped his retsina. "Patience, boys . . . patience."

THE PAINFUL
VIRTUE OF
PATIENCE

I.

It would be wrong to say that Aurora's descent into coma following her eating of the Apple had in any way broken George; his near freezing-to-death after Calliope's exit had taught him his lesson, and he would not fall into the trap of despair again. Still, it would also be wrong to say that the loss of Aurora was anything less than hell.

The doctors at Tompkins County General could find nothing wrong with her, no physical reason for her slumber; under lab analysis the apple she had bitten proved to be quite ordinary, completely non-toxic. Despite this the Princess slept on, as Monday became Tuesday became Wednesday became the Eve of the March Ides, and if the physicians had no clue to the cause, they had even less notion of a cure.

George had a few ideas on the matter. He might occasionally be foolish, but he wasn't stupid, and he would have been a bad storyteller indeed not to recognize a fairy tale when he saw one. But even if he chose to believe what the sheer madness of this past year made it possible to believe, that someone in Power was recreating a Brothers Grimm fantasy, what could he do about it?

Tuesday and Wednesday were passed in the stacks of Uris and Olin Libraries on the campus, searching for an answer to that question. Olin was one of the most comprehensive book repositories in the country, but not even the self-help craze of the Eighties had produced so much as a single pamphlet on how to escape from someone else's daydream. George buried himself in the literature of Malory, Chaucer, and even, God help him, Edmund Spenser. In an ancient edition of *The Catholic Encyclopedia* he read about St. George, who three times had been put to death only to be resurrected, and who had bled milk instead of blood when a beheading finally finished him. None of this was remotely inspiring, or very cheerful, either, and when George returned to Aurora's hospital bed Wednesday evening he acted on instinct rather than learning, trying the most classic cure for enchanted sleep: The Kiss.

It didn't work. The critics might call him a Saint, but no one had ever accused George of being a Prince, and Aurora slept on. Feeling that he had failed her in some fundamental way, he went home fuming at himself, ate a disgusting amount of take-out pizza, and slept fitfully for six hours.

It wasn't fair; it was like Writer's Block, that most horrible point in the telling of a story when you had no clue what was supposed to happen next and the mere sweep of the second hand on your watch was enough to scatter your thoughts, foil your attempts at concentration. And George wasn't even in charge of this Story, that was the worst part.

Rising before dawn Thursday morning, determined to do *something*, George burst from his house with a fiercely hopeful look on his face that scared hell out of a passing jogger. The only plan of action that had occurred to him—and a sketchy one at that—was that he must somehow prove himself, like a true knight of old, through brave or charitable deeds. *Then* his Kiss would have the potency it now lacked.

Only trouble was, bravery and charity didn't seem to want to have a thing to do with him that day. Strolling along the edge of Cascadilla Gorge while darkness still lay on the land, George heard what sounded like desperate cries from below; but after nearly killing himself trying to reach the Gorge bottom, he found a contented—though chilly—couple who needed nothing except, perhaps, a thicker sleeping bag. Embarrassed, George followed a path down into town, where he attempted to offer his protective services to children on their way to school, but they all ran away from him, terrified by the look on his face; a dowdy old matron he tried to help across a busy street left him choking on a breath of Mace.

This sort of thing went on, literally, until well into afternoon, by which time he had ranged back up and around far north of The Hill, beyond Cayuga Heights. The rain caught him in open country, out of sight of any shelter, and while it brought chaos to Ithaca it brought nothing to George other than a good soaking. Worn out, his desperation to revive Aurora changing to anger at the still-unseen Author of his miseries, he plodded the back roads shouting dire threats at the clouds, from which he imagined he could hear the faintest echoing of laughter.

"What are you waiting for?" he bellowed. "I'm ready to take whatever you've got, so let's bring it on already!"

A new sound: a siren, approaching from behind him. George turned expectantly, feeling incredible release, the moment come at last, a task to perform for the glory of his Princess. But he was wrong; the red pick-up truck that came flying down the road, a police car close on its tail, was not the test of chivalry he'd been searching for. There was nothing he could do but jump back out of the way, stumbling blindly under the spray of mud the two vehicles kicked up as they roared past. They were gone as quickly as they had appeared, Sam Doubleday's cries to "Pull over, you fuck!" lingering longest in their wake. Then no sound but the pattering of the rain, George's angry exhale, and the faint heavenly laughter.

"All right," George said, furious. "All right, that's the way you want to play."

Freshly determined, he set off in the direction the truck and cop car had gone. But it was past dark by the time he finally found someone in need of his help, and by that point, he almost wasn't paying attention.

II.

If George was nearly untouched by the madness raining down on Ithaca, Ragnarok found himself practically swimming in it as he raced up University Avenue toward Fraternity Row, eager to do to Jack Baron what Jack had done to his bike. The mayhem seemed to have concentrated itself along his chosen route, like a Dali painting brought to life and scattered in a line along the Hillside. In one house he passed someone with a lunatic's cackle was hurling model trains through the individual squares of a many-paned living room window; twenty yards beyond that, another someone had decided to toss their furniture into the middle of the Avenue: a warped highboy, a rain-soaked divan, a shattered standing mirror.

Not far beyond that, as he was cursing the slowness of his legs, Ragnarok came upon another Daliesque apparition: a purple-maned horse, led by a hairy man in leather with a six-pack clipped to his belt. Z.Z. Top had been on West Campus when the Dark Rain began and things got decidedly weird. A polite argument between two passing Cornellians had metamorphosed without warning into a rib-smashing brawl that took the efforts of six other bystanders to break up.

"Got the hell away from that scene," Z.Z. Top would have explained, if Ragnarok had given him time, "and then I saw Lion-Heart's horse zipping down the road with no rider. Took me half of forever to catch up and calm him down."

But Ragnarok did not stop to chat. As it was the Top barely had time to recognize him before the stallion's reins were torn out of his grasp and he was roughly shoved aside.

"Hey!" the Top shouted, as Ragnarok slipped one foot inexpertly into a stirrup and tried to lift himself into the saddle. "Rag, what do you think you're do—"

"Need the speed," Ragnarok barked at him, and with a determined lunge managed to get himself astride the stallion. Still clutching his mace in one hand he gave the reins a vicious yank to turn the horse, which neighed in protest.

"Ragnarok," the Top began. "Ragnarok, wait, you don't know how—"

Too late. A stout kick, a cry of "Giddap!" and stallion and rider were off at a suicidally fast gallop.

" . . . don't know how to ride a horse," Z.Z. finished. And watched them vanish into the rain.

III.

Rain pounded against the walls of Rho Alpha Tau, but the Brothers paid little attention to it, or to the chaos going on outside. A party of five—Bill Chaney, Bobby Shelton, and three others—had gathered in the House game room for a game of True Stud Poker, a special variant utilizing nude playing cards. Even as Ragnarok was taking the horse from Z.Z. Top, Chaney took Shelton for a twenty-five-dollar pot.

"Two pair, Linda Lovelace high," he announced, to which Norris Mailer, another Brother, could not resist adding: "Looks like *four* pair to me, Bill."

Bobby Shelton gave him a black look. "You know any jokes that *aren't* as old as Martha Washington's underwear, Norris?"

Chaney took the pot; Mailer, chastened, gathered in the cards and took his turn as dealer. They were in the middle of the next hand when Jack Baron came in. His step was almost silent and at first only Bobby Shelton noticed him, but soon they had all turned around to look. Norris Mailer goggled openly.

The House President was still damp from his early sojourn in the rain. His hair lay close to his skull, and his eyes were wide, searching. One fist was curled tightly around the sledgehammer he had used to demolish Ragnarok's motorcycle and house; at the moment he looked very anxious to try his hand at demolishing a skull or two. This look was not deceiving.

"Doing some yardwork, Jack?" Shelton asked, eyeing the sledgehammer. "Putting up a tent, maybe?"

"Where is he?" Jack studied each of them with extreme suspicion. "He ought to be here by now. Who's seen him?"

"Seen who?" said Bill Chaney. *He* was studying the door, wondering how quickly he could get through it in a pinch.

"*Ragnarok*, of course! Son of a bitch should have been here a long time ago!"

"Why would he be here, Jack?" asked Shelton. Jack made no answer to this question, turning his attention instead to the grandfather clock that dominated one end of the room. Its ticking was slow and not particularly loud, but to the Rho Alpha President, who had heard it from three rooms away, it sounded almost mocking. When it began suddenly to chime the hour he stepped up to it and planted the sledgehammer in its face.

"Hey!" Norris Mailer cried, definitively demonstrating his stupidity by getting up to interfere. "Hey, hey, my old man *paid* for that cl—"

Jack whirled on him, felling him with one stroke of the hammer; with equal swiftness, Bill Chaney bolted from his chair.

"*Where is he?*" Jack roared at the three remaining poker players, "*I want him here now! I WANT HIM HERE NOW!*"

On the floor, Mailer clutched at what was left of his nose and screamed through broken teeth.

IV.

Ragnarok would have been more than happy to oblige Jack, but his cavalry charge on Rho Alpha Tau was destined for a premature end. He got as far as the Cayuga Heights Bridge before his luck, and the stallion's tolerance for abuse, ran out. He had driven the horse as he would have driven his bike, to break all speed records, and despite his lack of riding experience he thought he had everything under control right up until the moment the animal threw him. They were halfway across the bridge, Gorge roaring below, when all at once the stallion seemed to skid. Its shoulders dropped; its hindquarters came up, catapulting him into the air.

With perfect detachment he watched the world turn over. He fully expected to go flying over the side, and somehow it was not important that this would keep him from reaching Jack. His last thought before crashing bodily into the guardrails was that the rain seemed to be slacking off.

The shock of impact rang in his head; his sunglasses broke in half, falling into the Gorge while he himself dropped back onto the cold metal of the bridge, blood running from a cut above his eye, pupils wide to the thinning rain. The stallion seemed to study him for a moment, then snorted and moved on across the bridge, where it began cropping the dead grass by the entrance to Carl Sagan's house.

A half hour passed while Ragnarok lay unconscious on the bridge. During that time the rain stopped completely, and Stephen George found his way back to The Hill, wet, muddy, exhausted. After a brief and fruitless march down Fraternity Row during which, still, no damsel in distress or other potential good deed showed itself, the storyteller decided to return home and reconsider his strategy. It was about two minutes after making this decision that he came upon the fallen Bohemian . . . whom he very nearly walked past without noticing.

This time George felt no surge of victory, no release. He simply checked to make sure that Ragnarok was still breathing and then hurried to call an ambulance.

Naturally, it did not occur to him that he had finally found what he had been yelling for all afternoon.

AT THE HOSPITAL

I.

When Ragnarok's senses returned to him he was lying in a private room in Tompkins County General. His forehead was bandaged and one of his ribs had been taped up, but other than that he was in remarkably good shape, except for the drained and ashen pallor of his face.

"You look like tofu," Myoko said affectionately, when he blinked his eyes open.

"Maybe next time you decide to steal my horse," Lion-Heart added, "you'll remember to ask for a few riding lessons first."

Wincing, Ragnarok raised his head a few inches, looked around curiously. "Did I kill him?" he asked, his voice weak.

"Charlemagne's fine," said Lion-Heart, thinking he meant the horse. "Luckily enough, and no thanks to you. What the hell were you up to, anyway?"

"Never mind that now," Myoko interrupted. "How do you feel, Ragnarok?"

The Black Knight's head dropped back against the pillow. He seemed not to have heard them. Withdrawn, he whispered to himself: "No, I didn't. Not yet."

Myoko and Lion-Heart exchanged glances. Then she said, more tentatively: "Ragnarok? Visiting hours are almost over, but Jinsei ought to be here in about fifteen minutes. Do you want to see her when she gets here?"

"Not yet," Ragnarok repeated, and all at once he was sitting up, struggling to get out of bed.

"Wait a second, Rag," Lion-Heart said, alarmed. "Doctor said you're supposed to rest. They don't know if you've got a concussion or not."

"I have to talk to Stephen George," the Black Knight insisted.

"You can thank him for bringing you in tomorrow, Rag. You can call him on the phone, OK?"

"Don't need to." His feet tested the floor for firmness; he tried to stand, did stand. "Don't need the phone, he's here in the hospital."

"No, George went home a while ago. Said he hoped you'd be—"

"He's *here*. Visiting Aurora."

"Aurora?" Myoko said.

"How do you know that?" Lion-Heart asked. "How do you know that, Rag?"

Ragnarok paused, puzzled by the question. "How? . . . I just *do*. Some-one—" he glanced briefly at Myoko, "—someone must have whispered in my ear while I was out. In a dream, maybe. I've got to give George a message."

"Tomorrow, Rag. You can give it to him tomorrow, OK?"

"Tomorrow's too late," said Ragnarok. He fought his way out of the thin blue hospital robe someone had dressed him in, looked around for his own clothes. "Tomorrow's what it's all about. . . ."

II.

There were two other beds in Aurora's hospital room, but both were empty. The lights were out, leaving the moon—the clouds had dispersed—to shine in and illuminate the sleeping Princess. The storyteller sat in the darkened half of the room, watching her; she was, as he had told her, a beautiful sleeper. Radiantly beautiful now, despite three days in a sickbed. As much as anything else, this beauty gave him hope.

It still had the feel of a fairy tale, that was the thing. He had been made a fool of today, in his quest for a chivalric act to perform (in his mind, his discovery of Ragnarok did not come close to qualifying), that much was true, but it didn't change the basic situation. The Poisoned Apple; the Sleeping Princess; the test of valor waiting to be taken. Being drenched by the rain and laughed at by the clouds had not caused George to doubt his sanity, or, for long, dampened his optimism. He had been balked, he was still angry; but he wasn't ready to quit.

Loosely cupped in his right hand were four seeds from the Apple; every so often he shook them like dice, listening to the sound they made. He had them rattling like wind-up teeth when he became aware of a third presence in the room, a figure standing directly behind him.

For an instant George thought it must be Calliope. When he turned and saw Ragnarok instead, though, he wasn't really surprised.

"In The Boneyard," Ragnarok said. The Bohemian spoke with the voice of a ghost reciting lines in someone else's play.

"What's that?" George's fist was clenched tight, the apple seeds silenced.

"It's in The Boneyard." Ragnarok told him. "What you've been looking for. Calliope left you a present."

He slumped a little, his duty discharged. A hand stole its way up to touch the bandage above his eye. "Tired," he said, in a voice more his own. "Headache."

"Wait," George said, as he turned to go, and Ragnarok waited . . . but there didn't seem much point in questioning him. Instead the storyteller reached for something on the nightstand beside Aurora's bed, offered it, a return gift. "This is yours, I think. It was lying next to you on the bridge."

Ragnarok flinched a bit at the sight of his mace. At first he seemed reluctant to claim it, but then a burning in one eye called up a memory of Jack Baron, and his hand closed around the black handle of the weapon. "All right," he said, accepting it. And then: "I'll see you tomorrow, George. You do what you have to do tonight, and I'll see you tomorrow."

He turned, shambled out of the room. Alone again with the Princess, George wondered if he might have hallucinated the whole thing. But not for long.

He called a taxi, and fifteen minutes later was on his way back to The Hill. To The Boneyard.

FRACTOR DRACONIS

The Boneyard was large, but it wasn't hard for him to guess where he had to go. He entered the cemetery from the downhill side, scrambling up a slope between jutting mausoleums, heading for the far north end.

The wind blew at his back as he made his way through the trees; it blew cold, offering no comfort. George moved as swiftly as he could, and soon entered the area where the main body of Rasferret's army was preparing for a pre-dawn march up The Hill. George passed the demon-adorned tombstone of Harold Lazarus without noticing it. The marble gargoyle crouched atop the stone watched him pass; so did the company of Rats clustered at its base. As the storyteller topped another rise, a cordon began to close behind him.

He stood at the crest of a burial mound, the bones of Ithaca war dead beneath his feet. Moonlight cast a circle around him, ringed the mound with shadow. From these shadows came the first sound, a rustling of rotten leaves like the approach of small animals. The second sound was harder to identify, a faint twanging.

He was on his way down the far side of the mound when the first tiny crossbow bolt struck him. George felt a sharp sting in his ankle and reached down to pluck a sharp sliver of bone from his pants cuff. More missles flew, some bone, some metal. George jerked around as pain flared in his calves; his feet tangled and he fell, landing in a shallow gully.

Small dark shapes came swarming over the burial mound after him. All the storyteller could think of was Gulliver and the Lilliputians. He scrambled backwards, groping for some sort of weapon. One hand clutched a stone and hurled it, felling two of his opponents.

The Rats returned fire. George's chest became a pin-cushion; only luck saved him from a serious puncture or the loss of an eye. He continued to retreat, yanking the miniature bolts out of himself as another volley flew.

All at once he felt something cold and hard beneath him. He gripped it in his fists: an iron bar, left lying in the grass. Using the small crosspiece at

337

one end of the bar like a mallet head, he swept through the advancing ranks (he still could not clearly see what they were), batting them right and left like croquet balls.

Crossbow bolts were no longer flying; now it was the Rats who were airborne. Suddenly overmatched, they routed, scattering for safety, and George let them go with one last swing. "Send something bigger next time!" he called after them, only later reflecting that this might not have been a wise thing to say.

Bleeding from a dozen pin-sized wounds, the storyteller stood up and continued his walk. Coming to The 'Yard's northern fringe, he found Calliope's present easily enough; the moon led him right to it. Though the **PANDORA** stone was no more, the spearhead that Calliope had thrust into the bole of an oak tree on her way out of town still remained. Its exposed portion glimmered like a beacon.

George grabbed at it and tried to pull it out, succeeding only in slicing a finger. The spear blade *wanted* to cut something, yet the oak held it fast. George had another idea. He raised the iron bar, inserting it into the square socket at the base of the spearhead.

It fit perfectly.

"OK," George said. "OK, I think I understand."

"Understand?" a chuckling voice said behind him. "You make it sound as if you really do know something. But then I didn't choose you for humility; that's not a storyteller's trait."

George turned, pulling as he did the bar which was now a shaft, drawing the spearhead out of the oak easily, revealing the inscription: **Fractor Draconis.**

"Who are you?"

Mr. Sunshine smiled from his seat atop a squat tombstone. His sandaled feet were crossed one over the other, and in his hair a circlet of laurel leaves rustled with the wind.

"Someone very old, that's who I am," Mr. Sunshine said. "And a Storyteller. You've guessed that much correctly."

"You put me in a fairy tale," George replied. "That's what all this is, isn't it, a fairy tale brought to life?"

"Close enough. I didn't have to Meddle much to fit you in the Story, though. You're a very lucky coincidence for me, George—if I'd ever Written about Ithaca before I'd have to wonder if the Monkeys had something to do with you. Your first and middle initials are almost too much to believe."

"St. George," the storyteller nodded, a last piece of the puzzle falling into place for him. "And the Dragon Parade's tomorrow."

"Now *that* I had a little more of a hand in," admitted the Storyteller.

"So the Princess is asleep," George continued, "and what happens next is the Dragon comes to life somehow, and I kill it to save her and the town from—" But here he stopped, for Mr. Sunshine had burst out with a familiar-sounding laugh.

"I kill it," the Storyteller repeated, amused. "Ego! Ego! We're not rewriting *Romeo and Juliet* here, George. It's *my* Story, and no one said you're obliged to survive it, or live happily ever after with the woman. I like tragedy; after all, I'm Greek."

"But your fairy tale's about a Saint, with the Brothers Grimm thrown in for good measure, so how Greek . . ."

"My Story," the Storyteller insisted, "is about a Fool on a Hill, a Fool who has put the wind at his beck and call, a Fool who accepted without question when his Uncle told him that artists were the only beings other than the gods who could grant immortality. Which is a dangerous attitude to take, whether you're Greek pagan, Christian, or Jew."

"But if you're a storytelling pagan," George countered, "it's the *only* attitude to take."

More laughter. "Pity you aren't *really* immortal, George—I have a feeling we'd have made good friends. Same pride, same spirit of hanging on to the end, never admitting defeat. Who knows, maybe the Fool who rushes in really can save the day"—he raised an eyebrow—"or at least die in a truly interesting fashion, one worthy of a Story."

"Promise me," George pressed him, "promise me Aurora gets to live if I win."

"*Promise* you? Oh, please, I—"

"It's a *good* ending, damn it! Save your damn tragedy for some masochist who'll get off on it, not me."

"*Patience*, George. The Ending hasn't even been Written yet. But if I were you, I'd be more worried about the Dragon than the Lady."

"I'll win," George insisted. "I'll win whether you want me to or not. But when I win, Aurora gets to live, OK? Deal?"

"Go home and get some sleep," the Greek Original said. "Tomorrow I'll call you when it's time, and we'll write the last Chapter together."

"*Wait*—" George reached out, to restrain him or run him through with the Spear, it did not matter which, for all at once Mr. Sunshine flickered like a projected image and faded out.

"No, no, no!" George cut the air with the Spear blade as if trying to bleed it. "You come back here! You come back here!"

Fool or Saint, he received no answer, not even a mocking laugh, and all was still in The Boneyard except for a light breeze that wafted the scent of hills, and rain, and laurel.

Book Four

THE IDES OF MARCH

1866—AT THE
HILL'S CREST

. . . And so at the last they reach the top, the gullied pasture that is the crest of The Hill. There are no school buildings here yet, no students, but Mr. Sunshine can sense them like phantoms still to be. The thing he does not sense, no matter how hard he squints into the Future, is the one thing that would make his Story idea complete.

"No Dragon," he sighs. "Not even a statue of one. Maybe at Oxford . . ."

"Ahem," says Ezra Cornell, his boots caked with mud, his strength sapped by the long climb.

"Well Hades," continues Mr. Sunshine, ignoring him. "Hades, I've got this much, I suppose I could Meddle out a Dragon. Did you say"— all at once Cornell is present again—"that you planned to have instruction in every study?"

"Eventually," Cornell agrees. "But as you can see, there's not much to see right now, so I'd really appreciate it if we could—"

"Engineering?" Mr. Sunshine presses him. "Architecture and design?"

"Of course engineering and architecture. What—"

"Then that's it." The Greek Original withdraws into his own musing. "A budding architect or engineer, sort of fellow who likes building things. I could send Calliope to inspire him. And it could be a yearly event, a college tradition, the Annual Snow Dragon, maybe . . ."

"My dear sir," Cornell tries once again, "I'm cold. I would like to go home now."

"Certainly," Mr. Sunshine surprises him by saying. "Certainly, you need your rest. You have a great undertaking in the works here—and I have quite a Story." He hands Ezra the lantern. "Build your University well, Mr. Cornell. I have interesting things in mind for it."

"Do you?" Cornell sounds less than fascinated; his thoughts are already on the long walk down to town. He is more than a little surprised when Mr. Sunshine vanishes into thin air a moment later; even before that, he is startled by Mr. Sunshine's last words to him.

"There will have to be women here, of course," the Greek Original says in parting. "Your plan for coeducation is a good one. If Denman Halfast gives you any more trouble warn him that he'd better start listening to reason or risk waking up one day with the ears of an ass."

He smiles, fading.

"I can still do that, you know . . ."

Fading.

Gone.

And then Cornell is alone, and all is still on The Hilltop except for a light breeze that wafts the scents of hills, and rain, and laurel.

DAWN OF
THE IDES:
THE DEATH

I.

Five A.M., pre-dawn of the March Ides.

Blackjack woke from nightmare. He'd crawled into a dark place out of the wind to sleep and at first did not remember where he was. A dog crouched near him, its scent mixing and fusing with the scent of another dog from his dreams.

"Luther?" he said, confused.

"It be Rover. Rover Too-Bad." The Puli was a blacker outline against the black velvet of the sky, still unblemished by first light. The moon had set an hour ago.

"What do you want?" Blackjack demanded testily, secretly glad to be awakened. He retained no shred of what had passed through his mind during sleep, but it had not been pleasant. There had been blood in the nightmare, much of it his own. . . .

"I an' I be sent to tell you 'bout an 'emergency assembly' Boss-Dahg be callin' at sunrise. Everyone be there, he say: dahg, caht, whatever."

"Assembly? What the hell for? It's not time yet for the graduation ceremonies and I'm damned if I'd go to them anyway. I want more sleep, thank you. Or, hmmm—" He sniffed; the scent of rat was surprisingly strong in the air. "—hmm, maybe an early breakfast would be nice."

"Blackjack," said Rover, "why you give me shit, eh? T'ink I an' I *want* to bother you? Listen—meetin' called by Boss-Dahg. The Dean. You have to go."

"I don't have to do anything," Blackjack said warningly.

"There's been a death, Blackjack. A killin'. Do you understand that?"

"A killing? Human or animal?"

"Bulldahg. Some Bulldahg torn to pieces."

"Torn to pieces by what?"

"That's why Boss-Dahg call assembly. Some t'ink it was dahg wit' the rabies, even wolf, but others . . . it be very bad, Blackjack. You remember

345

Lady Bucklette, Collie bitch wit' long teeth? She goin' aroun' half the night, tellin' everyone who listen that mongrels do this t'ing, 'mongrel agitators' she say."

Blackjack understood at once the need for an assembly. Bad enough to have a rogue predator loose on The Hill, but if Purebred began to turn against mongrel in suspicion . . . "There'll be no end to trouble," he finished the thought.

"You come now, Blackjack?" Rover asked him. "I an' I got others to find."

"Sure, I'll come," the Manx agreed. "But what do you think it was, Rover? Could there really be a wolf here?"

"I an' I don't know 'bout wolf," replied the Puli, "but this be one big mother, wolf or not. I an' I see the body—Jah love, Bulldahg torn apart."

II.

"Order!" Excalibur III, Sheepdog and Dean of Canine Studies, barked fiercely at Ezra Cornell's statue. "Quiet down, why don't you!"

The sun was just creeping over the horizon, and the scene on the Arts Quad was very similar to that seven months ago at the initial Dog's Convocation, but with about twenty times the hostility. The mongrels had once again drawn into a tight, protective knot, with the campus cats—on direct request from the Dean—placed unwillingly in a ring around them, to create a buffer zone. Many Purebreds were openly antagonistic, and Bucklette the Collie continued to exhort them.

"Damn it!" Excalibur fumed. "I want order!"

With some difficulty his Doberman aides got him turned around to face the crowd, after which his pleas for order had a much greater effect. Bit by bit the assembled dogs quieted, but the silence, when achieved, was a very uneasy one.

"That's better!" said the Dean, squinting beneath the thatch of hair that covered his eyes. "Now what the jolly hell is going on here, eh? Have we got the jolly rabies, one of us? Frothing? Feral? Speak up!"

"It's anarchy!" Bucklette spoke up.

"Anarchy?" beneath Excalibur's sternness there was a note of fear. "What's this?"

"It's no secret!" the Collie went on. "We all know they've got it in for us."

"*They* who?" piped up Denmark from among the mongrels. "Which they are you referring to?"

"Jus' so, sister," added Rover Too-Bad, the only Purebred to openly cross party lines. "I an' I would also like to know."

"Listen to me!" Bucklette appealed to those around her. "Listen, it's common knowledge that certain dogs take a very negative view of the Fourth Question. With no concept of or respect for proper scholarship, it shouldn't surprise us that they'd resort to organized violence."

"What's all this 'us' and 'they' garbage?" Denmark demanded. "You—"

"Don't insult my intelligence!" Bucklette snapped ("What intelligence?" muttered a tabby on Blackjack's right). "You mongrels are nothing but a bunch of self-segregating snobs who live in the past and try to blame Purebreds for your feelings of paranoia. We don't ostracize you, you ostracize yourselves, and I for one am sick and tired of having to be afraid every time I run into one of your packs. I don't want revenge taken on me for imagined prejudices that I never had anything to do with."

"Imagined prejudices?" cried out another mongrel who was missing half an ear.

"If we're paranoid," questioned Denmark, "how is it that you're the one who's always afraid?"

"I asked you not to insult my intelligence!"

"Well I'm sorry, my dam raised puppies, not miracle-workers."

"You insolent—"

"Order!" Dean Excalibur overrode them again. "Order, order, order, this is going too fast and I'm getting confused! Now I don't want any more quibbling, I want bloody facts. *Slow* facts."

"Begging your pardon, sir," one of the Dobermans put in, "but we have an expert witness ready, if you'd like. Sureluck?"

A very ancient and dilapidated Bloodhound detached himself from the throng of Purebreds and came forward, moving slowly but not without dignity. Excalibur squinted at him.

"At your service, sir," the Bloodhound said respectfully.

"Eh? Who's this fellow?"

"His name is Sureluck," a Doberman explained.

"He's rabid, you say?"

"No sir, not at all. He's a *witness*, sir."

"Well, he certainly doesn't *look* rabid. I see no foam, no—"

"Begging your pardon, sir. Sureluck *isn't* rabid. He's the one who found the body, and he's done some sniffing around for us."

"The body? What body?" Then, after a pause during which one could almost hear the Sheepdog's scattered thoughts crawling back toward each other across the battlefield of his mind: "*OH!* Oh, *that* body, of course! The Bulldog, you mean. Jolly good! And tell me, do we know who this Bulldog was?"

Sureluck answered: "Yessir, Sergeant Slaughter has already identified the victim as one of his own." Slaughter, who sat ringed by Boxers, affirmed this.

The mongrel Denmark turned to one of his companions. "Beats all, doesn't it?" he commented discreetly. " 'Bred victim, 'Bred witnesses, a 'Bred bitch howling for blood, and a half-senile 'Bred running the whole show. You suppose we'll get to play any part at all?"

"Half-senile my wagging tail," came one response. "Try three-quarters."

"Oh Denmark," said another, "the Accused is a very important role, didn't you know that? So's Martyr."

"Where and when did you find the body, Surelatch?" Excalibur was asking. "Begin at the beginning, end at the end, don't go too fast, and all that. . . ."

"It's Sureluck, sir," the Bloodhound corrected him patiently. "Well, I was out scrounging for a bite to eat some good time before dawn—the moon was still high, sir—and my wanderings took me down by the Western Campus. I smelled blood, sir, and at first I thought some kind Master had thrown out a steak or two, but I soon discovered I was mistaken. He'd been ripped in pieces—the Bulldog—torn in half, and then again, and partly eaten, I'm afraid." The Bloodhound's tone was calm and almost matter-of-fact, but more than a few of his listeners were horrified. Bucklette could barely contain herself.

"That's barbaric!" she snapped, growling accusingly at the mongrels. "But not entirely surprising!"

There were answering growls; caught in the middle, the cats tensed nervously, ready to scoot out of the way and mind their own business should a riot erupt.

"Sir?" said Sureluck, tensing a little himself.

"Yes, please excuse me," replied Excalibur. "Order!" he demanded. "Please continue, Shotluck."

"Yessir. As you may have guessed, sir. I'm not very fast going upslope, and I knew you'd want to be informed as soon as possible. Fortunately I was able to find Rover, there, in the vicinity."

"I an' I be visitin' the Lady Babylon," offered the Puli. "Long may she live."

Sureluck continued: "I sent Rover up-Hill right away with the news. As for myself, I sniffed around carefully a bit longer, trying to see where the killer might have gotten to. I had to be most careful, of course—it must have been a very large animal."

"What about a pack?" queried Bucklette impatiently. "It could have been a pack, couldn't it?"

"A pack?" echoed the Bloodhound. "Oh no, no, it was one animal, I'm quite sure. I picked up only one scent."

Another Purebred spoke up. It was Skippy, the Beagle, for once too frightened to hop about: "Was it . . . was it really a wolf?"

"Eh? No, no, no, a dog, I should think. How would a wolf get here?"

Bucklette again: "What kind of dog?"

"A big dog, as I said."

"Yes, as you said, but what kind of big dog?"

"I'm sorry, I don't understand the question. The four-legged kind, what other kind is there?"

"Purebred or mongrel, you idiot!"

Sureluck stared at her. "Can *you* smell the difference?"

"Well," the Collie faltered, "well no, but you're supposed to be an expert witness."

Sureluck glanced discreetly at the mongrels. "How did it go?" he said. " 'My dam raised puppies, not miracle-workers.' I'll know what it is when we track it down, not before."

"Hmmph," exclaimed Denmark. "An honest dog. How about that?"

"Maybe you're just too old," Bucklette suggested. "Maybe your nose can't be trusted anymore. I still say it was mongrel agitators. Everyone knows you can't trust them."

"Enough of that." Gallant, the St. Bernard, stood glowering behind her. "You've had your say, why don't you quiet down for a while, now?"

"Why should I?"

"Because I say so, because I'm tired of your manure, because I'm a big dog too and can quarter you as easily as any wolf."

"Oh! Maybe *you* killed the Bulldog, then!"

"Eh?" Sureluck broke in. "Oh no, didn't I mention, I don't believe I'd ever scented this dog before. And I've been around here a long time. Of course, if the Dean wishes I'd be happy to double-check everyone." He sniffed loudly. "Say, who's been eating rats and farting?"

"Oh yea, oh yea," Dean Excalibur said abruptly, once more confused and trying to catch up with the conversation. "Did somebody say something about a search party?"

THE SPIDER'S WEB

I.

The sun came up high and bright, the sky clear at first but smelling of another storm in the making. All over North and West Campuses, and in student apartments in Collegetown and down the Hillside, the weekly ritual began, the deciding whether or not to blow off classes and start the weekend early.

For the Architects at least it was an easy choice: their studies were suspended for Dragon Day, freeing them to concentrate on the last-minute business before the noon Parade. By ten-thirty many of them were already gathered on the Arts Quad, most in costume, many drinking steadily, working up toward critical mass. Costumes ranged from simple green greasepaint on the hands and faces to elaborate cardboard shells in the shapes of famous buildings. One extra-tall undergrad came as the Tower of Babel; he mingled with the crowd, quite drunk, making sexist remarks to the women and accusing the men of multiple acts of bestiality. Because he spoke in Esperanto and because the smile never left his face, nearly everyone felt flattered by his gibberish and complimented him in turn.

Campus security was out early, high-strung after yesterday's pandemonium, watching for any sign of further trouble as more and more people drifted into the Quad. By quarter past eleven a fair cross-section of Arts, Ag, ILR, Hum Ec, and Hotel students were out waiting, along with delinquent faculty, Bohemians, Blue Zebras, and a handful of zealous Engineers acting as forward spotters. Following tradition the Dragon would begin its journey in the Sibley Hall parking lot, come around the side of the building into the Quad, cut over past Lincoln Hall to East Avenue, and travel down to the Engineering Quad. There the Engineers would attack it, throwing mudpies, tomatoes, rotten cabbage—aerodynamically sound rotten cabbage—and, if the weather changed radically over the next half hour, snowballs. Then, unless the Dragon was overwhelmed—and the only Dragon ever to fall down, last year's, had done so without any help from the Engineers—it would complete the circuit, right on Campus Road, right again on Central Avenue, and so back up to the Arts Quad for burning.

"Good day for it," Curlowski commented, overseeing the connection of the Dragon's tail to the rest of the body. Midway through the linkup a cat without a tail and two dogs hurried by; Modine bent to pet them, but they avoided him neatly and continued on, moving with a purpose.

Larretta Stodges, the Mastermind, strode across the parking lot, elbowing her way through the crowd of onlookers. "Is everything going all right?" she asked.

"Couldn't be better," Curlowski told her. "The weather's perfect: not a breeze since early this morning, no clouds, and not freezing cold like last year."

"There's a storm coming," Larretta responded, not so pleased as he. "Can't you smell it?"

"Guess I don't have a nose for storms. It looks fine, and the radio said—"

"Never mind the radio. How's the Dragon holding up?"

The main body of the Dragon reared up vertically forty-five feet, and the inner wooden frame was set on wheels, like a siege tower. The skin was thick canvas, overlaid with dark green paper-plate scales. Set atop the body was the specially designed head, flame-thrower in place; below the jawline two taloned arms jutted from the body, large and menacing. The Dragon's wings were also canvas, like the skin, but of a lighter weave and rigged to collapse against the body should the wind become too strong. On the ground, now fully connected, the Dragon's tail stretched out another thirty feet behind it. It had no wheels but would be lifted and carried by a select group of Architects standing inside, while a second group pulled the body along with ropes.

"It's holding up very well," Curlowski said, justifiably proud. "Better even than expected. I thought there might be some trouble with the head, but the extra weight from the flame tank doesn't seem to have hurt the balance."

"So we're ready to go at noon?"

"Barring a disaster. Listen, though . . ." He lowered his voice. " . . . that flame tank's still got me a little worried."

"Why? All the kinks were worked out of the design two nights ago. There shouldn't be any problem."

"It's not the design I'm talking about." Curlowski lowered his voice still more, to a whisper. "There's a fire marshal here, you know. For the burning, afterwards."

"And?"

"Well come on, Larretta. This fire-breathing business was never officially approved. If a fire marshal's watching and that thing starts spuming at the crowd . . ."

"The angle of fire is way above everyone's head. You know that, you helped build it. Unless Mary Poppins comes sailing by on her umbrella, there's no danger to—"

"I know there's no danger," Curlowski interrupted, "and you know there's no danger, but what's the fire marshal going to say?"

The Mastermind pondered this; it was an unsettling thought, that the marshal might shut them down in the middle of the Parade.

"No," she decided. "No, he wouldn't cancel the Parade, but he might make us stop and take the tanks out. We'll have to keep it a secret until we get to the Engineering Quad. One good blast to scare the daylights out of them and I don't care what happens afterwards."

"All right," Curlowski agreed. "If worse comes to worse we can always send somebody up to pull the tanks."

"Right." Already Larretta had put the problem behind her. She glanced at her watch. "Thirty-three minutes until we start. How long is the Parade supposed to take?"

"An hour, maybe an hour and a half to complete the circuit. Why?"

"My nose. I've got a bad feeling about this storm. . . ."

II.

The storm surrounded Ithaca in a shrinking ring, like a spider's web drawing tight. Barely had Curlowski commented on the calmness of the air when the wind *did* pick up, blowing uncertainly, now this way and now that, bringing clouds from every direction. Mr. Sunshine—letting the style of the Story override his personal taste in weather—guided them in, spun the web.

Now it is, of course, difficult to imagine a city the size of Ithaca becoming isolated from the outside world. A small town, some rural backwater out in Iowa, perhaps, could conceivably vanish off the face of the earth without anyone noticing, at least for a while. But a city of thirty thousand souls, with a major university and a smaller college on opposite hills, is another matter entirely. There are telephone calls, deliveries, commutings in and out every day, every hour. Ithaca, most would agree, could not be cut off without somebody taking notice very quickly.

Yet that is exactly what happened. As the Ides marched on, as the storm drew nearer, as the web tightened, Ithaca began to sever its ties with the surrounding country. It became enchanted, a darkly enchanted fairy city; fewer and fewer communications passed in and out, and travelers chose another Road, to another place.

One of the last beings to enter the enchanted city before the web closed completely came on four legs.

III.

The sign said ITHACA—2 MILES, and though Luther could not read it, he knew that his journey was almost over. Ragged and lean from many long weeks on the Road, he padded along a deserted stretch of Route 79, the same road he and Blackjack had come into Heaven on the first time.

Heaven was just ahead of him now, rich and rain-smelling; Hell followed close on his tail. From this vantage point it was already possible to see the rapidly converging clouds, thick and grey and darkening near to black at the horizon. Lightning flickered within them, and cold fog swept the ground below, eating up the visibility. Terror of the storm kept Luther moving at a brisk pace, yet he knew it would overtake him long before he reached The Hill.

"Oh Blackjack, please be alive when I get there," Luther pleaded, moving still more quickly. Memories of recent dreams haunted him, dreams in which he came upon the savaged corpse of his old friend, and standing over it another, larger beast, sometimes the light-and-shadow-demon Raaq, sometimes the Purebred Dragon. *I've been waiting for you, mange. . . .*

The wind shifted suddenly, purposefully. For the barest instant it blew directly from The Hill, and Luther caught a brief whiff of a familiar scent, a scent he was no doubt meant to catch.

"He *is* waiting," Luther whimpered. "He is waiting for me, he's there ahead of me, just like in the dreams. . . ."

Was it a test, a last test of courage from God or Raaq? *I will not kill another dog, even my enemy.* But if the Wolfhound was waiting, and found him, as he no doubt would find him . . .

"It's hopeless," he told himself. "I'm dead. I'm a dead dog."

Yet he did not slow or falter in his course, did not let the knowledge of coming death overwhelm him. During his journey he had thought long about many things, among them Ruff's philosophy about the purpose of life. Maybe it *was* all just a story, an entertainment for God and His angels. Luther believed at least that there must be some plan, a plan he did not understand but would not turn against.

"But I'm afraid. I'm so afraid, Blackjack, please, *please* be still alive."

The first clouds were directly above him, now, and the leading edge of the fog snaked chillingly between his legs . . . like tendrils of smoke from the breath of a monster. He kept moving.

HOBART TELLS
A FINAL TALE

I.

Eldest sprite Hobart let out a low moan.

"Julius? . . ."

Zephyr sat on the edge of the bed—a padded matchbox with four headless Strike Anywhere posts—and wiped his brow with a cold sponge. Hobart jerked beneath the covers, exhibiting more movement than he had in months, but his eyes remained unfocused.

"The fever seems to be breaking," Butts, the physic, observed. "That's a hopeful sign, at least."

Zephyr shrugged noncommittally. Her face was drawn and tired, and she bore the look of one who has lost or is on the verge of losing everything, hope included.

"He's been speaking in his sleep ever since he was brought here," she said. Her voice was cold, like old embers. "It doesn't mean anything."

"Yes, but the signs . . . well, to this practiced eye, I'd say he might very well wake up—"

"I've had enough of practiced eyes," Zephyr interrupted. "Most of them seem to be in need of more practice. Two months ago you were telling me almost the very same thing, that he would either wake up soon or die, and either way it would be over and done with. Two months ago Hamlet was reassuring me that any day they'd find Puck, and that would be over too. And now . . . now, can your practiced eye tell me when they'll find Hamlet?"

Despite her words there was little anger in her tone; Zephyr had no energy for a proper fury. Nonetheless Butts backed away nervously and said no more.

"I'm going to fly up to the Tower," Zephyr told him, dropping the sponge into a thimble of water. "I have to tend to the Chimes. Watch him until I get back."

"Yes, ma'am," replied Butts, not unhappy to see her go. Her temper had become frightful lately.

Zephyr exited the healing rooms quickly, following a passageway that ran above the false ceiling of the Straight's main lobby. Though she passed many sprites she knew she paused to speak to none; those few who attempted a greeting of their own were ignored. Puck would have recognized her mood, had he been there—it was the same mood that had consumed her the day she had led him on a ragtag chase through the skies down to The Boneyard. At her core Zephyr felt cheated, in the same way she had felt cheated by Puck's infidelity with Saffron Dey. Fate had robbed her, with no explanation, of her lover and a good friend, and put her grandfather deep in coma; yet unlike a straying boyfriend, she could not kick Fate out of her bed or deny it her presence. That was the hardest thing: not having a concrete being to blame for her troubles.

A hidden stair took her upwards, to the highest reaches of the building. There was no hangar, but a hatch opened at one of the roof peaks, and there was moored the gossamer glider, newly repaired, bucking in the swelling wind as if anxious for flight.

The weather surprised her; the sky had been perfectly clear a few hours ago, yet now clouds threatened from all directions, leaving only a small pool of sunlight that centered directly over the crest of The Hill. Lightning flashed in the distance; the storm looked to be a nasty one.

Zephyr climbed into the pilot's sling and slipped the moorings. The wind took the glider immediately, yanking it into a climb. Zephyr banked toward the Tower—the Clock said ten to noon—her thoughts turning once more to Puck, and then, for the first time in a long time, to George. There was another one that Fate had, in a sense, robbed her of. Oh, she understood well enough now the truth that sprite and human could never match, yet it would be nice, *kind*, if she could talk with him about all her other losses. Surely he would be sympathetic, even though, now that he was in love, she found it difficult to imagine that he would have any real problems of his own to face.

Wondering where George might be—and keeping one eye on the approaching cloud bank—she winged up to the Tower, paying no mind to the crowds swarming on the Arts Quad, and certainly not noticing the two tiny figures below her who were racing with utmost speed toward the very building she had just left.

II.

"Go!"

A freshman with a knapsack slung on his back knelt in front of the Straight to tie his shoelace, and Puck and Hamlet each caught hold of the end of one of the shoulder straps. The shoelace-tier finished his business and stood back up without the slightest inkling that he now carried two invisible piggy-backers. Moving with a stride greater than the broadest-jumping sprite could hope to match, he hopped up the Straight's front steps and shoved through the swinging doors, headed for Oakenshields Dining.

"Jesus, Troilus, and Cressida!" Puck cried out, as the freshman turned sideways to squeeze past a fat woman and nearly brushed him off. "Walk right, why don't you?"

"Calm down and get ready to move," Hamlet suggested, as they passed through the second set of doors into the main lobby. Imminent Dragon Parade notwithstanding, the Straight was packed, some students here for lunch, others hoping to make a withdrawal from the bank to pay for this weekend's partying. The lobby floor was a shifting mass of heavy feet, yet the two sprites dropped to it anyway, clutching at the freshman's pants legs to slow their fall. The Cornellian felt the tug and hitched at his jeans, and then Puck and Hamlet were loose on the floor, weaving and dodging through the forest of feet. Twice Hamlet was nearly stepped on; a girl in an Angora sweater and matador boots almost did for Puck, but her boyfriend came up behind her and swept her fortuitously off the ground at the last moment.

At the base of one of the walls, beneath a bench, a secret door gave access to one of the sprite passageways. Safe inside, they rested only a moment before rushing up to the healing rooms. Like Zephyr before them, both ignored the sprites they passed, but they got a good deal more attention in return. Ghosts often do. Macduff, leader of the ill-fated Lab Animal Freedom Raid, watched Puck and Hamlet go by in astonishment and turned to follow them. So did his brother Lennox.

And so it happened that all four sprites came bursting into the healing rooms, all babbling questions at once. Puck, by virtue of having the loudest voice, managed to get the amazed physics and attendants to show them where the Eldest was quartered. The babbling died down abruptly as they were ushered in.

Hobart was sitting up in the bed.

III.

"Not trace," Rover Too-Bad commented, nose to the ground. "Not single trace of it. I an' I be t'inkin' our wolf, he long gone."

"Pity," said Blackjack, not feeling very pitying at all. "I can still smell rat just fine. Anyone for lunch?"

The three of them—Blackjack, Rover, and the mongrel Denmark—were on a dirt trail on the south side of Fall Creek Gorge; the suspension bridge was just ahead on their left. They had been combing this general area for some hours now, the search hampered by the fact that only Rover knew the scent they were trying to pick up. Most of the dogs at the assembly had trotted first thing to West Campus to get a whiff near where the killing had taken place. Denmark, however, had wanted to get clear of the Purebreds as soon as possible, and Blackjack simply didn't care to bother with the Slope.

"I wish we could stop and eat," Denmark said now. "But if this 'wolf' isn't found soon . . ."

"You're nervous about Bucklette, aren't you?" asked Blackjack.

"All 'Breds make me nervous." He glanced at Rover. "Most 'Breds, I mean. That St. Bernard did surprise me this morning, speaking up like he did."

"Jus' so," said the Puli. "Maybe, Denmark, there be hope yet for us all."

"But is there?" replied the mongrel. "One or two dogs taking a stand isn't exactly overwhelming. Sometimes I wonder if life isn't meant to be a setup. Things like the Fourth Question, the density of some dogs—it almost seems designed to keep the old feud going. Maybe it isn't meant to end."

"Jah love, Denmark, you really believe the world could be designed in such a way? I an' I t'ink not—"

" 'Design?' " interrupted Blackjack. " 'Meant?' Spare me, please. Basic animal nature is a good enough explanation for all this Purebred-and-mongrel nonsense. You don't have to go dragging superstition into it. That's just the mentality that got this mess started in the first place. Why not try being a little bit feline in your outlook? You might rest easier."

"Never talk God to a cat," said Denmark, quoting an old proverb.

"If there is a God," the Manx retorted, "and if He's really on the ball, then obviously He must have intended me not to believe in Him. Which would mean that, out of the three of us, I'm the only one content to fulfill my role in this life without pestering Him with stupid questions. Am I right?"

Denmark fell silent, either considering or sulking. They moved on a little farther, coming closer to the bridge. Across the gorge they could see the approaching clouds, hear muted thunder.

"That storm looks foul," said Blackjack.

"This whole place is foul," said Denmark. The words were his last. All at once the wind changed, bringing a new scent, causing Rover to start and Blackjack to bristle in sudden recognition. Only Denmark did not sense the danger immediately.

A mound of rotting leaves on the slope to their right exploded, and death fell snarling among them, white fur and teeth.

IV.

"I've dreamed a great deal," Hobart told them, sitting on the edge of the bed, flexing his bedsore muscles. "Dreamed and dreamed. And learned. Yes, I understand a great many things now that I didn't before. Or think I understand."

His eyes found Puck's, and the younger sprite thought Hobart looked strangely revivified, stronger and more alive, despite his long sleep, than he had on New Year's Eve when they had flown into ambush at the Tower.

"Rasferret the Grub is alive, of course," Hobart said. "We did not kill him at the end of the Great War—that part of the history is a lie."

Shock registered on the faces of Macduff and Lennox. Butts the physic gasped aloud, though he was a simple fellow, not much for stories, and knew less than any of them about the War. Of the other sprites in the room—and a good many of them had come crowding in to see the miraculously recovered Eldest; physics, attendants, and patients from elsewhere in the healing rooms—their reactions ranged from startlement to barely controlled terror. Only Puck and Hamlet seemed impassive, unsurprised by the revelation. Perhaps they had been doing some dreaming of their own. Why else had they both awakened this morning with the sudden inspiration to end their period of hiding and come here?

"You remember the story I told on Halloween, the Death Story Laertes so wanted to hear?" Hobart spoke directly to Puck and Hamlet, but a good number of the others also nodded. "Most of the details were correct: the final assault on The Boneyard involved two contingents, one large one to draw off Rasferret's main force, a second smaller one led by Eldest Julius to take care of the true business at hand. But we did not go in with the intention of killing the Grub—we were afraid to try that, not even sure it could be done.

"No, we tricked him instead, attempted something so unexpected that perhaps its very unexpectedness is what allowed it to succeed. We imprisoned him. We hunted him down, drew him out with his own overconfidence by pretending to fall back immediately before his magic and his personal guard. A series of our own illusion magics completed the trick—Rasferret was trapped in a box, a magic box designed to hold him, alive but powerless.

"We put him in the box, then put him in the ground. It was far more difficult than you can ever imagine. The Rats did not let us alone for a moment, and there was the rainstorm raging around us, and . . . and Rasferret himself. He did not go quietly. Every seam and crack of the box was sealed in such a way that his own magic could not get out, but there was a hole in the seal, and through that hole he performed one last animation. It happened just as we had finished digging a deep enough pit for the box, just as we were lowering it in. My own crossbow—I do not know why it happened to be mine—turned in my hands, fired of its own volition." Hobart touched his left breastbone gravely. "Julius was struck right here, through the back and out again through the front. He faded almost instantly.

"There's little enough to tell, beyond that. The breach in the seal was fixed with panicked swiftness; the box went into the ground. We filled in the hole, and then those few who remained alive tried to make an escape, for still the Rats did not give up. And only I—a very young sprite in those days—actually got out of The Boneyard. Only I knew the secret of what had really been done. Before long the Rats *did* disperse, either dying or returning to their original form, I'm not sure which. But The Boneyard remained a haunted place, and in time I saw to it that a ring of magic stones was placed over the burial site, stones enchanted to frighten off animals and sprites. I did not think that the Big People would desecrate one of their own graveyards, and did not worry about them digging up the box. Perhaps I should have worried; but perhaps I was not meant to. In any case, Rasferret the Grub was never killed, though I had hoped after a century that he might simply have died in his box. Yes, I hoped that very much."

"Begging your pardon, sir," Butts the physic spoke up, after a long silence. "But what exactly does this mean to us?"

"Rasferret's got out, of course," Puck spoke up.

"And he has enough Rats assembled," added Hamlet, "to destroy us all."

"Good God!" Macduff exploded. "Och, we're not prepared for war. If—"

"We're a sideshow," said Hobart, and all attention turned back to him. "It's one of the understandings I've come to," he continued. "We didn't kill Rasferret the Grub then, and we're not going to kill him now. He's got another purpose, he's someone else's foil—just whose I'm not sure."

"What are we supposed to do, then?" piped up Lennox.

"Organize and defend ourselves as best we can," said Hobart. "Until Rasferret *is* killed, or his power broken—if it's broken—we're all in very grave danger." He stood shakily and buckled on his sword, which had lain beneath his bed for the past two months. "One way or another, there's going to be a great killing before this day is over."

V.

You're all done, cat," Dragon said, blood flecking his teeth. "All done."

Denmark was dead, Rover Too-Bad nearly so. The Wolfhound's attack had been unbelievably swift—he had moved more like a serpent than a canine—and both Puli and mongrel were out of the fight before they had had any real chance to react. Only Blackjack had dodged the initial assault, propelled by the memory of the Hell-town where he and Luther had almost been torn apart by the Purebred pack. Moving with a serpentine swiftness of his own, the Manx had slashed at Dragon, scoring on his flank and then scuttling away . . . into a death trap. Stupidly, he had run onto the suspension bridge, inviting, but a mistake since it was flat, narrow, and gave no cover. Ten feet in he had realized his error, turned to backtrack, and found the way behind already blocked.

"Go ahead," Dragon challenged him. "Run, cat. Run for the other side. You'll never make it—I'm fast, faster than you, and I'll snap your spine halfway across. But go ahead, try it."

"You're looking pretty thin, Dragon," said Blackjack, terrified but determined not to show it *(Out, out, how do I get out of this?)*. "Maybe you're not as fast as you think anymore."

"Oh, I'm fast." And indeed, though the mark of the Road was heavy on the Wolfhound, Blackjack had seen well enough that this was true. Dragon might have grown lean, his once pure-white coat might now be tangled and dirty, but he still looked every inch a killing machine, slimmed down to its most basic outline. "I'm fast like death, cat. Where's the mange?"

The question caught Blackjack by surprise and he could almost sense Dragon probing him, using that uncanny mind-reading ability that some few animals had. Though Blackjack had no answer to the Wolfhound's query, still he thought to evade him.

"Why did you kill the Bulldog?" he asked in return.

"I was hungry," said Dragon. "Where's the mange, cat? Gone away? Not back yet? *Yes*, that's it . . . so the dreams were true."

The Wolfhound began to advance, jaws wide and dripping. Blackjack backed up, keeping an even distance between them.

"Dreams, Dragon? What dreams?"

"Dreams that I killed you. Both of you. And guess who dies first, cat?" He poised to launch himself forward, and just then, back on the gorge path, Rover Too-Bad struggled to get up. The Puli had one leg broken and another torn nearly off, but he got halfway to a crouch before collapsing again.

"Jah," he said incoherently. "Blackjack, I an' I t'ink—"

Dragon was distracted from his prey for the barest instant. Blackjack was off like a shot, tearing for the far side of the bridge. But the Wolfhound was after him almost immediately, and the Purebred had not lied: he was fast, fast as death, faster than the Manx. Midway across the span he caught up and angled his teeth to break Blackjack's back. But Blackjack rolled, losing only a chunk of flesh and hair out of his side—that was bad enough—raking Dragon in return with both sets of claws. The Wolfhound recoiled briefly, his muzzle torn, then darted his jaws down again for a second bite. The Manx did not give him time to clamp on—he shot between Dragon's legs, heading for the dog's rear quarter, for that which was the most sensitive target on any male animal. But what he found—or rather, did not find—stopped him short.

Castrated! he thought, stunned. *Someone's castrated him. The 'catchers must have—*

"All done, cat!" Dragon caught him by the hind leg and tumbled him over onto his back. There was pain, blood, but no snap of bone, not yet. Blackjack reacted with a fury, clawing and spitting as never before. Bloodied but still by far the stronger, the Wolfhound released him, and they faced each other nose to nose, ready for a last grapple.

"You can't win," Dragon told him, triumphant. Blackjack, still wondering how this murderous apparition had come to find him, knew it to be true. The Purebred was too powerful and too full of hate—he was hopelessly overmatched.

"You'll pay in blood, though," the Manx said, hissing. "I'll leave you some scars to remember me by, 'Bred."

"And I'll carry your corpse in my mouth, to show to the mange when he comes. What do you think he'll say, cat? When he sees you dead?"

"Maybe," said Blackjack, filled with sudden inspiration, "maybe you won't have my corpse."

"What?" Dragon's eyes narrowed, and Blackjack sprang—not at the Wolfhound, not forward or backwards along the bridge, but sideways. The bars on the safety fencing were set too close together to squeeze through but the Manx flattened himself out, slipped beneath them.

"*NO!*" Dragon roared, moving to stop him. If Blackjack had had a tail he might well have been caught and drawn back, but he did not, and was not. He passed under the fence and tumbled from the suspension bridge, falling just as Preacher had fallen, and from almost exactly the same spot. But the river below was not the same as it had been on New Year's Eve. Then it had been frozen, the ice snow-swept; now it was thawed and roared with the body and strength that yesterday's rain had given it.

Blackjack's last thought before he struck was *Christ, I hate the wat—*

THE BATTLE OF WILLARD STRAIGHT HALL

I.

The Parade got under way two minutes early. The Green Dragon was ready to roll, and the Architects were becoming increasingly nervous about the weather. The clouds had closed ranks above The Hill, cutting off the last bit of blue sky, and the wind was dervishing.

"Rain, do you think?" Modine asked, as dozens of students bent their backs to get the Dragon moving.

"No," Larretta told him. "Feels like an electrical storm. Fireworks." To the crew: "Let's *GO*, people!"

The spectators on the Arts Quad—it was packed near to overflowing, now—cheered appreciatively as the Dragon first appeared around the side of Sibley Hall. Yet apprehension about the darkening sky dampened the festivities: several bright green kites that had been lofted, tentatively, at the wind's first stirring, were now being rapidly reeled in.

"Come on, come on!" Larretta was shouting at the pushers and pullers of the Dragon. "Double time, let's beat this damn storm!"

One minute to noon. The Dragon completed its transit between Sibley and Tjaden Halls and entered the Quad proper. Its makers need not have hurried so—the beast was destined to go no farther than here.

Not until the Story was finished.

II.

"Has anyone seen Zephyr?" Puck asked, as they gathered themselves to move.

"Oh, she's gone to the Tower, sir," Butts told him. "Flew up there just a short while ago."

Puck and Hobart exchanged glances, remembering New Year's Eve.

"But there's no time," Hobart said firmly. "If the Rats have gotten in there again, she's on her own and we can't help her."

"If there's another glider around here," said Puck, "or a plane—"

"No, Puck—"

"Or I could go on foot. It might take a long time, but—"

"No," Hobart insisted. "The Rats will be all over The Hill by now, preparing to attack. I'm quite certain of it. If they're not already in this building I'll be very surprised. We have to muster a fighting force of our own as quickly as possible."

"Aye, an' you'll find a great lot down below," Macduff spoke up. "In the Oakenshields kitchen with the Big People. There's t' be a banquet tonight o' sorts, and with all the cookin' . . . well, many a tidbit's to be had. Look for your army there, Hobart."

"Good," said Hobart. "We'll go there first. Lennox, I want envoys sent throughout the campus as swiftly as possible to warn the rest of our people."

"I could be envoy to the Bell Tower," Puck offered.

"No, Puck," Hobart replied, with a note of finality. "My granddaughter is an able enough duelist . . . either she'll hold her own against whatever comes there, or one extra sword won't help very much."

Puck disagreed—it was obvious from his face—but Hobart held his eyes a moment longer, willing him to obey. Then the Eldest said to them all: "Very well, swords ready! We go!"

They moved as a body, picking up extra fighters as they went. Lennox turned off early, seeking out envoys, but the rest proceeded downward, toward the lower level of the Straight where the human dining rooms and kitchens were. The kitchen complex serving Oakenshields Dining was huge and sprawling, and the sprites had put in many secret entrances and exits for their convenience. As the war party drew nearer to their destination they began splitting off into the various forking passageways that gave access to Dining. At one such fork Puck broke away from Hamlet and Hobart, taking a different path. Hobart let him go; as Eldest he expected to be obeyed, but as a grandfather he would secretly be relieved should Puck double back and head for the Tower against orders.

Good luck and godspeed to you, the Grandfather thought, as Puck vanished from his view around a corner. *I only hope you're not too late to help her.*

It was the last Hobart ever saw of him.

III.

The kitchen was bustling. In addition to the serving of the lunchtime meal, preparations were well under way for that night's Cross-Country Gourmet Special. The guest chef was a burly blond Norseman imported from a restaurant in coastal Maine. His name was not common knowledge—the regular Oakenshields cooks simply called him "the Swede"—but he bore the look of a mad Viking and might well have numbered Grettir and Beowulf among his ancestors. He made most everybody in the kitchen distinctly nervous, puttering around humming a nonsense tune ("Duh-heen, duh-hyun, duh-heen!") under his breath, and the student work supervisor, statuesque and a touch Nordic herself, did her best to keep out of his way. Mad or not, though, the Swede knew what he was about, and dinner prep progressed rapidly.

"Ah, but Little Peoples must earn their keep also—duh-heen!" barked the Swede, facing a table crowded with pies. The other cooks could see no one whom he might be addressing and shrugged, pretending not to notice, but the baker's dozen of sprites who scurried here and there on the table top—they had been preparing to siphon one of the pie fillings—were suitably impressed. The Swede was in good health and did not appear to be drunk, so if he could see them then it followed he truly was insane. The Little People paid attention as he barked out instructions to them. Shortly thereafter the human kitchen workers began to find small tasks being completed, as if by magic, when their backs were turned.

Humming away—"Duh-hyun! Duh-heen!"—the Swede went from one end of the kitchen to the other, impressing every last sprite into the work force and offering encouragement to Big and Little Persons alike. Things ran even more smoothly now, though the humans were damned if they knew where the extra efficiency was coming from. The Swede just clucked happily. "By Loki!" he cried, "Little Peoples should be more often!"

There were well over a hundred sprites in Oakenshields that day, ducking around the pots, pans, and people; all of them wore their swords and some carried crossbows on their backs as well. Even lacking advance warning, with so many pairs of eyes the Rat assault force should have been spotted relatively quickly, and a battle engaged. But now, busy with the tasks they had been given, the sprites didn't see as the first of Rasferret's vermin came up out of drains and holes where only cockroaches had tread before. These lead Rats had tasks of their own to perform, swift acts of sabotage.

Actually, one sprite did see the Rats, yet said nothing: it was Laertes, the angry brother of Saffron Dey. He had been out walking in the Rain yesterday when something fell stinging into his eye; today his mind felt strangely . . . clear. He saw two of the vermin scuttle out from under the big dish machine carrying an object like a cherry bomb between them. He raised an eyebrow and went back to his business.

Until the explosions began.

IV.

Lightning struck the Clock Tower at precisely noon. The bolt—crackling and blue—contacted the pinnacle of the Tower, but the whole structure seemed to surge briefly with electricity; the Clock stopped, hands frozen at twelve. A frightened murmur ran through the crowds below.

"Jesus, Larretta—" Curlowski began.

"Shut up!" The Mastermind wrung her hands in despair. The clouds boiled darkly in the sky above, and fog was creeping steadily up The Hill; to an observer standing on the crest of Libe Slope, the world would seem to end just below West Campus. "Damn it!" Larretta demanded of the weather. "Why did you have to pull this today? We had history made, here!"

Curlowski was shouting to the Architects surrounding the Dragon now: "Get the wings folded! Get them down! Oh, f—"

The wind gusted; another, louder murmur escaped the crowd. Larretta turned around and her heart broke.

The Dragon was tottering.

A moment later, it fell.

V.

The deep friers in the south end of the kitchen were the first things to go; those standing nearby heard a low blatting noise followed by a *whoosh!* and the oil was blazing. Half a breath later a sequence of explosions—it was impossible to count how many—rocked the place from end to end, damaging equipment, shattering pipes, spreading more flames. Throughout the Straight an alarm sounded as fire doors swung automatically shut. The human occupants of the building began a speedy exodus, and none so quick as the kitchen workers. A panic gripped the cooks, the pantry staff, the student help, sending them running. Someone hit a black EMERGENCY button on the wall in passing, activating mounted extinguisher jets that doused the friers, but other than that there was no attempt at fire control: the Big People just wanted out.

Which left the sprites alone on a sudden battlefield filled with smoke, steam, and a host of enemies. "To arms!" the cry went up, as the Rats swarmed out in full force now, swords and bows drawn for the kill. Caught by surprise and in no small state of shock, the Little People reacted slowly at first, and were nearly overrun. Yet even as the first swords were crossed, Macduff arrived at the south end with one of the groups from upstairs (Puck was no longer among them). They counted not so much for reinforcement value as for the sense of battle-readiness they brought with them.

"Aye, ye bastards!" Macduff cried, striding into the smoke unperturbed and impaling a Rat on his sword. *"Aye!"*

The killing began in earnest.

VI.

The crowd watched the Green Dragon topple. Many of them had been present to see last year's Dragon fall as well, had seen it land in a wreck, frame snapping under its own weight.

Curious that it did not happen that way this time. The Dragon's carven talons touched the ground and splayed out instead of breaking; the short arms bent to absorb the shock of landing. *We didn't design those to be flexible*, Curlowski thought, his heart beating a little faster. The snout of the beast kissed the earth, yet rather than accordion in on itself, the neck—which had also not been designed to be flexible—bent smoothly, so that the Dragon's chin rested comfortably on the grass. The wings ceased to flap in the wind and folded up neatly against the body. And the tail . . . the Dragon's tail, which had originally connected to the whole at a ninety-degree angle, now ran smoothly out with no hint of such a sharp bend. The Architects who had been walking under it scurried out, and when the last of them moved away it became impossible to tell where the juncture was, or what had happened to the wheels beneath the main body structure.

The thing no longer looked like an artificial construction. In the dimming light, it began to look more and more like it might be alive, or almost alive.

Larretta caught her breath. As did Curlowski. And Modine. And the other Architects. And the campus police. And the crowd. They were all waiting for something to happen; they all knew, somehow, that something would. But none of them saw the sandaled figure perched on the roof of Goldwin-Smith Hall, a figure who had left his Writing Desk and come down to the World to take a ringside seat at this Story.

"Hey-ho," Mr. Sunshine spoke to the clouds. "Let's clear the field, shall we?"

The wind screamed; lightning flashed anew, lighting up the Sibley Hall Dome. A second bolt hit an old tree on the Quad, scattering branches and breaking the crowd's paralysis. A stampede began, identical to the stampede at the Straight; as the thunder crashed over them like a wave, even Public Safety forsook their duty and scrambled to escape.

"That's right," Mr. Sunshine said. "Run home, run hide. And sleep."

Doors flew open on the buildings surrounding the Quad; more refugees swarmed out. A group of Bohemians led by Lion-Heart linked arms and fought against the press of the crowd. Even with this safety precaution Z.Z. Top, well oiled on cheap beer, managed to become separated from his companions. While the rising tide of panic forced the others to abandon him in a rush for Risley, he blundered into the bushes along the western face of Lincoln Hall, crawled under, hid his face in the dirt, and passed out, waiting on the end of the world.

The fog crested The Hill and crept over the floor of the Quad; the spider's web was almost sealed.

VII.

Hobart's group came out in DMO, Dish Machine Operations. This was a long rectangular area near the north end of the kitchens. Along one wall was the Dish Machine itself. Directly opposite it was a conveyor belt that brought in trays and dishware from the two dining areas. Running parallel to the last twenty feet of the belt was a trough through which water jetted constantly. Uneaten food scraps, napkins, and other garbage were dumped into the trough before the dishes were run through the Machine. Water swept the debris down the trough and into a nasty-looking device aptly named The Grinder, after which it was never seen again.

Both the Dish Machine and the conveyor belt had shut down immediately after the explosions; steam now hissed from within the Machine's belly. Water still jetted in the trough, however, and The Grinder pounded on at full speed, making the stilled conveyor belt a distinctly dangerous place for a battle.

"Somebody help me, here!" Hamlet cried, as a sprite faded beside him on the belt, leaving him to face two Rats on his own. *Puck, where are you when I need you?* He ducked back around a dirty drinking glass, parrying desperately. The Rats pressed him hard, not letting him off the defensive, and Hamlet found himself being backed toward the edge of the trough. "Damn it! *Somebody!*"

But the other sprites within hearing distance had problems of their own; Hamlet was not the only one outnumbered. He twisted to avoid a sudden sword thrust and felt empty space at his heels; he heard the rush of the water.

Something crashed into the Rats from behind, sending one tumbling past Hamlet and into the trough, where it was swept away. The other tried to turn toward this new assailant but was dead before it completed the motion.

"Jesus, Troilus, and Cressida," said Hamlet, "that was—"

He stopped, seeing the face of his savior. And the expression he wore.

"So you're alive," Laertes greeted him, hand tight around his sword hilt. He continued, in the most conversational of tones: "And where's the sprite who murdered my sister? Is he here too?"

"Murdered your sister?"

"Puck!" The point of Laertes' pinsword quivered. "Where is Puck?"

"What are you talking about, Laertes?" Hamlet said warily. "Puck didn't kill Saffron. The rats in—"

"The Rats are everywhere," said Laertes, and Hamlet saw the madness in his eyes.

"You've gone insane," he whispered, wonderingly. "You've lost your mind."

"Oh no," came the reply. "No. My mind is clear. *Very* clear. I think maybe you're the insane one, Hamlet. But I know just the thing for that. . . ."

Laertes attacked without warning, but Hamlet parried automatically, redirecting his thrust so the sword point passed without touching him. Laertes continued forward, slamming bodily into Hamlet. Together they tumbled over the edge into the trough.

The water jet was cold and strong, the floor of the trough slick with muck. They began to slide, struggling to hold on to their swords, grappling, rolling over and over as they were drawn inexorably toward the maw of The Grinder. Hamlet caught a glimpse of it, a huge grey metal hulk just ahead. The trough emptied into a square vertical opening like a mouth in The Grinder's side. Directly over the mouth was a sign: SMALL BONES ONLY!

Not two feet from the dropoff a melon rind had gotten jammed sideways in the narrow trough. Hamlet and Laertes were very nearly carried right over this low barrier, which would have been the end of both of them. Instead they fetched up against it. Hamlet had a second to ponder the ludicrousness of this salvation—spared by a melon rind! Then he and Laertes drew back from each other and raised their weapons.

Somehow they had exchanged swords during the tumble. Hamlet felt an absurd flash of annoyance—*This is no time to be picky*—but the matter quickly became academic. In a lightning move, Laertes disarmed him before he had a chance to make a single attack. The pinsword vanished into The Grinder.

Hamlet was defenseless; Laertes tensed for a final thrust. "*Very* clear," he said, and chaos slammed into them.

Two Rats and another sprite had fallen into the trough farther up. They arrived unannounced, struggling fiercely, and the weight of their impact dislodged the melon rind. Hamlet felt himself begin to slide again and made a valiant leap; using a Rat's head as a springboard he launched himself up the side of the trough, catching onto the lip with both hands.

"Yaaah!" he grunted, straining to pull himself up and out. Fingers clutched at his foot; he glanced down and saw that it was Laertes. All the rest—melon rind, Rats, sprite—had washed into the maw.

"Jesus and Troilus!" Hamlet cried. He swung his free foot, and, by some lucky chance, caught his enemy square in the face. Laertes gasped and lost his grip. He uttered one last word of protest—"*Clear!*"—and then The Grinder ate him whole. A whirlpool of water and chopping blades drowned out any screams he might have uttered.

Exhausted, wanting only to rest, Hamlet pulled himself back onto the conveyor belt, back into the dubious safety of battle.

VIII.

Far up the length of the belt, near the beginning of the trough, Hobart slew a Rat and found himself momentarily alone. All around him were the sounds of combat, but swirls of steam made everything into vague shadows, isolating him. He rested briefly and thought back, for a last time, to that other long-ago battle in The Boneyard.

A familiar echo in his mind: *Ho-bart* . . .

The crossbow bolt struck him in the left breastbone, piercing him clean through and out the back. Hobart grunted, muscles tautened near to snapping by the sudden pain; he felt his heart try vainly to continue pumping around the impalement.

Ho-bart. The General of the Rats materialized out of the steam, limping as always, crossbow cradled in his arms. *Thresh ends you.*

Hobart fell to his knees. His life wanted to swim away but he would not let it, holding back death for a few bare seconds with the heat of sudden fury that flared in him. Of course it made infinite sense that it should happen this way, that Rasferret's special envoy should be here to deliver his demise. And the thought that his death would bring satisfaction to the Grub—that was what infuriated him, gave him a last strength.

The Rat General came nearer; Hobart looked up, into his eyes. *Thresh ends you* . . .

"And *Hobart* ends *you*," the sprite said softly. In a supreme effort he drove his sword upwards, striking the absolutely surprised Rat in the abdomen. Thresh let out a squeaking scream and dropped the bow.

"Can your master see us?" Hobart choked out. "Tell him I think his time is short."

Still screaming, Thresh clutched at the sword in his belly. He swayed, staggered too far, and fell into the trough. The water carried him away. To The Grinder.

Hobart slumped onto his side. Eldest sprite of The Hill, veteran of the First Great War with Rasferret the Grub, and one-time secret admirer of Jenny McGraw, he exhaled a last breath and faded from this world.

IX.

The death of a leader is rarely insignificant; when such a death occurs during wartime it carries even more import, sometimes in a supernatural as well as mundane sense. Coincidentally or not, the moment of Hobart's passing marked the critical point in the Battle for the Straight. It was in that same moment that the Swede woke up.

In a remote corner by the south end of the kitchens, the Swede opened his eyes and shook his head to clear it. One of the explosions had knocked him cold, and in the panic the other Big People had left him behind. He pushed himself up on his arms now, an awakening giant. He sat up . . . stood. And looked around. His already severely addled brain was addled still more by the ringing in his ears, and he saw everything.

He saw the sabotage.

He saw the fires, and the smoke.

He saw the sprites, fighting for their lives.

He saw the Rats.

His eyes widened, and a berserk rage worthy of Beowulf himself flowed into him.

"Vermin!?" the Swede growled, from deep in his hairy chest. "Vermin in *my* kitchen? *DUH-HYUN!"*

A meat tenderizer the size of Norway hung within easy reach. The Swede grabbed it, swung it once to test its weight, and blasted the nearest Rat into Valhalla. Another dozen and a half had been annihilated before either of the warring sides realized what was going on. Then the sprites, not sure what to make of this avenging colossus, began to cheer.

"Little Peoples," cried the mad chef, "follow me!"

Wielding the tenderizer in one hand and a fire extinguisher in the other, the Swede strode forward and put the enemy to a rout.

"Aye!" said Macduff.

X.

Everything was ready, now. The spider's web had closed.

Ithaca lay dreaming under its enchantment; it had been cut off, forgotten without and within. The humans in the town, with but a few exceptions, were caught by a magic slumber similar to the one that had taken Aurora Smith, and Sleeping Beauty before her. In the Straight the fire alarm wailed on, but no engines would come in answer to it; just as well that the Swede was on the job, for a little longer anyway. Shortly he too would crouch down, lower his head, and dream of vanquished Rats like so many Grendels. The sprites were wide awake and fighting for all they were worth, but animals, again with only a couple of exceptions and excluding Rasferret's Rats, were likewise affected by the magic, and slept. The Green Dragon lay awaiting the spark of life.

Time.

On the roof of Goldwin-Smith Hall Mr. Sunshine cupped a hand to his mouth and whispered a single word to the wind.

"George."

GEORGE'S ASCENT,
AND WHAT HAPPENED
DOWNTOWN

I.

George.

The storyteller opened his eyes and was lying in his bed. Waking felt unreal, yet the events of last night had been no dream—without sitting up he could see the Spear, standing erect and ready for action against the bedroom wall. Dim grey light leaked in through the window, and even this poor illumination was enough to make the spearhead glimmer wickedly.

"Time," George whispered to himself, getting up. His head was very light. Almost floating. "Time."

He tiptoed naked into the bathroom—*How did I get home last night?*—and bent over the sink, splashing water on his face. It was cold and rinsed the sleep from his eyes, but did nothing for his head. He felt as if he had taken a hit of something.

Why? To help suspend my disbelief? Make it easier to write without paper?

Easier . . . his own overconfidence was one of his greatest dangers. Back in the bedroom, hefting the Spear, he felt invincible, every inch the knight. He would control the Story, fight the good fight, defeat the Dragon. Aurora would live. All very easy.

Sure.

Yes, sure . . . but as long as there was an outside chance his pride was only leading him to a fall, there would be no harm in hedging his bets. The Spear made a formidable-looking weapon, but it might be wise to bring along something else, something that harnessed the wind.

Dressing, he glanced around the room, trying to remember where he'd left his kite.

II.

High in the McGraw Hall belfry, Rasferret the Grub laughed ecstatically. He was in the power seat now; his Sense had returned to him, and now The Hill

371

and the city below were laid out in his mind with all the clarity of a highlighted map. His magic was at a pinnacle, ready to take on all comers. And there would be only one.

He knew of the events at the Straight, had Sensed them, but the death of Thresh and the Swede-authored rout did not concern him in the least. Hobart was dead, too—at last!—and one lost battle meant little. His Rats were everywhere, pressing home their attack throughout the campus, in many places overwhelming their enemies. The sprites were, ultimately, doomed.

Stephen Titus George remained the only stumbling block in the path to victory. And yet, Sensing him, Rasferret was again struck by the apparent weakness of his opponent. What magic he had in him was hardly a threat; nor was he physically anything special. Whereas the Grub had magic in abundance, and the perfect—perfect—vehicle for animation lying practically at his feet.

He is nothing, Rasferret chuckled to himself. *How easy it will be to kill him, and how foolish to think he could be any sort of threat to me. How could he be?*

The feel of his own power, ready for use, washed away all cautionary fear Rasferret might have had. The storyteller did not feel dangerous, therefore he wasn't dangerous. Nor was he moving very quickly—it would be some small time yet before he found his way up to the Quad.

In the meantime, the Grub focused his Sense on downtown Ithaca, searching for any still-wakeful beings in the slumbering city with whom he might amuse himself while he was waiting. It did not take long to find some, or to figure out something to do to them.

III.

"Don't close your eyes, Doubleday!" Hollister barked, bolt upright behind the wheel of the patrol car. She struggled to keep her own eyes open, fought the fear that wanted to hustle her into the nearest house and put a locked door between her and the Outside.

"Huh! Jesus, I'm tired," said Doubleday (it was about the fifteenth time he had said it in the past ten minutes). "What the hell is going on in this town?"

Hollister did not reply; she knew no more than he did. They had been out on Route 13, stopped for coffee at Mano's Diner, when the storm had passed overhead. Thunder rattled the windows and as the sound died away two thoughts struck the patrons simultaneously: first, that it might be very dangerous to go out, and second, that the chairs and booths in which they sat made extremely comfortable resting places. So nice, so *safe,* to just nestle back and relax . . .

Nattie Hollister had almost let herself go under. What stopped her fall into sleep was a sudden vision of the mannequin, the impossibly alive mannequin that had nearly killed her on New Year's Eve. And so she was struck by a third thought: It's out there.

She brought her fists down against her thighs as hard as she could, and used the blossoming pain to fight her way back up, onto her feet. She slapped Doubleday to break his descent, and dragged him toward the exit past others who were already snoring.

Now they drove. And fought the spell. Across his lap Doubleday held a shotgun.

"Check and make sure that's loaded," Hollister instructed him.

"I already did. Twice."

"Check it again." Groggily, Doubleday did as he was told. Hollister swung the car carefully to the right, turning onto State Street. She kept a light touch on the accelerator; the fog thickened conspiratorially in front of the headlights, throwing back glare and nearly blinding her.

"Loaded," Doubleday said. He looked out his window and could see no other signs of illumination; the city's power seemed to be out. "So . . . where are we going, anyway? The station house?"

Hollister considered. The station house seemed a good choice, but they had already tried radioing in and gotten no answer. Besides, headquarters was not where they were needed.

"We're going up The Hill," she told him. "Whatever's wrong, that's where it's coming from. I can feel it, can't you?"

After the briefest pause, Doubleday nodded.

"Yeah," he said. "Jesus. Jesus, I'm tired."

IV.

The building stood dark on East Clinton Street, not far from The Commons: City Police Headquarters, repository of local law and order. Repository, also, of evidence from unsolved murder cases.

The building stood dark, offering no comfort to the passerby—if there had been any passersby—and nothing should have moved in its silence. Nattie Hollister and Sam Doubleday were out driving, and the rest of the force had succumbed to enchantment: they snored at their desks, lay slumped in hallways, nodded over dispatches. Nothing should have moved, save for brows furrowing in nightmare.

Nevertheless, the front door of the station house swung open, and a figure exited into the fog. It was no cop, but it had donned a parody of a uniform: an oversized policeman's jacket hung from its shoulders, and on its head was a regulation cap set at a rakish angle.

Its eyes glowed blue; it wore a plastic woman's grin.

V.

George stepped out onto his porch, Spear in one hand, kite in the other. The fog formed a curtain around the house, thick but not impenetrable: he could make out vague shapes. Lightning shot a glow through the mist as if a giant flashbulb were popping at some distance; the thunder was unmuffled.

George took another two steps and the wind sliced through the curtain. A path opened for him as far as the curb, and one shadow-shape resolved itself into the figure of Ragnarok in full black regalia, sitting astride his motorcycle.

"Afternoon, George," the Black Knight said. "Or whatever this is." He glanced at the Spear, then nodded at the dragon kite. "Nice."

"Ragnarok?"

"Nice," Ragnarok repeated. There was something different about him, and after a moment's thought George realized that it was the absence of sunglasses. He had been too preoccupied to notice last night at the hospital, but Ragnarok's eyes were intense and surprisingly humane after their long time in hiding. "So George, you need a lift somewhere?"

"This is going to sound like a stupid question," George responded, "but what are you doing here, Ragnarok?"

"Doing?" The Bohemian seemed perplexed by the question. "Doing . . . well . . ." He rubbed one eye with a dark-gloved fist. "Unfinished business, I guess. Tell you the truth, I'm still trying to figure out who put my motorcycle back together."

He looked so lost that George asked no further questions of him. Careful of the Spear, he climbed on the back of the bike, saying: "OK, let's go." Ragnarok gunned the throttle and they drove off, up The Hill, up to the Quad.

For once in his life, the Black Knight did not break any speed limits.

VI.

Up ahead, Luther told himself. *Just up ahead.*

Almost home, almost back in Heaven now. Except that he came alone it was just like the first time, fog shrouding everything, the town quiet around him. Luther longed to climb up, pass through the arched gate and stand again on the top of The Hill, but did not rate his chances on making it even so far as the foot; for this *wasn't* the first time, and now death waited in ambush for him. As he padded along State Street not a block and a half from the beginning of The Commons, the mongrel's nose came alive with the scent of his adversary.

Just ahead, he's waiting, any second and you'll be face to face. And then, even if

*you were a fighting dog, it would be death for you. Your only chance is to run, run
away now, hope you're faster and he loses the trail. . . .*

Luther let his mind waver and wheedle, but his legs carried him forward
without faltering. For he was, finally, a good dog, and not without courage;
he would not back out so near to the end.

A few more steps, a few more and the fog will clear, and you'll see—

"Mange . . ."

The fog did not clear; but it thinned, enough at least to see the now-dark
digital clock at the west end of The Commons, and the animal that crouched
at the foot of it. Luther had become rib cage–thin during his long walk and
expected to find Dragon in similar condition, yet the first sight of him was
still a shock.

"You look like Raaq," Luther exclaimed, resolve draining away to terror,
and he was abruptly very sorry that he had not run when he could.

"No," the Wolfhound replied, baring his teeth. "Not Raaq. Not a devil.
I'm an executioner, mange. Yours."

"An executioner. And look what killing's done to you. Your soul belongs
to Raaq, now."

"He may have my soul, but I have my life. And my revenge. I'm going to
tear you limb from limb, mange. Slowly. Will you actually just stand there
and let me do it, without resisting?"

The Wolfhound studied him for a moment.

"You're worried about the cat, aren't you?"

"Where is Blackjack?" asked Luther, fearful of the answer. "Did you—"

"I wanted to have him here," Dragon replied. "His body, I mean. To
show you. But you'll never see him again, mange. Even if you've convinced
yourself that you're going to get past me somehow, have no doubt about that.
He fell. He fell a long way."

"Cats are good at taking falls."

"Not this fall. And they aren't much for swimming. He's dead."

"But you don't have his body." Luther felt a sudden, irrational hope.
"You didn't actually see him dead, did you?"

"He's dead," Dragon repeated.

"You aren't sure, are you? You don't have proof."

"He's *dead*, I know he's dead, and I don't need to prove anything." Rage
kindled in him. The cat was certainly done for—nothing could have survived
that drop—but damn this mange for planting the slightest seed of doubt.
"He's *dead*. Now it's your turn."

Dragon got off his haunches and came on, moving swiftly but not
running. "I think you might fight," he said, when he had closed half the
distance between them. "I think the pain might make you frightened enough
to fight me."

In that moment Luther was not sure whether he would fight, or try to run, or simply stand his ground and be slaughtered. What he finally did do, without knowing why, was ask one last question.

"How did you get away from the 'catchers, Dragon?" he asked.

And Dragon stopped, seizing on a sudden inspiration.

"'Catchers aren't so terrible," the Wolfhound replied. "They have soft throats, mange."

Luther understood, and was horrified, as Dragon had wanted him to be. "You killed a *Master?* You killed a *human being?*"

"Two of them, mange. One 'catcher, and another on the road, a woman. I was hungry, so very hungry . . ."

"You're damned," Luther told him. "You're damned for this."

"Funny, being damned doesn't frighten me. It makes me feel stronger. But if it disgusts you so much, why not fight me? I'd like that. Take out your revulsion on me. Try."

"No," Luther said, with no hesitation. "I won't kill another dog, not even you. Never. Raaq will not have my soul."

"Coward. Simple little pup—"

"You lie" the mongrel pronounced firmly. "You're so much bigger than I am, I refuse to fight you, and yet still you'll kill me, even though I've done you no wrong. Who's the coward, Dragon?"

"Coward or not, you're a dead dog," the Wolfhound told him, but before he could spring, they were both distracted by a sound.

Boots against concrete. Footsteps.

Something was walking toward them along Cayuga Street, hazy in the fog.

"Would you like to see how I kill a human being, mange?"

"No." Luther begged. "No, Dragon, you can't."

"It's easy," The Wolfhound assured him. "But you can always try and stop me."

"Dragon, *NO!*"

Too late. The Purebred was already in motion, teeth bared. Luther barked a warning to the approaching Master but the human seemed not to hear and came right on. In that moment Luther was caught on the horns of a greater dilemma than he had ever known before.

Then Dragon reached the Master and leaped up, and in a flash the mongrel's decision was made. "Damn you," he said. "Damn you, then." He rushed forward himself, intending a suicidal attack on the Wolfhound's flank. What he did not know was that the Wolfhound's decision to attack had been just as suicidal.

Dragon's front paws slammed into the Master's bosom—it was a woman—and he put his full momentum behind knocking her over. But the Master did not oblige. She did not fall; she did not even stagger. Instead she raised her arms, and as the Wolfhound angled his jaws in for her throat, locked strong hands around his neck.

Cold hands.

Plastic hands.

"*Whub*—?" Halted just as surely as if an iron leash had been pulled taut, Dragon's head jerked back, and he found himself staring into the glowing blue eyes of the Rubbermaid. Luther saw the eyes too and stopped short, terrified.

"Raaq . . ." he whispered.

"*No,*" the Purebred insisted. Dragon struggled to free himself, but he could not bring his jaws close enough to bite, and it would have been useless anyway. The Rubbermaid's body was hard, unyielding; only its hands flexed, and those only to tighten around the Wolfhound's neck.

"What are you?" Dragon demanded, trying to bark but finding no air to do it with. "What are you?" He tore at the 'Maid with his paws but it felt no pain, just kept on smiling a synthetic smile as it wrung the life out of him. Darkness closed in around his mind, and near the end it seemed that the Rubbermaid changed. Its eyes remained the same, but the face swelled, expanding, became that of a dog, an impossibly huge dog composed of light and shadow. *Welcome home, 'Bred,* it greeted him.

"*NO!*" Dragon roared in his mind. Luther could not see what he was seeing, but felt the torment. The Wolfhound's back paws scrabbled desperately against the pavement, scraped themselves bloody as he made a last attempt to escape. "I'm alive, I'm alive, *I'm alive, I'M*—"

The crack of his neck breaking was a small sound compared to the thunder. The Rubbermaid tossed his carcass aside like a toy in which it had lost all interest. It turned its eyes to Luther.

"You stay away, Devil," the mongrel told it, backing up. The mannequin cocked its head—the police officer's hat was still firmly in place—and walked toward him, not hurrying, moving in slow and easy strides.

That was when the patrol car came barreling out of the fog.

VII.

Hollister sensed the Rubbermaid up ahead even before the headlights picked out its shape in the fog. She stomped on the gas, giving Doubleday just enough time to cry "Wh—" before the mannequin whipped into view and was struck by the front fender. Hollister had thought to either run the 'Maid down and under or knock it out and away, broken, but neither of these things happened. Instead the Rubbermaid fell deliberately forward across the hood, reaching out for them as if that were exactly what it had intended to do.

"Oh fuck!" Hollister spat, for the beginning of The Commons was just ahead and she was out of driving room. She switched from the gas to the brakes and swung a hard left; the car spun onto Cayuga Street and slammed sideways into a parked van, stalling. Doubleday's head racked up against the passenger window hard enough to star the glass.

Hollister couldn't believe her eyes. The Rubbermaid had lost its hat but continued to cling effortlessly to the hood, like an unwanted ornament. With the patrol car at rest it reached forward again, smiling. A plastic knuckle rapped at the windshield and cracks spiraled out from the touch.

"Doubleday," Hollister said, but her partner was out cold, blood running down the side of his head. She snatched the shotgun off his lap just as the Rubbermaid thrust a fist through the windshield. The hand grabbed eagerly at the front of Hollister's jacket.

"Wrong," Hollister told it, and as she brought the weapon up she could hear a dog barking outside somewhere. The sound of the gun going off was the loudest thing she had ever heard; the windshield erupted outwards and the right side of the Rubbermaid's head evaporated. The mannequin reeled back all of two feet . . . and then leaned forward again, fingers questing.

Hollister had her seatbelt off before she knew she was doing it. She yanked at the door handle, which stuck; threw herself at it, and spilled out onto the street when it abruptly gave way. She landed hard but held onto the gun, pumping another shell into the chamber as she rolled away from the car.

The Rubbermaid came down off the hood, the cruel grace of its movement unchanged. Its head was a cracked ruin but one eye still glared blue, and whatever remained of its mouth might well be curled up in a grin, though that was hard to see. Hollister raised the shotgun and fired a second time, taking off the other half of its head, eye winking out like a shattered beacon.

Decapitated and blind, the mannequin kept right on coming. The stolen police jacket it wore swayed loose on its shoulders.

"Anne Boleyn on a cross." Hollister was sitting on the asphalt and did not waste time trying to get up. She pistoned her legs and slid backwards on her ass, pumping the shotgun. She fired again, hitting the 'Maid in the left shoulder; its arm sagged, then dropped whole out of the sleeve, fingers still clenching and unclenching as it landed on the pavement.

Hollister pumped the gun, and fired again; the blast struck the mannequin in the thigh, and at last its stride altered, its leg dragging. Hollister fired again—last shot—and the entire leg fell away. The Rubbermaid twisted and dropped, its upper torso striking Hollister's boot as it toppled. She scampered back, kicking at it.

"Goddamn you stop moving!" she shouted, as the Rubbermaid's still-attached arm stretched for her. Its fingers stroked the asphalt searchingly; as they crawled closer Hollister raised the butt of the shotgun and prepared to use it as a club. But at last the mannequin seemed to give up the ghost. Its fingers froze all of a sudden; its mutilated body grew rigid. Still Hollister did not relax, expecting some trick. But the Rubbermaid did not move again.

A little black-and-white dog—no doubt the one that had been doing the

barking—padded into view now. It went over to the remains of the 'Maid,
cautious at first, and sniffed at them. Then, as if to make a final statement on
the matter, the dog raised a leg to the mannequin and urinated briskly on it.
Lightning flashed to give a better view of the action.

"Jesus . . ." Hollister let out her breath in a gush and nearly passed out.
In the aftermath of fear exhaustion swept over her, fighting to drag her down.
And it would be good, good to just lie down here on the pavement and
sleep . . .

In a moment, the dog came over and began to lick her face.

VIII.

The motorcycle drove north past the law school, past the great courtyard
between Myron and Anabel Taylor Halls. George thought of Richard Fariña,
who had written of this place in his Cornell novel, calling it a perfect place for
duels. So it was; but Stephen George knew of one place even better.

North, north up Central Avenue. In the fog George could not see the
Tower, but he knew it was there. And just beyond, the Quad. As they drew
near his hands were damp, and not merely from the moisture in the air.

"Far as I go, partner," Ragnarok said, stopping the bike just beyond the
Campus Store and the Straight, just short of Uris Library. "I think you know
your own way from here."

"Do you know where you're going?" George asked him.

Ragnarok rubbed his eye. "I think . . . I think I will. Not far. Good luck,
George."

George only nodded at this. Ragnarok set his hand back on the throttle
and drove off into the fog.

"Well," George said, when the Black Knight had gone.

Lightheaded, as in a dream, he hiked the last stretch to the place of his
trial.

ST. GEORGE
AND THE
DRAGON

I.

The dank gloom ended at the entrance to the Quad. Curls of fog wove in the grass like restless vines, but for the most part this battleground was clear, the view hazy but unobstructed. Like the hall of a great king, the Quad stretched long and north, and there, at the far end, lay the Dragon.

It was big.

It was very, very big.

Oh, they'd built it big, its makers, bigger than any Dragon before it, but if Larretta or Curlowski could have seen it now, they would have been shocked at how it had grown still larger, and even more life-like. Folded in upon itself as if in slumber it resembled a small mountain, and a mantle of darkness surrounded it, giving it yet more substance. Behind it, Sibley Hall could only barely be seen.

"Wait a minute," George said, an expression on his face as if he'd just been dipped in ice water. The Spear in his hand felt suddenly very small. "Just wait a minute . . ."

A laugh rang out from the roof of Goldwin-Smith on his right. On his left, in the belfry of McGraw Hall, there was a second laugh, too tiny to be heard.

"Wait," George said. "Wait."

It did not wait.

With a flare of blue light and a bustle of unlimbering wings, the Dragon came to life. It unfolded like a flower of gargantuan proportions, wings spreading in a slow explosion of dark canvas. Shadow girded it and made it a giant black silhouette, a blue fireball-eyed shape, unreal and real at the same time. *But will it bleed?* George wondered. *If I stab it with the Spear, can it feel pain? Or fear? And how do I kill it?*

The Dragon beat its wings to test them; George's hair was tousled by the rush of air, and all at once he was very aware of the empty space at his back, temptingly fog-filled avenues into which he could run and hide. Only it would find him. He knew that as surely as he knew that heroes never run; it would find him.

Fighting the mounting fear, George brought his foot forward, took a step toward the Dragon. The Dragon replied in kind, reaching forward with one claw, then the other, gouging grass and earth like clots of flesh, wings beating like tremendous fans above, churning the air. It did not actually look as if it were stalking toward him; it looked as if it were turning the Earth beneath itself, dragging George closer with each tug of its talons. Its tail beat the ground like a felled oak striking a drum of soil and stone.

Light-headed and -hearted with terror—the Dragon was *huge*, impossibly huge, and it might not even bleed—George forced himself to keep moving with a Fool's resolve, holding the dragon kite before him like a shield.

When half the distance between them had been closed, the Dragon dropped its jaw open, and the storyteller prepared himself for a lunge and a snapping of mammoth teeth. That the Dragon intended to burn him where he stood—he did not even think to expect that. Instead he raised his Spear high and hunched his body low, ready to jab at the thing's snout when it tried to bite.

"All right, here we go," George said.

And marched straight into his own barbecue.

II.

Ragnarok drove through the abandoned tangle of Hooterville. He rode alone but the fog around him was haunted. Coiled within its muting dankness he thought he could hear the whisper of old sounds: the light thump of a robe in a gift-wrapped box; the tear of razor sharp mirror shards on skin, a noise rarely heard above the clamor of breaking glass but there all the same. If the fog had suddenly resolved itself into a dozen threatening white shapes, thinned out into smoke from a guttering cross around some nearby corner, Ragnarok would not have been surprised.

But if it was haunted, it was also enchanted, woven with strange possibility. Along with the dark fantasies it also occurred to him that he might through some sleight of hand reach inside himself, grab that part of the past that he carried with him and tear it out. Leave it behind; lose it in the gloom.

Unfinished business . . .

He turned, drove up between Day and Stimson Halls. Coming out on East Avenue he slowed the bike, listening, pausing long enough to pluck the black-handled mace from its tube rack. His eye prickled in warning.

"Where are you, Jack?" he called out, moving north down the Avenue at a steady fifteen miles an hour. Three heartbeats later he had his answer as the sledgehammer simply swung out of nowhere, clotheslining him, a single thought—*Not supposed to happen like this*—flashing through his mind as the oak handle cracked across his chest like a baseball bat, toppling him over backwards while the bike rode itself to a wreck a few yards beyond.

"Here I am," Jack Baron said, standing over him. "Here I am, you fuck." Ragnarok had lost his grip on the mace and he groped for it with his left hand, but Jack swung the 'hammer with crushing force, shattering four of the Bohemian's fingers. For only the second time in his life, Ragnarok screamed.

"Here I am," Jack repeated, driving a foot into Ragnarok's side, flipping him over on his back. "Looks like I might have sprung a rib there, *partner*, are you frightened yet?"

He aimed another kick but this time Ragnarok risked his other hand, catching the foot in mid-swing. They strained against each other, Jack struggling to bring his foot all the way down, Ragnarok trying to throw him off balance . . . and then Jack jabbed at the Bohemian's groin with the butt of the sledgehammer, breaking the deadlock.

"I could kill you now, *partner*," Jack Baron said, as the Black Knight curled himself into a protective ball. "I thought about that all last night and today, how good it would feel to kill you. But I think I'd like a game of tag first, how does that sound, eh, *partner?*"

One more kick, a fresh bruise in the small of Ragnarok's back, and then the Rho Alpha Tau President was moving away, footsteps and laughter retreating off to the left, toward Goldwin-Smith.

Not far away, on the Quad, a wind was rising.

III.

The fire seemed to come out of the Dragon's mouth in slow motion.

George had time, more time than should have objectively been possible, to see it coming and react. Mentally react; for physically he too seemed to have slowed down, leaving only his mind to race, stretch out the event.

Two bursts of emotion he felt, one after the other. The first was simple surprise, for approaching the Dragon to attack was like approaching a black fortress; it was imposing enough at first glance, overwhelming enough, that any further enhancements seemed unnecessary. It was so much bigger than George that he could not help but be shocked that it *needed* to breathe fire. Tooth and talon should have been sufficient.

The second emotion was less rational, and therefore saving: indignation that he should be overmatched in this way; *he* had no fire to breathe. Angered, with the bolt of flame jetting down at him, he forgot the limits of possibility and let instinct take over. His mind gripped the air around him like a matron grabbing the corners of a sheet, and tugged. All at once the wind was with him, turning the flames so that they encircled him in a cyclone but did not touch him.

The firestream cut off; the Dragon's mouth snapped shut. Unharmed, George struck with the Spear, tearing a gash across the monster's snout. The Dragon cut easily and bits of material scattered into the rising wind, but it did not bleed. Nor did it seem to feel pain.

"Wait," George said, "wait just a minute here . . ."

A claw reached for him, seeking to mash him down. Near panic, George swung the Spear like an ax, leading with its sharp edge, at the same time concentrating, trying to Write with his mind: *This must hurt you, this* must *hurt you.*

The Spear edge neatly lopped off a talon; the Dragon's wounded claw hovered in mid-air, not bleeding, no, but had the blue glow in its eyes dimmed a bit? A touch of pain, perhaps? The Dragon drew back, seemed to reappraise the situation.

"Got you!" George cried triumphantly, too quickly. "I got you! I got you!"

"Ego," Mr. Sunshine whispered, shaking his head.

George had forgotten the tail. The Dragon only seemed to hesitate. It brought its long tail around like a whip, and George's elation was shattered abruptly as it thundered across his back, hurling him to the ground, ears ringing like dinner gongs. His arms stretched out before him like a diver and his face ploughed grass and dirt.

It felt as though his spine had been broken. Trying to push himself up, for he knew the Dragon would be on him almost instantly, his body was a cord of pain. No time to lie and suffer; he heard a roar behind him and rolled to the side, grunting at what this did to his battered back. A line of flame shot past him with no room to spare.

The Spear lay on the grass ten feet to his right, too far. He got halfway up and went for it anyway, but the Dragon was over him and with another explosion of pain he went flying again, the undamaged claw batting him this time. The storyteller landed in a tangle of hurt, tried to move, and couldn't.

Rasferret's turn to be triumphant: *Have you, have you, HAVE YOU NOW—*

Concrete beneath him, not grass. Fighting the paralysis, uncertain how many seconds he had left before the Dragon either tore him in half or burned him to ash, furious that he should be losing so quickly, so easily, George realized that he had fallen on the walkway between the statues, the two statues of Ezra Cornell and Andrew D. White. His mind grasped at legend for salvation.

What time is it?

He turned his head toward the Tower, sought out the near Clock face.

Fog would have hidden it from him but again the wind came to his aid, clearing it for half a breath.

Both hands were still frozen, still stuck at twelve; and though that had meant noon when the lightning first struck, it was midnight that George thought of.

At midnight, if a virgin passes between . . .

He was seven years beyond virginity yet still he tried, bringing all his remaining strength to concentration, willing it: *Get up, get up, Ezra, Andrew, help me!*

Then the Dragon was there, poised for the kill, pausing indecisively as it sifted through the various ways it might finish him. Rasferret exulted in his hiding place.

And there *was* a third figure moving on the Quad, not Andrew White, he sat tight on his bronze chair, but near the pedestal where Ezra had stood for so long. It held some long and slender object in one hand, and even as the Dragon/Rasferret made the decision and opened wide for a breath of fire, the figure raised the object to its shoulder, pulled a trigger.

A sound like an explosion, and buckshot punched a hole in the Dragon's hide, just below the neck. It forgot George and turned with fresh outrage to face this new antagonist. Searchlamp eyes picked out the intruder.

It was not Andrew D. White, not Ezra Cornell.

It was Nattie Hollister: master shotgunnist, mannequin slayer extraordinaire, and last waking member of the Ithaca City Police Force.

At the moment, she was seriously considering a transfer to Cleveland.

IV.

Wishing for once that he could be as burly and hulking—and as long-legged—as one of the Big People, Puck raced through the fog with as great a speed as he could muster toward the Tower. If only he had his biplane! A touch of the throttle and he would be up there, ready to fight at Zephyr's side. In his mind Puck pictured her, fighting alone against dozens of Rats. . . .

Come on, come on, come on! Puck recited in his head as he raced along. And though Mr. Sunshine's attention was focused on the Quad, it might be that some other Power with a sense of humor saw his plight and decided to throw him a reckless chance. He had gone only a few more yards when an object appeared on the asphalt in front of him: a wood-frame paper diamond, dropped by a fleeing Parade-goer, its green tint appearing almost black in the fog.

Puck saw it and stopped short, immediately grasping the possibilities.

But he had never flown a kite before.

V.

"What!?" Mr. Sunshine cried from the roof of Goldwin-Smith. "What sort of deus ex machina crap is this?" He glared at the sky. "Somebody's going to be very sorry if I find out there's been Monkey-business at my Writing Desk. . . ."

Hollister looked at the Dragon and felt she must surely go mad. Walking mannequins were one thing, that she could almost handle, but this . . . this defied both law and order in a way that had nothing to do with the justice system. Fairy-tale monsters such as this simply *could not be.*

She had not succumbed to sleep downtown after finishing off the Rubbermaid; struggling harder than ever to stay awake, she had dragged herself back into the police car, forced it to start, and driven up The Hill with the black-and-white dog perched on the lap of the still-unconscious Doubleday. Stalling out just beyond the Quad, continuing on foot, the dog had ultimately shown more sense by choosing to wait in the car. But not Nattie Hollister; driven by duty and drawn on by an unshakable certainty that something of great importance was taking place here, she had charged in, weapon reloaded and ready, only to come face to face with impossibility.

"You can't exist," she told the Dragon, which seemed unimpressed with her claim. It took a first step toward her and she cracked off another two shots, punching a pair of holes in the Dragon's chest that hurt it not at all.

The Dragon paused, once more deciding whether to bother wasting a breath. Mr. Sunshine, who had Meddled to save Hollister's life on New Year's Eve, concluded that he didn't want her mucking up his Climax. He acted before the Dragon could, glancing again at the sky, which flickered in answer.

"You're under arrest!" Hollister shouted hysterically at the Dragon, pumping the last shell. "Got that? You're under arrest, motherf—"

Lightning lanced down from the clouds, blew her off her feet. The shotgun shell exploded in the barrel, destroying the weapon; Hollister crashed in a heap at the base of Ezra Cornell's statue, eyebrows singed off, jacket smoldering. Out cold.

"Nothing personal," Mr. Sunshine said. "You're a wonderful Character, but this is storytellers only. Sorry." He turned his attention to George, crawling across the grass toward the Spear, still unable to stand. "How disappointing. How very disappointing. For all your talents I think you lack the proper motivation, George."

Then a smile played at Mr. Sunshine's lips. A terrible, mischievous smile, more Faustian than Greek. "Look here, George," he said.

Stephen George, one hand on the Spear, heard the voice and turned to look. His heart nearly stopped at the sight: a bed had materialized on the walk in front of Andrew D. White's statue, a hospital bed like a bier for the perfect sacrifice, and on it Aurora Borealis Smith, still locked in slumber, wreathed in enchantment. Defenseless.

"No," George said. "No, you bastard, that's not fair, not fair. . . ."

The Green Dragon, momentarily spellbound by the felling of Nattie Hollister, now took notice of this second woman. The corners of its fireproof mouth pulled back in a parody of Mr. Sunshine's smile; like the Greek Original before it, the Dragon focused its concentration, and its magic, at the sky, seeing if could repeat the trick it had seen. Electricity flickered across boiling clouds of black, gathering at a central point.

"*No!*" George roared, and function returned to his legs, to his feet, lifting him up, sending him pounding across the Quad. Without losing its grip on the sky the Dragon fired a blast of flame at him, withering the grass at his heels, toasting his backside. Feeling the searing heat George ran all the faster, intent on reaching Aurora, uncertain whether his hair had caught fire yet or was only about to.

Then the sky opened, firing a huge blue bolt at the Earth. With a last desperate bound George sprang to the bed, spent a precious half instant gathering up Aurora, and leapt away. A brilliant flash, a thunderclap breaking directly behind him like a wave, and the storyteller landed hard at the base of Andrew White's statue. Stars swam in his head, but he still had the Spear in his hand and Aurora unharmed in his arms. The hospital bed was a burning, melted wreck; the air was sick with ozone.

And the Dragon was coming. It bore down on them like a juggernaut, but George took the time to give his Princess a brief kiss. She did not stir, but the kiss gave him the strength, the steel, that he needed.

The Dragon came on, dragging shadow with it. Its jaw dropped open as it came in range, and George sprang up to meet it, whirling around once, twice, three times. "All right then, fine," George shouted, "come on, COME ON!" and hurled the Spear up and out. Fire welled in the Dragon's mouth and the Spear flew straight to it, thrusting between the massive jaws, sticking fast at the back of the monster's throat.

There were two sounds. The first was the disconsolate *thuk-thuk-thuk* of the broken valve on the Dragon's fire tanks, unable to dispense more fuel.

The second was a cry like a sonic boom fed through a bad amplifier: the Green Dragon, screaming. Impossibly stung, it jerked its head back in anguish; in the McGraw Hall belfry, Rasferret the Grub convulsed, feeling an invisible spike at the back of his own throat.

"*Does it hurt?*" George shrieked at it. "*Does it hurt, you bastard?*"

The Dragon, whipping its head around in anguish, trying unsuccessfully to dislodge the Spear. The force of its cry rebounded the length of the Quad, shaking buildings, shattering windows.

As the beast reared back, George looked and saw his kite lying in the grass by the Dragon's tail. And all at once he knew how the Story should end.

VI.

"Where are you, Jack?" the Black Knight bellowed, staggering along the first-floor corridor of Goldwin-Smith Hall. Ragnarok had the mace in his right hand, while his left rested against his chest like a beloved but broken toy. Walking the corridor was like walking the depths of a tomb, and the Bohemian watched each dark classroom doorway. But the President of Rho Alpha Tau failed to appear; Ragnarok reached the center of the building and paused, listening. To his right, wide steps descended to a lobby where doors opened on the Arts Quad. Sounds from the battle outside echoed dimly in the Hall.

Gunshots; and at the same instant Jack Baron materialized from behind a bust of the Hall's sponsor, rocketing the sledgehammer overhand at Ragnarok's skull. The Black Knight side-stepped the blow, sweeping a knee up into Jack's stomach. The Rho Alpha grunted, doubled over . . . and then, half letting go the sledgehammer, seized Ragnarok's wounded hand and squeezed it tight.

"Painful?" Jack inquired. The Black Knight let out a roar and crashed bodily against the Rho Alpha, spilling them both down the steps, Jack still gripping the broken hand for most of the tumbling way down. At the bottom they rolled apart; above the agony of his ruined fingers Ragnarok realized that he had once again lost his weapon. It lay halfway up the steps, too far to reach.

Jack Baron laughed as he got to his feet, sledgehammer secure in his grasp. "What's the matter, *partner?* Drop something?"

Not three feet behind him, another open staircase, narrower, steeper, descended into the basement. A handmade sign taped to a pillar announced that this was the south entrance to the Temple of Zeus Coffeehouse.

"You're disappointing me, Ragnarok," Jack taunted. Outside, more gunshots. "This is too easy. I thought you were supposed to be a killer, sold your soul to the Devil."

"A killer," Ragnarok whispered, his eyes narrowing, burning. "A killer, is that what you want?"

"Come and get me," Jack said, and lightning struck on the Quad, the flash coming in through the windows on the doors, dazzling the Rho Alpha Tau President for half a second. In the time it took him to blink Ragnarok had crossed the distance between them, landed one punch to stun him a half-second more. Standing too close for the sledgehammer to be any use, the Black Knight seized Jack Baron by the throat with one hand and began slamming his head up against the pillar.

"Is *this* . . . *what* . . . you *want?*" Ragnarok shouted at him, accenting each slam. The Coffeehouse sign slipped to the floor, flecked with blood.

"*Is this what you want?*" he shouted again, turning, pivoting Jack around toward the narrow staircase. At the last moment Jack's eyes refocused, he seized Ragnarok in a clumsy bear hug, and once more they tumbled together.

The southern doors of the Temple of Zeus burst their hinges as Ragnarok and Jack plunged through, not as two separate combatants but as a single coil of fury, a symbiotic union of hate. Like a giant's skittleball they rolled into the Coffeehouse proper, scattering chairs and tables. From a shelf along one wall a pantheon of Greek statue replicas—some missing arms, some missing legs—watched this action; a plaster Apollo seemed especially attentive, as if recording the moment for posterity.

Only Ragnarok got up from the floor. Jack was flat out on his back, blood all over his face, eyes blinking rapidly like defective shutters. The Black Knight stood straight and tall, sledgehammer in his good hand, and placed one boot on the Rho Alpha Tau President's chest, steadying him as a lumberjack steadies a chopping block from which an ax is about to be pulled.

"If you want it," the Black Knight said softly, "you'll have it. Partner."

"No," Jack croaked, too weak to move, too weak to do anything. "No, please . . ."

And Ragnarok tucked the sledgehammer beneath his arm, freeing his hand, freeing it to swipe at his eye, where fury burned in a single teardrop. Outside the Dragon screamed, and the windows set high up near the ceiling of the Coffeehouse broke and fell inward, even as Ragnarok wiped his vision clear.

"Now," the Black Knight said, taking the sledgehammer in hand again. He raised it above his head, paused for an instant, a blacksmith ready to strike. "Now I win."

Jack Baron screamed aloud, a scream that rose as the sledge descended . . . and cut off abruptly as it struck.

Ragnarok let out a breath.

Wind gusted through the broken windows.

And Jack, eyes wide, looked to the right, to the place where the sledgehammer had struck the floor, leaving barely three inches to spare.

"Surprise, you son of a bitch," Ragnarok said. "I *win*."

Jack's eyes rolled up in his head. His head dropped sideways in a faint.

A moment later, with a satisfied smile on his face, the Black Knight of Bohemia did the same.

VII.

Leaving Aurora at the base of the statue, hoping he would not be made to pay for leaving her unprotected, George raced forward while the Dragon still choked on the Spear. In its convulsions it stood almost upright, though it had no rear legs to support itself. Skirting the monster, George passed beneath one mammoth wing—it was like running beneath an eclipse—and hurried to snatch up the kite, which danced ahead of him for a moment, propelled end over end over the grass by the gale the Dragon's movements kicked up.

"Got you!" George said, grabbing it by the crosspiece, and the ground erupted in a shower of dirt two feet to his left as the Dragon thrust down with a claw.

The Dragon's head swung down, its eyes seeking to pin George with their blue intensity; the impotent *thuk-thuk-thuk* of the firetank valve kept a steady beat. The claw struck again, tearing up more landscaping. George rolled to avoid it, felt something hard beneath his back.

The ball of kite twine.

That was even better than the kite.

"Try this on for size," George said, grabbing the ball, hurling it as he had hurled the Spear, giving it just the right twist of the wrist. The ball shot upwards, twine unraveling behind it in even coils, and as it flew into the Dragon's mouth three of these coils fell around the shaft of the Spear, drawing tight.

"Finished!" George yelled, standing up, dodging away. "You're finished!"

Again it was the tail that got him. Bullwhip quick, bullsnake sinister, it knocked his legs out from beneath him with more force than a line tackle. Now the Dragon claw descended at leisure, not smashing down but scooping up.

"I smell Epilogue," Mr. Sunshine said, as talons closed like an iron fist around the prone storyteller, picking him up. George shook his head dizzily as the monster grabbed him, saw the kite on the grass again. Too far; couldn't reach it.

Didn't matter.

The Dragon, Spear jutting out of its mouth like a headless lollipop, lifted him up so it could see better as it crushed the life out of him. George did not meet its eyes, those eyes that were the blue that is the hottest part of a flame. No; he let his head loll back while the claw tightened around his torso, cutting off his air. He lolled his head back and looked at the sky, studying it, as if searching for a familiar face there. And though he could not turn in place, could not speak the magic phrase, still he managed to smile.

Come on, he thought, feeling the first of his ribs begin to crack, *come on . . .*

A new wind, one not caused by the beating of the Dragon's wings, began to blow. The kite stopped dancing on the floor of the Quad and began to rise, purposefully, a slender umbilicus of twine still tethering it to the Spear shaft.

Thuk-thuk-thuk, went the fire tank valve.

Have you now, have you now, have you now, went the babble of Rasferret's thoughts.

Up, up, went the kite, *up*, above the Quad, above the Princess, above Saint George, above the Green Dragon. Reaching for the clouds.

In those clouds, electricity gathering, gathering . . .

Now George lifted his head, met the Dragon's gaze. Smiled the fiercest smile he knew.

Finished, Rasferret thought.

Finished, George agreed.

"BEN FRANKLIN!" a slurring voice boomed. It was neither storyteller nor Storyteller, but the Bohemian Z.Z. Top, who rose from enchanted sleep beneath the bushes by Lincoln Hall to let out a drunken bellow.

"Ben Franklin says burn in hell, _burn in hell_, _BURN IN HELL!_" he roared and George thought _Come on_ and Mr. Sunshine said "Aah . . ." and Rasferret thought _No, NO, cannot, MUST NOT_— as lightning struck the kite, incinerating it. Like a moving finger the crackling bolt continued to Write, dancing down the string, finding the metal Spear shaft at its far end, so much like a lightning rod. There was a last cry _NO!_ from the Grub that seemed to stretch out for eternity as blue fire—a gift from another Saint, Elmo—danced over the skin of the beast from nose to tail.

Then, with a sound like the end of the world, the Green Dragon exploded.

VIII.

A tremor shook The Hill, rolled down to the town below. The enchantment shivered and broke, and as one the human and animal populations of Ithaca twitched, sighed, and eased into a more natural state of sleep. In the world of the wakeful, Rasferret's Rat troops lost their battle courage in the blink of an eye and fell into a shrieking rout before the remaining sprites.

In the open-air belfry of the Clock Tower, Zephyr stood beside the half dozen bodies of the Rats that had found their way up to her; she watched the Dragon blow apart and cheered its demise even as she screamed in fear for George, who was lost in the glare of the blast. Yet all at once there was another sound behind her. She whirled to face a new opponent . . . and boggled at the sight of the dark diamond shape that came sailing out of the fog, crash-landing in the middle of the belfry.

Zephyr lowered her sword, her arm stiff from exertion. The fog was evaporating, and in the growing visibility she studied this second, miraculously unroasted kite with curiosity. It jittered here and there, and all at once a corner lifted and Puck crawled out from under, looking disheveled.

"Hey there, Zeph," he greeted her, smiling sheepishly. "How's it going?"

IX.

Pieces of the Dragon littered the Quad, spreading smoke in the wind. Near the center of the blast a hot, fragmented fire burned, and it was in the midst of this inferno that George had fallen, knocked semi-conscious by the explosion. He felt the heat around him, tried dazedly to crawl to safety, managed as much as to kick away the remnants of the Dragon claw that had held him, but no more; the last of his energy was spent. He collapsed and began to go under as the smoke thickened.

Then Luther came running. Barking in alarm as he dodged through the burning debris, he revived George with a series of sloppy licks, drenching his face until he lifted his head weakly, shook it. For all the acridness of the smoke, Luther could still smell the scent on him, the Heaven scent of hills and rain.

Taking a firm grip on George's arm with his teeth, he once again began to lead the storyteller out.

X.

"The end," Mr. Sunshine pronounced, rubbing his hands together in satisfaction. "Or almost." He gazed across the Quad at the far statue and winked. "Told you it'd be a good Story, didn't I, Ezra? Now, just a little cleaning up to do around here and then I think I'll see how World War III is coming along. . . ."

A KISS AT
DAYBREAK

It was early morning of the next day when the town of Ithaca reconnected fully with reality, and became once again just an ordinary part of the world, however ordinary that ever is. One by one the townspeople awoke, and like a cat who had dreamt remembered nothing of what had taken place the day before. Even if some suspected an important occurrence, no evidence remained to help them puzzle it out. Nattie Hollister and Sam Doubleday, for example, started from sleep at about nine o'clock in the front seat of their undamaged cruiser, stiff but uninjured, wondering how they had come to be parked out front of the head shop on State Street. Ten yards away at the beginning of The Commons, the remnants of the mannequin and the corpse of the Wolfhound had been swept away, carried off by the receding fog. Ragnarok opened his eyes in his dark, unvandalized house, wondering how he had sprained his left hand. And Jack Baron . . . well, the circumstances of his waking were somewhat indelicate; it is enough to say he wondered where his clothes had got to.

The town awoke, but first up, ahead of everyone, was a pale-cheeked Princess who preceded even the dawn. As the sun rose in the east she stood on the crest of The Hill, seeming to lead the new day above the horizon, the hospital gown she wore glowing like the finest of dresses in the rose light of daybreak.

She walked across the Arts Quad, illuminating it, illuminating the ashen debris of the Dragon that lay on the otherwise unscarred Hilltop. Remnants of yesterday's Parade, nothing special . . . but the storyteller was not here, he had wandered some distance once he had escaped the fire, so Aurora moved on, seeking him out. The new day was warm and fine, more like June than March. She walked out by the Slope and passed the Johnson Museum, pausing to listen to the wind chimes, then continuing on along the same route that Preacher had taken to his death. But this morning it was safe, safe as daydreaming.

She found her love on the suspension bridge, covered with soot, looking more dead than alive. The dog had curled up to sleep beside him, offering what warmth he could to a kind Master. At Aurora's approach Luther opened his eyes and barked a joyous welcome, recognizing her. She bore the Heaven scent now as strongly as the storyteller, and the mongrel began to hop about like a young Beagle, certain that she would set all things right.

"Oh, George," Aurora said, kneeling beside him and cradling his head. "Poor George . . ." He did not stir as she touched him, did not seem even to be breathing.

Aurora didn't worry about this, though; she knew what to do.

"Because I love you," she said, an enchantment of her own making, and kissed him. A tremor ran through the bridge that even Luther felt. Called back from slumber the storyteller opened his eyes, reached up his arms to embrace her, and returned the kiss. They stayed that way a long time.

"Hooray!" Luther said, yelping, hopping about in a perfect imitation of Skippy. "Hooray! Hooray!"

And as if this happiness were not enough, the mongrel looked down at the near entrance to the bridge and saw something which nearly bowled him over. The bodies of Denmark and Rover Too-Bad had vanished with the fog as sure as the Wolfhound's, but another animal that should by all rights have been a corpse had appeared, fur muddy and unkempt, badly scarred, and as always lacking a tail.

"BLACKJACK!" Luther burst out, racing down to meet him, his feelings one with paradise now.

"Oh shit!" the Manx responded, as Luther knocked him down with a barrage of sloppy dog-kisses. "Shit, no more water, please, Luther *Luther,* don't bark so loud, I have a splitting headache for Christ's sake! Luther, would you *please stop it!*"

But Luther wouldn't, and Blackjack was forced to suffer the affection while uttering many a "Shit!" and "Fuck off, would you please?" On the bridge, the two human lovers continued their embrace, while the sun came up and chased away the remaining chill from the air.

"Jesus," George whispered. He did not know how he had come to be here in the early hours of the morning, with the breeze from the gorge tangling his hair with Aurora's, but it surely felt grand. "Jesus, what a day to be alive."

EPILOGUE

I.

March gave way to April, and April to May. On the last day of that month Aurora Borealis Smith graduated the Cornell University, along with two dozen Bohemians and several thousand more normal people. George stood in the stands, no longer a Writer-in-Residence but a free agent again; he would travel west from here with his Lady, to where an eventual wedding awaited them both, and whatever might come after that.

The canine graduation went less smoothly. Tension over the Fourth Question of Ultimate Wisdom—and other related issues—had reached the breaking point, but The Hill's mongrels still had a long crusade ahead of them, a crusade of many years. Luther and Blackjack would see much of it, for they remained in Ithaca the rest of their days; they lived long and fairly well on the occasional purloined chicken, though Blackjack never really got used to all the rain.

The Bohemians scattered to find their various fortunes. Lion-Heart and Myoko went to Europe to found a dynasty; Z.Z. Top ended up shearing sheep in Tierra del Fuego, though how he got there is something of an epic tale in itself. Ragnarok, purged of the burden of his past though he did not quite understand how, roamed for a while and eventually settled in the Midwest. He and Jinsei remained lifelong friends.

Late that August, on a particularly hot night, Rho Alpha Tau burned to ashes, as the Dragon had before it. It was no small coincidence that the Brother responsible for the fire, nodding off with candles still lit on a paper-strewn table, had drunk himself to sleep with a couple of bottles of retsina; nor that so many of the Rho Alphas, homeless now and under investigation by the Inter-Fraternity Council, came to bad ends. Jack Baron was not spared, though his reckoning was the most abrupt: he was simply yanked from the stream of history one evening, like a character edited out of the last pages of a novel. He was not missed.

The sprites lived on in secrecy as they always had, helping the University keep its files straight, seeing to it that alumni got their student loan repayment notices right on schedule. The romance of Zephyr and Puck

395

remained something of a roller coaster, and many more stories could be told about them; but suffice it to say, for now, that though they never suffered another War, between themselves they saw a fair amount of combat.

And Rasferret the Grub? Who could say? Perhaps he faded into nothing when the Dragon was defeated; perhaps, bereft of all magic, he fled and hid in lonely places for the rest of his wretched life. One thing sure, on The Hill he was never seen nor heard from again, and as far as the Little People were concerned, that was all that mattered.

II.

On a windless summer day in an uncertain year, more than a century after the founding of Cornell, a man who told lies for a living climbed to the top of The Hill to fly one last kite. He was a young man, a surprisingly wealthy one even for a professional liar, and the woman who accompanied him up the Slope was as perfect a companion as he had ever had any right to hope for.

They sat on the Arts Quad and assembled the kite together, the man and the woman; it was a white diamond crossed with red, and at its center was a representation of a Tarot card. The card depicted a man standing at the edge of a precipice; his eyes were turned skyward, and at his feet barked a black-and-white dog very much like the one that even now ran happy circles around the two kite-flyers. Across the bottom of the card was written the legend: THE FOOL. It made a beautiful design, altogether.

When the kite was ready to go the man took it and stood up. The little dog yapped expectantly, and in another corner of the Quad a lounging St. Bernard turned to watch with a bit more restraint.

The man stared up into the sky, as if searching for a familiar face there. He began to turn in place, holding the kite in one hand and a spool of heavy twine in the other, facing first west, then north, then east, then south. Three times around he turned, smiling all the while, as if casting a spell that was as amusing as it was powerful.

He stopped turning and gazed deep into the face of the sky once more. "Come on," he coaxed softly, the woman mouthing the same words, and the wind began to blow. It came out of the east where it had been waiting all along and lifted up the kite with unseen hands.

The little dog was barking furiously now, and even the St. Bernard could not resist a bit of noisemaking. Smiling, the man offered the kite string to the woman, and they shared it back and forth between them while the Fool rose higher and higher above The Hill, borne aloft in a diamond cage.

The wind blew strong all summer.

Matt Ruff
Ithaca / New York City
May 1985–April 1987